playing HIGH

Perfection SAGA
BOOK TWO

BETH PELLINO-DUDZIC

My 3 Girls
PUBLISHING

Playing High
Perfection Series Book Two
Published by My 3 Girls Publishing LLC

ISBN: 979-8-9896803-1-3
FICTION / Romance / Contemporary

Cover and Interior design by Victoria Wolf, wolfdesignandmarketing.com, copyright owned by My 3 Girls Publishing LLC.

My 3 Girls
PUBLISHING

To my closest family and friends who believed I could write this series and support me on this journey. The belief in the positive forces in the universe which has guided me on this path and taught me writing is my passion.

SECRET
WEDDING

GINA STIRRED. "Good morning, baby. Why are you staring at me like that? Are you still high?"

After a grueling three-month tour, Perfection was beginning to get traction on the music scene. With songs on the top rock charts, the band was getting attention on a national scale. They were an opening act on tour, and with their music playing on the hard rock radio stations, people were taking notice. As lead singer, Gina Poole drew people in with her voice and the sexy way she toyed with the audience, and with the love of her life, Trevor McNaughton. Trevor and Rio Poole, the two guitar players for the band, added the hard rock quality with their tremendous guitar playing. They traded off lead guitar roles, but they were both high-energy guitarists. Trevor added the spice when he and Gina sang lead together and their interplay onstage became a hot commodity.

The entire crew of Perfection had some time off to relax and recharge before Brown Fence Records wanted them back in the studio to record another album. Trevor and Gina relaxed at their Hollywood Hills home, dropping acid, which heightened their sexual appetites.

Trevor had to tell Gina what he was thinking. The words from Brent Nolan, lead singer in a competing band, haunted him. "You better marry her or somebody like me could easily take her away."

Trevor blurted, "Gina, it's time …"

"Trevor, you're scaring me, what do you mean its time? What the hell, baby? What's going on in that head?"

"I want to go to Vegas and elope. Let's do it. It's time."

Gina woke up fast. "Are you serious? Are we doing this? Are you sure you're not still high?"

Trevor gently lifted her face to his. "We should have done this sooner, but I want to get married right now."

Gina's head was spinning. "You know I want to be your wife more than anything. But can you give me a day to find a nice white dress, please? We are being unconventional, but I want a pretty dress to marry you in." She kissed him. "I'll look for a dress today, and we can leave on Saturday."

Gina had an idea. "Wait, wait … Trevor, I never thought I would say this to you, but we need to change our look. If we go looking like this, every paparazzi is going to be there with their cameras in our face. I don't want that. I'm willing to cut my hair and dye it. Are you willing to do the same? I love your beautiful long blond curls. I hate the idea, but I'm sure I will still love you with short hair. I found this new chic hairdresser in Beverly Hills. Tammie. I trust her. I'll get her to come to the house. But leave your facial hair. Don't fuck with that."

Trevor grabbed her up in his arms. "Go get a dress, and call Tammie. You're right, we need to be stealth. I don't want to have people coming up to us in Vegas. I'll try and get us a private jet."

She rushed through her shower, this time uninterrupted by Trevor. Showering together was part of their love language, but Gina was in a hurry.

Gina pulled her ponytail through a baseball cap and put on oversized sunglasses. As she walked out the door, she gushed out the words, "Love you baby. We're getting married, and I'm the luckiest woman in the world."

While Trevor was working on private jet reservations, Gina visited a few of her favorite boutiques, avoiding Rodeo Drive. There were always paparazzi there.

Wandering into Topical, she asked the salesgirl to see white or ivory dresses, in a size two or four. The young clerk placed five dresses in the dressing room for Gina to try on. The first three didn't make her feel like a bride. The other two were different. When she put them on, she felt a spark of something special. One was an ivory lace halter dress falling slightly below the knee, a contender. The last one was a maxi high neck halter dress with lace insets and intricate beadwork along the bodice and hem. This was the one.

The salesgirl brought out a pair of beaded stiletto heels, saying to Gina, "It's like they belong together."

"So, Gina Poole, that comes to $1,249.54. Credit card I assume?"

Worried that she had been recognized, Gina gave the girl a pleading look. "Please, forget you saw me today. I promise you backstage passes at our next concert if you don't say anything."

"I will take you up on that. Don't forget. I like your band. Next time you play in LA, remember those passes. You're going to Vegas, I'm guessing?"

Gina declared, "I'm not saying anything more. What's your name?"

"Jaimie."

"Okay Jaimie, backstage passes at our next show in LA. Here is a special number to call to get those passes."

Gina was already into Jaimie for backstage passes, so she didn't mind asking if she could use her phone for a minute. She took out Tammie's card, hoping she could get an appointment since she was on everyone's radar as the new thing. "Tammie, it's Gina Poole. Can you manage to come to my house today? … Okay, tomorrow would work. It's both of us. Bring blonde dye. Thanks so much. You have no idea how much this means to me."

Gina couldn't believe this was happening. She scored the dress but would have to wait until the next day for Tammie to change their hair. She would have to tell Trevor to move reservations out a day and leave Sunday. Hopefully, they could get a jet. Now to find a wedding chapel that wasn't tacky, and a place to stay. They could make this all work. It was their time.

When she got home, Gina started talking before she was all the way through the door. "Babe, Tammie can't be here until tomorrow. It's one extra day. I'm sorry."

"It's okay. I can't get a private jet until Sunday evening anyway. I booked us at Caesar's Palace. Get this, the Honeymoon Suite, for Mr. and Mrs. Knott."

Trevor checked out the bags hanging from Gina's arm. "You found a dress? Let's see it."

"You're nuts. You have to wait. Do you know how you want your hair cut?"

Trevor was slowly getting used to the idea of not having long hair. "No, but I'm sure she'll come up with an idea. What about you? Gina Poole's lovely locks go away."

Gina loved the idea of changing her look. "I'm going for total sophistication. I want to create my own look—short on one side and in the back, with a beautiful long swag in the front, cut on an angle."

Trevor smiled at her and pulled her into his lap. "I want to marry you, and we can have babies, and we can perform in a rock band. We can have everything."

Gina stared into his eyes. "I know we can. This is the life that is important. This needs to be Perfection—us, and this life."

Tammie pulled up to their bungalow the next morning, carrying her bag of makeover magic. She did a two-step process on Gina's hair. Creating a blonde undertone and adding heavy highlights made Gina look like a natural blonde.

Tammie was trying to figure out how much of Trevor's hair was coming off. She cut his beautiful curls, left it a little long in the back and cut it short on the top and sides. Trevor stared

at himself in the mirror. "Wow, that's different."

Gina looked over at him. Even with his beautiful blond locks gone, he was somehow more handsome. His face, his blue eyes. Gina fell in love all

4

over again, "Trev, you are so handsome, I'm dying. I'll miss the long hair, but I love your face."

Gina's hair was also coming off. One side of her head had short hair. The back of her head had a fade with a wispy back. The drama came with a massive amount of hair pulled forward. It was long, shaping one side of her face and cut on an angle. Behind her ear were strands of long hair which separated the short hair and long hair. It made her look sexier in a grown-up way.

Trevor gazed at her in awe. "You look amazing. Why didn't we think of this sooner?"

Gina reminded him. "No, then people would recognize us. We're doing this to *not* be recognized."

Gina told Tammie, "You can use our haircuts and say we are your customers, but can you wait a few weeks until after our marriage becomes public?"

"Sure, I work on being discreet. Don't worry your heart."

Gina walked Tammie to the door, putting a generous stack of cash in her hand, and told her she would be their special guest at the next concert in LA.

Gina and Trevor stared at each other. Gina spoke first, "Baby, we may look slightly different, but we are the same people we were a couple hours ago. I think you are sexy as hell. I just have to get used to no long hair."

"Okay, G. I loved your long hair, but woman, you're so sexy right now."

Moments later, they were in bed, looking at each other.

Gina got teary, "Trevor, I love you so much. Baby you're my everything."

Trevor kissed her gently and held her close.

The next morning, the Cessna Citation chartered for them made it to Vegas in just over an hour. A limo was waiting for the Knott party on the tarmac and whisked them to Caesar's Palace. They were directed to a front desk clerk who knew who they were and took care of their check in. Gina leaned over the counter and whispered, "Do you have anybody at the hotel who can marry us? We'd rather not go to a tacky wedding chapel."

The clerk, Cliff, said the justice of the peace would be there on Monday.

At this point, another day wouldn't matter. Gina asked one more question, "Can I get a bridal bouquet made?" Cliff confidently told Gina, "When you're in Vegas nothing is a problem. You can get anything within twenty-four hours."

The next morning Cliff told them that the justice of the peace would marry them in the hotel's Tuscana Chapel at four o'clock that afternoon.

Gina got dressed in a small room off the chapel. Her bouquet was waiting for her—all white flowers. The manager asked Gina what song she would like to walk down the aisle to. Despite being a singer, Gina drew a blank. She took a deep breath, suddenly it hit her. Paul McCartney's "Maybe I'm Amazed." Gina's eyes welled up with tears with the meaning behind the song.

Gina had no idea what Trevor was going to be wearing. He wasn't a dress-up guy, but she didn't care. She loved him unconditionally. Anything he wore would be acceptable.

The music started and Gina glanced down the aisle to see Trevor enter the room, looking handsome in a black jacket, black shirt, black leather pants, and a pink tie—the same thing he had worn to their album release party.

As she stepped onto the golden patterned aisle, her eyes filled with happy tears and focused on Trevor. She loved how private their special moment was. They stood holding hands, and panic reached Trevor's face when he realized he had no rings.

While Gina had been waiting for the music to begin she had taken the rings she had custom made years before out of their boxes and tied them to the ribbons on her bouquet.

Gina was first to say her vows. She untied her ring and handed it to Trevor. He appeared puzzled as he gazed at the beautiful diamond wedding band and placed it on her finger. As Trevor said his vows, Gina untied his wedding band she had made for him, featuring black diamond strips on the top and bottom, and a replica of his favorite guitar on the band.

They were now husband and wife. She was now Gina McNaughton. Could life get better? She hoped so.

The justice of the peace congratulated them and told them to wait while he completed their paperwork. As they lingered at the altar, Trevor was still puzzled as to how Gina had rings. "You want to tell me how you had those rings?"

Gina was proud of herself. "Sure, when we were in New York, I went to our family jeweler to have wedding bands made for us. I was either going to look like a loser, or we would get married eventually and use them. Take off your ring, only this time, never again, and read the inscription." Trevor took off the ring and read the inscription. *Found You Forever*.

His eyes watered. "G, you think of everything. I'm grateful because I don't think of these kinds of details." The justice of the peace came with their paperwork showing they were legally married. They only needed to sign, and it would be official. They walked out of the chapel a newly, happily married couple.

After their ceremony they were anxious to get back to their room, order room service and do what newly married couples do. As the elevator doors were about to close, another couple rushed toward the elevator, and Trevor held the door open for them. Thankfully they were too busy arguing over how much the wife lost at the craps table to recognize Gina and Trevor.

As they approached their suite, they noticed a butler standing at the door with a room service trolly. They were confused because they hadn't ordered dinner yet.

They asked the butler if he had made a mistake, and he answered, "This is from Caesar's Palace to congratulate you on your nuptials. You'll find we chose only the special items on our menu and have included a bottle of our best champagne."

Gina was genuinely touched. "Wow, this is truly endearing. Thank you so much."

Trevor unlocked the door and lifted Gina in his arms. "I'm carrying you over the threshold, wife."

Gina laughed at this conventional custom, after their not-so-conventional wedding.

The butler wheeled the trolly into the room after them and set the dining room table. "I hope you both enjoy your wedding dinner."

Trevor thanked and tipped their server who silently slipped out of the room. "What's on the menu? Duck a l'orange, steak au poivre, salad topped with edible flowers, potatoes Romanoff with caviar," he read from the card. There was even a tiny wedding cake.

The newlyweds shared dinner and toasted to their marriage. Gina picked up the cake and champagne bottle and headed toward the bathroom. Trevor asked, "What are you doing woman?"

"You'll see. Give me a minute." Gina set the cake and champagne flutes on the edge of the bathtub, poured in scented bubble bath, and turned on the tap. "Come in here."

Trevor followed her into the bathroom and Gina unbuttoned his shirt. Soon his pants were off too. She slipped off her wedding dress and climbed into the tub. "Let's be that couple, who eat cake and drink champagne in the bath."

Trevor placed one foot in the water. "Gina, its fucking hot in this tub."

"You'll get used to it. Here, take a bite of the cake." Gina gently fed him a piece of cake. "Is it good?"

"It's delicious. Here, you have some." He smashed it in her mouth.

"Gee thanks. You had to do that, didn't you? She wiped the cake of her face with a soapy hand. "This is perfect. Can I have some champagne, please?"

"Sure, the more drunk you are, the easier it is to take advantage of you."

"Trev, did you ever have to ply me with alcohol to take advantage of me?" She put her glass down on the floor and swam on top of him. "I love you forever, you know that. You look so handsome. I love everything about our wedding, our wedding night, so maybe we get out of the tub now."

The McNaughtons had a wonderful wedding night.

They woke up late. Too much champagne and too much … wedding night. Gina had spent the night curled up in Trevor's arms. She always felt safe with him, and now she felt safer, believing he would always be there.

Trevor growled, "What time is it? Is it really ten? Shit, we haven't slept this late for a long time."

Gina reached for the bedside phone. "I'm going to have coffee delivered to the room. Want anything special for breakfast?"

Trevor pulled her back in bed. "Yes, I do. Come here."

"Trev, I never turn you away, but at least let me order breakfast."

NOT A SECRET WEDDING

THEIR ORDER ARRIVED QUICKLY, accompanied by the morning paper. They climbed back into bed and placed the breakfast trays over their laps. Trevor sat up, almost spilling the coffee. "What the fuck?! Oh shit, Gina you are going to be pissed. I'm totally telling you now. I assumed we covered everything. Baby, I hate to tell you—we have been made."

"What are you talking about?"

"You should see these pictures. It's us getting on the plane in LA. They have been following us. This way if we do anything they are there to cover it. It's like we go to Vegas, and they are waiting."

Gina was fuming. "Are you telling me these pieces of shit are watching everything we do now?"

"Yes, that's what I'm saying. I think we may have to move."

Gina realized, "Holy shit, I need to call my parents. If they see this, they will be devastated that I didn't let them know. Although I always told them we would do exactly this. I have to call them, I'm sorry."

Trevor was resigned to the fact the Riccis needed to know. "No, we don't want to piss them off. Go ahead, call them."

Serena picked up on the third ring. "Hi Serena, it's Gina. I'm good, thanks. Is my mother or father home? Oh, that's right, they're at work. I'll call them there … yes, love you too."

Gina dialed the office line. "Hi Misty, this is Gina. Is my mom or dad there? … Yes, I'll hold … Mom, hi it's me. Mmm … Trevor and I have something to tell you and Dad. Is he around? … I'll wait … Okay, so you're both there and on speaker? Okay … well we want to tell you before you find out somewhere else."

They said together, "We're married!"

Gina continued to fill them in. "We got married yesterday, but the paparazzi took pictures of us as we flew out on a private plane. So, we wanted to tell you before the papers in New York got it."

"Gina Annamarie! In the eyes of the Church, you aren't married. You and Trevor need to get married in Church, so God can see you. What would happen to your babies? No, you two have to get married at St. Mary's." Franny's voice got louder with each proclamation.

Trevor rolled his eyes.

Gina eyeballed him as she replied to her mother. "Mom, I always said we would do this. We don't want the whole wedding chaos. It's not us."

Until now, Mario hadn't said a word. "Listen. This would make your mother happy, Princess. I want her to be happy. It will be small."

Gina knew better. "Dad, your small is two-hundred people. If we do this, a quick meaningful prayer at church with Father Vincent and a small party at the house. That's all we are willing to do."

After a silent pause on the other end, Franny spoke. "Gina that would be beautiful. I'll look for wedding dresses …"

"No, no Mom. I'm already married. The virginal white thing has been over for years, okay? I'll find something. By the way, we may have to move. Our house is being overrun by photographers, fans, and newspapers. We can barely leave. We don't want to sell the Hollywood Hills house because it's close to the studio. But we can't live there daily. No, we haven't started looking … no I don't want to live in Malibu, too many celebrities and photographers. I'll look, wait what … no you don't have to come out next week."

Gina covered the receiver and whispered to Trevor. "Oh, shit babe, they're coming out to look at houses with us. Fuck."

Trevor laughed. "G, at least we're married."

Gina was focused on her handsome man. "I fucking love you."

They spent the next day and night in the Honeymoon Suite before they decided to go back home. What would be waiting for them? More importantly, would they be able to leave Vegas without being noticed? A limo took them to a waiting private jet. They asked the limo driver if he could look around for photographers before he stopped. He told them it was clear, and they left Las Vegas unnoticed.

NEW HOUSE SEARCH

THE MCNAUGHTONS COULD NOT IMAGINE what they would find at their house. Would it be covered with journalists, paparazzi, and fans? Once their pictures appeared in the paper, the secret was out that the hottest couple in the rock scene had gotten married. They were greeted by a circus as they pulled into the driveway. Photographers, fans, entertainment news outlets were camped out on their front yard. Out of nowhere, Gina's cousin Rio showed up and yelled at the crowd, "Fuck off and leave. Private property."

Gina could always count on Rio. They grew up like brother and sister. Living five houses away from each other, Rio even had his own bedroom at her parents' house. Their use of colorful words made for a playful banter, which to others could sound cruel or crude. It was the New Yorker in them, that's the way the family talked to each other. To them it was fun. When Rio started his band, Gina was there, always insinuating herself to become the lead singer. Rio relented because Gina had a good voice and was sexy onstage. Because they didn't want to be recognized by their family connections, they changed their name to Poole. A name they chose while they were stoned, sitting around the pool at Rio's house.

They had become even closer now that they were business partners. Rio was there when Gina and Trevor met, calling the moment "electric." Rio was there when Trevor had to go back to Canada. Rio was there to help fix the visa situation. Rio cared about Trevor and knew they were a great tandem in guitar playing. Knowing that he cared about Trevor endeared Rio to Gina even more.

Rio stomped into the house. "Thanks for letting me know, you two pieces of shit. Really?"

Trevor tried to calm him. "No one was supposed to know anything until we were ready."

Rio took a closer look at the both of them. "What did you two fucking do? You cut your hair? Both of you? Wow, I guess you really didn't want people to know who you are."

Gina was losing it. "That's right asshole. We did this whole fucking thing so we could have our privacy. You know Perfection isn't the only life I want. I want this too—my husband and a semi-normal life."

Rio laughed at her. "Well that was never going to happen, doing this for a living."

Gina was worried. "Well now we need to move. We can't live like this."

Rio had a thought. "North of Malibu is an area called Montecito. It's where celebrities who don't want to be found go. Extremely exclusive. You should check it out. You could probably get a beachfront house. You could find a place for $800,000 to a million. Not a problem."

Trevor liked the idea. "We should take a drive and check it out. Technically we are still on our honeymoon."

Rio said his goodbyes and told them to let him know what they found.

They didn't have much to unpack after their short trip to Vegas. Gina threw some laundry in the washer and they soon climbed into bed. Rio had given them pause to think about this Montecito he talked about. They sat up in bed and discussed the idea of moving. Trevor hated the idea of leaving the bungalow, but also hated the idea of coming home to throngs of people in front of their house. Exhausted by all the changes in their lives, Gina and Trevor fell asleep in their perfect cloud of a bed.

They woke up the next morning and decided they were definitely going to take the drive to Montecito. Gina called out to Trevor, "I'm going to make breakfast, some pancakes and bacon. You good with that?"

Trevor walked into the kitchen wearing his crappy sweatpants. "I'm good with whatever you make. I just want to get going on our drive. Are there people outside the house?"

Gina peeked outside. "There are a few people, not a huge mob. Let's eat, we have a two-hour plus drive. Once again, let's try to get around the people outside."

After a quick shower, the two got in the car and drove up the Pacific Coast Highway. The trip was scenic, and they enjoyed being able to drive free, no onlookers. As they cruised down the streets of Montecito, they liked what they saw. On impulse, they parked in front of a realtor's office.

The realtor recognized them but was notably discreet and told them he had several homes that would work for them. One even had an outbuilding that could be used as a studio—a beachfront with a long staircase leading to the beach. The pictures showed an open living room with floor to ceiling windows revealing the ocean view. Open kitchen, four bedrooms upstairs, with a master bedroom that took up at least half of the first floor. They didn't want to seem pushy, but they were wondering if they could look at any of the houses right away.

The realtor said a few of the homes were empty, so no problem. They followed him in their car and viewed three houses. They knew they needed a house with a gate, like the Ricci estate—something that projects, "You can't come in."

The first house they looked at had a front yard that must have covered an acre, with a fence and gated driveway. The living room opened to a sleek kitchen with grey wood tone colors. The center island measured fourteen feet, with a sink, cabinets, and bar height seating.

Wide plank light grey wood floors led to the master suite on the east side of the house. On the other side of the kitchen was the living room leading to the deck which ran the full length of the house. Every room had an ocean view. Four wide steps descended to a small pool out back of the two-acre property. Gina never thought of having a pool.

Through the privacy hedges were a steep set of stairs that led down to a quiet beach, where a few people were walking their dogs.

After breathing in the ocean air, Gina and Trevor returned to the house and followed stairs to the second floor while the realtor remained outside. Gina ran her fingers along the handcrafted iron banister, similar to one in the house she grew up in. They walked through the four bedrooms, each with its own bathroom.

Returning outside, they walked around to the side yard and saw a building that may have been a barn or a garage at one point. Barn doors slid open to reveal a two-story room with a bathroom in the back, nothing else. Gina turned to Trevor. "Could we make this like a private studio setup? I know nothing about the equipment or anything, that's you and Rio. Could this work?"

Trevor poked around. "It definitely can be a practicing studio, with some offices maybe."

The realtor rejoined them, and Gina asked, "Okay, how much?"

"It's listed at one point one." When he saw Gina's eyes grow large, he added. "But it's been on the market for a while. A deal could possibly be made."

Shrewd like her father, Gina asked, "So how much action has there been with this house?"

"We get lookers. That's about it."

They got back in their cars and viewed two more houses that afternoon. The other two were older, darker inside, and way too ornate. As they all shook hands and prepared to leave the last house, Gina smiled. "Thank you so much for your time. We did like the first house. I was hoping to bring my parents to see it next week."

"No problem. I'll be waiting."

On the drive home, Gina started thinking out loud. "My mother with this church stuff. I knew she would do this. Trevor, I don't want you to think for a moment that this is something I want. We are married, but I need to keep Franny and Mario happy. Do you think they are going to buy this house?"

Trevor proclaimed, "With your parents it's anyone's guess. Do we want to spend a million dollars on a house? That scares me."

Gina had a thought. "I know it's a lot of money. Maybe we can find something not on the ocean that might be cheaper. I absolutely know we need a gate and a long driveway to keep prying eyes away. I am determined to have a private life."

MOVING?

THE TIME AWAY FROM THE BAND was good for everyone's soul to relax and get their creative juices flowing. Rio was writing but was also getting a reputation as a big LA party guy. Rio Poole, Jeff Wainwright, and Brian Mayfield were spotted at the clubs, the strip clubs, and anywhere there was a good time. Jeff was now sporting a ponytail, kind of a chick magnet for some. He was getting a lot of action with that ponytail.

Brian Mayfield was Gina's nemesis. Gina didn't understand why he was given a visa to the US, didn't understand why Trevor, Ian, and Kevin needed him. Gina got a bad vibe from him immediately. She believed now that he was trying to disrupt her relationship and band. She knew he was bringing drugs into the band's practices, and probably women too.

Jeff was an original member of Vision Skye, Rio and Gina's first band. He didn't need much of a push to go wild. Ian and Lisa were levelheaded and had moved into a little house not far from Trevor and Gina. Ian was Trevor's best friend in Vancouver, who played drums in their band Stanley Park. He was also the friend who had lived with Trevor's demons—drugs and alcohol—since they were young teenagers, the juvenile detention stays. Ian beat those demons totally. He married Lisa who was an intelligent, attractive woman. They both felt lucky to have met each other, truly a love story. Lisa and Gina became close friends, their husbands good friends. Would Ian and Lisa be upset if Trevor and Gina moved farther away?

Franny and Mario arrived by private jet the next week, as they had threatened. Everyone was thankful they were staying at the Beverly Hills Hotel, but Gina invited them over and cooked an Italian dinner.

Franny surveyed the house. "Exactly as I remembered it. It's cute, but I do see the crowds. How do you get sleep?"

Trevor explained, "They aren't interrupting us when we are home. It's when we walk out the door."

Franny stiffened. "That's not good for babies. They would disturb my grandchildren."

Gina retorted. "Mom that's not an issue right now. Stop. Seriously, I'm newly married."

Mario was impatient. "When do we see this house you keep telling us about? It's up the road—how far? Is it on the water?"

Trevor chimed in to give Mario the details. "It's north of here, past Malibu, about two hours away. It's a quieter beach community, more protected. Private. We went to see three houses but liked the first one."

That was all that needed to be said. The next day Franny and Mario went to look at the house. Franny walked around casting a critical eye. "This is what California houses look like? No formal rooms? It's a big house for sure, lots of room for grandchildren. Gina, are you going to have time to keep up this house?"

"We will probably be living downstairs for now. Please, no more talk about children. They will come when it's time. What do you think? It has a private drive, which we need, and the outbuilding would be great to set up as a studio."

Mario interjected, "I like it. Sounds like you have given thought to the future of this place. You have a beautiful view of the ocean. Hopefully Gina, it will remind you of our house on the Sound. It's a nice house—not your mother's and my style but we're not living here. I'm a New York guy, so I don't get this California living bullshit. If you and Trevor want this house, let me talk to this guy and cut a deal. He probably hasn't met a guy like me who's going to lowball the shit out of him."

The four of them went to the realtor's office and Mario put his offer in. The realtor had no idea Mario Ricci bought real estate for a living. The seller was desperate—a divorce situation which meant they wanted it sold quickly. They got the house for $895,999 and could take possession in thirty days with a quick closing.

As they were walking out of the office, Franny told Gina, "You and Trevor are getting married October twelfth at St. Mary's Church. A small luncheon after, at the house, that's all."

Gina felt more at ease now she would have her sanctuary.

Now she had to tell all the members of Perfection about the move. Plus, tell them about their upcoming "wedding."

THE NEW HOUSE, BAND REACTION

IT HAD BEEN A FEW WEEKS SINCE Gina saw Lisa. She loved spending time with Lisa, a girl from Queens, which is on Long Island. Gina loved Lisa's genuine, easygoing nature. Gina always thought no matter how famous Perfection became Lisa would never change and become some spoiled rich rock star wife. Gina was afraid to tell Lisa about the move, although she couldn't wait to tell her about her mom's wedding plans.

Gina met Lisa for lunch and told her about the farce that her mother wanted. "She told me I had to wear a wedding dress, all white and virginal. Is she nuts?" They had a laugh.

Lisa asked, "What's next?"

Gina spoke hesitantly. "First Trevor and I are moving. We can't live in the Hills any longer. Next, record another album and probably have to go out and promote that. It's a sick cycle, and more people know you, and you lose a bit of your privacy every time. Have you found that people are around your house?"

Lisa gave Gina a faint smile. "No Gina people leave us alone, sorry. Where are you thinking of? Beverly Hills?" Gina tried to find the words. "Actually, my parents bought us the house. It's in the town of Montecito. It's sort of what Malibu was like decades ago. It's where people who are rich, famous, or whatever go not to be found. There is an issue. It is over two hours away from here. I'm concerned how that affects the band. There is a space that we were thinking of making into a studio. Again this is a concern for everyone in the band."

Lisa did look concerned about what would it mean for the rest of the band. "That's quite a distance to be driving during rehearsals. You both really want to have your privacy. You are correct Gina. This would likely affect us all. I'm happy for you and Trevor. I have a feeling every member of the band will have some thinking to do."

Lisa decided to change the subject, not wanting to think of the ramifications of the McNaughtons' move. She quickly went back to wedding dress shopping. "So, when do we shop for your "not wedding" dress?"

Gina smiled. "We can go now."

BACK TO THE BUSINESS OF MUSIC

SKIP GLAZER, THE BAND MANAGER, made it clear the band needed to start writing music for the next album. He was responsible for business-related issues and worked as a liaison with the record company. Skip worked hard for the band—promotion, tours, recording—always keeping the band's interest ahead of everything

The Realtor in Montecito told Gina and Trevor the seller would be open to closing faster, knowing it was a divorce situation. The McNaughtons jumped at the opportunity to move quickly.

Rio and Jeff needed to be reeled in from partying and find a place to write. Trevor offered up the Hollywood Hills house. He and Gina were in the process of furnishing their new house and if needed they could vacate the Hills house and move into the house in Montecito.

Although Gina loved to be involved in the writing, she wanted to leave Hollywood Hills as soon as possible. She enjoyed decorating the new house herself, sending pictures to Franny for her approval. She chose a color scheme of grey, white, dark blue, and dark plum.

Gina ordered a white baby grand piano for the living room, which featured a two-sided fireplace with a marble surround. On the other side was an area Gina set up as an informal living room and office. She chose a glass top table with grey driftwood legs for the dining room, covering the chairs in a dark blue and white pattern.

The walls in the master bedroom were painted deep blue and furnished with antiques Gina found at an estate sale. She set up one bedroom as a guest room, and one was furnished for Trevor to write music until the other building was ready. Gina left two rooms vacant. She didn't need to worry about those. At this moment she needed to move, leaving all the paparazzi and adoring fans behind.

Gina stopped by the music writing session to see how things were transpiring. There were people around the house, which was getting to be annoying, but they had to write. Rio jumped up, "Oh, look who's here. You care to write some lyrics today? We could use a soft side to what we came up with."

Gina was interested. "Yes Rio, I'm here for a couple of hours. Let me see what you have." Rio handed her a sheaf of papers. Gina glanced through them and glared around the room. "Seriously? This is what you came up with? It stinks. It has no soul, no hook. Wait, are you all high right now?"

She saw Brian Mayfield walking out of the bathroom and her anger ratcheted up a notch. Gina had taken an instant dislike to him the minute she met him at Trevor's father's house and credited her feelings to intuition. He still had no official position with the band and Gina could not figure out why he was on the payroll. He was a small guy with red hair and always had a fake smile on his face. He constantly reminded her of someone, and she couldn't figure out who until she was watching TV one night and a commercial for Lucky Charms cereal came on. The leprechaun inspired her nickname for him.

She never got a good answer why Trevor got him a visa to come to the US. Gina felt he wanted to reawaken Trevor's demons. She needed to find a way to remove him from the Perfection umbrella. Maybe try to revoke his visa. She hated him and didn't understand why Trevor couldn't see what Mayfield was doing.

"Oh, Mr. Lucky Charms, are you writing music now? Why are you here, to get everyone high, so they can't put a cohesive bunch of lyrics together? You know what? I feel like walking out right now, let you all feel the pressure of meeting a deadline. But this is my band too. I want to hear the music for these songs."

Rio and Trevor started playing to give her an idea of how the song would go. Gina was pissed. "Are we now trying to write corny rock ballads, or are we a true rock band? We aren't that soft crap. We need edgy. When you guys get your shit together, without fucking Lucky Charms getting you all high, let me know. I'll sit and think about the lyrics. Right now, I'm going to my new house to enjoy the beautiful Pacific Ocean. Trev, baby, I don't know what to say to you right now. Come home when you're not shit-faced. Hey Brian, stop fucking with my business."

Gina slammed the door as she left. Trevor knew he would have to deal with her wrath when he got home. As Gina drove the two plus hours home, she kept hearing the music that Rio and Trevor played. When she got home, she immediately started writing a song, and titled it,

"Who Knew Life Would Be Like This?"

I wanted the life of lights and glamour; I did everything to make
it work. Once the lights hit you, you're a star. They love you, they
want you, you give them your soul everything you have they give you
applause, but they want more they want to see your life they want to
live through you then you're theirs, like animals in a cage
Who knew life would be like this, who knew life would be like this
I didn't know how life would change but I'm taking it back
I didn't want life like this, People evading your space,
Wanting to know about hair, clothes, and your sex life
I have nothing to say, go figure it out, my life is not yours
I feel I have nowhere to go, who knew life would be like this.
I'm taking it back, and then you can go to hell.

Gina went into the kitchen and made a salad with chicken for dinner.
She didn't know when Trevor was going to make it home. She didn't like
the vibe she got from him, especially because of Brian. Trevor didn't try
to catch her and apologize. She left knowing he was incredibly high. She
only hoped Trevor wouldn't drive if he was really messed up. She worried
because she knew he had demons waiting to escape. Was this going to be a
fight, the second in their whole relationship? It remained to be seen. They
had to leave in two weeks for her mother's wedding. How would that work
with her and Trevor at odds with each other?

About an hour later, Gina heard the front door open.

Trevor walked right toward her. "What's wrong with you? You lash
out at us because we were a little high. In an instant you look at our work,
criticize it, and walk out. What goes on in your head when you make those
accusations? I love you, but I need to understand."

Gina was feeling cocky. "Okay baby, this is it. Brian Mayfield makes
you all look like the band that is all about drugs, drinking, and womanizing.

That's what he thinks of our band. That's what he wants. He doesn't respect our marriage, or Ian's either. Or anyone's sobriety. I'm a member of this group. He is not going to have that power over me, our marriage, or this band. I see him for who he is, even when you don't. I don't want this to be a thing between us. I love you so much. I even came home and wrote some lyrics. Yes, I was mad, but I'm over it."

Trevor leaned heavily on the counter, a stance she never saw before. "Damn you G! Brian cannot and will not get between us. I keep telling you that. He may have Rio and Jeff out partying all night, but I'm home with you. If I wanted that, would I have married you? Think about that. I even agreed to get married again to make your mother happy. Have I ever pushed back on you? You know I haven't."

Gina started to cry. Trevor never spoke to her in that manner.

He walked over to her. "Okay, stop. Don't cry. I hate when you cry. I'm sorry for coming down on you. Why do you feel so insecure? You're beautiful and talented, but you're also jealous as hell Gina, and you don't need to be. Come here." He opened his arms. "Come here and stop crying."

Gina felt his arms around her and cried into his chest for a few minutes. "Are we good now?" she choked. "Are we? I don't like this feeling."

Trevor hugged her tighter. "It's all good baby. It's all good. What did you make for dinner?"

She wiped her eyes. "I got lazy, a salad with chicken."

"Sounds good. Let's eat. Later show me those lyrics."

After dinner, things seemed more normal. Trevor changed into his old sweatpants. Gina put on one of her sexy nightgowns. "Here, this is what I wrote." She was nervous about what Trevor would think about it.

"How long did it take you to write this?" he asked.

"Honestly Trev, not long at all. It was what I've been feeling. Moving here has calmed me. I know no one can break through the barrier."

Trevor eyed the lyrics. "We need to work some lines out, but this is better than what we came up with. We need you to write your perspective. You're important in the songwriting."

"Okay, Trev I hear you. I will get this place in order so I can spend more time writing. But the drive is a killer for sure."

Trevor calmly said, "Let's go to bed. You good with that? Can I take advantage of you?"

Gina smiled. "I think we can work out a deal."

Trevor hoisted her over his shoulder and carried her into the bedroom. Gina had a sexy surprise. She opened her nightstand and brought four long silk ribbons. "Baby, I bought these the other day, so you can tie me up and do whatever you want."

Trevor was stunned. "So, I can do whatever I want and you're helpless?"

"Yes, that's right. Want to—" Before Gina finished saying those words, Trevor pushed her down on the bed and had her hands tied to the headboard. He tied her legs and ripped her nightgown off. He teased her for a long time using his mouth over every sensitive part of her body. She was helpless to take in the pleasure he was giving her. She loved the feeling of being powerless under his control. It was erotic. After they were done, Trevor was out of breath.

She whispered, "Baby, can you untie me now?" They laughed and slipped under the comforter. She nestled under his arm and began to drift off to sleep. "I love you always. Remember that."

Trevor was satiated. "I do. I love you too. Let's not disagree. I hate it. I much prefer this."

FRANNY'S FAUX WEDDING

IT WAS BACK TO REAL WORK on the album. Gina sat with the guys for a couple of days trying to sort out the music and lyrics and was making headway. Perfection thought they had a solid four songs, but that wouldn't be enough. However, it was time to go to New York. The McNaughtons wanted the entire band of Perfection to attend their wedding. Even Brian Mayfield was invited. He would lay very low for this event. However, Brian Mayfield would prove to be problematic down the road. Skip Glazer and his wife June were part of the band family. Skip was always working on the band's business, even when it was an off day.

Tommy and Anne Whelan were invited to the wedding. Tommy worked for Brown Fence Records; he was the producer for Perfection. And had asked specifically to work with the band. Tommy was a well sought after producer in the music world. He wanted to take Perfection to the highest level. He had a close attachment with them. Gina and Trevor hired a private jet so their guests didn't have to pay airfare. Everyone wanted to attend this wedding since no one was there for the first one in Vegas.

Gina was keeping a huge secret. It might slow down the rehearsals, maybe the recording, certainly now wasn't the time to share it, though. She wondered when and how she would tell Trevor.

Lisa sat next to her on the plane and asked, "Are you nervous?"

Gina laughed. "Why would I be nervous? I'm already married. This is solely so my mother can say I got married in the eyes of God. It's silly. Get ready for a lot of Italians. Why? Are *you* nervous?"

Lisa's response was unexpected. "I *am* nervous. I am busting. I have a big secret to tell you, and Ian would be mad if I told anyone without him but … I'm pregnant!"

Gina's heart completely sank. "I'm so happy for you two. When is the baby due?"

"March eighteenth—something like that." Lisa was glowing. "Ian said he was going to tell everyone on the plane."

An hour later, as Ian made the announcement, Gina worked to hold back her tears.

Trevor noticed Gina's effort to hide her emotion, but he didn't bring it up. He would wait until they had situated themselves in New York. He didn't think it was jealousy, since Gina and Lisa were such good friends. He knew something was going on with Gina, though. He had lived with her too many years not to recognize her moods.

The plane landed and limos were waiting for all the guests to take them to the Inn at Great Neck. Franny and Mario picked up Trevor and Gina, who would stay in the carriage house. Franny had to add, "It is bad luck for the groom to see the bride."

Gina reminded her mother, "Mom, I told you I am already married, so please stop."

The ride back to the estate was filled with chatter about the wedding. They entered the carriage house and turned on the lights like an old habit. Gina realized that she and Trevor had taken the cloud mattress from the master bedroom, so they would have to sleep in the other bedroom.

Trevor asked, "You want a drink?"

"Umm, maybe a tiny bit of wine, and I mean tiny," Gina hedged.

Shawn McNaughton, Trevor's dad, was coming in for the wedding.

Gina hoped his presence would help heal the relationship between father and son. Franny and Mario insisted he also stay at the Inn. Shawn was about to be overwhelmed by Italians and rock stars. It would be a culture shock for sure, but he was there to witness Gina and Trevor getting married again and in church.

Shawn may still have his issues with Trevor, but he cared deeply about Gina. She showed him unconditional love. As long as she had to go through with this farce, Gina felt it was important for Shawn to be there. She asked her parents to keep a watchful eye over him and make him feel like part of this crazy bunch of Long Islanders. Franny felt her daughter's wedding was the most paramount event in her family and the Ricci family would all be present. She had hoped and planned for this day and now it was here.

Gina's brother Frankie and his wife, MaryAnn, would be there with their three children. Frankie was still Mario's heir apparent and relished his position. Gina's younger brother, Ant, decided on a law career. He was a senior in high school and had been looking at colleges. His first choice was Villanova, a good Catholic University in Pennsylvania. Of course, Serena would be there as a member of the family, not the woman who ran the house. Everything was set for a beautiful event, even though it was a "redo" wedding.

Gina and Trevor had succumbed to what Mario and Franny wanted and played along. But Gina had a bigger secret for Trevor. This wedding would be memorable.

GINA HAS
A SECRET

MARIO AND FRANNY WANTED TO ENSURE that Gina and Trevor's marriage was sanctioned by God and Church, and any children would be protected by the Holy Sacrament. Gina and Trevor owed much to her parents. They had bought them two homes in California worth over a million dollars. How could they not indulge her parents in making them happy? This was a simple request. It was surely a Ricci family event.

Trevor and Gina were back in the home where they had begun their relationship, the carriage house on the Ricci estate. It was like an old friend. Trevor noticed Gina was a bit weepy and had to find out what exactly was bothering her. Trevor asked, "Babe, we are getting married again tomorrow, so please, tell me what's wrong, because I know as soon as Lisa told you she was pregnant, your face just got teary so—"

Gina stammered, "I've been keeping a secret from you for about three weeks. I'm late, and sure that I'm pregnant. I didn't want to say anything, writing music and all this shit. I was afraid to tell you. I wasn't sure how you would feel because we didn't plan it. I'm about six weeks along. I figured out that the baby's due date would be around early June. I still need to see a doctor. I'm not sure how tight my body-hugging wedding dress will fit and I'm scared about your reaction." She paused to wipe the tears falling freely from her eyes. "Trevor, please say something."

Trevor had tears in his eyes too. "We're going to have a baby. That's what you're saying?"

"Yes, absolutely. No mistake. You didn't realize I haven't had my period?"

"I don't count the days or watch for that stuff. But why not tell me sooner? Was it this wedding thing?"

"I didn't want it getting out until after. I was afraid one of us would slip. I'm so sorry. This should be the happiest moment in our life, and I ruined it."

"G, you didn't ruin it. Maybe it would have been nice to share the fact you thought it was possible. But how can I be mad? You're thinking the baby will be due in early June? A summer baby.

"Yes, but we can't say anything. I don't want to take the spotlight away from Lisa. She's so happy. I couldn't do that to my friend."

"You did it again Gina McNaughton. You have left me speechless. I'm going to be a father."

Gina was weepy. "I guess that's why I've been so emotional. This is what I wanted for us. I just can't believe it's really happening."

"Come here. I'm going to happily marry you all over again. Is it safe for us to—?"

"Make love? Yes, it's safe. I don't know how you will feel when I'm fat, though."

Trevor reassured her. "Stop, you will be even more beautiful. Let's go to bed, and let me show you how happy I am."

WEDDING DAY

THE NEXT MORNING, FRANNY had hired makeup and hair stylists to come to the house. "Gina why did you cut your beautiful hair?"

"Mom, just let it be the way it is. Can you fasten my dress?"

Franny struggled to zip and button Gina into her dress. "This is a beautiful dress, but it's very tight."

"Mom, it's not tight. It's made to fit this way."

Franny was a bit upset. "You didn't get a veil?"

Gina made a face again. "Mom I am a married woman, and we are doing this to make you happy, so please just go with it."

As Gina, Trevor, and her parents drove to St. Mary's Church, Gina recalled her days attending high school at St. Mary's. Those feelings of never fitting in came back. While Mario drove, her mother asked Gina and Trevor for their wedding rings. Gina was in a bit of a daze and riding to the church was the first time seeing Trevor all day. She noticed he was wearing a midnight blue suit. She wondered if that was Franny's idea. Gina was waiting to see her brother Frankie and MaryAnn and their three spoiled rotten children. But it's family.

Gina stared at St. Mary's. How many times had she entered through those doors? Franny would have the church decorated elaborately with the finest of everything. As she expected, there were pure white and soft pink roses, mixed with lilies of the valley, hydrangeas, and lush greenery in tall vases that lined the pews. At the altar were the largest floral arrangements made with the same flowers. Brass candelabras graced the altar, giving the church a candlelit look. Gina was amazed and realized that this was truly a special moment for her mother. Instead of the organ music usually played at the church, her mother had hired a string quartet who were playing Bach.

Gina went into the bridal room that was inside the church. Franny handed Gina a beautiful large bouquet and Gina placed a wrist corsage on her mother's wrist. There were boutonnieres for her father, Trevor, Shawn, Ant, Frankie, and Ian. Franny also made sure that MaryAnn, Lisa and Serena had wrist corsages. Lisa and Ian were standing in as witnesses and held the wedding rings.

Gina heard the beautiful music coming from the sanctuary and the quiet chatter of people filling up the church. This wasn't going to be a small affair. Franny asked Gina, "You okay Gina? You look a bit pale. I know you're not nervous since, as you said, you are already married. Is there something bothering you?"

Gina seemed a bit lost. "Mom, promise me we aren't having a High Mass, that Father Vincent is only going to say a few prayers and then read our vows. No communion either."

There was a knock at the door and Franny got up to let Aunt Deidre and Lisa in.

Aunt Deidre said, "In about two minutes, they are going to start the processional. Tony and I are getting ready to walk down. The church looks exquisite Franny, but you always do the best. Gina, Trevor is already at the altar. He looks so handsome in that suit. Oh, and after Uncle Tony and I walk down, Shawn will be walking down." Aunt Deidre walked over to Gina and gave her a kiss. "You already did this once, so you're fine."

After she left, Lisa spoke up. "Ian is already there with Trevor. You look beautiful."

At that moment Ant and Mario came in. Ant said, "Mom, let's go. It's your turn Mother of the Bride."

Franny teared up. "Princess, this is the happiest day of my life."

Ant walked Franny down the aisle to Bach's concerto in D minor. Tears trailed down Gina's cheeks as she remembered Trevor loved classical music. *Maybe it's the pregnancy hormones,* she thought.

"Daddy, wait. Let me quickly fix my makeup. I'm good." The knock on the door was from the woman who helped with weddings at the church, "Okay, your turn."

Gina grabbed her father's arm.

"Princess, you're doing this again. Let's go." Everyone stood as Mario and Gina walked down the aisle. Gina tried to look ahead at Trevor, but got distracted by her parents' old friends, wishing her good luck. The Perfection group sat together.

She glanced at Rio, who had tears in his eyes. She mouthed to him, "Please don't. I'll lose it." The scent of the flowers was strong and sweet.

Mario and Gina stopped before the altar. After a beat, Father Vincent asked, "Who gives this woman for marriage?" Mario choked out the words, "Her mother and I do."

As he stepped away, Trevor walked over and grabbed Gina's hand. "You're good, relax. Remember we're married already."

Father Vincent started with a prayer and instructed everyone to sit down. He said a few heartfelt words about knowing Gina since she was a little girl. Franny was crying. Father Vincent led a prayer for the couple and beseeched the Blessed Mother to watch over them. He asked for the rings Lisa and Ian were holding. He took the rings, blessed them, and instructed the couple to say the holy vows. Father Vincent led one more prayer to have God and Jesus watch over Gina and Trevor. At that moment he pronounced them Man and Wife in the eyes of the Catholic Church and the State of New York.

"You may kiss your bride." Trevor leaned over, touched her face, and drew her in for a soft, loving kiss.

He said out loud for everyone to hear, "I love you Gina McNaughton, you are my life."

Gina smiled through her tears. "You are the only man I will ever love."

They turned around and returned down the aisle to Brandenburg's Concerto No. 3. Franny went up to the couple and kissed them. The whole service only took twenty minutes.

A reception line formed in the vestibule of the church with Franny, Mario, Shawn, and the happily married couple. Well wishes, hugs, and tears were shared. All would have been perfect if it weren't for Frankie's kids running in and out of the reception line. Franny wrapped it up, "Princess there is a limo ready to take you both to the house. We will see you there."

Gina asked, "Are there going to be pictures?"

Franny smiled. "You're silly. Of course there will be, but at the house."

The happy couple climbed into the waiting limo as family and friends threw rice. Trevor turned to Gina. "Happy you married me again?"

Gina grabbed him lovingly and gave him a lustful kiss. She was the happiest woman for the second time. "I would marry you every day if I had to. We are going to have a baby. I'm happy and nervous at the same time. I probably need to get help at home. Trust me we will not be getting some young twenty-year-old to help around the house. It will be someone like Serena. She was there when my mother couldn't be."

Trevor was fidgeting in the suit. "I can't believe I agreed to wear this."

Gina grabbed his face, "Baby you look awesome all dressed up. What would you do if we ever got invited to an awards show?"

Trevor easily replied, "I wouldn't dress like *this*."

Gina laughed, "You'll have to. Red carpet babe. They judge you. Remember we're the sexy couple."

RICCI WEDDING RECEPTION

A VALET SERVICE PARKED THE CARS that were unloading more people into the house. There seemed to be more people at the house than at the church. The couple walked through the house and was stopped by a photographer taking candid shots. They made their way straight to the backyard where, although the day was uncharacteristically warm for October, a white tent with zippered walls and electric heaters had been erected. The same type of flowers that filled the church were splashed all over the tent in massive floor arrangement and tall table arrangements. Candles at various heights filled the tables. Spheres of white roses hung from the ceiling with pale pink silk ribbon cascading down. Once again, the smell of the flowers was intoxicating, but were becoming overwhelming for Gina's delicate condition.

Partygoers cheered the couple as they entered, and the photographer snapped more photos. Lounge sofas surrounded a dance floor. The DJ her father hired from a club was set up in a corner, already playing soft rock as guests arrived. There were three bars and all the best food imaginable—lobster, chateaubriand, and all types of Italian food. It was a Ricci event, that's for sure. Franny directed the couple to a spot where the family was to take more photos. The event reminded Gina of what it felt like to be at a record label "meet and greet." It wasn't that bad if it made her parents happy.

Gina never had a chance to escape the wedding her mother wanted. Thankfully no one knew Gina was going to have a child. Gina and Trevor walked through all the people as the DJ played "Lovin', Touchin', Squeezin'," a Journey song. Everyone looked at them expectantly, waiting for them to start dancing, and they quickly obliged with a couple of moves. The music was not what they were used to dancing to, they moved to a much harder beat. But they weren't onstage, this was a wedding.

Shawn McNaughton had never been to a party of this magnitude and was somewhat out of his element, so Gina made sure she introduced him to the important people in her family: Uncle Tony, Aunt Deidre, Serena, Ant, Frankie, and MaryAnn. Shawn had talked to Rio on the phone many times regarding the visa situation when the band was first getting started. They had never met in person, but they felt like they knew each other. Shawn was happy to see Ian, Kevin, and Brian. Ian introduced him to Lisa and told Shawn they were expecting a baby. Before long Mario took Shawn around and introduced him to Vinny and Sal, Ricci Construction guys, and a few select friends. Gina was sure Shawn had never met a group of people like this in Vancouver.

Gina decided to rescue Shawn. "Are you having a good time, Dad? It means so much to me for you to feel like a part of my family, our family. You doing okay?"

"My son is very lucky to have found you. I'm mystified that you have so much love for him, knowing that he has many faults. Gina, I'm proud to call you my daughter-in-law. Thank you for loving my son so deeply."

Gina gave Shawn a kiss on the cheek. "I will always watch over him. No demons."

Gina made sure Shawn had someone easy to talk to and went in search of Trevor. "Babe, you need to spend some time with your father. No matter what is between the two of you, please try to spend some time with him. It means so much to me."

"If it makes you happy I will."

Rio came up to the happy couple, laughing. "Well Aunt Franny sure outdid herself again, especially since the two of you are already married. How does it feel to get married again?"

Gina confessed, "Honestly, it feels better the second time." She winked at Trevor because they knew they were going to be parents. Jeff and Kevin joined them, and Rio suggested, "Hey, Gina for old times' sake, let's all go smoke a joint in the pool house, come on."

She looked at Trevor not wanting to give away her secret. "Okay Rio if you insist, but just one hit, because I have to deal with all this shit. I don't feel like talking to some of these people while I'm high. This may be my parents' wedding, but I can't be mad. My parents have been very generous to us, so I'm being a good daughter and enjoying the party."

A happy memory came over Gina as the five of them walked to the pool house. She remembered sitting by the pool at Rio's house, being very stoned when they came up with their stage name—Poole. Rio lit up the joint. "Here Gina, you need this more than us."

Gina was perplexed. "Why do I need this more? Because I'm already married and my mother is pretending like today is my wedding day? Or is there something about the band I need to know? Is it that I told Skip I wanted to be more involved with the business side? I want to protect our interests."

Trevor took the joint out of her hand. "G, maybe you should just write with us for now. You don't want the stress of the business side of things. That's why we have Skip."

"Skip is great, I just want to make sure we never get screwed."

Rio knew he would piss off Gina, but he said it anyway. "We also have Brian." Rio couldn't stop laughing, "He's your favorite."

Gina smirked. "You must be high, or I would beat the shit out of you right now." They started walking back to the tent as the DJ called Franny and Mario to the dance floor.

Gina had never seen her parents dance before and wasn't about to miss this. "You Are the Sunshine of My Life" started to play. Mario and Franny truly displayed their love as they glided effortlessly across the floor. Watching her parents dance in perfect unison, Gina started weeping and couldn't stop. Trevor drew her closer, seeing how emotional she was. Mario walked over and dragged Gina to the dance floor. Franny grabbed Trevor and brought him out to the floor as well. Gina continued to cry as she listened to the words, dancing with her father, knowing he would always watch out for her. Everyone started clapping. The emotion was too much for her. The hormones of her pregnancy were kicking in. She kissed her father.

"Princess, you are the daughter every man should be happy to have."

She tried to get the words out between sobs, "Thank you Daddy. I love you too."

As the dance ended, Gina turned away and started walking fast to the house. Trevor caught up to her. "That was a beautiful sentiment, and I can see you're emotional. The hormones are catching up with you. What can I do?"

Gina was sobbing. "Just hold me for a minute until I get myself together. I never saw my parents in love like that. It got to me."

Lisa came over. "Gina, you okay?" Trevor answered, explaining that seeing her parents dance made Gina a little emotional.

Lisa stroked her back. "Oh Gina, that's so sweet. We're having a blast. Now I know why money is never an issue for you. This place is spectacular."

Gina got herself together. "It's a blessing and a curse. My parents have been very generous to Trevor and me. That's why we agreed to this party."

The evening went on, everyone drinking, having a great time. The food was delicious, and the DJ played old favorites that kept everybody on the dance floor. Gina said hello to all her parents' friends who all thought it was her actual wedding day.

Gina brought Trevor over to his father to make sure he was having a good time. Shawn looked around. "I've never seen anything like this."

Trevor hung back in his security zone—with Rio and the other band members. Gina was fine with it.

They were called to cut the cake. How far was this going to go? She looked at Trevor and mouthed, "I'm sorry." Gina cut a piece and gently fed it to Trevor. He repeated what he did in Vegas—took a piece of cake and jammed it into her mouth. Gina mouthed, "You really suck."

People started to leave, thank God. Gina turned around at one point and there he was, Mr. "Lucky Charms." What a hot mess this was going to be.

"You know Gina, I misjudged you. You are very savvy. I guess you got that killer instinct from your parents. I need to watch out for you. I get you now."

Gina walked right up to his face. "Brian if you get me, you should know not to fuck with me. Don't. It won't end up well for you. Respect my position in the band, and most of all respect my marriage. If you don't? Well, we will see. That's a friendly reminder."

Brian walked away without responding.

The party was ending, the band members were shuttled to their hotel, and tomorrow they would head back to Los Angeles. Gina felt saddened every time she flew back to Los Angeles, like she was losing a bit of her New York edge. LA was home now, but she was still that Italian girl from Long Island.

In the morning, she thanked her parents and told them to come and visit their new home. She told them she would miss them, her hormones getting the best of her.

BACK HOME
TO CALI

THE BAND AND THEIR GUESTS BOARDED the private jet to head home. Gina curled up next to Trevor. She was completely worn out. Now that she was pregnant, she felt she never got enough sleep. During the flight, Lisa sat next to them. "Gina, I had a wonderful time at your parents'. They are so sweet. Your house, I mean unbelievable, it's hard to imagine you growing up that way—so privileged. You're so levelheaded."

Gina looked up at Lisa, "Thank you Lisa. That's very nice of you to say. I try not to let myself be that spoiled woman."

Gina excused herself to run to the bathroom. She locked the door and started puking her guts out. *It's real*, she thought. *Now I have morning sickness.* How long would it be before she couldn't hide it anymore? She wasn't showing of course, but people might start recognizing her symptoms.

Trevor got up and excused himself from Lisa and knocked on the door. "G, let me in. Please open the door."

Gina, still hanging her head over the toilet, flicked the lock. Trevor knelt next to her. "I know you feel like shit. I wish I could do something."

Gina was visibly worn out. "I know. I wonder how long I can hide this from everyone."

"You don't have to hide this. It's our joy. Just because Ian and Lisa told us they were having a baby, doesn't mean we have to hide our news. We probably should tell them soon, because I don't want you to spend long days writing music, and when we go into the studio, you can't work until ten p.m. Let's be smart about this. The baby is the most important thing. We don't have to say anything right this minute, but sooner than you intended. Let's get you some ginger ale. Come on babe, I got you."

Gina knew he was right, and it seemed like he wanted to share the news, but not today. Together, they would tell everyone once they went to the Hills house and started to write. Gina wobbled her way back to her seat. Trevor got her a pillow and blanket and she lay across his lap.

Lisa was very perceptive and could tell something was up. She kept her thoughts to herself and wondered why Gina wouldn't tell her.

The ride from LAX to Montecito took two hours and twenty minutes. They should have flown directly into Santa Barbara Municipal. They would remember for next time.

It was nice to pull through the gates and drive up to the house without onlookers. Gina wondered when they would catch on. Trevor brought the suitcases in and dropped them in the foyer. Gina walked to the floor to ceiling windows and stared at the ocean, calmed by the gentle waves. Trevor came up behind her and put his arms around her, resting his chin on her head. "We good? Can I get you anything to eat?"

Gina turned around. "Trev, I love you very much, but you can't cook for shit. Let me see what we have. We were only gone four days. There must be something I can put together. Hey, we have wine in the wine fridge. I don't remember filling it."

"G, baby should you be drinking?"

"Honey, I can have a sip. Would you like some? We're home, in our beautiful house, let's enjoy it and sit outside. I'll make some pasta with meat sauce."

They sat on a large chair on the deck, sipping wine. Gina looked up at Trevor. "I wish our life could always be this ... calm. But we chose a path where this is an anomaly. We chose chaos. I want to take the baby with us when we tour. I don't want to leave my child."

Trevor looked puzzled. "Gina we can take our child with us wherever we want. It's our band. We get to do what we what. Don't let that worry you."

They finished eating. Jet lag and pregnancy sent them to bed early. Gina turned to Trevor. "Baby, is it okay if we don't make love tonight? I just want to cuddle with you."

Trevor smiled, "Of course it is."

THE TRUTH
COMES OUT

GINA WAS WELL INTO HER PREGNANCY. She had to tell Perfection. They were working on writing more songs for their second album. Gina and Trevor worked on lyrics while Rio put guitar and keyboards together. They wrote four more songs, bringing the total to eight, but wanted two more. Everyone in the band came up with two more songs, making a total of ten songs. They picked the best eight of the ten songs. Rio seemed to be a bit more settled, not that he wasn't smoking weed all day, but he wasn't at the strip clubs or the bars every night. His antics weren't newsworthy, and Gina took note.

The Hollywood Hills house became a magnet for fans and paparazzi. Gina wanted the building on their new property to be made into a rehearsal studio and offices, sooner rather than later. Rio would help with equipment. Unfortunately, most of the band were in Los Angeles, a good two hours away from the Montecito house. They would keep the Hollywood Hills house in case of a late night at the studio, even though Gina was approaching her third month of pregnancy. She was going to investigate placing a fence around the Hills house, to help keep the gawkers away. A zoning issue for sure.

They had spent the entire day writing and going through the new music and now it was getting late. Gina asked Trevor if they could just spend the night there and not drive home. She was worn out.

Trevor responded, "We need to tell everyone, it's time."

As everyone was packing up, the McNaughtons announced they were expecting their first child. Trevor wanted it known that Gina's time in the studio would be limited. More of a reason to get Montecito ready.

Rio was a bit hurt at hearing the news with everybody else. "Gina, I'm your cousin, like a brother, why wouldn't you tell me sooner?"

Gina hugged him. "Listen, I wanted to tell you, but when Lisa said she was pregnant I didn't want to trample on her news, so I kept quiet. I'm sorry I should have told you sooner."

Rio patted her on the back, "I get it Gina."

"I even waited to tell Trevor, so please don't be hurt."

"Seriously? You didn't tell Trevor? Christ Gina. You can keep a secret."

"I also didn't want to slip up at the wedding. Trevor and I could have easily said something by mistake. Oh, shit Rio, I haven't told my parents yet."

"You haven't told them either? Okay, now I don't feel so bad."

"Please don't say anything. What time is it in New York? Nine-thirty? I can call them."

"You better let Aunt Franny know as soon as possible. She's going to lose it. But how about that? I'm going to be an uncle, how cool. Just so you know I have a secret too, but I would rather show you than tell you."

Gina jumped at this. "Yeah, buddy I do love you. You will make a great uncle. I'm intrigued by your secret though."

Gina got the phone. "Trev! I have to tell my parents. You want to hear the hysterics that come out of Franny when I tell her?"

He laughed. Of course he wanted to hear this.

Mario picked up, "Yeah?"

"Hi Dad. It's me, umm, is Mom there too? I need to talk to you both."

Mario sounded concerned. "Princess, is everything okay with the marriage?"

Gina ignored the question. "Dad, can you just use the speaker? Mom, can you hear me?"

Franny was a bit anxious. "Yes Gina, what's going on? It's late. Is everything okay with you and Trevor?"

Trevor shook his head. The faith they had in him, that he would hurt their daughter. But Franny and Mario would hold that thought.

"Okay, I'm just saying it. We're pregnant. I'm about three months so you will be grandparents again."

Franny shrieked, "I've been waiting for this. My true grandchild! Oh Gina, how do you feel? I'm just so excited I don't know what to say. Do you need me to come out?"

"No, please we're good. I just needed to let you know, and you will be updated. I'm still feeling sick at times. I'm not showing either, in case you are wondering. Now you both know, and we are very happy. I guess that's it for now. Congratulations. You got what you wanted."

Gina could tell Mario was choking back tears. "Princess we are so happy for you both! Trevor, you take care of my Princess."

Done. Dot the I. Everyone who needs to know, knows. Except for Skip Glazer, Perfection's manager, and Tommy Whelan, Perfection's producer with Brown Fence Records. Tommy took a very personal interest in Perfection; it would come into play in the future. They needed to know so they could figure out the studio time. Tomorrow, they would tell them.

It was weird staying at the Hills house. Gina was afraid that some sicko would walk right up to the door or look in a window. She wouldn't get a good night's sleep. She found a fancy nightgown and put it on. Why not? Trevor was looking at some of the music Rio wrote. "Hey G, I think we have some good music here. I want you to figure out what lyrics would go best with the music."

"I got it. No worries, babe. Can I interest you in going to bed early?"

He looked up from the music. "You mean bed, or bed?"

Gina gave him a sly look. "What do you think I mean? I may be pregnant, but I keep telling you I want to make love to my husband. Is that something that still interests you?"

"Yes, I just want you to tell me when you feel good enough to play."

"Trev, I'm not even showing yet. My body is still the same and I still want you. Please don't treat me like I'm fragile."

Trevor put down the music, then checked the locks on all the doors and turned on the motion sensor security lights. "I'll be right there."

Gina was waiting for him, already naked under the comforter in their cloud of a bed.

By the time Trevor got into bed, he too was naked.

Gina turned on her side and traced his face with her finger. She thought he was handsome before. But since the makeover, he looked so much more sophisticated.

She moved her body as close to him as she could without starting the lovemaking process. She ran her hands all over his body, stopping where they both wanted her to go. "May I have this? I really do want it."

"It's yours to do what you want Mrs. McNaughton. Show me what you want."

She stayed on her side and wrapped one leg over him. He wasted no time in how this would go. She wrapped her hands around his neck, and started kissing him like she hadn't seen him for months.

"Is this the hormones working? Because I can get used to it."

Gina used her sexy voice, "Maybe, but I always want you to know how much I need to have this part of you. It completes me and takes me to a place where only you can take me. Silly?"

Trevor was excited. "No, you sound like a woman who loves her husband. You're the only woman who can have me."

They always finished with ultimate satisfaction. His words were something Gina never doubted, until she did.

MUSIC WRITING AND
SECRETS REVEALED

IN THE MORNING, they showered, Gina made coffee, and started making breakfast. There was a knock on the door. Ian and Lisa. Lisa ran in and hugged Gina. "I can't believe it. We are going to have our babies a few months apart. I'm excited we will be going through this together."

Gina certainly wasn't expecting that first thing in the morning. Lisa continued, "I knew there was something wrong with you on the plane, but you never said anything."

"I didn't want to take away from your happiness, that's all."

"You're a crazy lady, Gina."

Gina asked, "Do you plan on staying for music writing, and fighting, and a million other things?"

"No, I just dropped Ian off and wanted to see you. I'm going to let you go to work."

Jeff showed up an hour later, hung over.

Gina looked at him. "Hey guy, get your fucking head in the music. We need you. Stop with the star fuckers and strippers. Isn't it enough? Are you doing a lot of coke too?"

Jeff was pissed. "Hey Trevor, tell your wife she isn't my fucking mother."

Gina got in his face and pointed her finger. "Look you cocksucker, this band, Perfection is what we created. If you can't cut it, then get the fuck out! Get your shit together and do whatever drugs you want on your own time. This is Perfection time. And never speak through my husband, you speak to me directly, you piece of shit. Have some coffee and straighten up."

Jeff knew better than to piss off Gina, however he hated when she called out people in front of the group. "Gina I'll take the coffee to help with this hangover. When it comes to my personal life, can you not voice your opinion?" Gina stared at him. "No Jeff, we need you so I'm begging you get your shit together." Jeff took the coffee and knew not to press Gina.

Rio showed up two hours late, which was unusual for him. He walked through the door with an alluring woman trailing behind. Maybe Asian descent? Mixed like Rio.

"Hey everybody this is Jae. Jae, everybody."

Gina was instantly intrigued by the newcomer and moved to make her more comfortable being thrust into this group. "Hi. I'm Rio's cousin, Gina, I'm so happy to meet you." And jumped right in with the questions. "Where did you two meet?"

Jae answered in a soft voice, "A gallery opening about a month ago."

Gina to herself, *This is a decent girl, thank you.* "Well Jae, can I get you anything? Coffee? Please make yourself at home. I also want to stress, there might be some fighting and nasty words going about. But we all love each other."

Jae smiled and Gina, *Is Rio growing up? This woman is cultured, not a plaything.* Gina couldn't wait to dig into this relationship, but first, write lyrics.

"We have a fast beat song with some lyrics I came up with. Trevor singing one line, and me singing a different set of lyrics, marrying those together, it must be upbeat ass kicking. The title is, 'She Got It.'"

She Got It

She got it, she got it, that's my lady she is walking around with a
Special air, walking around like she just don't care, I just want to get her
In my bed, she's saving it for me. When she sings, I know she's singing
For me. When she dances in that seductive way, I know it's for me
On the floor she got to get you hot. She got it, she got it, she got
me hot, got to have her now, she drives me crazy in every way.
Got it, she got it to take me and get me off, she got it, she got it I'll
Be making her tonight

Separate lyrics

It got It, I got it, I want to make him mine, to take you just a little
Higher, I got it, I got it, I'm going to take him home. It got it, I got it
I'm going to blow his mind

"This is just a jumping off point. Everybody can add whatever."

Rio looked, "Yeah, this could be an ass kicker for sure. Gina coming through, get your head around one or two more."

"I'll try, but my pregnant brain doesn't work so well some days."

Ian chirped in, "Yeah, Lisa can't remember where she leaves things, then it's a hunt around the house."

Gina became serious with everyone. "Trev and I are concerned about everyone because work is being done on the Montecito studio. You all live two plus hours away."

Rio spoke first. "I realize you both felt you couldn't stay here with all the nonsense outside. Uncle Mario and Aunt Franny bought you two the new house. I honestly don't have an issue moving. You said you are getting the studio ready, that's great for Perfection. What about Tommy? Skip is our manager; he does what he needs to do for us."

Looking directly at Jeff, Gina reiterated, "We can certainly use this house for rehearsals and music writing, if it helps Jeff get over partying too much."

"Gina, is this your way to keep me from all the parties here in LA? I like living here. For a single dude this is great. However, I'm not into driving two hours to get to a studio. I'm renting a studio apartment. It's really not a big deal for me to move if I need to. But you two should have asked what we thought before you bought a new house."

Trevor interjected, "Jeff man, you see the crap we are dealing with outside, come on. We don't feel safe and now with a baby. We went to look, and you know Gina's parents, they bought the house we liked. I'm not apologizing. I think it would be great for all of us. You get it now Jeff?"

Jeff shrugged it off, knowing it was a battle he wouldn't win.

Gina added, "I love this house and I know I'll miss it, but honestly, I don't know how many times a week I can make the drive."

Ian took it all in. "Listen I'm not interested in driving two hours to meet up. With Lisa being pregnant we were looking at buying a house. Maybe this is a blessing. This area is expensive as shit. Maybe moving farther away we can get a higher quality house. It's going to be disruptive with Lisa pregnant. Rather do it now than when the baby comes. I'm in, let's move."

Skip showed up at the end of the conversation. "What are we talking about here? The band is moving from here to Montecito? You bought a house there? Don't you think that's a discussion for the band?"

Gina was a bit incensed by that comment. "Skip, do you live here? Are there fans, paparazzi, reporters outside your house? If so, please let me know. This is what Trevor and I have to deal with every day. I'm sorry I need a place with a gate to block out those people. No matter where we are, Baby McNaughton will be with me. I'm very clear about it."

Skip asked, "Does Tommy know yet? That's a factor."

"Skip, you missed the part when I said we can still use this house, close to the studio. That will work for a few months. Once our studio is ready, then we have to speak with Tommy. Feel free to talk to him now if you think it's an issue."

Skip retorted, "It might be an issue."

Rio looked at him. "Let's deal with it when we need to. Right now, we all need to think about moving."

Gina turned her attention to Jae. She had gotten an instant good vibe from her. Could she have a friend now, an ally? "Hey Jae, you want to grab lunch?"

"Most definitely. It's not fun listening and watching musicians decide which chords to play."

Gina whispered to Trevor, "I'm hungry so I'm going to take Jae for lunch, get details about this new relationship. Should I bring back something for you?"

He kissed her. "Whatever you bring back, I'm good. Don't ask the group. You'll get four different answers."

Gina waltzed out the door with Jae. "Us ladies are going for lunch. See ya."

Gina drove to her favorite little spot that offered fresh salads, inventive appetizers, and fantastic drinks. The hostess recognized her and seated the two women right away.

Jae thought it was cool. "It must be nice to be recognized. You get special treatment."

Gina shook her head. "Not really. It means you can't walk down the street or go grocery shopping without having a camera in your face. Fame is intoxicating until it changes the way you live your life."

Jae responded shyly. "I knew who Rio was when I saw him in the gallery. I thought he would be stuck up, or even a persuasive charmer. He was surprisingly real though, telling me all about the different art styles. I was amazed he knew so much."

Gina could break that down. "Well Jae, my Aunt Deidre, Rio's mother, was a famous model back in the day. Her friends are all artists, photographers, and writers, so Rio was exposed to it at a young age. But what about you? It appears you're intelligent and know about art. Are you studying art?"

At that moment the waitress came over. "Mrs. McNaughton, do you know what you are having?"

"Yes, the avocado and crab wraps with calamari." Jae ordered a Cobb salad.

After the waitress took their order, Gina got right back into it. "Jae, I'm not going to lie to you, and I don't want to scare you away. Rio needs a rock, someone who will steady him when he gets a bit out of control. I'm sure you have seen articles about him, the bad boy. He is a very caring, down to earth guy. I bet you see that, or you would have run. He needs a Jae in his life, and I just met you. I'm sorry I cut you off before you could answer."

Jae wasn't an over sharer for sure. She did tell Gina she was an art major at UCLA working on her master's.

Gina confessed she never had many female friends because the girls in school thought she was a mean girl. "Now that I'm older, I think having female friends is essential when you work with men all day long. They are always judging your music, sexualizing you. Jae, I know this is crazy, but I think we will become great friends."

Jae looked Gina in the eye. "I hope so Gina. Rio loves you very much."

Gina felt reassured. She and Rio hadn't been spending as much time with each other, like back in the early days. Good to know he still feels close. She ordered food for the band, and they headed back to the house.

THOUGHTS ABOUT BABY MCNAUGHTON

TREVOR AND GINA DECIDED TO ESCAPE back to their oasis, nirvana, the home in Montecito. On the drive, Gina turned down the radio and broke the silence. "Jae seems like a nice woman. I can't believe Rio convinced someone of her caliber to date him. I like her, I could use another friend. I have Lisa, but I would like another friend."

Trevor took his eyes off the road for a second. "I thought I was your best friend?" He laughed.

"Baby, you're my everything, but sometimes a woman needs to talk to another woman. We are complex creatures, what can I say. Speaking of little creatures, have you given any thought to baby names?"

"Holy shit, G. We need to think about that now, with a new album?"

Gina shook her head at him, "Are you serious? This is our baby. You have no idea what you would like to name our child? No thought whatsoever?"

"I'm thinking about it now, okay?"

"I know what I'm thinking."

"G, I never doubted you would have an answer. Tell me. I may hate it but go ahead."

Gina sighed, "If it's a girl, I thought Melody. And if it's a boy, Dakota. You hate them, don't you?"

"You will be surprised; I don't hate either of those names."

BACK TO
THE STUDIO

SKIP GLAZER CALLED A BAND MEETING, "All hands on deck" he said, which meant everyone connected with Perfection—the band, Kevin their sound man, and the road crew. It even included Brian Mayfield. Gina still wondered what he did for them. Skip announced the label wanted them in the studio after Thanksgiving, Monday, November twenty-sixth. He wanted them to have songs locked in and ready to go.

Maybe even a cover since the last cover gained Perfection attention. Since it was the beginning of November there wasn't much time to polish things up. However, Perfection knew Tommy Whelan would have his own ideas about the arrangements in the songs, maybe try some different things.

Gina and Trevor's announcement of moving sparked everyone in the band to address new living arrangements. They all decided to relocate. Kevin was in charge of the road crew and anyone who worked on Perfection's live performances. The crew members decided to find a rental house in Santa Barbara. Rio was closing on a house in Montecito, thanks to the generosity of Uncle Tony and Aunt Deidre. It was in a gated community not far from Gina and Trevor. Jae would be living in Rio's house, so she transferred from UCLA to Antioch University to finish her master's. Ian and Lisa were looking in Summerland.

The studio at the McNaughtons was almost complete. Sound equipment was arriving daily. Skip and Gina had their offices set up. Perfection was ready to move their operations away from the prying eyes of photographers, gossip rags, and fans. They still needed to go Los Angeles to record with Tommy Whelan. Gina was debating with herself if she wanted to host Thanksgiving for everyone at their house. Was she up for it? Gina asked Lisa and Jae if they would help with the menu. Of course, their answer was a resounding yes. Gina would make the turkey, gravy, stuffing with Italian sausage, cranberry sauce—homemade never bought. And she would make a New York cheesecake. Lisa would make mashed potatoes, green beans, and pumpkin pies. Jae would make a butternut squash soufflé and pecan pies. The men could worry about the alcohol situation.

Trevor was checking their wine fridge and looked at Gina. She looked tired.

Trevor was worried. "G, Baby come here and sit down. I think this is too much for you. I know you want to have a bunch of people over. I worry we need to go in the studio the next Monday."

Gina sat as close as she could to him and lay her head on his shoulder. She loved the way he smelled, wearing her favorite men's cologne she bought for him. When he used it, she would inhale deeply. "I'm good. I hired people to set out the food and clean up—that's the worst. It's a good thing I got a table that could seat eighteen people. You thought I was crazy. I am tired though; little Melody or Dakota is zapping my energy."

Trevor placed his hand on her blossoming belly. "Hey kid, can you give your mother a break?"

Gina laughed, "You're so cute. I always say this to you, but I love you more watching you enjoy this baby. Kiss me."

"Are you asking me to make out with my wife?"

Gina looked lovingly at Trevor. "Yes please, and anything that could come after that."

Afterward, Gina looked out the bedroom windows at the Pacific Ocean and saw herself as the luckiest woman alive. Soon magazine covers would be proclaiming that exact thing, probing every facet of her life.

Thanksgiving was a success. The smell of all the rich food made Gina a bit queasy, but she made it through.

RECORDING
TIME

MONDAY, NOVEMBER 26, 1979, first day of studio work. Tommy was happy to see everyone and told Perfection it's time to work and make an even better album.

The road crew was responsible for regular maintenance of the equipment and had set up each band member's, guitars, drums, and bass. As Gina walked through all the equipment, she noticed a label on one, which read "GMac." She looked at one of Trevor's beloved amps and noticed it had been marked "TMac." Gina turned to Stu, a senior member of the road crew and asked, "What's up with the labels? What does it mean?"

Stu was a bit embarrassed. "Well, that's how we refer to you and Trevor. You're GMac and he's TMac. It's easier for us guys."

Gina smiled and put her arm around Stu. "You know what? I love it! I'm going to refer to us that way from now on. Stu that's awesome, love it, love it."

Gina was about thirteen, fourteen weeks pregnant, a little over three months and was showing a little baby bump. She was worried Trevor would find her undesirable, but pregnancy had the opposite effect, he was proud he helped create this little human. When she walked into the studio, Tommy and Skip congratulated her on the baby. "Guys I may have an additional player with me, but I'm ready to sing the shit out these songs. Let's go."

It was a grueling eight-hour day, going over guitars, drums, and bass. No vocals yet. Tommy wanted to hear the music of each song first to refine it and add vocals after the music was set. Gina added her opinions about the music. She was happy when Lisa and Jae showed up. "All I do is sit around; I can't wait until they let me sing. I did write some killer lyrics. Tommy has been perfecting the music for two weeks."

I FAILED

THE FIRST WEEK OF DECEMBER, taking a page out of Franny's book, Gina hired a company to decorate the house for Christmas since she had no time.

Gina and Trevor were getting ready to leave for the studio when Gina noticed she was bleeding. She screamed for Trevor. "Baby, somethings wrong! I'm bleeding. Call 911 right now!" Gina sobbed, "Oh no, oh no please don't let this happen."

Trevor was scared. He wasn't sure exactly what was going on, but he knew it had to do with the baby. Gina lay down on the floor, hoping that would put a stop to whatever was happening. Trevor sat next to her and stroked her hair while they waited for the ambulance to arrive. As soon as they heard sirens, Trevor jumped up to let them in. The emergency personnel asked Gina a few questions, took her vitals, and quickly loaded her onto a gurney.

Trevor was punching the studio number into the house phone before he climbed into the back of the ambulance with Gina. Rio picked up, "Hey man, where are—?"

Trevor cut him short. "I'm taking Gina to the hospital. Something's wrong, I think it's the baby. I'm not sure. It's not good. I gotta go."

Rio stood there, tears welling up in his eyes. He knew how much Gina wanted to be a mother; this would devastate her. He told Tommy he had to leave.

Trevor followed the gurney as the attendants rolled Gina into the emergency room of Santa Barbara Cottage Hospital. A stout woman in blue scrubs stopped him, holding up open palms. "I'm sorry sir. You can wait over there. Only medical personnel beyond this point. If you wait over there, someone will come out and give you an update."

Trevor could hear his wife crying, sobbing loudly. Gina knew she was losing the baby and Trevor feared the same. In pain and frustration, he banged his fists on the wall. Did they work her too hard? Was it his fault, having her write late into the night? He blamed himself and tears silently rolled down his face.

After an hour of pacing in the packed waiting room, Trevor jerked around at the sound of slowly approaching footsteps, squeaking down the hall. A tired looking young man approached him. "Mr. McNaughton?"

"Yeah. I'm McNaughton."

"I'm so sorry, we tried everything, but your wife lost the baby. She is still under sedation from the procedure and will be moved into a room as soon as she gets out of recovery. Do you have somebody to be here with you? We will let you know your wife's room location as soon as possible."

Trevor knew he had to call Franny and Mario. He wandered out of the hospital into the inside garden where there was a phone so he could find a quiet spot to give the devastating news.

Franny picked up on the first ring. Trevor could barely get the words out, alerting Franny that something was wrong.

"Trevor, what's happening? Is it Gina? Is everything okay?" She knew it couldn't be good news, because she could hardly make out what he was saying. "Trevor, where are you? Tell me you're not at the hospital."

"She lost the baby."

Franny sucked in her breath and cried, "My poor girl, my poor girl."

Mario grabbed the phone out of Franny's hand. "Trevor, is it the Princess?"

All Trevor could get out was, "Yes."

"You go be with her, and we will be there tomorrow."

Trevor found his way back to the emergency room where a duty nurse gave him Gina's room number. As he turned toward the elevator, Rio and Jae pushed out of the slowly opening doors. They knew from the look on Trevor's face the news couldn't be good. "Trevor, I don't know what to say, man I can't even put words together right now. Is she going to be okay?"

"No man. She's not going to be okay. We've lost the baby."

Jae had a desperate need to clarify, "But Gina …?"

"She had some procedure, probably to make sure everything was gone. They've just taken her to her room. I'm headed there now."

Gina was asleep when they eased the door open and tiptoed into the room. She was pale, looking like a broken marionette with the IV tube in her arm. Trevor climbed into the bed with her. At least when she woke up, she would see he was right there for her.

Rio looked at Jae, "I'm not leaving. I'll sit here until she wakes up."

Trevor added, "I'll sleep next to her like every night."

Rio looked over at Jae. "You don't have to stay. Why don't you go home?"

"No. I couldn't. I want to be here for her. But I should call Lisa. She would want to know as soon as possible." Jae kissed Rio and headed into the hallway to call Lisa.

A soft looking woman wearing well-worn scrubs with kittens on them walked into the room. Her eyes flicked from Gina to Trevor who stood up to greet her. Trying to calm Trevor, she reached over and patted his hand. "Sometimes this happens with first time pregnancies. Miscarriages are more common than what most people know."

Trevor wasn't accepting it. "She went to every doctor's appointment and there were no issues. I want to know why."

The nurse quietly replied, "We can't always pinpoint why these things happen."

Trevor raised his voice. "Not to my wife. She is the strongest person I know. Do you know who she is? Who we are? This doesn't happen."

She had no idea who they were, other than another devastated couple. "I'm sorry you two have to go through this." She turned around and padded quietly out of the room.

Rio tried to calm Trevor. "You need to be calm. When she wakes up you need to be strong, because she won't be. This is all she ever wanted—for you two to have babies. So, keep it together as much as you can."

Hours passed and Gina was starting to come out of sedation. She felt Trevor sleeping next to her, opened her eyes and touched his face. He woke immediately. Gina sobbed into his chest. "I'm sorry baby. I'm so sorry I wasn't good enough."

Trevor wrapped her up in his arms. "No. It's nothing you did. I pushed you. I'm the one to blame. We'll have more babies, you know that."

Gina heard Rio push the chair back as he stood up. "Rio, I fucked up … I lost my baby. I just fucked up."

Rio leaned over her and whispered, "It's not either one of your faults. The baby wasn't ready, Gina. You and Trevor know neither one of you did anything wrong."

Jae walked in with Lisa. They placed their hands on Gina's arm from the other side of the bed and told her how much they loved her; they would be there for her.

But Gina knew that Lisa still had her baby.

The next morning, Gina woke to a ruckus outside her room. The Riccis had arrived. A frantic Franny barreled through the door, followed by a stoic Mario. Franny burst into tears as soon as she locked eyes with Gina. Jae and Lisa walked out, too many emotions. Franny sat next to Gina crying, "My girl. I'm so sorry. You know you're still perfect. I don't know why God called our little one, but you will have more babies. I pray to Our Mother Mary; she will see to it."

Franny pulled Trevor over. "What reason did they give you for this?"

Trevor was rung out with emotions. "The nurse said it happens with first time pregnancies."

Franny angered, "That's some bullshit. That's not true. There's something not right. Do you know if it was a boy or a girl?"

Trevor didn't think to ask, nor did he want to know.

Franny charged out of the room, headed for the nurse's station, and demanded to speak to the doctor. The doctor answered the page and had no trouble finding Franny hovering by the station. He had barely introduced himself before Franny let him have it. "How dare you tell my son-in-law that these things happen the first time! That's not true, something's wrong." The doctor, keeping his voice calm and low, did his best to explain the possible scenarios that could lead to a miscarriage.

Calmer, but not placated, Franny demanded, "I want to know whether the baby was a boy or girl. We will want to acknowledge this child in a Catholic service. The child would have been baptized and I need the sex, to give the child a name."

The doctor had never met a force like Franny Ricci before and told her it was a girl. Franny caved a little hearing she lost a granddaughter.

She gathered herself and returned to the room. "Trevor, did you pick out names for the baby?"

"Melody if it was girl. Dakota if it was a boy."

"Thank you, Trevor. We will acknowledge this child. I don't know what we are supposed to think, their answers are no answers at all. I don't know the way they do things here."

Gina, grasping a snippet of her mother's conversation, asked, "Mom, was the baby a boy or girl? I need to know."

Franny wanted to shield her, "Gina, not now, it's too much for you."

Gina sat up. "No. I want to know. Trevor wants to know. What Mom? Please just tell me."

Slowly, quietly, Franny answered. "It was a precious little girl, your Melody. We will make sure that Melody is placed at God's feet to go to heaven. We will have a memorial at the nearest Catholic cemetery so you can visit her—"

"Mom, just stop …"

Mario who had been silently watchful, finally spoke. "You know what I think? We all need to give Gina and Trevor time alone for a bit." Mario had to practically drag the agitated Franny out of the room.

The room was once again quiet and Trevor climbed back into bed with Gina and whispered, "I love you so much. Don't you ever, ever forget that. We will be stronger. Don't give up on us."

She touched his face, "I love you always. as long as I have you, I'll be okay. Promise."

The OB/GYN came in. "Mr. and Mrs. McNaughton I want you to know our plan. We would like to keep you here for another two days in case there are any blood clots. Then we will send you home. Then you need to take it easy for a bit and no sexual relations for at least four weeks. You both clear on the plan?"

Gina questioned anyone who tries to tell her what to do. "We have an album we need to record, when can I go back to work?"

The doctor looked at Trevor, "I think a week at home, then light work three to four hours a day. Nothing more."

Trevor reassured the doctor, "That's not a problem."

A NON-CHRISTMAS

IT WAS CHRISTMAS BUT there was no celebrating this year. Franny had all the decorations taken down before Gina came home. Franny and Mario moved several of their appointments and parties to be with Gina for three weeks. They were situated in one of the guest bedrooms upstairs. She was determined to nurse her daughter back to health no matter what time of the year it was. Franny suggested that they get help as soon as possible. Gina had already been looking before everything went to shit and had found a nice lady named Marisol. The rooms above the garage had been converted into a small apartment for her.

Gina had convinced her parents to fly back right after Christmas and before the New Year's holiday. This New Year's would be the marking the beginning of the new decade. Surely 1980 had to be a better year, a better decade. There would be no celebrating this year, though, it reminded Gina of the first New Year's when she and Trevor were separated.

WORK WILL CONTINUE

THE NEXT WEEK, TREVOR AND GINA walked into the studio, which was happily buzzing. Gina could read the looks on everyone's face. "I'm back because I want to be. We have an album to put out. I'd appreciate it if we could focus on that and not, well everyone knows, okay, so let's do it."

Even Brian Mayfield stepped back. Trevor was still very raw emotionally.

Tommy asked Gina, "Would you like to sing the updated version of 'She Got It?' We made additions to your set of lyrics."

Gina leaned over. "Will I like the additions, Tommy?"

Tommy winked. "Yes, I think you'll love them. Ready when you are. Cue the music."

Gina didn't miss a beat. She knew they needed to get this on schedule. As a performer, you had to shake off the adversity and keep going. She was worried about Trevor after finding him in the living room holding a half empty bottle of whiskey one night. She told him not to go back to visit those demons. She needed him strong. He promised her.

Six weeks later, the final cut of the album was ready for Perfection to hear. Tommy suggested two songs be released: "She Got It" and "Time Is Now," both very strong rock songs. "Perfection has another winner, this time you will be the headliner, with the proper support of the label, which

I don't think will be an issue. Would you be ready to tour, if necessary? The label will want some type of commitment."

Gina spoke up. "Tommy, I think the way we would like to do this tour is maybe away for five weeks, come home, and do another five weeks. Can we break it up? I think being away from home three months is too long."

Skip stepped in. "I agree with Gina, and Ian is about to have a baby." Skip regretted saying that in front of Gina. "Gina, I'm so sorry … I didn't mean."

"Skip it's fine. It's the truth."

Now it was up to the label to give Perfection their orders. Brown Fence Records had Perfection under contract for four albums, this was their second. The record company would like to have an album release party once again. Of course, they would want Perfection to go out and promote the album, and most likely tour. This was the formula for a successful album. Brown Fence held the cards and Perfection knew how to play the game. They waited like they had before.

MONTECITO LIFE
AND MORE

TREVOR AND GINA TOOK ADVANTAGE of their beachfront property, taking long walks on the beach, chatting with people who didn't know or care who they were.

The celebrity gossip rags got word about McNaughtons losing their baby and were at least kind, respecting their space. But they knew a concert tour was coming up.

Gina and Trevor were just trying to relax. "Baby, it's the calm before the storm again. You ready to go back out there and tour?"

Trevor answered nervously. "I'm more worried about those demons this time, with everything we've gone through. I need you to keep me straight. Don't let anybody take that power away from you."

Gina looked at him lovingly. "Trev, do you think I could ever let that happen? Just remember, I'll punch out that asshole Brian Mayfield if he tries any shit, he'll be sorry. No one gets between us."

Trevor took her hand. "Let's head back to the house. I think it's time for us to have an afternoon playdate."

Gina smiled. "I always like the sound of that." Things seemed to be back to normal, but there was a dark undercurrent that the two didn't recognize.

Perfection had made it clear they would tour and talk to radio stations to get the word out about their new album. This time they would be co-headliners, with Brent Nolan and his band, Orange Wave. Brent had taken a brief interest in Gina a few years earlier and she shot him down immediately, saying, he could have any woman he wanted but she was not one of them. Trevor hated the idea of touring with them again, but they were Brown Fence Records' top act. There would be another album release party, but now Perfection was well known with their own fan base.

Skip Glazer met with Benjamin Blum, the director of operations with Brown Fence Records, technically Perfection's boss. They were working with John Dunn, a legendary rock festival promoter on their next series, "Brown Fence Records and John Dunn Presents."

If you wanted to become a top band you would want to be invited to play at one of his festivals. Both were ready to promote the concert series and wanted Perfection to be a co-headline band. Logistics needed to be worked out. Gina was in contact with them regarding the business part of the tour. The Montecito studio was done. Perfection would be recording in their own studio and have their own rehearsal space. The only problem would be getting Tommy Whelan, their producer, to come up to Montecito. That would be a discussion. Gina had an office with copies of music, contracts, and maps with potential dates. The word was out, Perfection was going to tour as one of Brown Fence's two hottest bands.

Before tour dates were discussed, there was one member of Perfection who had a more important date, Ian. Lisa gave birth to a beautiful healthy boy, Liam. Ian was on cloud nine. Everyone went to visit her. Gina could not. She didn't have the mental strength to go to the hospital. She sent a beautiful bouquet of flowers with a note, "Thinking of you. I just can't be at the hospital yet. Much love, your friend always, Gina."

Skip drove up to Montecito to go over the tour dates and plans for the album release party with Gina. She wanted to push the meeting to April, to give Ian some time home with Lisa and Liam. She would have wanted to do the same thing, but she would have taken Melody with her everywhere.

MAGAZINE ARTICLE AND DEMON SLAYING

SKIP ARRANGED FOR *Golden Pick Magazine* to do an article on Rio and Trevor. The article would showcase the two hottest guitarists currently playing. The bonus was they were in the same band. Gina loved the idea, especially if it came out before the album release party. She also wanted to tell Skip she wanted a more subdued party than the first album, *Perfection, Playing*. The first album release party was held at a new club on Sunset Boulevard with the hottest bands, movie stars, rock journalists, gold diggers, bunnies, and Hollywood wannabes in attendance.

The lights and loud music became too much for the Whites and the McNaughtons. Adding in the fact that Brent Nolan was hitting on Gina, and Brian Mayfield was trying get a hookup for Trevor with any bunny or starlet he could find. Both never happened. Gina and Trevor waited for their first album *Perfection Playing* to be played in its entirety then decided to leave. Upon leaving Perfection was asked to attend the White Lace Festival, a John Dunn Production. Perfection decided to wait a day until they agreed, they wanted to leave them guessing. Rio showed up the next morning declaring they had to tour. He also added that Jeff and he partied with half-dressed women and cocaine flowing. The band realized that they had to take the opportunity given. Gina wanted a conference call with *Golden Pick*. Of course, she wanted Skip to join.

The magazine was excited to profile both Rio and Trevor, talk about their styles, favorite guitars—material that wannabe guitar players would eat up. Gina wanted to know where the interview would be held. *Golden Pick* was open to the location. Gina offered up the Hollywood Hills house, not sure she wanted press at their new home. Jay Brooks was the journalist who would be doing the interview, and they set the date for Tuesday, April eighth, at eleven a.m. She didn't want Trevor making the two-hour drive too early in the morning.

Skip was uncomfortable with what he had to tell Gina next. "I am going to be busy arranging the schedule for the tour, so I'm going to have Brian hang around to make sure the interview goes smoothly. I know you have issues with him, but he is on a short leash, I promise you."

Gina shook her head. "If you have Mayfield involved, problems will ensue. He is a weasel and a snake. I'll talk to Trevor and warn him. But I appreciate your honesty. You know I hate him; I am baffled why he is still employed by us, do you know why Skip? I'm at a loss why we keep him on the payroll."

Skip promised, "Don't worry about him. I will try to reel him in."

The interview was four days away and she needed to talk to Trevor. As she walked up to the house she wondered where she would have made the nursery—next to Trevor's writing room? How cute would that have been. She walked into the kitchen and found Trevor sitting at the kitchen counter, looking a bit disoriented.

"Babe, how are you? You're looking off."

He smiled at her. "You know I love you right? I fucked up again. I drank half a bottle of whiskey. It's not good. I'm going to be a mess on the road. Remember, I need you to watch over me."

Gina was worried, "Trevor, why did you feel you needed to drink? What's setting you off?"

"I'm depressed. The whole thing with the baby just blew me away. I feel responsible for working you too hard."

Gina knelt next to him. "Trev, no one is responsible. The baby wasn't ready for us. I try not to think about it much. Now that Ian and Lisa have Liam, I'm reminded our baby would have come soon after. Trev, let's not do this. Don't go down to that dark place. We have both been there. Drinking is not going to help; it just numbs it. Come to me."

Trevor got off the stool and sat on the floor, the stink of whiskey strong on him. Gina stood him up. "Come on, let's get you in the shower."

Trevor was shaky. "Will you come with me?"

"Of course I will. Let's go." Gina struggled to undress him since he could barely stand. She had to get him straight for the interview in four days. Trevor was more fragile than she had ever seen him. He wouldn't leave her side at the hospital; she wouldn't leave him like this. She turned on the shower, hot then warm. Trevor hated hot showers.

Trevor flopped on the bed naked. Gina pulled him by his arms, "Let's go Trevor. Let's get in the shower. I'm taking off my clothes, see? Let's go."

She placed him under one of the two shower heads, the warm water on his face. He moved his head from side to side, wetting his hair. Gina shampooed his hair, then soaped up her hands and started washing his body.

He seemed almost oblivious to her touch. After a few minutes of the warm water hitting his face, Trevor seemed to straighten up, revived himself from being under the influence and felt more like himself. He kissed her. "I love this, keep going." She washed his legs and went to the spot he had hoped she would reach.

"Does that feel good?" The desire.

"You know it does."

They finished and Gina told him, "You seem to be more yourself." She stepped out of the shower and grabbed a Turkish towel to wipe him down. The shower seemed to help drive the demons away, for today. Would Trevor revisit them sooner than later?

"Don't you feel better? Showered clean, no more whiskey stink."

Trevor looked at her. "Why do you put up with me? Do you love me that much?"

Gina smiled, "You're being silly, we have been together for way too many years for us to have this discussion. I just fucking love the hell out of you and have since I first saw you. God, Trev." He was just lying there naked, begging her to love him. "Only if you are sober. No drunk sex, Trev."

He had that look in his eye that meant he wanted her. "I'm good, come here."

While they sat in bed, Gina told Trevor that *Golden Pick* was going to interview him and Rio about guitar stuff, how you create songs, guitar styles, favorite guitars. She didn't hold back; Brian was going to oversee the interview and she was concerned. Trevor promised he wouldn't let him spin things out of control. He kissed her. "No worries, babe. You're my number one."

PHOTO SHOOT
GONE WRONG

THE DAY OF THE INTERVIEW Trevor and Rio drove together to the Hills house and waited for Jay Brooks. Brian was all pumped up, saying he had a great addition to the interview, but they had to wait for it to be almost done.

Jay was very excited to meet Rio Poole and Trevor McNaughton. He probed their styles, and which was their favorite guitar to play onstage, and asked if they switch guitars during a performance. Who takes the lead on some songs? He was very thorough. Trevor and Rio felt that other guitarists would find their point of view, in methodology regarding writing music and guitar playing could inspire the next generation. Jay Brooks, Rio, and Trevor were having a great dialogue throughout the interview. All three felt this would be a dynamic interview and possibly a great cover story.

Mayfield was sitting back waiting for his opportunity to add some *color* to the interview, almost like he was salivating for his surprise. Brian ushered them out to his car and drove them to a Hollywood house that had a lavish backyard and pool. Rio looked puzzled as did Trevor the moment they saw what Brian had arranged. There were at least ten very young women, strutting around in string bikinis. He had hired a photographer to take pictures with the models standing around Trevor and Rio, some ladies almost on their laps.

Brian tried to ply them with weed and alcohol. Trevor knew this would be a big issue. Rio also knew Jae wouldn't like the scene at all. Jay Brooks wasn't sure if it would be appropriate for his article, but maybe a magazine cover could attract the guitar guys.

Trevor and Rio pulled Brian aside. Trevor asked, "Brian, what the fuck is this? You know Gina will kill you if this gets printed, why? I don't want my picture with a bunch of almost naked women. Not good for my marriage, dude."

Rio was equally pissed. "Hey Brian, tell me you aren't that asshole who doesn't understand that if your woman sees this, there is a lot of explaining to do. Why?"

Brian rationalized, "You're rock gods, these are just chicks to show how you are those guys. It's not like I'm telling you to sleep with them. It's just a sexy picture to sell your sex appeal. If you do find any girl interesting let me know."

Trevor was livid. "Brian, I am happily married but if Gina sees this it will be a problem for me and absolutely for you. Do me a favor, I don't want any one of these women actually touching me."

"But I paid these models and the photographer, so let's just take the pictures, we don't have to use them. Especially if you think *your women* are going to freak out."

Rio shook his head, "You are some piece of work, asshole. You better hope these pictures don't come out. You better not give Gina McNaughton a reason to come after you, because she will."

The two guitarists reluctantly posed for pictures. This was a mistake Brian had miscalculated on. It would backfire. Both guitarists did not want to pose, but somehow Brian Mayfield had a Svengali like magic. Trevor and Rio allowed a tamed version, no ladies touching them, still knowing how uncomfortable it made them. Why do it? They felt if it was a tamer version they might be able downplay the whole photoshoot. After it was over Trevor reassessed, there was no way Gina McNaughton would ever be agreeable to any pictures of this type. Trevor asked Jay Brooks not to publish the photos. He admitted he couldn't be sure his editor wouldn't want to use them. Trevor and Rio knew this was an issue. Rio told Trevor, "We need to make sure that Skip gets these pictures and destroys them. Skip needs to squash this, Trevor. Both of us will be in big trouble. I'll speak to Skip."

Trevor and Rio drove home knowing if Gina saw those pictures she would lose her shit. They just hoped the proofs wouldn't come to the office. Hopefully Skip would get them.

DON'T GET
GINA MAD

ABOUT FOUR DAYS PASSED after the photoshoot. Gina was working in her office and had asked to see the guest list for the album release party before invites were sent. She needed it to be a chill atmosphere, not a bunch of young actresses, models, and hangers-on. A manila envelope was delivered. Gina was excited, thinking it contained the article.

Meanwhile, at the Montecito rehearsal hall everyone was going over equipment that would be needed for any upcoming tour.

Gina opened the envelope, took one look at the contents, and screamed. She ran into the studio. "Where is he? Where the fuck is that motherfucking Brian Mayfield? Where, where is he?"

Everyone moved out of the way. Gina was on the warpath, and her target was in sight. Everyone knew not to piss off Gina McNaughton, it would end badly. She always prioritized her and Trevor's best interests. Do not fuck with her. So, when she was looking for Brian, everyone knew it was bad.

She grabbed Brian by the shirt with both hands, threw him up against the wall, and shoved her arm up against his neck. "You snake. You cocksucker. What the fuck are these pictures of almost naked women extremely close to my husband and my cousin? In what world did you ever think this would be appropriate?" She threw him up against the wall again and placed him in another chokehold. "I swear to you Brian, I could make your fucking ass disappear. One motherfucking phone call and you would disappear. And I mean no one would know you even existed. I promise you; I am one step away from doing it. But I'm not even going to waste the phone call on your slimy ass. *STAY THE FUCK OUT OF MY MARRIAGE!* You better run, and I mean it. I am working on firing your ass."

Gina spit in his face. "Get off the property. Right now."

Gina burst into the studio next. "What were you two thinking? Here. Why don't you take a look at these. So try to tell me how you let this happen. Were you high? Drunk? Because in my mind that's the only way you two morons would let this happen."

Rio and Trevor were stunned silent and didn't have time to reply before Gina started in again. "I don't want to hear the explanation now. I'm furious."

Gina was so worked up she didn't notice Jae walk in. "Gina, you look really mad."

"Oh, I am, and when I show you, I don't think you will be very happy either." She handed the envelope to Jae, who opened it with trepidation.

"What are these pictures of? When did they do a model shoot? How come Rio never told me about this?"

"Well Jae, because Brian Mayfield thought it was a great idea. Here's the note from Jay Brooks, the writer, and his editor saying they chose this picture for the magazine cover."

"I thought it was about guitars and guitar playing."

"Yes Jae, that was the point. I can't even look at Trevor right now. I warned him this would happen. I don't want Mayfield coming on this tour. I know he is trying to find a slight crack in my marriage and exploit it. I won't have it, nor should you."

Trevor spoke first. "G, I knew you would be mad. I told Brian that it wasn't cool, and I didn't want those pictures released. I can talk to Brooks and tell him not to print it. Please I had your back. I don't like it either."

Rio began to explain to Jae, "I would never do something that tacky. You know me. I don't know what to say, seriously both of you. You know us, we wouldn't want to hurt you."

Gina's rage had turned into tears. "Thousands of people are going to see that cover. I feel like a moron. It's hurtful, just so you know. You both honestly don't see how destructive this guy is. I don't want him coming on tour with us. I don't."

Trevor knew her anger. "Baby, I hear you. You went all New York on him—you threw him up against a wall and spit on him, Gina, you're a bad, bad girl."

Gina was enraged. "What would you have me do? Let him destroy Perfection? No, not happening. This has put me over the edge. I don't want to waste my breath on Mayfield anymore. When I think of him it frustrates me, it angers me that you don't see him for the person he is." She abruptly changed the subject. "Can we talk tour dates? I got the final from Skip. The label wants us to leave April twenty-second. Our first gig would be on April twenty-fifth. Skip already has the road crew leaving tomorrow.

Touring and Articles

The 1980 tour dates were as follows:
Concert Series brought to you from Brown
Fence Records and John Dunn.

April 25	Hartford, CT
April 30	Philadelphia, PA
May 8	Tampa, FL
May 16	Indianapolis, IN
May 21	Kansas City, MO
Break three weeks	
June 13	St. Paul, MN

June 18	Dallas, TX
June 26	Salt Lake City, UT
July 6	Portland, OR
July 12	Sacramento, CA

The schedule was set to hit secondary markets to promote the bands. Because the band had toured before, they didn't need that much promoting. They may not be the king of the label, but they were close. There would of course be interviews on radio stations and maybe some magazine articles— all expected the second time around. Gina agreed to do some women's magazine interviews as long as it didn't get too personal. They wanted to interview her at home, which let people inside her private domain. Gina was quickly gaining a reputation as an elusive rock star, so everyone wanted to know more. Even her haircut became something women were starting to copy. They called it "The GMac." Gina knew she should have been flattered, but she thought, *Why do you want to look like me? Get your own look.* But it became a thing. That's when you know people are watching everything you do.

April fifteenth was the second album release party of *Perfection, The Perfect Album.* Gina asked Mimi to come to Montecito with some dresses that would work for the album release party. Mimi was Gina's stylist who she used from when she first got to Los Angeles. Mimi didn't mind the two plus hour drive; Gina was a high-profile client. She could tell other clients she dresses Gina McNaughton and that would add to her cache. Mimi brought about five dresses. Gina and Mimi landed on a simple body-hugging beaded, iridescent blue spaghetti strap dress that made the most of all her curves. She had shoes made to match the dress. She wasn't worried about what Trevor would wear; he had amassed clothing for these types of events. He hated it, but he knew he needed to have a style.

Jae was excited this would be her first "official" outing as Rio's lady. Lisa was a bit stressed, due to having had a baby. She didn't feel her best and was still losing her baby weight, but she was a trouper. Jeff was always the loose cannon; would he bring another Hollywood starlet? Perfection was ready for this, a simple release, say hi to all the important people, then go home.

April fifteenth came, and the band stayed in Los Angeles at the Beverly Hills Hotel. There were a few paparazzi hanging around the front of the Hills house where Trevor and Gina stayed. Gina still wanted that fence. As everyone got ready, Gina noticed Trevor dressed in black. Gina looked at Trevor "Could you mix it up? Okay it's a bad boy look. I kind of get it."

Everyone in the band arrived at the venue around the same time. Pictures, more pictures, people shouting questions. How do you answer them? "Thanks. We are doing great. Excited about the album release."

"GMac, we love you!" Half the women and girls in the crowd had copied her haircut. A microphone was put in her face by some fashion magazine, asking her what designer she was wearing. Gina hated those questions, and would answer, "It's a famous designer. Can you guess?"

The party was held at a rooftop bar, which gave everyone the opportunity to get fresh air. Benjamin Blum and John Dunn introduced everyone and thanked them for their work, adding the concert series was almost sold out already.

Skip looked at the band expecting someone to get up and say something. Gina was becoming the spokesperson for the band and stepped up to the microphone, with Blum and Dunn standing to the side.

"Hi everyone, it's me Gina McNaughton. I want to thank everyone for coming. We think this album will kick your ass. I'm lucky to work with great musicians, including my husband. This is truly a work of love; we hope you enjoy listening to it as much as we enjoyed creating it for you."

Gina got whistles and some very pointed sexual remarks. She was used to it. She walked off the stage toward Trevor who greeted her with a kiss, and they walked arm in arm over to the bar. Gina looked at Trevor, "Please baby, just take it easy. No demons tonight."

Trevor kissed her hand. "You don't worry about that, I'm good."

They watched as Brent Nolan, the lead singer for Orange Wave, the hottest band in the country, took the stage. He said the usual things about how pumped the band was to go on tour and see their fans. The three had met for the first time at Perfection's release of their first album, *Perfection, Playing*, where Brent made a bold play for Gina's affections.

He walked off the stage and headed right for them. "Well look who's here." Looking at Trevor, he continued, "So I guess you took my advice and married this woman. I admit, I thought I could have had a chance."

Gina smiled while delivering his takedown. "I know you have tons of women who drop their panties for you, and good for you. I love this man, married or not. I am fairly sure I told you that last year. You told my husband he should marry me because you would have tried to hit that. You could never have come close to hitting anything. Here's the thing—we have to work together and I'm a fan of yours, but don't ever interfere with our private life, and then we will be good. Got it?"

The look on his face made it clear he got it. She hoped they wouldn't have a problem working together on the tour. Time would tell.

Jae and Rio came by. Rio commented, "This party is much more low-key than the first. They started playing the album, good. Jae, you doing okay, babe?"

Jae looked beautiful in her emerald-green dress, which complemented her complexion. Gina was happy to see Rio more settled with someone at his side.

Ian and Lisa always looked like they felt out of place, but they hung in. Jeff surprised everyone by bringing a date, some new starlet, the new "it" girl. Still better than him dancing on tables with half-naked women. Kevin, their sound guy, even brought someone. Everybody in the band believed he was secretly living with her. Gina thought, *Good for him*. The band was maturing, a great thing when you're ready to tour with one of the most out of control bands in the business. Drugs, groupies, and rock and roll.

TOURING, DRUGS AND OTHER

APRIL CAME, AND EVERYONE was packed up and boarded the private jet. Gina thought, *Here we go; I have to kick ass this tour.*

First stop—Hartford, Connecticut. The crowd was rowdy. Gina knew from experience that it could go bad fast. But Perfection had fans there because they had played clubs in Connecticut back in the day and it wasn't far from Long Island. Gina and Trevor stole the show with "She Got It." Gina closed with a cover of, "Brass in Pocket," making the crowd crazy. The band came offstage sweaty and went right to the dressing rooms to change.

Skip reminded them they had a bunch of fans who had won a backstage hello session. Gina hated those sessions, but it was part of the gig. She smiled and watched the girls who really only wanted to meet Rio and Trevor—clever ladies. Brian Mayfield couldn't sneak the groupies in past Gina and Jae, though. Gina told security and their road crew to watch out for him. They had strict orders from Gina to keep that garbage out of Perfection's area. There was plenty of room for the groupies over at Orange Waves' camp.

Lisa wasn't coming, it was too much with new baby Liam, even though her mom was staying with them. Gina thought to herself, *Marisol would have taken care of Melody while I was onstage.* She needed to get those images out of her head. They were sad and depressing.

Gina wondered when she and Trevor should try again. They had never used protection, which made her wonder if she had a problem. She and Trevor would make the decision together. After the tour certainly, she couldn't imagine getting pregnant until after the tour.

After the numerous interviews on local radio shows, the band became pros at answering questions. "What was the inspiration for this song? What did Gina think of her haircut becoming a fad?" She was sick of that question. Her answer was always, "If you can pull it off great, most people can't." Gina didn't care that she sounded cocky. She had a few interviews with women's magazines when she got home. Would her face be on the cover? She hoped not.

They arrived in Kansas City, the last stop before the band took a break. There were the usual interviews, sound checks, set lists—all the required work while touring. But their friends in Orange Wave were partying hard. So much cocaine, so much alcohol, so much everything. She watched Brian "Lucky Charms" Mayfield closely. Why was he here? She told Skip she didn't want him touring with them, but here he was. He was always trying to get Trevor and Rio to party with the other band. Trevor was on shaky ground. She promised him she would keep him "safe."

The temperature in Kansas City was in the sixties, and they were playing at an outdoor venue. Gina decided to wear one of her sheer outfits to create buzz about her sexiness—the way she sang and moved around the stage, always playing up to Trevor. The audience loved it. Gina did something she never did before going onstage. She smoked a joint with Rio for old times' sake. The crowd was pumped up and anxious for Perfection to go onstage. They opened the set with "Punch the Night," which got everyone standing up.

Gina stepped up to the microphone. "Hey Kansas City! It's awesome to be here with you. Thanks for coming out. We will get you dancing and sweaty with us. These stage lights are fucking hot and those pyrotechnics make it hotter. I'm going to find out if my clothes become see through.

My name is Gina McNaughton. To my right is my cousin Rio Poole, the hottest guitar player. In back of me is our great drummer, Ian White. On my far left is a guy who plays a mean bass, Jeff Wainwright. And right next to me is the sexist man I know—my husband, Trevor McNaughton. Give it up KC! We're going to rock your asses off. Let's go!"

The audience went wild. Gina was at the top of her game with her clothes stuck to her body, absolutely like she wanted. The first leg of the tour catapulted the band where her expectations said they should be. They even got praise from Orange Wave and Brent Nolan. It was time to go home for three weeks to relax and recharge for the next part of the tour.

Perfection took up about a third of the seats on the plane, and Orange Wave had the rest. They traveled with crew, groupies, drug dealers, anything you could imagine was there. Gina was trying to relax, a magazine on her lap, when a shriek was heard from somewhere behind her. At first, she didn't pay much attention, but when people started running down the aisle, Gina got out of her seat and walked to the source of the commotion. There, on the floor, a young woman lay passed out. No, more than passed out. She was overdosing. That got the band more than worried, this was their reputation. Gina was certain if she could make the girl throw up she would be okay. Gina rolled her over, face down and tried ramming her fingers down her throat. It didn't work. Shit. She didn't want to be on a plane when someone died.

She yelled, "I know there is a doctor on this plane for insurance purposes. Where the fuck are you?"

A chalky little man finally worked his way through the useless onlookers.

"You have to have something, adrenaline shot, something to bring this girl back."

He started rummaging in his bag. Gina was thinking of what else she could do before this quack of a doctor found the right drug to administer. She asked the flight crew for cold towels.

Gina looked at the doctor. "Hurry up asshole. This girl is going to die." She turned around and Trevor and Jae were behind her.

"Can you believe this shit? Come on hurry up."

The doctor kneeled next to the girl and injected a syringe into her heart. Nothing happened at first, but then she started to come around.

Gina looked at Brent Nolan, "Hey, you're welcome, I without a doubt saved you from a big public relations nightmare."

Brent looked at her. "I owe you one Gina. Don't forget that."

Trevor took Gina back to her seat, "You are fucking amazing, my wife. How lucky am I."

Gina snuggled up to him, "When we get home, I'll show how amazing I really am."

He laughed because he knew she would.

HOME IN MONTECITO, BABY TALK

THEIR FLIGHT WOULD LAND AT LA. The band preferred to fly into Santa Barbara but Brown Fence Records and Orange Wave were the ones paying for the chartered jet. Perfection hadn't the ability to request a separate plane nor an additional stop to Santa Barbara. Two limos picked up Perfection for the two-plus hour drive home. Gina couldn't wait to be in their beautiful house, watch the ocean, and walk around in next to nothing or nothing at all. Marisol was there to greet them with her homemade enchiladas, guacamole, and chips.

Trevor dropped their suitcases in the foyer. Gina was exhausted and felt dirty after the whole overdose incident. She told Trevor she was going to take a shower, their secret code that it's time for sex. Trevor followed her through the bedroom, and into the bathroom.

"Is this an invitation? Do you want me to join you?"

Gina opened the shower door. "Are you kidding me? When have you ever asked that question? Let's get the filth of that plane ride off us. Come here." Gina stepped out of the shower, stripped him naked, and led him by hand into the stream of hot water. "Doesn't that warm water feel good? Get all that shit off of us from the tour. The first part of the tour seemed a bit raunchy, didn't it?"

Trevor was ready. "You were a little raunchy yourself."

"That's a terrible thing to say. I was *sexy*. I gave them what they wanted. Maybe we get nice and clean and then we dry each other off. I know you're ready to go, but I promise I'll make it worth the wait."

"Woman, what do you have planned? I'm excited knowing there is a mystery."

Gina picked up two bath towels and they headed into the bedroom. "Come here, you're soaking wet. Let me dry you off." She took her time drying every bit of his body, highlighting all the sensuous parts. Simply looking at his naked body made her tingle. "Now dry me off, and make sure you get every part of me that's wet."

He laughed at that remark. "G, I think you're always wet."

"I get hot when I see you play onstage. Sometimes I fantasize I'm taking you right there."

Trevor was aroused. "Ugghh, that sounds very hot. Are you dried off enough?"

"Let me shake my hair a bit. You know what? Let me show you how much I love you."

Gina used satin ribbons to tie Trevor's ankles to the bedposts. She teased him with soft kisses between his legs. She tied his wrists to the bedposts at the top of the bed. "Now I get to do whatever I want to you. I'm starting from your feet and working my way up." She rubbed her entire body up his legs. She landed, where he hoped she would, using her tongue masterfully. She aimed to take him to the point where he begged her to have him one way or the other. She of course teased him. She straddled him, her movements were something very different, but so much more sexual to him. He was, after all, her captive, now begging her to finish him.

"Not so fast baby."

Trevor pulled his hands out of the silk ribbons and slipped off the ties around his ankles. He flipped Gina on her back and took her—again and again.

Gina loved being home. "I'm hungry, let's eat Marisol's food, it's the best." She put on her bathrobe. Gina went into the closet and handed him the robe she had him wear so many years ago when they first met. Trevor kind of hated that bathrobe but it had been around forever. "Here join me, you'll feel freer. I don't know why you hate the robe so much, you're naked underneath. I think it's more freeing than your boxers that you love."

Trevor humored her, "I will wear this thing, but you know I hate it." He kissed her wishing she would let him wear those damn boxers.

Gina took the enchiladas out of the oven and the guacamole out of the refrigerator. "You want to eat outside? It's nice. We never eat outside."

"G, you just blew my mind and everything else, so whatever you want."

She set the outdoor table and lit a couple of candles. "You want some sangria? Of course you do. I'll get the food in just a minute. I was thinking while we were on tour I want to try and have a baby again. What worries me is that we have never used protection, and I haven't gotten pregnant all these years except, you know. But I do want us to try, what are you thinking?"

Trevor grinned. "You mean I might have to make love to you every night to get you pregnant? Damn Gina. That's a lot. Twist my arm and I'll do it. Seriously, Mrs. McNaughton, I want us to have children. Let's put this plan into action during the last part of our tour. I don't want you going crazy onstage in case you do get pregnant. We have an understanding, I'll do my part, every night. I love you Gina, you know that. Thank you for keeping me out of trouble."

Gina leaned in. "Baby, that's my job. This food is delicious, isn't it?" After they finished eating, they went into the bedroom and watched TV, a luxury. They smoked a joint and Gina lit up one of her Sobranies. For good measure they made love again, just in case.

GINA GIVES INTERVIEWS

GINA HAD INTERVIEWS ARRANGED at the house with several of the leading women's magazines. They all asked, in one way or another, "How does rock stardom transfer into being a wife and businesswoman?" She hated that question. The first interviewer wanted to know all about the designers she chose, what she liked about fashion, what she didn't, what her views were about everyone wanting her hair style. She asked her about sex and the rock and roll lifestyle. Groupies. Does any of that affect her marriage? Did she have a good marriage? She believed it was evident that she had a great marriage and that she and Trevor were very happy.

Then the question came about children. She looked at the interviewer in disbelief and with tears in her eyes she told her, "You know, I had a miscarriage a few months back which devastated me. As an interviewer that logically would have come up in your homework. This is not a topic I care to discuss. How's that?"

The next interviewer was more interested in the choices she made in decorating her house and knew that Gina had been enrolled at the Fashion Institute of Technology back in New York for interior design. She knew that her mother had a thriving interior design business and asked if that helped in her design choices.

The last interviewer wanted to know more about her band and the relationships in the band. Gina was careful not to give too much away.

In a week's time Gina's face was on three different magazine covers. One used her favorite picture in the crochet dress sitting on Trevor's lap, when he had his long blond curls. They looked so young, but it wasn't that long ago. Her mom, Jae, and Lisa were excited to see her pictures on so many magazines, Gina didn't care, she was fixated on finishing the tour and getting pregnant.

She spent some time visiting Lisa and baby Liam; she owed her that. Because Lisa knew Gina so well, she understood why she had hesitated to spend time around the new baby.

Jae and Gina enjoyed lunches together and went shopping for the next leg of the tour. It was only five dates, but that was four weeks away from home. Gina asked Jae, "What do you think about touring? Do you mind all those boring sound checks and radio interviews we have to do? It can't be fun for you."

Jae gave Gina a look. "It *is* boring, but I love Rio and he wants me to come, so I have put off school to make him happy."

"Oh Jae, it makes me so happy that he found you. God knows where he would be without you. You knew his reputation, bad boy, parties, strippers, cocaine, and whatever. I was actually worried he would be a casualty to the rock and roll lifestyle. Oh my God, even worse find some chick who would take him for a ride and take half his money. Before you, his dating history was horrible. You saved him."

When Gina got home that afternoon, Trevor was in the studio working on some music and stopped her, "Hey, G have you seen all these?" as he pointed to an array of magazines.

"We don't need those. Did you buy them?"

Trevor shook his head. "No, they all came to the house with a letter thanking you for the interview. I hope we can slow down on this. I feel our whole life is being broadcast to the world."

Gina agreed, "You are 100 percent correct. I hate it, but you know the label sets these things up." She couldn't resist adding, "At least I don't have Brian fucking Mayfield throwing naked men in my interviews."

"Gina, don't you know how I felt about that?"

Gina sighed, "I promise I'll be the perfect wife for the next three days before we have to go back on tour."

Trevor was reminded of something. "Skip called and said the label is apeshit over what we did so far."

Gina was shocked. "So far? I don't know what else we are going to do to top what we have already done."

BACK ON THE ROAD
AND A SURPRISE

THREE DAYS LATER, they were back on a plane heading to St. Paul, Minnesota. Thankfully, it was summer. The weather would be pleasant. They enjoyed playing outdoor venues when possible. There were shuttle buses at the airport to take both Perfection and Orange Wave to the historic Saint Paul Hotel, first class all the way. Gina loved the old-world charm and the twenty-four-hour room service menu. It became a prerequisite for Gina. She wasn't fussy. This was one feature in travelling she demanded. They arrived at the venue did their sound checks, then waited to start getting ready for the show. Skip let me them know it was a sell-out crowd. The audience in St. Paul was hard to read. They sat quietly and listened to the songs—no yelling or profanities. The meet and greet was pleasant and the band genuinely enjoyed meeting the laid-back people.

The show in Dallas was a great success. The crowd knew Perfection's music and treated them like a headliner. Dallas was a large market; Perfection had a lot of airtime on the radio stations. The band thanked the crowd and promised they would be back.

The next stop was Salt Lake City, home of the Mormon Church. This would be a noticeably different show. Gina knew she had to ride a thin line with propriety, so she reeled in the sexiness for fear of getting arrested.

In Portland, the audience was clearly stoned so Gina let her freak flag fly high in the wind. Gina loved the Portland vibe and made note that she and Trevor could spend a few days there on a short vacation.

The last city was Sacramento, which meant they would be home soon. Sacramento considered both Perfection and Orange Wave their bands. After all, they both were from California. Gina winced every time they were introduced as a Cali band. Gina was still that girl from Long Island, New York.

Perfection booked a private plane so they could fly into Santa Barbara, close to home. They chose to book their own jet for their convenience. On the morning of that concert, Gina couldn't contain herself. She needed to talk to Trevor immediately. He was held up in set lists and arrangements, but she needed his attention. She pulled a GMac. "Listen guys, I'm sorry but I need to take this man away for a while."

Trevor looked at her like she was crazy, "G, come on, what's this all about? You know I need to take care of these things before tonight. Can't this wait?"

"No Trevor, I'm sorry. It can't." She took Trevor's hand and led him into the dressing room. She would have preferred taking him to the hotel where it would have been more private. "Okay, Trevor I need to show you something. Don't freak out on me, okay."

Annoyed, he asked, "What is it, Gina?"

Gina removed a piece of plastic from her pocket and held it up to Trevor's eyes. "Are you annoyed now?"

Trevor squinted at the pregnancy test, not sure what the faint blue line meant.

"Trevor, you dope! We're pregnant!"

Trevor looked from the stick to Gina. "Holy shit, it happened faster than I imagined. Well actually no, I have been your love slave for weeks."

"Get the fuck out of here. There have been no complaints on your end. You okay? You excited like I am?"

Trevor was overjoyed. "Baby I'm so happy, but can we not say anything yet?"

"My thoughts exactly. Let's wait a little while. After the last time I want to make sure everything is fine."

Trevor looked concerned. "G, please no crazy shit tonight, no going over the top with the crowd, no dancing all over the stage recklessly, reel yourself in. We want to make sure the pregnancy is fine. And please no see through clothes tonight."

She shook her head. "I promise, for our baby, I promise."

The Sacramento show was a bit crazy, but that was all Trevor and Rio. Gina did hang back a bit, she had a bigger, better picture to paint.

BABY
TALK

WHEN THE MCNAUGHTONS went to Gina's first OB/GYN appointment, they asked about her history and she disclosed that she previously had a miscarriage around fourteen weeks in. The urine test she took for the appointment confirmed they were pregnant. The doctor ordered an ultrasound test, and Gina and Trevor were excited to hear the whoosh whoosh sound of the baby's heartbeat. It put them at ease until the doctor voiced her concern that Gina's uterine wall wasn't as thick as it should be. Gina promised to make all her appointments and left the office feeling slightly worried.

The record label was ecstatic with Perfection's performance on tour. It was a sellout. The sales of their record were steady, and they offered a bonus. It would be incentive to get back into the studio for album three. They also believed they could be nominated for a possible Grammy. The labels love that shit. They knew they owed Brown Fence two more albums. However, they didn't realize at the time their contract had said something else. Perfection wasn't rushing into the studio to write more music. There were so many requests from top line magazines and music magazines for interviews, even the new entertainment TV shows wanted to have interviews, most with the McNaughtons. Something about the couple piqued people's interest. They wanted a peek behind the curtain.

Skip went to the home office, waded through the many interview requests, and prioritized them. Gina would make the final cut. She still thought it was an invasion of their privacy and kept reminding herself this was the lifestyle they chose.

When she was nine weeks along, Gina made the phone call to New York to tell Franny and Mario she was pregnant again but didn't want many people to know. Gina confided in her mother that she was concerned about the doctor's comments about her uterine wall. Franny was instantly worried but would never acknowledge it to Gina. No need to make her more nervous.

Gina made a call to Shawn. Trevor rarely mentioned his father and she wasn't sure how much of their life he shared with him. However, Gina saw him as a sweet man who had probably never recovered from his wife's death. Trevor was obviously still dealing with some traumatic issues over the ordeal.

"Shawn, it's Gina how are you? I'm sorry we haven't really spoken since the wedding. I've been thinking of you."

Despite the months that had passed, Shawn appreciated the phone call. "I see you and Trevor have been busy. And your picture is on the cover of half the magazines at the checkout in the grocery store. I tell everybody in line, 'That's my daughter-in-law.' I became a bit of a celebrity at the grocery store. Is everything good with you and Trevor?"

Gina wasn't sure what he was alluding to. "Everything is great. I wanted you to know that we are expecting a baby, and you will be a grandfather."

Shawn's response troubled Gina when he said, "I hope Trevor is happy about this."

Why would he think that? Gina quickly replied, "Yes, he is, very excited."

"Well Gina that sounds wonderful. I'm happy for you both."

Gina promised, "I will keep you updated. It was good to talk to you. I'm hoping you come visit us soon."

"Sounds good Gina. Thank you for calling." Click.

Gina couldn't shake the feeling there was something behind his words. Did Shawn know more about Trevor's demons that he wasn't sharing? But why? She got along well with Shawn. They had a connection. Was his relationship with Trevor so damaged that he refused to see how fortunate his son's life was? Gina assumed there was more to it than that, but didn't want to push, not yet.

BACK TO MUSIC AND AWARD SHOWS

MEANWHILE IN THE STUDIO, the band was starting to put together ideas on new music. Trevor wouldn't bring Gina in until he needed her for lyric writing. He wanted her to relax.

She spent her time visiting Lisa and little Liam. Babies grow fast. Gina took joy in watching Lisa go through motherhood and was happy for her.

She and Jae always found time to hang out and enjoyed sitting on the deck and eating Marisol's food. Gina knew she still had to keep her figure, even with a pregnancy. The entertainment business was fickle. If you gained weight, there would be some picture of you, with a caption, "Is she letting herself go?" Celebrities have babies. Most women gain weight while pregnant. The double standard was ridiculous.

The label called Skip and wanted Perfection to be presenters at a minor award show which meant spending a few days in Los Angeles. Gina wasn't a fan of the idea, but Skip pointed out they would get even more exposure because the show was being broadcast on television. That gave Perfection actual face time with a TV audience that may not connect the band name with their faces. That was the game—always getting some new demographic to know you and your music. Perfection agreed and showed up dressed like rock and rollers. Gina dressed as sexy as she could. Even though she wasn't showing yet, her clothes were getting a bit tighter. She glowed in a multilayered navy dress.

The media couldn't get enough of Gina and Trevor. It's like they couldn't believe a couple in the music business could have a great marriage. They never considered they were indeed in love. All the band members presented the award for the Top Rock Act of the Year, hoping that they would be considered for it next year. The audience shouted, "GMac we love you!"

"We love you too. Thank you." Gina smiled and walked off the stage.

Trevor and Gina stayed at the Hollywood Hills house. Even though Gina had been able to get a variance to put a fence around the front, the crowds were getting larger, and it was becoming a security issue. It's not like there weren't other celebrities in the neighborhood. Go bother them.

Gina was relieved to finally flick the high heels off her swollen feet. "Oh, Trev my feet are getting so fat, I won't be able to wear these kinds of shoes soon."

"Come here and I'll rub your feet. Just don't ask me to do this when you're not pregnant." They sat in the living room and reminisced how this place was where their journey started in California.

Gina couldn't shake the phone call to Shawn, "Hey babe, do you have any reservations about being a father? I'm just wondering."

Trevor did a double take, "Why would you say that? It gutted me when we lost our first baby. This is what I want. Why would you even think that?"

Gina was tired, "I'm just doing a sanity check. The band is finally a contender in the music world and our life will change with a baby, that's all."

"Gina McNaughton, you are a crazy woman. Give me a kiss."

"Is that all you want?"

Trevor laughed, "Of course not but a kiss to start would be nice."

They sat on the couch and made out like a couple of teenagers; Gina knowing it was wonderful foreplay. Trevor carried her into the bedroom. Even though they were very much in love, demons lurking way down below would resurface. Gina's love for her husband would be tested. She would do anything for their love.

MCNAUGHTONS' LOSS

THE MONTECITO OFFICES, rehearsal and studio rooms were running at a hundred percent. Gina was now four months pregnant. At her last baby appointment, the doctor advised her to take things easy. The lining where the baby was lying wasn't where the doctor thought it should be. This made Gina extremely nervous. Everyone knew Gina had a tenuous pregnancy and didn't want her to be aggravated or stressed.

Lisa felt worried for Gina when she heard about her condition. She could only pray this pregnancy went full term. Lisa tried to visit or call Gina every day when not running around catching Liam. Rio encouraged Jae to check on Gina as much as possible, even when he couldn't. They both sensed Gina's nervousness.

The label was hoping for some previews of songs for their third album. Trevor and Rio were firm, it would come, but not as fast as their other albums. Their lead singer was pregnant, and she was not to be stressed. Jae became almost a permanent resident at Gina's house when the guys were writing music.

Gina admitted to her that she felt left out. She was antsy and told Jae, "Let's walk down there, I want to see how things are progressing." She also wanted to check on Brian Mayfield. She heard rumors of him taking the "boys" out to the new strip club down in LA and needed to keep that asshole in his place. This was a perfect time to try and get Trevor, Rio, and even Ian in a situation that could have heavy repercussions with their home life. Brian didn't care, that was the worst part about it, he wanted to push that envelope and loved making Gina angry. It was almost a game with him. Why Trevor still kept him around was a mystery.

Jae asked nervously, "Gina, should you go down there? I mean when they need you, they will ask you to start writing, correct? You should stay calm; you know, the baby."

Gina was frustrated, "Yes, Jae, but I feel like an outcast from my own band. It's just a short walk, it can't hurt." Gina got up and felt a bit dizzy.

Jae looked worried, "Please Gina, stay here, I'll go check."

"Nonsense, I can walk a little bit. Jae, hold onto me, okay?"

Jae was not going with the plan, "Gina, I don't think you should go anywhere, please."

Gina got up anyway and immediately felt sharp pain in her abdomen. She had to see Trevor. She walked slowly, knowing what was happening. She needed to get to Trevor.

The pain quickly became excruciating, and she began to cry. Jae opened the door to the studio and immediately started yelling for everybody to come. Rio ran first, followed by Trevor. Gina fell on the floor screaming, "It's starting again."

Her shrieks scared everybody. Trevor leaned over her, "Baby, no, please hang in there. Someone call fucking 911 now!"

Jae started to cry and buried her face in Rio's chest. Rio was shaken. "Call a fucking ambulance now, Christ."

Finally, they could hear the sirens and the gate opened. Trevor was visibly upset, sobbing with Gina, "It's going to be okay, this time it will be okay, baby. Please hang in there, please."

Jeff ran out and led the EMS team to Gina. Everyone connected with

Perfection watched as their strongest member was in pain, and most likely going through the worst experience they could imagine.

Trevor, shaking, climbed into the back of the ambulance to ride with Gina, trying to calm her down, hoping against all hope this could be stopped. Trevor shouted to Rio, "You know what to do, make the call."

Jae was sobbing heavily into Rio, "I told her not to go. It's my fault."

Rio held her. "No Jae, it isn't. Stop. I need to call my Aunt Franny now. I'll be right back."

Jeff rushed alongside Rio. "I'm coming with you." When Rio got to the phone, he was choking back tears. This wasn't a call he wanted to make. Aunt Franny would be in LA in hours, he knew it. The phone rang. "Aunt Franny, it's Rio," unable to hold back his tears.

Franny knew. "Rio, is it Gina? Is it my girl? Not again, please don't tell me."

Rio couldn't stop his tears, "Aunt Franny, please come right away. Gina's bad. It's bad. Please come now."

Franny let out a mournful cry, "I'll be there as soon as I can get a jet. Where's Trevor?"

Rio still was trying to compose himself, "In the ambulance with Gina."

Franny asked what hospital they were taking her to. Rio had no idea. Jae said most likely Santa Barbara.

Franny said, "No that won't work, I'm going to have her airlifted to Cedars-Sinai in Los Angeles."

"Aunt Franny, I'll drive there now, what should I do?"

Aunt Franny was both determined and heartbroken. "Try to be calm. I knew there was something wrong with her, but no one listened. I'm getting the best doctor in LA. Please let Trevor know, so he's not surprised when they put her in the AirMed."

Jeff looked at Rio. "You head out. I'll go find Trevor and tell him."

Trevor was right next to Gina in the ER, where the staff were using ice packs to try to stop the bleeding—but there was no stopping what was happening. Gina's OB-GYN had been notified and walked into the room. She took her hand. "Gina, I'm sorry. I told you I was worried about the lining. I'm so sorry."

Trevor yelled, "You never told us once that she would lose the baby. You only told us to be careful. How was that a warning? My poor wife has gone through this twice. What the fuck? Don't you know anything? Damn all of you!"

Gina was in shock at this point and nonresponsive.

"Mr. McNaughton, we realize this is traumatic but please don't scream obscenities in the ER."

Trevor, "Fuck off all of you. Look at her. She's in shock, what are you doing for that?"

A nurse stood timidly in the doorway and told Trevor someone was at the nurse's station for him. "I'm not leaving my wife." Trevor's sobs were unstoppable. The nurse told him it was extremely important he got this message. He reluctantly walked out of the room and saw Jeff. "What the hell, Jeff? Gina's doing bad, please let me go back."

Jeff put his hands on his shoulders. "Listen to me. Rio and Jae are driving to Cedars-Sinai. Apparently, Gina's mother is arranging to have her airlifted there. Franny didn't take it well, as you can imagine. She will be there as soon as she gets a jet."

"When, when are they going to take her, soon?"

"Trev, that's the plan. Man, I don't know how fast, be prepared at any time. Can they save ..." Trevor visibly upset, "No, no this will break her, I don't know how I pull her out of this, I am at a loss. I don't know how to make this better." Jeff had known Gina before Trevor. "Trevor, she loves you more than life, it will be okay."

"No it won't." Trevor heard AirMed landing and raced down the hall back into the ER.

The ER doctor in charge said, "Well Mr. McNaughton, apparently someone very powerful is airlifting your wife to Cedars. You can accompany her. We have sedated her. She was sobbing uncontrollably."

Trevor cried into his wife's chest for the entire fifty-minute ride. When the helicopter landed, fifteen medical staff surrounded Gina's gurney. Trevor stood for a second not knowing what he should do.

One of the nurses recognized him. "Mr. McNaughton, come with me. We are going to get your wife a room. You can stay there until they take her in for, well it's a procedure. Mrs. Ricci has arranged everything. I'm sure you knew that. Come follow me."

Trevor felt like he was walking in some sort of horrible dream, this time worse than the first. He paced in a private waiting room and through the doors, raced Rio and Jae. Rio needed Jae to drive because he was so upset. He put his arms around Trevor, and through his cries he could only get out, "Hey, bro I'm so sorry. You know I love you both. How could this happen again?" They almost collapsed on each other.

While Franny was waiting to board the jet, she called Cedars-Sinai Hospital in Los Angeles. "Yes, my name is Franny Ricci. I'm sure you know my family. I want the best OB/GYN doctor at Cedars-Sinai in the next few hours. I need someone to evaluate my daughter who a few moments ago suffered her second miscarriage. I know there is something wrong, and *I KNOW* it can be fixed. Remember a few hours."

When Franny's plane touched down five hours later, a limo was waiting to take her to the hospital.

Trevor never left Gina's side throughout the night. Rio and Jae slept in the chairs in Gina's room. The next morning, Franny Ricci walked through the halls with purpose and found her daughter's room. Sitting next to her on the bed was an inconsolable Trevor. Rio got up out of the chair, crossed the room, and hugged his aunt.

"Rio, thank you my dear. You and Jae should stay at the house. You look tired."

Rio wouldn't hear about leaving. "Aunt Franny, I'm not leaving. I'll be around."

Franny walked over to Trevor and looked into his tearstained face. "Trevor, look at me." "Oh Trevor, why is not an answer we can know now. We will find out the reason why this is happening. Have they taken her for the procedure? Trevor, please answer me."

"They said they gave her some sort of procedure. The baby is gone, right? I don't understand this."

Franny touched him, "Yes, the baby is gone. I know this is very painful. Gina looks ashen. What have they given her? Anybody know? I am livid by this whole situation. Trevor, you need to be strong. But I promise this baby will be brought to God with Melody." Franny choked back her words. "I am having the best obstetrics doctor come and see Gina. She will tell us what's really going on. I promise, you and Gina will have your own beautiful baby, I promise you."

An attractive red-haired woman with a serious face walked into the room. "Mrs. Ricci, I understand you called for me. I'm Doctor Pamela Schear. We must take Gina down to make sure that everything is cleaned out of her uterus. We don't want her to become septic. Mr. McNaughton, I'm so sorry. I'm hoping to get a look at your wife's reproductive system and see what we can do. I'll have her back in her room in about an hour or so."

Franny spoke up, "Doctor Schear, we would like to know the sex of the child so that we can have the Catholic Sacraments said. If you can let me know, I would appreciate it. We would like to give the child a name so God can recognize it."

Dr. Schear said, "Yes, I'll be sure to relay that information to you. I'm sure the team that worked on her upon arrival will have that information."

A teary Franny looked at Trevor. "Trevor, what did you and Gina pick for a boy's name and for a girl's name?"

Trevor sat there, not like the rock star he was, merely a man who had lost his second child. "Drake, we picked Drake for a boy and Emma for a girl."

Franny looked at Trevor. "Trevor come walk with me." Trevor was on autopilot. Franny found a chapel; she walked in with Trevor. "Trevor, kneel next to me and pray with me."

"Franny, I don't know how. I don't know what to ask."

Franny put her hand on his. "I will lead us. Father, we ask you to watch over our Gina to help her through this unbearable tragedy, to help her heal from this pain. We ask Holy Father, that they find the reason for Gina's medical problem. Lay your healing hand on her. We ask Our Mother Mary, find a resting place for this baby, and we ask this Holy Father in your name, Amen."

Trevor started trembling. "I don't believe like you do Franny, but if this can help, I pray for that."

Gina was rolled back into the room, Dr. Schear following. "Mr. McNaughton, Mrs. Ricci, first I want you to know the sex of the baby was a boy. I'm so sorry. I think we know what's happening with Gina. She has a thin uterine lining, but we can give her medications and infusions to help build it up. When the baby reaches about three to four pounds, she miscarries. She can't hold the baby's weight after that. There is a procedure that will essentially create a drawstring, closing the cervix, and will keep the baby in place for the nine months. We of course will take the baby by C-section. I believe this will work. However, I'm not sure we can do this many times, twice maybe, but one realistically. This procedure has been successful for many women. Gina could be a candidate to have one successful pregnancy."

Franny took that information. "When does this have to be done?"

Dr. Schear answered, "We want her to get infusions to help build up the lining and give her the medications as soon as possible. We would need to wait about a month or so to start. Once she finds out she's pregnant, we need her to come in and have the procedure, it won't interfere with the pregnancy at all. Does that sound like a plan you could live with, Mr. McNaughton?"

Trevor was trying to process what was said to him. "So, let me understand we can have a successful pregnancy doing this?"

Franny smiled. "Yes, Trevor that's what the doctor is saying. Our prayers were heard." Franny wanted to know, "When can we take her home?"

"We would like to keep her here for about two days. I want to make sure there isn't any risk of hemorrhaging. I am concerned that she still appears to be in shock. We want to wait and see how she comes out of sedation. Now as far as getting pregnant again, I would wait for about four months. Let us build up that lining a bit. Of course, no sexual relations for about four weeks."

The doctor left and Trevor climbed into Gina's bed again. When Gina woke up, she immediately started crying when she saw Trevor, "I fucked up again, baby. Please don't leave me."

Trevor touched her face, "No Gina, that wouldn't happen. But your mom and I got some good news."

Franny leaned over and kissed her daughter's forehead. "Gina, Doctor Schear, a doctor I called in, said there is a procedure that would keep the baby for nine months. You could at least have one baby, maybe two. You will have to get some injections to build up your lining, but it's good."

"Trev, is this the truth? I would be happy if we could only have one baby."

"Yes, G that would be the most beautiful idea."

Rio and Jae peeked in the room, "Do you want visitors?"

Gina sat up. "Yes, come in." Rio and Jae were surprised to see Gina was in better spirits so soon.

An attendant entered the room with a huge arrangement of lavender, white, and pink roses. Gina looked at Trevor, "Are these from you?"

"G, I haven't had any time to do anything but look after you."

Gina read the card. "Gina, I am so sorry for your loss. Know I'm thinking of you. I know how it feels to lose a child. I lost my son while I was in London producing an album. That is why I don't leave LA, you never know. Sweet Gina, take your time, no rush, we will get an album out when you're ready. Much Love, Tommy and Anne Whelan." Gina teared up, this was something she understood and would only share it with Trevor.

After two long days, Gina and Trevor left the hospital to go home. Marisol cooked up a feast. Soon things would go back to normal. Perfection would take a month break before considering any writing or recording. Life was about to change for everybody. But how much change does a person need?

PERFECTION REACHES THE MCNAUGHTONS

FRANNY, MARIO, ANT, AND SHAWN were spending Thanksgiving with Gina and Trevor. Gina was excited to host a family dinner with the help of Marisol. Of course, all the band members were invited. It was a celebration this time. Perfection was starting to write music for their third album. There was no decision when they would be in the studio recording. Gina was taking injections for her pregnancy issues. Gina and Trevor's parents were excited about the possibility of Gina finally being able to carry a baby. The dinner was one of Gina's finest.

It was hard to keep all the conversations together for Gina. She and Trevor sat back and watched this mismatched group of people talk about everything, enjoying the frantic discussions. Mario entertained everyone with stories about how he got his business to a multi-hundred-million-dollar operation. Jae was wide-eyed. She knew that Rio's dad was part of this operation.

Shawn was invited to stay with Gina and Trevor. He was awed by the beauty of the Pacific Ocean; it was different from the Pacific Ocean in Vancouver. He sat on their patio taking in the fresh air. He promised Gina he would start an herb garden for her. Gina enjoyed taking walks on the beach with Shawn. He always seemed sad, and she knew he and Trevor weren't very close. While Shawn was there, Trevor spent many hours in the studio perfecting the new music. Gina knew something deeper happened to Trevor and she wasn't sure she wanted to dip her toes into that, yet.

Her parents also enjoyed the patio. Franny smiled at Gina. "This time next year, I'm sure there will be a little one. You will be a wonderful mother."

"Thank you, Mom, I can't wait to have the chance."

LATE HONEYMOON, CABO BABY

AT THE END OF NOVEMBER everyone had gone home. It was nice to have their home to themselves. Gina walked through the house in her sexy lingerie. It was twilight when she walked down to the studio. "Babe, are you finished playing with the progressions and solos? How many songs do you need lyrics for?"

Trevor looked like he hadn't slept in days. "I admit I feel spent ... the cycle ... write music, record, promote, tour. When do we get a break? Like go on vacation?"

"We can go on vacation now if we want. The label isn't pressing us for the album. Where do you want to go?"

Trevor thought, "We never went on a honeymoon."

"Want to go to Cabo? We can get a bungalow on the beach at an exclusive hotel where we probably won't be bothered. Let's go for five days before Christmas and get regenerated. We need this, just us, no intrusions. Relaxation, sun, sex, you, and me."

Trevor felt the weight disappear. "Let's do it. I'm burnt out."

Gina became excited. "I'll call a travel agent. I love you. This is an excellent idea. I'm not bringing a lot of clothes." She gave Trevor a huge kiss. "This is our Christmas gift to each other."

Two days later, they were on a private jet to Cabo San Lucas. A limo was waiting for them, along with a few paparazzi. How did they always know where they were? Just as long as the tip-off wasn't coming from within Perfection. They were dropped at a private entrance and were met by their personal concierge.

"So nice to meet you both. I'm a huge fan."

Gina smiled. "Thank you very much. Can you take us to our bungalow?"

A bellman immediately appeared. "Please follow me. We have you staying in our exclusive area. You shouldn't be bothered by the other hotel guests. You will also have a butler assigned to you for whatever you need."

They rode a golf cart to their secluded bungalow right on the beach. They could lay out in the sun undisturbed. A second cart followed with their luggage. Trevor tipped the bellman, who got in the second cart and rode off, leaving the first cart for the couple's use.

They walked through the bungalow to the lanai on the surf's edge. Gina went back inside, stepping out of her gauzy sundress as she headed for the bed. "Come here," she beckoned.

Trevor turned around and joined her on the bed. "This is how we're starting?" He quickly slid off his jeans and T-shirt and crawled up to Gina. "My head is clear from writing and my attention is on you."

"This isn't touring, this is just us, we have no schedule, we get to do whatever we want and have people waiting on us. Come get me. I'm so ready to have you with no intrusions."

Trevor was worried. "Are we going to be good? No problems with your injections?"

"They didn't say we couldn't make love. Come on."

Trevor got up. "I'm opening the sliders to hear the ocean then I'm coming back to get you Mrs. McNaughton."

"Please do."

They enjoyed the salt air and unhurried lovemaking. They ate at the hotel restaurant afterward, ordering silly frozen drinks. The meal, locally sourced, did not disappoint. They shared a dessert and took a walk on the beach after their meal.

Focused on each other, they didn't notice another couple approach them. "Oh, shit! It's GMac and TMac! We love your music," they gushed. "I wish we had something to get your signature."

Trevor looked at them, "Like you, we're here to recharge. We would appreciate it if you didn't say anything. If we run into you again, we'll give you an autograph."

"Wow, thanks cool. We promise we won't say anything."

Gina and Trevor kept walking hand in hand, like any other honeymoon couple. They had a drink on their lanai and made love again. Their lovemaking was never boring. They enjoyed each other every way possible. The McNaughtons were that sexy couple on stage. But behind closed doors they were driven by their insatiable need for each other. Their lovemaking was powerful, over charged. At times they seemed like two teenagers who discovered sex for the first time. Trevor even brought the *Kama Sutra* book they bought years ago. He wanted to try every position in the book or at least he wanted to see where they would end up.

Their five days flew by and when it was time to return, they felt invigorated, recharged, and ready to get back to work. Gina went to the studio every morning with Trevor. Rio would come by, and the two guitarists put together songs. Gina listened and started writing lyrics with them.

HOLIDAYS
PERFECTION STYLE

THE MCNAUGHTONS DECORATED for Christmas. Rio and Jae hosted Christmas Eve at their house. Their relationship seemed to Gina to be very serious. *Why not propose Rio?* She hoped his hesitation wouldn't turn Jae away. Rio and Jae had a very sophisticated dinner. It was a nice diversion. Ian and Lisa came with a crawling Liam. Jeff had another starlet girlfriend, maybe this girl could get Jeff to be more responsible. They enjoyed each other's company, it was a nice life, all of them enjoying the fact that Perfection was a top band in the country.

Gina and Trevor spent Christmas Day alone, but Gina cooked a special dinner. Gina called her family back home. Everyone enjoyed their gifts, which were always over the top. Gina missed being a part of it. Gina urged Trevor to call his father. Shawn was happy to hear from them, however Gina felt sad he was alone. Shawn let them know he was stopping by a friend's for dinner, making Gina feel better. He held a special place in her heart.

On New Year's Eve, the McNaughtons did what they loved: hung out in next to nothing, watched TV in their bedroom, and ate junk food. They weren't rock stars, just a regular couple chilling out at home.

SUCCESS, INTERVIEWS, RUMORS

NEW YEAR'S 1981 ROLLED BY, AND SKIP brought the band together. He told them they had three songs on the top rock music stations, their albums were selling off the charts, and Perfection merchandise was flying off the shelves in major record stores. Perfection was now the band everyone talked about. They were everywhere and everyone wanted an interview. The entertainment shows wanted interviews with the entire band, and one famous interviewer wanted an in-depth interview with Gina and Trevor as one of "the most interesting couples of the year." Did they want to open Pandora's box? Skip thought all this press would put Perfection in the stratosphere. He asked how far they had gotten on the new album.

Trevor responded, "We're working on it. We have four songs, with a few in the pipeline." They would start working to get songs together in about a month, no stress.

Perfection was invited to play a two-day charity rock festival in early summer. Skip and Tommy were positioning Perfection to play the second to last act on the second night, closing out the festival—the prime spot.

Gina went over the interviews and ranked them. She knew she had to do the interview with Trevor for "The Most Interesting Couple." She thought it was an intrusion into their personal life, but Gina always knew to hold back just a bit to keep their lives private.

There were tons of interviews over the next several months, with the whole band, Rio, Trevor, and of course the McNaughtons. Most people wanted to know about their marriage, how they handle the new stardom, shit like that. The interview for "The Most Interesting Couple" bordered on wanting to know intimate details of their marriage. They always told interviewers, "We have been together for years, that should tell you that we love each other very much. Nothing has changed that; it's only gotten better." Once an interviewer sat down with them, it was apparent that they were very much in love, case closed. No room for questions on that subject.

Gina was trying to write some lyrics. She thought about the last months of promoting themselves and the band. The more they gave, the more the public wanted, it was a hamster wheel. Perfection was her band and her business. She knew there was a bigger prize for her and Trevor, a baby. Gina continued with her injections and Dr. Schear liked the progress. She gave Gina and Trevor high hopes that when they became pregnant, it would go full term. She was almost there.

Skip and Tommy went to Montecito. Tommy was fine making the drive; he even preferred the smaller studio. "I think we could make some great music here. It's private with fewer distractions. How many songs now?"

The group had seven new songs, all collaborative, so everyone would share royalties. That's the way Perfection worked, preferring to be united. They watched some top bands break up over songwriting. Gina wrote a song she thought was topical—the way they all felt about losing privacy, named, "What Do You Want to Know?"

What Do You Want to Know?

Here I am, here I am. See me, I'm on the stage, I'll give you a
good show. I'll make you feel some soul and rock and roll. I
adore you all when I'm up on the stage, I will give you everything
and so much more. I try to give you a sexy show, but then you ask for
more, pictures snapped when you don't know, it's out of nowhere,
where do I go. People always stop to say hello, I just want to
know, what do want to know, what is it that you need to know?
My life is open for you to see, however, could you just let us be
for a moment, just a moment for me to catch my breath, I love
you all but what is it really that you need to know, what do you
want to know, what do you want to know?

Trevor read the lyrics and smiled at his wife. She made people think,
he liked that. There would be revisions but the song itself was making
a point.

Gina would often visit Lisa and Jae. They understood what it felt like to
live in a fishbowl. That annoyance, Brian Mayfield, started to snake his way
back with the band. *Why hadn't Perfection cut him loose already? What was
his hold on Trevor?* She couldn't stand him, and now he was telling the band
about great parties, except the ladies weren't invited. That excluded Gina,
but she was a force you needed to deal with. Mayfield would tell anyone
who would listen about a great party in Beverly Hills or Bel Air given by
some record producer or band. He could persuade Jeff, but no one else was
interested, yet. Rio used to love the parties, but the only way he would go
now is if Jae went with him. Jae went to one or two of those parties but felt
extremely uncomfortable. She didn't think that they were the right "fit" for
parties filled with drugs and half-naked women, who were looking for some
celebrity to latch onto. Jae and Rio were more sophisticated and intelligent
than that kind of California life.

Ian and Trevor weren't interested, they had wives. But Mr. Lucky Charms tried every way to include Trevor, sometimes even lying to him to lure him away from Gina. There were whispers that Brian had gotten Trevor to a hedonistic party where Trevor was no angel. This angered Gina to maximum strength. She didn't believe the rumors, but at the same time the thought of it was swimming in her head. Brian Mayfield was becoming a bigger problem that Gina would have to tackle.

The band was at a point where they thought they should record some of their music, finally. Skip came to Montecito two or three days a week and had an office next to Gina's. Their little outbuilding grew into a nice building, with additions that made it a fully equipped studio. Tommy said he would try coming a couple days a week also. He was confident in Kevin's knowledge of the soundboard.

Tommy stopped by Gina's office. "So, Gina how are you? I heard you were getting help from Doctor Schear, she's good."

Gina smiled at him. He knew her pain. "Tommy, I'm not sure I ever really thanked you for the flowers and your words. I know you know how I felt, a two-time loser—losing two babies. Does that pain ever go away, losing a child? I mean I never got to know mine, but you did. It can't be easy, even today."

Tommy sighed, "No, the pain never goes away, but you to try to prevent it from happening again. That's what you're doing. You hang in there Gina."

She assured him she would be successful the next time.

HUGE OPPORTUNITY

AT THE BEGINNING OF MAY, Skip rallied the band. One of the biggest gigs of the summer, a concert benefiting several big charities, was happening on June twenty-seventh. Every act was donating their time. They all wanted to be a part of history. It wasn't going to be a free-for-all like Woodstock, but two days of scheduled bands and no sleeping at the venue. The doors would open at nine a.m. The acts would start at eleven a.m. and end at eleven p.m. Skip read through the acts for day one. It was a who's who of bands, mostly rock, but some R&B, some pop—all big names. The acts scheduled for day two were the cream of the music world and Perfection had a great spot at nine p.m., with one act following them—Brown Fence Records biggest act, Orange Wave, with Brent Nolan. Perfection had made their way to elite band status. They didn't care how or why.

Trevor asked the most important question, "Where is this taking place?" Washington, DC, located perfectly for the I-95 crowd up north and the I-95 down south. Otherwise, you fly or drive to get there. The tickets were based on a lottery system.

Gina sat back and looked at everyone. "I know we have new music, but these people want to hear our old stuff, a couple of our good covers, throw one or two new songs in the mix."

Skip agreed this wasn't the concert to promote new music, however, maybe add two new songs to get the buzz going for their new album. Skip added another nugget. There was talk there might be a show in London with some of the same acts that played in DC and a few well-known English bands. If it were to happen it would be the week before with the same set up.

Rio looked at everyone. "We're in, right? We don't say no to this. Who cares if we get paid? What a platform. We will have national and European exposure. This will propel Perfection even further. You see that right?"

It was agreed that this was a gift in their lap. Tommy walked in at that moment and asked, "Skip, you told them the news, right? Your producer has just been asked to produce these concerts live for television. This is a must for all of us."

It was settled, they were going to DC. London hadn't been locked down yet, but Perfection knew they would be in if it happened.

Trevor looked at everyone. "Well, let's figure out set lists, equipment, and what covers we should do. Obviously, we will be highlighting my wife's sexual nature."

Gina looked up. "Why say it like that? When did that ever bother you?"

Trevor shut her down. "We will discuss this later."

Gina was furious with his tone, he never spoke to her like that, ever. She would address this with Trevor immediately. Everyone in the band, Kevin, and the road crew would tackle the logistical nightmare of moving equipment and staging. Skip was there to sort out some of the work and there was Brian. What was his job? Getting a different kind of talent? Gina still couldn't believe he was on their payroll; he was a problem. He would try to play on Trevor's demons for sure. Gina started walking up to the house, pissed off at Trevor. It was extremely rare that they ever fought, but that tone in his voice, what the hell was that?

Trevor started walking faster to catch up with her. "Can you stop? I didn't mean it like that."

Gina turned and snarled at him, "Well then, can you explain how the hell you meant it? That tone Trevor, where did that come from? What the fuck is your problem right now?" Gina kept walking toward the house and entered through the side door into her home office.

Trevor caught up and pulled her arm, "Hey, wife, can you stop so I can talk to you?"

"I don't think I have ever been so pissed off at you. You talk about 'my wife's sexual nature.' When was that a problem for you in all these years? You loved it. I swear Trev, what's going on in your head? Are you drinking again?"

Trevor exhaled. "Gina, you are my wife, my lover, and my best friend. We are trying to have a baby. Remember? It's okay for sexy Gina to show up, but can you just tone it down? You're going to be someone's mother one day. If they are showing it live, your performance is going to live on by being recorded and played anytime. Probably on some music show on TV. I bet you didn't think about that, did you?"

Gina succumbed to what Trevor was trying to say. "I hear you and I apologize. But that tone in your voice, I've never heard you use that with me. It shook me. I have one more round to go on the injections and we will see how everything looks. Then it's time to try to have a baby, then get the procedure. Trev, I can still be sexy … it's always been for you." Gina started to tear up.

Trevor pulled her in. "Come here. I hate it when you cry. I probably shouldn't have said it that way, but I can't help it. I see those guys staring at you. It's like they get to see my wife put on a sexy show. I see their eyes even when you don't. That's all."

Gina put her arms around his neck. "Baby, you're silly, the show has always been for you. I want you to say, 'Yes that's my wife' and be proud of what I do, for you. I'll calm down a bit. You're right, a baby, that's the goal. Do you think we are going to go to London? I haven't been in years. I love it."

Trevor laughed. "Of course you have been there, you'll have to take me around."

"Baby this is going to be difficult work for our crew. We have about six weeks to get our music, light show … are we allowed our own light show? What about pyrotechnics? We will have to ask all those questions, then have all the necessary equipment." Gina's head was spinning around the business side of the concert. She and Skip had some work to do over the next weeks. The guys would be working on music set lists for two different shows. They would try to keep as many of the songs the same for each show but knew the London show would be tweaked. Also in consideration was what covers Gina McNaughton wanted to do. She tried never to open with the same covers. There would be practice for that also. May to June would be a busy time for Perfection, but it would be worth all the hard work.

The band met every day at the studio to rehearse their set lists for each show. Gina considered the following songs: "Hold the Line," "Long Live Rock," or another Who song. After many long days at the studio, Gina and Trevor enjoyed the short walk from the studio to their house.

Marisol knew the McNaughton's were working hard, she would let Gina know every morning what she planned for dinner. Gina always told her, "you are in charge of the kitchen when I'm too busy to be around. It's your choice and we will be happier for your thoughtfulness. One night after a long practice session, Trevor felt he needed to have that special time with his wife. The hard work made them eat dinner and collapse in bed. Trevor was hoping for his *special time.* Marisol had left a note telling them her Chicken Adobe with rice was in the oven and made her flan that Trevor loved. She hoped they would have a lovely evening and relax. Trevor looked at his wife, "I think I need my own Gina McNaughton time, not sharing with the band or Skip. Just us." Gina touched his face tenderly, "Let's eat this wonderful food Marisol made and hang out in the bedroom and do whatever."

Trevor looked playfully at Gina. "Seriously, do whatever?"

Gina smiled. "Yes, the dirtier the better. Use your best moves."

PREPARATION, CHARITY CONCERT

THE PERFECTION CREW HAD BEEN HARD at work, readying equipment to get to DC. With so many bands, there were many restrictions to set up your own equipment. Their road crew was loyal and hardworking. Rio and Trevor had the playlist, the band had practiced, they knew Gina would want at least one of her moments. She chose her songs, and they had been practicing those also.

Skip was still busy handling logistics, planes, and hotels. London was happening. The London concert was going to be on June twentieth at Twickenham Stadium. A logistic shit show. The bands would bring their personal instruments and any smaller equipment. The show would have amps and such. It would never work with each individual band bringing their whole set of equipment. Skip had to fly the road crew out ahead on commercial air. The band would hop on a private charter with other US talent going over. All those different bands would make it an interesting flight. Jae and Lisa were excited for their first trip to Europe.

They stayed at The Ritz Hotel in London, first class all the way. Lisa and Jae were excited to go sightseeing during their two free days before the show. The ladies all went window shopping at Harrods. Gina did actual shopping, loving the British style of clothing. She bought some rocker outfits for herself and Trevor. In the evenings, the band would meet up at a restaurant and enjoy dinner together, which was unusual, but this concert had a different vibe. Many different bands had come together. Some bands from the UK were the top talent and then the US bands. The US bands were all top performers, Rock, Pop, and R&B.

Trevor and Gina took the second day to walk around London and let Trevor experience London for himself. Gina suggested they find a fish and chips place; she wanted him to experience the newspaper wrapped around the food. They walked freely around the city, because no one really knew who they were, or at least didn't bother them. However, when they neared the hotel, they noticed the British tabloids were perched in front, eager for any picture of a band member. As they got closer to the lobby, someone shouted, "Its Gina Mac!" Her hairstyle gave her away. Trevor kindly asked that they just take one picture and back off, and it worked.

Trevor was tired when they got back to their room. "I had a great time taking in London with you. I wish we were able to have more adventures, but we need to check out the acts tomorrow. You okay with that?"

Gina smiled. "It was nice just being a regular couple, walking around, I loved it. But seriously, you can't think of another adventure tonight?"

Trevor smiled. "I knew we would get to that eventually."

The first night they went to see selected acts perform. The next day, the band was due to arrive at seven p.m., two hours before show time. Perfection was getting a European following. Their set list was varied, with old material, some popular covers, and two new songs.

They killed it, and the crowd loved them. The last song Gina and Trevor did was their version of "Gimme Shelter," which had the audience standing. Perfection conquered the UK, a big deal for the band and the future of growing their fan base.

Back from Europe, direct to DC, Perfection was ready for their place in rock history. The set list was carefully selected. They wanted the crowd to see a true rock band on the rise. There were no distractions, and the band took the moment seriously.

The US Charity Concert was a week later. Perfection was staying at the Four Seasons. Gina needed her twenty-four-hour room service. As Gina was walking through the lobby to find coffee, she saw Skip, and pulled him over. "Listen, you better neutralize Mayfield. I don't want groupies or drug dealers around. You need to watch him. No surprises."

Skip promised to handle it. Perfection took the stage, in high gear for this televised event. The crowd went crazy when Gina introduced herself and the band the way only she could and had done for years. The crowd loved them so much they did two encores. They nailed it.

Perfection chartered their own jet back to Santa Barbara where everyone had two weeks off before any recording or work had to be done. Gina and Trevor locked their doors and dedicated the next two weeks to relaxing. Gina finished her injections, and they were free to start trying to have a baby and stayed in bed for two days. Taking a brief rest, they were flipping through TV channels and found a rebroadcast of the concert, weird to see it since the concert was just over. They analyzed their performance, laughing at the faces they made onstage.

When the concert was over, they found a music channel and Trevor started to make moves on Gina. She turned to him, "Did you want something? Is there something I have that you want?"

Trevor begged, "Come on G, you know what I want. Watching you on TV has made me want you, bad."

The banter. "Just watching me on TV, not always?"

Trevor looked at her. "I want you now, let's make that baby."

Gina fell in love with him like the first time she saw him. "Trevor, I love you so much. I want you any time, any reason."

They held each other, and she gave him sweet soft kisses around his face. He came back with deep irresistible kisses. She whispered, "Put a baby inside me."

He was happy to oblige. In the middle of their lovemaking, the song "Roxanne" came on, and they started singing along for fun at the same time. In the afterglow of their lovemaking, Trevor mused, "If we have a baby girl, we should name her Roxanne." Gina laughed and agreed.

Gina and Trevor never had an issue with the "trying" part of getting pregnant, they proved their love for each other almost every night, and sometimes on midday breaks.

Six weeks later, Gina was late. This time, she told Trevor right away. He was excited but knew not to get his hopes up until they were sure. Gina went to the doctor where they confirmed she was going to have a baby. Dr. Schear scheduled her to come to Cedars for the procedure four days later.

Trevor told Rio they would be driving to LA for Gina to be admitted to Cedars. Rio and Jae wanted to take the drive with them, for moral support. Rio wanted to make sure his cousin would have her wish, and that Trevor had someone to lean on.

Everyone stayed at the Hollywood Hills house. Gina was grateful to have Rio and Jae there for an extra hand to hold. Gina didn't even let Franny know until she recovered from the operation. It was at that point they would tell her parents and Shawn. No false alarms this time. After three hours, Dr. Schear came out of surgery and gave Trevor a congratulatory hug, the surgery went well, both mother and baby were doing well. Trevor had a huge bouquet of flowers waiting for Gina when she woke up. Rio and Jae had a cookie bouquet sent to the room.

Gina woke up and saw them all sitting in the room, and she got scared, "Trev, did everything go well? Are we still having a baby?"

Trevor smiled, "Yes, baby we're good, we will be having a baby in less than seven months."

Gina started to cry. "This time for real, right?" They all chimed in "yes." She saw the flowers and read the card, "I will always love you and our new little McNaughton. Your loving husband, Trevor."

Jae handed Gina a cookie. "Here, now you can indulge in some sweets."

Trevor called Franny and Mario and told them the good news. Franny wanted to come out, but Trevor told her there would be a time when they would need her to come out, but not now. Mario was elated. Trevor even placed a call to his father and let him know the news.

Shawn simply said, "Let me know when I'm a grandfather." Trevor felt that went better than expected.

Over the next months the band wrote music for album three. Gina would come down and listen to the music and thought which way the song should go and write lyrics. She went shopping with Lisa and Jae for baby clothes and all the necessary baby equipment. Lisa was helpful, making sure she bought everything she could possibly need. Gina started to get baby belly and was happy to get fat. As usual she was concerned that Trevor would not find her desirable and Brian Mayfield would be more than happy to arrange a hookup. Seated at the piano in her living room, looking at the ocean, Gina started crying. Would Trevor love "fat" Gina?

Trevor walked in from the studio and saw Gina sitting there. "G, baby, what's wrong? Is everything okay with the baby?"

Gina was hysterical. "Trevor, I have never been this big in my life. I'm so afraid you will find one of those big-boobed blondes that you will want rather than me. I know Brian would love to make that happen for you."

Trevor sat down next to her. "Gina, you're having our baby, I couldn't love you more. Why do you always feel like I want something other than you? You have been my life, my wife, and soon the mother to our child. Don't cry. I love you so much. Do I have to show how much I love you? Would that make you feel better?"

Gina looked up. "You still want to make love to me?"

"Gina McNaughton, I'm sure it's your hormones. Come on baby, let's go and have a playdate."

"I love you Trevor always."

BABY TIME

GINA MADE IT TO HER EIGHTH MONTH. Franny would be out soon. They knew the baby's birthday would be March 3, 1981. Gina felt comfortable setting up the nursery in soft pastel colors, with a garden mural painted on one wall. They didn't want to know the sex of the baby. It was to be a surprise. Franny swung into Montecito with brand new baby clothes, and many other baby trinkets. Franny couldn't resist buying everything she could for "her" grandchild. She just couldn't contain herself, this joy, her daughter to have "her" grandchild.

Lisa and Ian had their second baby—another boy they named Malcolm. Babies were coming into the world of Perfection.

Gina's bag was packed. She would be in the hospital for a few days with a C-section birth, not caring how the baby came into this world, just so it did. Trevor, Gina, and Franny arrived at Santa Barbara Cottage Hospital at six a.m. and met Dr. Schear who was allowed surgery privileges there. Trevor was allowed in the delivery room, wearing a paper gown and hat. Gina already had a spinal to numb her. Trevor was already teary, seated by Gina's top half. The nurse asked if she wanted the mirror to see them perform the surgery. Her answer, "Absolutely not."

She asked Trevor, "Please count all the fingers and toes."

He laughed and said, "If I could see to count. Once I meet our child, I'll lose it."

Gina felt nothing but intense pressure, then fifteen minutes later, she heard a cry.

"Congratulations, you have a baby girl," Dr. Schear beamed. The McNaughtons cried to each other. They did it. Baby Girl McNaughton was seven pounds, six ounces and nineteen-and-a-half inches long, born at 10:10 a.m. The nurse laid the baby on top of Gina's chest, and the three of them were already a family. The baby was taken to get cleaned, Gina's incision was stapled, and she was rolled into recovery. Trevor took off the gown and ran into the waiting room to tell Franny.

Franny was happy anxious. "So, is it a boy or girl?"

Trevor cried, "It's a girl Franny. We are naming her Roxanne."

Franny hugged Trevor tightly. "I'm so happy my little girl has a little girl. I have to call Mario. When can we see her?"

"As soon as they clean her up, she will be in the nursery." Franny and Trevor found the nursery where Roxanne already had a little name tag on her bassinet, Roxanne McNaughton. She was beautiful with a head of brown curls.

Trevor left to meet Gina when they wheeled her into her room. The nurses moved her onto the bed and Trevor sat down in the bed with her. They cried, this time for joy, with love and gratitude their perfect little girl was born.

Franny came running in, "Oh Gina, she's so beautiful. She reminds me of you when you were born."

Gina was excited. "I'm still waiting to see her."

Within the hour a nurse wheeled in Roxanne Harmony McNaughton, a perfect little baby. Trevor started calling everyone with the good news.

Rio and Jae arrived first, looking like rock stars, but with flowers and stuffed animals. Rio looked at his cousin. "Gina, you did it. You did good. She's beautiful. I'm so excited to be her uncle. I'm already thinking of things to do with her. Maybe I can teach her piano."

Jae just cried and couldn't have been happier.

By the end of the day, Gina's room was filled wall to wall with flowers and balloons. One arrangement surprised her. It was from Brent Nolan. How he found out, she would never know. The card read, "Congratulations Mrs. Gina McNaughton. I guess it's the real deal. Congratulations on your baby girl. Brent."

Trevor was exhausted but wouldn't leave. Franny went back to the house to make sure everything was perfect. Trevor fell asleep in a recliner next to Gina and she threw one of her blankets over him. An hour later, the sound of crying babies coming down the hall woke Trevor. When Roxanne was brought into the room, she wasn't crying, but making little sounds, indicating it was time for her to eat. Gina had decided against breastfeeding, so Trevor could bottle-feed Roxanne whenever he wanted. The nurse handed Gina a pink, sweet-smelling little bundle, and a bottle, telling her what to do. After a few moments, Gina handed Roxy over to Trevor.

"Really? I can feed her?"

"Yes babe, you're her father. Feed your daughter and don't forget to burp her." Gina's heart was filled with love, joy, every good kind of emotion, watching her husband with their daughter. Many years later, Gina would remember this moment, when Roxy and her father would have a bond that seemed unbreakable.

When the new family arrived home a few days later, there was a crowd of photographers and well-wishers outside the estate. Gina scowled. "It's not like I'm going to show them my daughter." The gates closed after them, shutting off the outside world. Gina and Trevor could relax at home, with their baby girl next to their bed. Franny and Marisol helped with feedings so they could get their rest, curled up next to each other, vowing to always love each other forever and swearing nothing could break them, not knowing how harshly those vows would be tested.

FINDING HER VOICE

THREE MONTHS AFTER ROXY'S BIRTH, Perfection's album three, *Perfection Personified*, hit the airwaves. This album had a harder edge to it. They were, after all, now a truly hard rock band. Brown Fence Records wanted Perfection to start work on their next album. It seemed very close to Album Three, *Perfection, Personified*. The record company knew they were hot and wanted to use that momentum for delivering their next album. Gina went to the studio and started to sing, but felt she couldn't find her voice. It had left her; she was flat or pitchy. What happened? Could hormones affect her singing? She knew she had to get it together. Maybe a phone call to Simon Beauvaux, her old voice coach, was in order. She wondered if she still had his number, but Aunt Deidre would have it.

"Simon? It's me Gina." Simon Beauvaux was the person who Gina felt made her the singer she had become. When Gina started with Vision Skye, Gina and Rio's first band, she knew she could sing. She also knew she could improve the quality of her voice. Simon was a friend of Aunt Deidre's who coached many Broadway stars. Aunt Deidre convinced him to take on her niece. Simon did so with trepidation when Gina was late to her first vocal lesson. When she got to his studio, she found a very attractive drag queen. She asked for Simon, he told her he *was* Simon, and he was getting ready for his night job. Simon and Gina developed a great friendship after that and he told her she would become a butterfly. She did, thanks to Simon.

"Oh no, girl. Gina, the rock star girl, that I helped make famous?"

"Simon, you know it's me. I need your help. Since I had the baby, I can't find my voice, it's like it left me. Can you come here and help me? I'll fly you private, put you up in a beautiful hotel, I'll even …."

"Stop, stop Gina. You don't have to ask me twice for a free trip to Cali. I'm on the next plane. How's Rio doing?"

"He's great. He has a wonderful lady in his life. Let me know your details. I'll send a car. I appreciate it so much. You can stay here at my house. I'm sure you will be very comfortable."

Simon laughed. "Gina, I know you. It's probably better than any hotel."

Perfection had months to finish the next album. Gina was in tears when she told Trevor her old singing coach was coming out to help her find her voice.

Being a good husband, he reassured her, "It's the hormones. Stop. You'll be fine."

Six weeks of no sex while she recovered from the birth felt like a lifetime. Gina yearned to reconnect with Trevor. Especially since Brian Mayfield had once again come out from under that rock of his.

Simon stayed for two weeks, reminding Gina of her fundamentals. She practiced by herself in a recording booth, listening to her voice. She felt it was getting better, but it had to be gold. Simon taught her some tricks to make her voice come across sultrier, no high notes. Kevin had a good mix of the instrumentals and now it was time for the vocals. Gina had hoped the magic she had harmonizing with Trevor would still be there. Simon had Gina feeling she was getting her voice back. He was an excellent coach and made Gina's vocals better.

Simon loved her house and home life. "Gina, I wasn't sure that you could make it, but girl you have shined. I am so proud that you stuck with it."

Coming from Simon, that was a huge compliment. She was sorry he needed to go back to New York.

Something is Wrong

Back in the studio the music was coming together for a few songs that had been recorded and next would be the vocals. She summoned all her energy to get through the first takes and find her groove. The mixing of Gina and Trevor's song tracks sounded great. She had hoped they would sing together and harmonize but each sang separately. Gina felt a distance from Trevor that couldn't be explained. She went to the house to spend time with Roxy, and hoped Trevor would do the same. She was determined to find out what was going on in her marriage or was she imagining it? Was it hormones or was it Brian Mayfield having Trevor's ear?

She walked into her bedroom as Roxy was waking from her nap and picked up the beautiful baby she so longed to have. She carried Roxy into the living room and gazed out at the ocean as she gently rocked her in her arms. Trevor came in and Gina handed her to him, "Say hello to your daughter."

Trevor made a sweet picture as he wove through the living room with Roxy, telling her about all the things they would do together as she grew up.

He sat down next to Gina. "What's wrong with you lately? You seem like you are on another planet. I need you to help get this album done."

Gina looked at him with disbelief. "Are you kidding me right now? I've been doing nothing but working on this album. Let me ask you, when did we ever record separately? When did you stop paying attention to me? We had a baby almost three months ago and you haven't tried to get close with me, no intimacy at all. You stay in the studio all night. You don't even come out to have dinner with Roxy and me. Are you unhappy? What did I do?"

Trevor was harsh. "Are you seriously bringing this up? We have an album to get out."

"That's it? The music? I gave you a child and that's it. Are you that stressed?"

"Actually Gina, I am. This album has to be a winner to follow up on everything we have done to get here."

Gina was pissed, "You know what Trevor, I used to mean more to you than just the music. I thought Roxy and I were the most important thing." She took Roxy and went into the bedroom.

When Trevor finally came to bed hours later, Gina had Roxy next to her in bed. Trevor picked up his daughter and put her in the bassinet and attempted to wake Gina. "G, get up. I want to talk to you,"

Gina wouldn't let Trevor's dismissive behavior go. "Fuck off. Let me sleep. That's all I do in bed anyway."

Trevor begged her, "Gina, please get up."

"What? What can I do for you?"

Trevor was confused.

"Why are you talking to me like this? Do I deserve this?"

Gina tried to keep her voice to a whisper so they wouldn't wake up Roxy. "I don't know. Do I deserve you having me record my lines to cued up music? When I sing with you, I have more energy with you. You cut me out, just like you have cut me out of our marriage. Roxy is three months old. I've been waiting for you to want me. You come to bed when I'm asleep and wake up before me. So, tell me. What the fuck is wrong with this picture?"

"I'm just obsessed in getting this done. That's all I can focus on. I haven't given you or Roxy the attention I should. But I want this album out."

Gina sat up. "You want that more than you want us. Got it, got it. Good night, Trevor. Let me know when my husband comes back."

Gina watched him walk out and cried silently into her pillow. The next morning, she fed Roxy and gave her to Marisol to watch while she took a shower. She thought she heard the door close but continued washing her hair. And there he stood, looking at her. She felt so undesirable. "Can I do something for you?"

"I'm just looking. Am I not allowed that privilege anymore?"

"I don't know what that means Trevor. Let me ask you, what are you doing to keep you up? To keep going all hours like you do. Are you doing lines? Is that why you don't want me around you when you record? Brian is feeding you coke to stay awake. Tell me you're not doing that shit."

Trevor ignored the comment about coke. "Gina, I want to deliver the album early, there would be bonuses."

"Trevor seriously. I could give two shits about a bonus. You have a problem. We have more than enough money. Stop blaming your addiction on worthless shit."

Trevor undressed and got into the shower. "Listen to me Gina. I have it under control. I never want you and Roxanne to feel I'm not present."

"But you're not. You're not. You just keep convincing yourself that you are."

Gina turned to get out of the shower, and Trevor grabbed her arm. "What are you doing?" she asked.

"This is our time for playing. I want to play."

"Let's play then. Let's see what you can do." She taunted him, knowing that cocaine made him unable to perform.

"Gina come on help me."

After several fumbled attempts nothing seemed to get Trevor's motor going. Gina stepped out of the shower, and he followed her. "Gina, please I need your help."

"With what Trevor? Getting it up or doing something about your cocaine addiction? What do you want from me?" She was shouting now, and realized they were actually fighting. "What does Brian say? That you're good? I need my real husband, not this half man I'm looking at. Let me know when you want my help, because it doesn't feel like it right now. The cocaine is more important to you."

She reached for her bathrobe and Trevor blocked her. "I need you to help me. You promised me you would make sure I didn't slip. But I have slipped, bad. Coke. Whiskey. Other drugs. I'm sliding Gina. I need your help. Help me, please."

Gina wondered how he had gotten here so fast. From being excited about the birth of his daughter to now. Brian Mayfield.

Gina couldn't help loving him. She walked out of the bathroom in her favorite bathrobe. She sat on the bed and pondered what her next move with Trevor would be. "Come here. Sit next to me. I love you, that hasn't changed, but I won't let you destroy our family with this crap. Tell me where your stash is now. I don't want anyone at the studio for the next couple of days. I need you to stay home and dry out, okay? That's how we are going to do it. The label will get their album. But we need to get back to our family, no discussions, this is it," she said firmly.

He leaned over and kissed her. "I love you and miss you."

"Trevor, I have never left you and I never will. Just be straight with me. We're good." She held him and told him to stay in bed. She went to the kitchen and brought back a sandwich and made him eat. While Trevor was eating Gina walked in another room and placed a call to Skip.

"Skip, I'm fed up with Brian Mayfield. I want him gone. I told you this a million fucking times, but you don't do anything. Please make this happen. I don't care how. He's ruining my family. Did you know he's feeding Trevor coke, whiskey, and God knows what else? Did you know this? Answer me truthfully."

Skip breathed a big sigh. "Gina I did see some lines going around. I didn't know how much was being consumed. Trevor has an issue?"

Gina raised her voice, "Skip, you need to watch this shit. I have a baby and need to record and write. But now I'm recording my lines alone with cued up music. That is not how we work. Tell me you are not happy with this. I'm Gina fucking McNaughton, the person people want to see, and I'm being sidelined by my husband and the band I helped create. Skip, we need to fire Brian Mayfield. I know you use him for … what the fuck, I don't even know. Please tell me we can do this."

Skip knew Gina would be furious with the answer. "He signed a five-year contract and he's in year two. We would have to pay him out."

Gina jumped at that. "Are you kidding me? Pay the motherfucker off. I mean it. I don't know what weird hold he has on Trevor, but he will destroy him. I can't have that."

Skip said he would see what he could do—not the answer Gina wanted to hear.

GETTING
WELL

GINA GAVE TREVOR SOME SPACe to get "normal" and told him he had to stay away from Roxanne until he was better. She thought that would be motivation, and it was. Trevor had bouts of nausea and the shakes. He looked like shit—all the signs of withdrawal. He was in

heavy withdrawal and would be turning the corner slowly.

Gina made chicken soup with orzo and fed it to him since he was unable to hold the spoon due to constant shakes from withdrawal. She needed to know where his head space was. "Trevor, how are you, really?"

Trevor was resigned. "I'm missing the whiskey bad, that's always been my demon, but coke and Vicodin has fucked me up. I'm feeling the withdrawal. I'm trying to work it out. Promise me you will take care of me."

"I love you more than anything in this world, but this is the third time you have needed my help to get you straight. I don't want you going to rehab—too much publicity. Can we get you right at home? Can you do it? I'll be here for you, promise, but no more, baby. I can't do it again."

Trevor placed a shaking hand on hers and kissed her on the cheek. "I miss you Gina, just know that I miss touching you and your little kisses. I miss your body. I miss seeing our daughter."

Gina had to be harder with him. "Trevor, get right and all those things will come back to you, promise." When she leaned over to kiss him, he pulled her into him and gave her a passionate kiss. Gina walked away with hope.

The next morning Gina walked down to the studio and found everyone there except Brian. She was greeted with hellos and questions about Trevor's whereabouts. Gina took everyone by surprise when she launched into them. "Trevor needs time to get his head together. I didn't realize that you all decided to assist your performance on this album with cocaine and whatever other kind of shit you are taking. Plus, drinking. What the fuck are you all thinking?" She was getting wound up. "That's not how we work, you know that. Is that the band you want to be in? Smoking a joint is one thing, but you are all guilty of using while recording. I won't have it, you assholes. When have we become a band on substances?"

No one had an answer.

"Rio seriously, don't pretend. Who's supplying it? Brian Mayfield? If he is, I'll be kicking his ass way out of California. Why is he allowed in our recording sessions anyway?"

No answers.

"I'm putting you all on notice. I don't want that shit in my house or in this studio. Nowhere. I'm a mother now. Do I need to be your mother too? I want this album finished, and for you fuckers to get straight," she spat. "Does anyone have anything to say?"

Rio spoke first, "Gina, we just needed a little help with the long hours of..."

Gina stopped him. "Rio don't give me excuses. It's done. I'll be coming down tomorrow to record my vocals. Get your shit together. This is your only warning. Don't you dare fuck with Gina Ricci McNaughton, don't."

Gina turned around and stormed back to the house. Everyone in the room looked stunned but knew Gina was dead serious.

After about ten days, Trevor seemed like himself and asked to see Roxanne. Gina brought the baby in, and they sat on the bed with Trevor.

"Damn Gina, it looks like she grew. She's so beautiful. I love you both so much."

She repeated to him the conversation she had with the band. "I told everyone that we are not the type of band that uses those kinds of substances, not here, not at our house. Weed is one thing, but I won't have cocaine or whatever else you all have been taking, and no more whiskey. You need to write and record clear, it's the only way."

Gina gently pried Roxy out of Trevor's arms and placed her in the bassinet. She was almost getting too big for it. She marveled that every day she could see her personality coming through. Lucky for Gina she was a good baby.

Trevor got up from bed and walked into the shower. Gina followed him into the bathroom. "You good? Feel better?"

Trevor opened the shower door. "Aren't you coming in? I think it's time for a playdate."

Gina missed him physically. She got undressed and joined him under the pouring water.

"I missed you," he groaned. "I need to have you. I know I have been a mess; can you just love me?"

Gina wanted him badly. "I'll wash you, get all that crap off you." She started slowly washing his hair, moving down the length of his body. She got to the place that they both wanted. He responded immediately. "G, let me have you, it's been so long." He leaned over and started kissing her. She could never resist him, no matter how angry she was with him. She put her hands around his neck and let him take her. Their passion for each other overtook any anger she had with him. This was the first time they'd had sex since Roxanne was born. They stepped out of the shower dripping wet and made their way to the bed. He couldn't get enough of her, and she of course had to have him. Their lovemaking went on for hours, until Roxanne started to wake up. They picked her up and placed her on the bed with them. This little person came from their love, and they adored her. Gina adored, no more, she loved and lusted for her husband.

ALBUM FOUR, A WRAP

EVERYTHING CAME BACK ON SCHEDULE once Trevor had dealt with his demons. They rerecorded the vocal tracks with Trevor and Gina singing together, their harmonizing was perfect.

Tommy was present for that session and liked what he heard. "I think we are so close; we should be able to give it to the label by the end of the week. Anyone have different ideas?"

Rio stood up and addressed Tommy. "You are the producer. If you think it's good for Brown Fence, then let's do it. Wait, what songs are going to be released first?"

Tommy looked at the band. "Let me make those choices. That's why I'm the producer."

Gina stepped up. "Tommy, does this mean we have to tour? I'll bring Roxy wherever we go, but I don't want to go on a long tour."

Tommy added, "We should be making videos before any tour dates. The music industry has changed, and MTV is hot. If the song is hot, MTV will have it on a quick rotation that gets out to millions. If the video is sexy, people will request it and tune in just to see it. Videos will take you from zero to a hundred in as quick as a week. Perfection has that high energy the viewers are craving. This album will top the charts in days. Bars, clubs, and people at home have the station on all day. Exposure, big time. This is the future. All the bands are making videos to sell their songs, get the buzz. We can make two videos, then see how the public responds. I believe that's the way to go. We will need some Hollywood director's help in what type of video you want to put out there. My instinct is to have the band playing the song and have some sort of story that intertwines with the song."

Ian and Jeff were on board immediately. Gina, Rio, and Trevor knew videos were the ticket to a fast-paced sale. Then touring wouldn't have to happen right away. The decision was to make a video of "What Do You Want to Know?" The second video would be the hard-edged song "Like Marble." They would add more videos as the album got traction. Tommy said he would produce the videos and look for a director. He told the band the label would want the album release party and the videos would follow. They named this album *Perfection Pumped and Powerful*.

There was no way they would be ready for a release party, although that would have been optimal. Gina took control. "Listen if we can get a director for "What Do You Want to Know?" it would be easy, have clips of the band playing and show all the paparazzi and tabloids following each individual of the band. Like they do all the time. We could drop the video at the release. Done."

The label loved the idea of dropping the video at the release party. They would wait for a thirty-day turnaround. Tommy found a director who was between projects. Although it was a rush job, it turned out perfectly. Gina was in the spotlight in that video. There was a small album/video release party. The McNaughtons didn't want to spend precious time on the party. Also, with Trevor's flirting with demons they believed the whole partying thing was something they would avoid. The label and party guests loved the video. They picked the perfect song and loved Gina. There would be four videos released from that album. Trevor and Gina stopped in long enough to show their faces and didn't linger at the party. They thanked the people responsible and told everyone they wanted to get home; they had a baby to enjoy.

DOWN TIME/
FAMILY TIME

AFTER THE RELEASE PARTY and the four videos in rotation, the band took several weeks to think about a tour. Gina was happy she wouldn't have to see Brian Mayfield for a while. They took baby Roxy to visit grandparents so she could be around family. They started in New York where the Riccis couldn't get enough of their granddaughter. It was a nice break for Gina and Trevor. They enjoyed the beach along the Long Island Sound. When they weren't at family dinners, Mario set them up at some nice restaurants in Manhattan where they wouldn't be noticed. Trevor and Gina soaked up the family time. Now they had their own circle, the three of them.

Their next stop was Vancouver to visit Shawn so he could meet his granddaughter. They arrived without fanfare, which they loved. Shawn hadn't been around a baby in a very long time and was nervous at first. Quickly, he became comfortable enough to take Roxy to the garden and point out all the different plants. It was easy to see the love Shawn had for Roxanne.

Gina was secretly hoping she could find out why Trevor was so defensive about Brian Mayfield. Still a mystery and still a problem. Gina's biggest kick was taking Roxanne for a walk around Stanley Park, where it all began.

Back home in Montecito was their safe place. The McNaughtons enjoyed a quiet life, where they could go to the grocery store and people may have known who they were, but they didn't care. It felt safe. When the tabloids found them, they would wave hello and ask for some space. Sometimes it was given, but most wanted a picture of Roxy.

The holidays were approaching—always a crazy few weeks. Between Halloween and Christmas, time seemed to fly by. Roxanne was dressed as a pumpkin for her first Halloween. Gina and Trevor took her house to house in her stroller. They knew she was too little to understand what was going on but wanted to have their moment of her first Halloween. Gina and Trevor dressed up too. Gina found the red wench costume she wore so many years ago at The Sunset.

Thanksgiving was scaled back, just the McNaughtons, Rio, and Jae—a family affair, no big presentation. Gina was grateful that Marisol agreed to do the cooking, although Gina felt badly, she loved cooking. Everything was delicious, of course. They insisted Marisol join them at the table. After all, she had done all the work, and she was part of the family.

Gina loved Rio and she loved Jae. She still wondered why Rio hadn't made his relationship with Jae more permanent. It was obvious they both loved each other. Jae had given up her education to be with him. Gina decided she had to have a private conversation with Rio. Feel him out. She didn't want Rio to lose Jae. She was the perfect complement to his life. Yes, she would talk to Rio. He was always there for her during the worst times of her life, and she didn't want him to overlook his future.

HOLIDAYS, PROPOSALS

GETTING READY FOR CHRISTMAS was fun for the Perfection ladies. Lisa, Jae, and Gina shopped for kiddie toys and grown-up toys. Gina decided this year she would decorate the house. Why not? She had the designer touch. She remembered that first year in Hollywood Hills when she and Lisa shopped for Christmas trees and decorations. It was all new to Gina, but she pulled it off. This year she would buy a huge tree and decorate it with a Victorian theme. She placed huge wreaths on the front door and windows. Gina felt she had matured, motherhood did that. Trevor helped with the tree and warned that this year he would be going Christmas shopping for his girls. Everything was perfect for Roxanne's first Christmas.

Gina called Rio. "I thought maybe we could have lunch. There's something I want to talk to you about."

Rio immediately asked, "Is Trevor okay?"

"Oh yeah, he's fine."

"I would love to go to lunch, just the two of us like old times. Is this Perfection stuff? I'm simply curious Gina. Love you, but I don't want to be blindsided."

Gina wasn't completely honest when she replied, "Can't we go to lunch and just be us? I feel like we need to hang out. I miss that."

"Yes, Gina I would love that. When? Why wait? Let's go tomorrow. Maybe you could give me some ideas for a gift for Jae."

Gina had her in. "I would love to help you with ideas. How about twelve-thirty at Lancaster's?"

Rio sounded happy. "Great. I'm excited to spend time with you that isn't connected to Perfection."

Gina smiled. "Me too buddy, me too."

Gina had a plan of action and was sure Jae wouldn't be upset with her. Gina met Rio while Trevor spent some time with Roxy. They were seated and had a glass of wine.

Rio looked relaxed. "So, Gina what's up? I like the idea of us just hanging out. We get so caught up with music, we sometimes forget what is important—family. Think back to when we first started this adventure. Did you think we would get this far?"

"It's everything I dreamed, Rio."

"I can't believe how far this venture has gotten us. We did it Gina, and you found the man you love unconditionally. Now you're a mother. Who thought that two Long Island kids would reach this kind of life."

Gina looked at him. "Rio, all that is true, but it's not like we came from a bad life to begin with. I mean we are Riccis after all. We left that name and life behind, for sure. Look at you, you have a beautiful home and a beautiful woman who loves you unconditionally. You do realize that Jae loves you so much, she put her life on hold for you."

Rio grinned. "You're right, when I think of all those bar sluts I used to hook up with I can't believe I ended up with an intelligent, beautiful woman."

Gina smiled. "Exactly. So, when are you going to make that beautiful woman permanent, if you don't mind me asking? Seriously, she's the perfect woman for you. Are you waiting for something? Have you two discussed the next step in your relationship, like marriage?"

Rio looked stunned. "Why? Has she said something to you? We talk around marriage, but never really said those words. Do you think that's bad?"

"Look Rio, I never discussed this with Jae directly. I wouldn't do that to you. That's why I wanted to talk to you, see where your head is at. If you both are okay with the way your relationship is, it's not for me to interfere. I just want you to have something more. I believe Jae is your *one*. I just don't want you to miss out on having that person."

Rio was thinking out loud, "I should buy her a ring for Christmas? I was hoping to wait until after our next tour. But you think I should do it now?"

Gina grabbed his hand. "Rio, this is your decision, I have no right to tell you when to ask her. I just wanted to know that you were considering it, and you are. I love her. She's always been there for me. Just do some soul-searching. Listen to your heart. I want you to know what Trevor and I have. A perfect love. Let's order, eat, and drink some more wine. I may need Trevor to pick me up."

The two Ricci kids enjoyed each other and their lunch. Rio and Jae invited Gina, Trevor, and Roxanne over for Christmas Eve, keeping it family. Rio bought a Santa suit, enjoying his role of uncle. Jae made a massive buffet of Korean specialties and served eggnog. Rio would wait just a bit longer to ask Jae to marry him.

Roxy's first Christmas was overwhelming with gifts from all over for a baby who was nine months old. It was Gina and Trevor's first Christmas as parents, and they savored every little moment in their love-filled home. The McNaughtons donated some of Roxanne's gifts to the children's ward at Santa Barbara Cottage Hospital where Roxanne was born.

New Year's for Gina always seemed bittersweet when she remembered the first New Year's she met Trevor. Visa issues kept them apart and she always reflected on the pain she felt being separated from him. Since then, they spent every New Year's quietly together, but this year would be different. Ian and Lisa invited the band over for drinks and snacks. It was a relaxed evening with the kids playing on the floor.

Ian told stories about when he and Trevor were kids in Vancouver and all the shit they caused. Gina laughed at all the trouble they got into and wondered if any of those times accounted for Trevor's distance from his father. Ian made their escapades sound goofy and funny, but maybe there was more to one of those stories. Gina also wondered how Brian Mayfield fit into this.

With the beginning of the New Year, award shows started popping up. The videos sold Perfection's fourth album, earning them some music award nominations. They hoped they would earn the award for Best Video of the Year. The band decided to tour in only ten cities. Family life was a focus for several members of the band and was more important, especially since sales of the album broke records due to the videos. The tour would start after March so Roxanne could celebrate her first birthday at home, not on the road. It was going to be a family affair—all the Ricci's Mario, Franny, Ant, Serena, including Frankie, MaryAnn, their three children, Shawn, and the Perfection family. It was over the top, but why not? Roxanne would be their only child.

Touring

The ten-city schedule started April 1 and ended May 28.

April 1	Cincinnati, OH
April 9	Raleigh, NC
April 16	Nashville, TN
April 22	New Orleans, LA
April 30	Little Rock, AR
May 7	Boise, ID
May 14	Lincoln, NE
May 21	Tucson, AZ
May 28	San Diego, CA

Venues were chosen to impact Perfection's sales in those cities. They already had a huge market share in the large cities. Brown Fence thought the smaller markets would extend the sales. This tour had a less stressful vibe to it, and everyone seemed at ease.

Gina made sure that Brian Mayfield had his wings clipped. He was only allowed to be backstage when Skip was with him. Gina told Skip to minimize his presence and keep trying to get rid of him. Gina also never let Trevor be alone with him for more than a few minutes. Trevor had issues with his sobriety when they toured. Gina promised not to give away her power to anyone. Having Roxanne with them leveled Trevor out. He was a father who enjoyed spending time with his daughter. Ian and Lisa brought the boys to a few of the shows and the band was maturing.

Rio was still waiting to ask Jae to marry him. Jeff was still dating that starlet, and Gina couldn't believe it was still a thing.

The first three weeks of the tour Cincinnati, Raleigh, Nashville were electric. Perfection rocked the cities. Nashville, the home of country music, showed they were rock and rollers, too. When the band hit New Orleans, Gina wanted a date night with Trevor to hit the French Quarter and taste the spicy cuisine. Arrangements needed to be made so they wouldn't be disturbed by fans and onlookers. Trevor knew Gina would be watching his drinking and New Orleans is a drinking city.

Gina was getting ready at their hotel, while Roxy stayed with Marisol, who traveled with them. She was looking forward to time together that didn't include the band, just the two of them. Trevor came into their room. "I'm really looking forward to having you all to myself tonight, not sharing you with the band, or thousands of people. I feel the last couple of weeks we have had a bit of a disconnect. I've been wanting you, but we have both been exhausted and always have Roxy to consider. Can we just have a moment like we used to that's just us?"

Gina touched his face and gave him those little kisses he loved. "Baby, you are the only thing on my mind tonight. We have had an easy tour but haven't had our usual playdates. That makes me sad. I need that part of you. We know that about each other. You know I always want you. How did we let weeks go by?"

Trevor grabbed her by her waist. "I plan to make up for that tonight, our own Mardi Gras celebration. Come on wife, let's get out there." Trevor found an excellent restaurant where they were given a private room to dine. After dinner, they walked back to their hotel unnoticed. Either people were too drunk or didn't care who they were. Gina wanted to stop by one of the voodoo shops to buy a voodoo doll. Trevor knew what she had in mind and indulged her. The voodoo doll was meant for Brian Mayfield. Gina took it seriously and picked up some spells to place on the doll. Trevor shook his head, knowing Gina would do everything in her power to banish Brian, even use a voodoo doll.

They got back to their hotel suite and checked on Roxy, asleep with Marisol in the next room. Their bedroom was on the other side of the suite. Trevor wasted no time in letting his wife know what he wanted. Gina showed him how much she missed him. Trevor reminding her, "Don't be too loud."

Trevor slowly undressed Gina, he wanted her badly. Gina loved when Trevor took his time, she knew that he was trying to calm his libido. He started kissing her hard and thirsty. Gina melted with his kisses, she loved him, lusted for him. Anything he would do to her would be totally acceptable. She stood naked. He stripped down and told her he wanted her on all fours, promising her he would take her hard. He started whispering in her ear how much he wanted her and how he was going to leave her, pleading for him to stop. Once he started it was difficult for Gina to be quiet. Trevor was highly stimulated by taking her from behind and was going hard. Gina used a pillow to muffle the intense pleasure Trevor was giving her. He became unstoppable and his movements became that much harder. Trevor was an animal, the weeks without a playdate made him into a sexual powerhouse, leaving Gina begging him to go harder and faster.

About twenty minutes later they were satiated. They lay on the floor telling each other how much they loved the other and it would always be this way.

Perfection knew what to expect when touring, this time it was only their band, no opening act, no headliner. There were five more weeks to push on. Radio appearances were arranged in the local markets of each city. Perfection were pros at this point, giving interviews usually lighthearted and fun, no heavy talks. Each of the remaining cities had contests for a special *Meet and Greet* with Perfection before the performance. Gina usually hated these. She believed that these fans would be grateful to have a band of their caliber come to their city. Perfection heard that Little Rock was a little city with a big city vibe. Gina was looking forward to Boise. She heard it was a hidden gem with lots of beautiful homes. She thought maybe she and Trevor would buy a winter house there, learn how to ski, and teach Roxanne to ski early. San Diego would be exciting since it was a military city. Perfection heard that sometimes the crowds in San Diego could be a bit rowdy. Perfection hoped to make the military feel special, they served our country and deserved a great show. They knew once they played San Diego, they would be going home.

Tour never felt overwhelming. Gina would be coming off stage and Marisol would have Roxy waiting backstage. A benefit for sure. Even though this tour sounded easy, Perfection would wait several months before they toured again.

Perfection had four videos released, and each one became a bona fide hit, playing hourly on MTV.

SURPRISES, ALBUM FIVE?

A FEW MONTHS AFTER THE TOUR, they had all become home-bodies. A few days a week, they would get together to write new music. Perfection believed that they produced the four albums due to Brown Fence. Skip and Tommy called Perfection together for a meeting. They had bad news for the band that was overlooked. Perfection believed they met their obligation to Brown Fence and they would create their own record label. What they didn't know was that Brown Fence had a clause that was added late in negotiation. It gave Brown Fence the ability to get a fifth album from Perfection if their music was a bestseller. Rio and Trevor went ballistic, the band would have never agreed to that condition. However, there it was in their contract. It became a huge catastrophe. Rio had wanted to hire an Attorney to explore that clause. Tommy, while still employed by Brown Fence Records, told Rio it was an iron clad part of their contract. He understood their destress but they had to think about one more album. They knew once Perfection created their own label Tommy Whelan would still produce their music and leave Brown Fence Records.

The band wrote new music for a good part of the year. They wanted to collect all new written music for Perfection to keep for their new label. Then they would decide what they were willing to give for their last album.

FAMILY LIFE

LIFE BECAME VERY STABLE and family oriented. Gina and Trevor couldn't believe that Roxanne was now two and a half and ready for preschool. How time flies.

They did their homework and found the best preschool in Montecito, which was more than welcoming to the McNaughtons. Who wouldn't want the rock stars as part of their school? The other parents knew who they were but didn't care.

Lisa and Ian had Liam and Malcolm in school and were enjoying parenthood.

Rio and Jae did some traveling, and Gina was still waiting for Rio to pop the question to Jae. It was time.

Jeff was a good guy, however he had two paternity suits against him that needed to be resolved. It became a bit of a public relations issue. Gina cared a lot for Jeff, an original member, and suspected these women were taking advantage of him.

Kevin mixed recordings for some minor bands in his time off.

The road crew always had work to maintain and buy new equipment.

Skip was busy with the business of Perfection—interviews, scheduling and planning their calendar.

Articles were written in tabloids, airing some of Perfection's dirty laundry. Brian Mayfield was always involved. He created a bad image for himself by being a party guy and procurer of everything related to drugs and women. Some of those women thought he was a real member of the Perfection inner circle. Those stories came out in the tabloids. But Brian leaked some stories knowing it would piss off one Mrs. Gina McNaughton. Gina needed to find a way to neutralize him. The best would be to fire him. Mayfield was a partier, he wanted the rock star life, but he didn't do anything. He aligned himself with record producers, wealthy do-nothings, and bands on their way up. He leveraged his relationship with Perfection to get himself into drug-fueled sex parties. There were some unsubstantiated rumors that Trevor and Rio attended these parties that were wildly over the top. Gina and Jae didn't believe those rumors were true, their men were with them, but why cause this tension? But was there any truth to these rumors? It disturbed Gina and Jae hearing the whispers.

Trevor couldn't have been a better husband and father. Gina knew she was lucky to be in love with her husband and he with her. They agreed to some national magazine articles to show their happy marriage. The McNaughtons didn't understand why they needed to prove they had a great relationship and anyone who knew them could see how much love they had for each other. They had an unbelievable sex life and didn't feel they needed to let anyone into their bedroom. Some of the interviews had Trevor furious. One reporter for a national magazine asked Trevor if their relationship was a "real partnership" or was that for show.

Trevor became visibly upset and retorted, "I've been in love with my wife since I first saw her. I don't need to demonstrate to you or anyone else the commitment we both have to each other. If you hear anything different, it's bullshit. I won't have that crap out there. Would people be happy to come into our bedroom and prove the love we have for each other? I hate these questions."

It was usually Gina who reamed an interviewer, so she was shocked when Trevor spoke up. After that exchange, she leaned over and touched his face, kissed him, and told him, "I love you always and forever. Thank you for protecting our love."

Many of the other interviewers took their cue from that quote—never try to separate the McNaughtons. They were the real deal, a pair of true rock stars who were actually in love. The questions became more about their home life and their daughter. They refused to talk too much about Roxanne. They wanted her to grow up without too much press coverage. Would they do that her entire life? Of course, they would.

Perfection had been nominated for several awards, and felt if they took home even one award, they would consider it a "win." Perfection dressed up for the American Music Awards, the guys in black outfits, perpetuating their bad boy image. Gina and Jae were dressed by a designer who solicited them to wear his clothes. Gina negotiated to keep the dress after the show. Lisa always dressed appropriately, but never designer wear, not her style. Gina had explained the event to Jae like this: "Everyone shows up. The band takes pictures together. Then each couple has their picture taken. It takes time, especially when you just want to get in your seat and wait to find out if we have won. The fans scream out to their favorite band members. Give a wave and say, 'Thank you.' The key is where are you sitting. The closer to the stage the more important you are."

Perfection had decent seats. Gina confided to Trevor, "I don't know why I'm nervous. I don't really care about this bullshit award stuff. We know our fans love us."

Trevor smiled. "If we win an award, it elevates our status in the music community. You know they love this shit. No matter what, you will be a winner tonight."

When they won for Best Video of the Year for "What Do You Want to Know?" Gina and Trevor exchanged a deep kiss and walked up to the stage with the rest of the band to accept the award. People in the audience started shouting, "GMac!"

Gina waited for the audience to quiet, and spoke calmly into the microphone, "Thank you to Skip Glazer, Tommy Whelan, Brown Fence Records, and the guys standing here on the stage with me. I love them all, especially this guy right here." Trevor hugged her and kissed her.

In the weeks that followed, Perfection started writing music again in Montecito. Gina would add her imprint with the lyrics. The were no tours scheduled. The band loved playing pop-up concerts at the smaller clubs on the LA Strip. They dropped into a few clubs in Seattle, Nashville, Miami, and of course in New York. They surprised their New York hometown fans with a free concert in Central Park, which was only promoted on the local radio stations.

Gina gave her family advanced notice and invited them backstage. They agreed it would be an experience but did not want to be part of the "shit show in the crowd." Gina couldn't imagine Mario and Franny Ricci out in the mass of humanity but wanted her family near her. They invited an up-and-coming band they liked, Airport Blues, to open for them. Central Park was crowded with concert goers and the smell of marijuana was powerful. Gina loved the feeling of letting loose for this show. These were her people. The band performed their old music and a few covers. The fans loved the covers. Gina sang solo but went crazy when she and Trevor started singing together—the way they seemed to make love to a song.

It was a sweltering summer day. Trevor asked, "Baby please be careful of what you wear. No more see through numbers."

Gina laughed, "Okay, I get it. Besides I don't think Mario and Franny want to see that. I have a cute off-the-shoulder number. It's still a little sexy. Only for you baby. It's always been for you."

Perfection took the stage at eight p.m. The crowd went crazy, shouting, "Welcome home, Perfection! We love you. Kick some ass."

Gina teared up as she was introducing the band. "New York, I love you and I will always be one of you. Thank you for loving us. It's so powerful. You have no idea." She barely got those words out when Rio walked over and gave her a hug. Trevor planted a huge kiss on her lips, leaned into the microphone and said, "Thanks New York for giving me this unbelievable woman. Thank you. Enjoy the show."

Perfection did three encores then rushed offstage into waiting limos to a private dinner with the Ricci family, Lisa's family, and others connected to the band. Mario and Uncle Tony arranged a private room at one of the best restaurants. Gina loved everything about the dinner. She was in New York and with her family. A truly special night … until she looked across the room and there he was. Brian Mayfield. She hated the fact he was enjoying her father's generosity, benefiting from this special dinner. Gina's mind was racing. She needed to find a way to rid herself of this pest.

ROXANNE GOES
TO EUROPE

ROXANNE WAS SIX AND A HALF YEARS OLD and beginning to understand her family's lifestyle was different from the other kids she knew. She was happy to be in New York and see her Nonna and Poppi—a normalizing effect for her.

There was buzz around the label that a European tour should be scheduled. The European market was starting to discover Perfection's early material and wanted to see the band. If the band decided to go, it would have to be in the summer, so the children wouldn't miss school. The logistics would be a nightmare to hit all the European cities, which would mean going to two cities a week. Gina and Skip would need to plot a schedule that made sense. They would also need to get a bigger road crew and charter a jet to carry all the equipment, luggage, and band members.

While eating dinner one night, Trevor asked Gina, "Baby, are you sure you want to go to Europe on this tour? Our life is so relaxing now. I love having you all to myself, enjoying every moment with you. I feel like our life is like when we lived in the carriage house. I like this simple life, with us just enjoying each other and Roxanne."

But that really wasn't true. As soon as they left their home, people followed them. Fame is great until your life becomes abnormal. Life had also become a bit different with Roxanne around. Locking their bedroom door became a necessity after Roxy came in one night while they were making love and wanted to know why Daddy was hurting Mommy. They explained Daddy was helping Mommy's back. Gina threw her robe on and ushered Roxy to her room. They both had a laugh and knew life was changing quickly. Hopefully, Roxy would forget that event. Maybe the European tour would be a great family trip.

Skip and Gina researched which European cities had a market for Perfection with an appropriate and available venue. It was tedious work. They knew they were big in the UK and wanted to hit London, Manchester, Glasgow, and Birmingham. Germany was another hot spot, with huge military bases. Did it make sense to also try for Paris, Italy, and the Netherlands? They would look at the numbers. Skip did heavy research and came to the decision that Italy would be a go. The Netherlands was another go, but they put a hold on France. Gina let Skip address all the venues. Most were outdoor locations.

They booked the late Spring tour in Europe. They would leave at the end of May and would come home sometime in June. It was a hectic schedule, but Gina and Trevor were excited that Roxanne would experience Europe. They employed a bodyguard, so interruptions would be at a minimum. The other band members had their own plans for Europe. It seemed all the stars were aligned for this trip.

Their first stop was Glasgow, where they visited castles and Roxanne asked if princesses lived there. Trevor explained that the princesses all moved out, so people could come visit the castle. Roxy was a Daddy's girl and hung onto every word her father said. Gina wasn't jealous about Roxanne being a Daddy's girl, she loved it. While shopping in Glasgow, Gina remembered that McNaughton was a Scottish name, and couldn't resist buying a kilt for Trevor and a blanket for Roxy in the McNaughton tartan. Glasgow proved to be a beautiful place to play. The crowd loved their music and responded by singing their songs. Maybe because there were a few McNaughtons in the band.

Three days later, they were in Birmingham, UK. Roxy had heard about leprechauns and was hoping to see one. Trevor told her that leprechauns were in Ireland not in England. Roxy said she saw a picture of one and laughed because they were funny. Gina believed they did indeed know one, but he was an evil leprechaun, and he must go down. They went to Birmingham Botanical Gardens and took a boat ride down the Birmingham Canals. Roxanne only talked about the flowers and boat ride. Perfection had no idea how popular they had become in the UK. Add another level of stardom.

Manchester and London, where they had a huge following, were the next stops on the tour. Perfection played a charity concert in the UK a few years back and folks in England followed the band after that concert. All the Perfection videos where played and that helped propel them in the UK. Trevor and Gina took Roxy to Buckingham Palace, Stratford-upon-Avon, and Windsor Castle. They wanted to introduce Roxanne to historic venues and hoped she would remember the visit.

Netherlands had a bit of a language barrier, but was a very open society, known for smoking weed anywhere. All of the band members took advantage.

The stop in Germany was mainly for the American soldiers stationed at Ramstein Air Base. Perfection played a larger than normal playlist and did three encores to shouts of "Please come back." It was a huge success for Perfection and appreciated by the Americans who knew the band. The McNaughtons, Rio, and Jae visited castles and beer halls. Rio loved to watch Roxanne fixating on castles, thinking every castle had a princess. Trevor told her she was the princess at their house, which satisfied her.

Perfection was going worldwide. Skip told the band, "Europe was a great success. We may want to think about Japan and Australia in the future."

Gina, marvelled. *Shit that is really far away, let's put a pin in that.*

The month after Europe was lazy for everyone. Ian and Lisa took their boys to Disneyland. Jeff was still dealing with the paternity suits. Rio and Jae chose to stick close to home and visited with the McNaughtons several times a week. Rio loved to grill, proclaiming himself a grill master. It was funny to Gina, who never knew Rio to have any interest or skill in cooking.

One day Rio gave Gina a call. "Gina, I think I need your help. Can we meet for lunch? I really need to talk."

Gina was a bit worried. Rio sounded troubled. "Of course. Is everything all right? I just saw you two nights ago. Should I be worried?"

Rio brushed past her questions. "Great. Let's meet at Lancaster's. One o'clock.

"Okay buddy, I'll be there."

Trevor overheard the call and asked, "What's up? Something with Rio?"

"He sounds worried. I don't know what it could be. We were just at their house. I hope he and Jae are okay. Do you know anything?"

"I'm sure it's nothing to worry about, Gina. Could it be something Ricci related?" He kissed her. "It will be fine." Quickly changing gears, Trevor winked and said, "I was thinking of a playdate."

Gina smiled. "When Roxanne goes to bed or when Marisol is watching her."

"How about both?" Trevor replied greedily.

Gina agreed. "I would love that idea."

Later that afternoon, Roxy was helping Marisol in the kitchen. Trevor led Gina by the hand into their bedroom. As he slowly began taking her clothes off, Gina laughed. Trevor was puzzled. "Is there something funny, or should I continue?"

Gina apologized. "I'm sorry, but this reminds me of our first night together. You slowly took off my clothes. It was sexy. If you continue, you will find my white lace panties, just like that night."

Trevor got more turned on. "That night was the beginning of everything we are today. I love you."

"I love you more. Let me show you how much. Let me get you naked."

Gina proceeded to take off his clothes. Without any hesitation, she was quick and hungry for her husband.

They moved onto the bed. Gina used her mouth, bringing him to the point where he would want to take her. He rolled her over and got on top. He looked at her and started to tear up. "G, I always tell you how much I love you. Right now, I can't tell you how much you have been a perfect, beautiful wife. I don't deserve you. I can be an asshole sometimes; you never stop loving me. I'm grateful as fuck. I want you so much."

Gina ran her fingers through his hair. "Baby, I'm here. Love me." She wiped his eyes. "Make love to me. I'll always want you." She wrapped her legs around him and kissed him.

"Love me baby. You have me so excited. I can't wait."

He slowly and purposefully made love to her, their eyes never leaving each other. Their eyes were saying what words couldn't. Gina's hands, touching his body, his arms, his face. She sat up and they moved together slowly, then together they felt that unbelievable sensation. They fell on the bed, not a word was spoken, again just staring at each other, and sharing small kisses.

Gina said, "I think we forgot to lock the door." They laughed, knowing that Roxy would be looking for them soon. They got dressed and made their way to the kitchen, where Roxanne was having a snack.

"Mommy, Daddy, I was looking for you." Trevor sat down next to her and stole a cookie from her. Roxy shouted, "Daddy, you took a cookie. I get to have another one now."

Gina went to the cookie jar, "Here you go sweet girl. Share this with Daddy. He loves you." They enjoyed the afternoon and early evening, walking on the beach, lying in the living room, listening to Roxy read. *I have such a wonderful life*, thought Gina.

That night, when Roxy went to sleep, Trevor showed Gina once again how much he loved her, mostly how much he needed her.

AWKWARD PROPOSAL

GINA WOKE UP THE NEXT MORNING and couldn't wait to find out what was bothering Rio. She kissed her family goodbye and drove to Lancaster's. She arrived before Rio and was seated right away.

Rio walked in, looking a bit out of sorts. He wasn't wearing his sunglasses. He sat down at the table and Gina began grilling him right away. "Bro, what's going on? You look like you have something major going on. Is it Jae? Please tell me you two are fine."

Rio drew a big sigh. "Yes Gina, we're fine. I want to ask her to marry me, finally. But what if she tells me no? What if she likes things the way they are? I waited so long, I fucked up. I want what you have—that person who will always be there, no matter what."

Gina looked straight into his eyes, "Will Ricci be her last name? It's about fucking time. I'm so excited for you. She loves you. She won't say no. Marry her Rio. Don't think about it. Do you have a ring?"

"Well, that's why I asked you here," Rio admitted. "Can you come with me to pick out a ring? I don't know from that shit."

Gina was flustered. "Rio, I'm not sure what style she would like, however I think we can find something. Where are we going to get this ring?"

"There's a jeweler in Malibu. Let's go now. I don't want to wait any longer."

Gina was eager too. "Yes, we can go right now. I need to let Trevor know I'll be out a bit longer. Let me ask you this, are you going to drag this out or get engaged and set the date?" Without giving Rio time to answer, she went on. "Please plan the wedding once you give her the ring. We haven't had a family wedding since my 'faux wedding.'"

Rio laughed. "Aunt Franny, she was something with all that Catholic stuff. Holy shit, do you think I'm expected to do the same?"

Gina laughed. "Umm, yeah probably. Uncle Tony made you go to Catholic school and Aunt Deidre never pushed back. I'm thinking at least a priest would be present. Let's forget this and let's go find Jae a ring."

They drove to a top-notch jeweler in Malibu. He took out every style of stone in the five-carat range. Gina surveyed the stones. "I think she would like an emerald cut or pillow cut."

The jeweler pulled out a six carat and an eight-carat emerald cut, and a six-and-a-half carat pillow cut.

"Rio, I think the emerald cut suits Jae. It all depends on what you want to spend."

"When was cost ever an issue for us? I want to give her something special since it took me so long to do this."

"We have to find a setting. The diamond needs to look beautiful in the setting, so bigger doesn't mean better," Gina advised.

Rio laughed. "That's why I have you here."

They agreed on a six carat in a princess style band. The jeweler said to give him about an hour. They walked around Malibu and noticed some paparazzi. Luckily no one was paying attention to them.

Gina pressed, "So when are you going to ask her? I won't be able to contain myself, so you better do it soon."

"Tonight. I'm going to do it tonight. Like you said, I shouldn't wait any longer."

Gina stared at him. "Did you have a fight? Why do you feel it has to be right away? Or is it just that you've been a dick, and you realize it now."

Rio smirked. "I realized when we were in Germany with all of you. I want that love you and Trevor have."

The two of them headed back to the jeweler and picked up the sparkling ring, nestled in a black velvet box.

Rio surprised Gina when he said, "I would like you and Trevor to be there and bring Roxy. Jae won't say no if you're there."

Gina laughed out loud, "Seriously, that's such a private moment. You want us there? Rio, you'll be fine. Jae loves you."

"I have a cook coming to make a fancy dinner, candles, the whole thing. I'll feel more relaxed having you there."

Gina surrendered, "It sounds incredibly intimate. I'll tell Trevor what's going on. He may want to witness Rio become a married man. Just imagine all your female fans will be so disappointed. I'm so happy for you. It's the right move. I love you and everything that has happened to us. Perfection is something we created. Now create your family. Let's head back. What time do you want us there?"

"The cook will have dinner ready at seven, so about six-thirty?"

Gina was excited. "Is this a Franny Ricci dress-up dinner?" Gina couldn't contain her laughter.

Rio shook his head. "No. Just be yourselves. Jae might think something was going on if you came all fancy as fuck."

Rio took Gina back to her car and she drove home. She shouted as she walked in the front door, "Babe, Roxy, where are you two?" Trevor was playing guitar, watching Roxy paddling around the pool. She had recently learned how to dive off the side.

"Hey, you two having a good time?"

Roxy shouted, "Mommy, I learned a new trick, want to see?"

Gina looked at their beautiful child, an unmistakable mix of Gina and Trevor. She had his blue eyes and was tall for her age. She had Gina's hair and face. Gina knelt down. "Of course, I want to see your trick. Did Daddy teach it to you?"

Roxy got out of the pool. "Sort of, Mom. Watch!" She jumped into the pool with her legs tucked up. She went under the water and bounced up. "See Mommy, Daddy told me how to use my legs to come back up."

Gina marveled at how vibrant her daughter was. "Roxy, that is something special. I'm glad Daddy helped you."

Gina sat next to Trevor. "Are you in the middle of writing something? I'm dying, I have something to tell you that will blow you away. Let me know when you're ready for it."

Trevor put the guitar down and looked at Gina warily. "Am I going to get pissed off at this information?"

Gina blurted it out, "We're invited over to Rio and Jae's tonight. He's going to ask her to marry him. We picked out a ring this afternoon. But for some reason he wants us there. He thinks if we are there, she won't say no. She's not going to say no. She loves him. We need to start making moves to get ready. Can you believe it?"

Trevor remarked, "It's about time. Shit, Rio is going to settle down completely. Yeah, I want to see this." He grabbed Gina. "Remember, when we get home, we have a playdate."

Gina pulled him up by the hand. "I will never say no to a playdate." She kissed him.

"Roxanne McNaughton, time to get out of the pool. We are going to Uncle Rio's for dinner."

Roxy looked up. "Okay. Why do you and Daddy kiss all the time? It's funny."

Trevor helped her out of the pool. "You should be happy that your mom and dad kiss each other. It means we love each other very much."

Gina barked orders, "Okay everyone, showers and get dressed for dinner."

Trevor saw an opening—maybe a playdate in the shower. As normal, Trevor grasped the opportunity to make love to his wife. All those people who think their marriage was "just for show" had no idea how much they truly loved each other.

Gina told Marisol to take the evening off since they were going to Rio's for dinner.

When they got to Rio and Jae's house, there was soft music playing. The table looked romantic. Gina felt they shouldn't be there for this.

Jae greeted them. "Isn't this sweet and a beautiful dinner? I'm so glad you could come. Roxanne, my kiss?"

Roxy hugged Jae and gave her a big kiss.

Rio walked into the dining room. "Hey man glad you can join us. This dinner is going to be epic. This chef comes highly recommended." They had cocktails and some appetizers and sat down. Gina threw Trevor a glance, *When is this going to happen?*

As soon as dinner was served, Rio got down on his knee and proposed. Jae was shocked. Everyone was waiting for her answer.

Jae started to cry, "Yes, yes I love you."

Rio placed the ring on her finger. There was more crying and hugging and I love you's. Trevor and Gina felt awkward, being present at such a private moment.

Trevor spoke first. "Well congratulations, maybe we should let you two celebrate alone."

Jae disagreed. "No, it's even more special with you here. I want to talk wedding plans with Gina."

Gina smiled at Jae. "I'm happy to help of course. What time frame are you thinking?"

Rio and Jae answered in unison, "As soon as possible."

"Great, I guess we have shopping to do. Where is this going to be? Here in California or New York?"

Rio without hesitation answered, "Here at our house. Everyone can come here. Jae's family lives here and my parents will have no problem coming out to California."

Gina prompted, "Rio, don't you think you should call Uncle Tony and Aunt Deidre now and tell them … and Jae's parents?"

Rio firmly said, "We will after we share this dinner with you. Both of you were my inspiration to finally get this beautiful woman to marry me. We want what you have. I've watched the two of you from the beginning. You're so much in love. With everything you have gone through, your love always wins. We want that too."

Gina again flustered, "Rio, thank you for that. Sometimes I think I can't love this man more. Then there is always more. I'm happy to help with whatever you need me to do. Does this mean no songwriting? We still have a band to think about and one last album. I'm sure we can do both."

After a somewhat awkward dinner, the McNaughtons said goodnight. On their way out the door, Gina added, "Call your parents, now."

On the way home Trevor asked Gina, "Well that was interesting. Didn't you feel funny? I mean, I'm glad they're getting married, but it was just weird for us to be there."

Gina looked in the backseat where Roxanne had fallen asleep. "It was awkward as fuck. But it's done. I admit thinking about the part that we inspired them was sweet. I'm sure I will be getting a phone call from Franny in the next couple of days."

When they got home, Gina and Trevor walked upstairs, put Roxy in her bed, and kissed her goodnight.

They tiptoed back downstairs, and Trevor poured two glasses of wine. "We are an inspiration. You are the inspiration. You have handled me leaving you, my demons, my fucked-up attitudes. Baby I would not be this man without you."

Gina sipped her wine. "You're being very sexy right now. I love it. Come sit next to me and look at the ocean." They curled up on the couch and stared at the beautiful backdrop of the Pacific Ocean. Gina rested her head on Trevor's shoulder. "Trev, life should always be this perfect. Now let's go to bed." She winked at him knowing what she had in mind.

RIO GETS MARRIED

TWO WEEKS LATER, everyone in the band knew about the engagement, and the tabloids got wind of it somehow. Gina made an appointment with a specialty wedding gown maker and Jae wanted her mother to join them at the salon for such a big decision. Gina was thrilled to finally meet Jae's mother, Nari. Gina knew at once who she was when she walked through the door of the salon. Her jet-black hair was smoothed back into a tidy chignon. Jae's striking looks clearly came from her Korean/African American mother. *Aunt Deidre will love this woman.*

Jae chose the third dress she tried on—a body-hugging lace and beaded dress with long sleeves and a plunging back. Everyone in the bridal salon looked on as Nari slowly nodded her head up and down and her eyes filled with tears.

Wedding preparations moved swiftly. Jae and Gina sampled food at a few caterers. Jae made decisions quickly and soon the caterer and florist were chosen. Rio hired the wedding music and chose the tuxedos for himself and the groomsmen. Perfection wouldn't be performing since of course they were guests. Rio chose a string quartet for the ceremony and a DJ friend for the reception.

Franny called Gina as soon as she heard the good news from Deidre. "Gina, Rio's wedding is happening quickly. Any reason I should know about? Your Aunt Deidre is over the moon. Can you give me any details?"

Gina laughed because she knew her mother was alluding to a baby. "Mom, Rio has waited forever to propose to Jae. Now he wants the wedding to happen sooner than later. Why wait? The band is writing music, we have downtime, it's time for them to get married. Do you and Dad want to stay with us? You will have a special time with your granddaughter."

Franny was in heaven. "What a wonderful idea. We would love that. I guess Ant and Frankie and MaryAnn can stay at a hotel nearby."

"Yes, Mom, Rio is handling that, but Frankie isn't bringing the kids. This is more of an adult affair."

"Of course, Gina, don't be silly. I'll let you know our flight plans. This is happening fast."

No sooner had Gina hung up with Franny when the phone rang gain. It was Lisa. "Gina, I'm so excited about this wedding, but I need your help. Can we go shopping for a dress?"

The answer was yes of course. Lisa could now afford something special. Perfection was a success, and everyone reaped the benefits. Rio and Jae asked Trevor and Gina to be maid of honor and best man and wanted Roxanne to be a flower girl.

Everyone from New York flew in. All the Riccis were in California. Uncle Tony and Aunt Deidre were staying at Rio and Jae's, and Rio's worst nightmare unfolded. Uncle Tony said he had gotten a priest to marry them. Gina laughed when he told her because she knew that was the Ricci way.

The McNaughtons hosted the rehearsal dinner. Jae's Irish father, Guy Reynolds, charmed them all when he told the story of meeting Nari while he was an Air Force pilot stationed in Korea. Nobody knew Jae had a brother. He lived in Alaska, a real live-off-the-land guy. Jae was surprised her brother was actually attending.

Ian and Lisa were happy to have a couple of nights away from the boys. Jeff showed up with a new starlet, who seemed to be smarter than the others. Maybe Jeff was getting more stable. Aunt Deidre pulled Gina aside.

"Sweet Gina, you promised me years ago that Rio would find a woman who was decent, smart, and beautiful. You did it. I love Jae. She's perfect for him. I know I'll be crying the whole time. I remember you two practicing downstairs and thinking to myself, *They could make it.* I'm so proud of you and Rio. The lives you made are wholesome and good."

Gina wanted her to know, "Aunt Deidre, Rio met Jae at an art gallery, so you should take credit for exposing him to the art world. It was fate that they met, a good thing. I love Jae too. How wonderful for her to be part of our family."

Aunt Deidre stood up and hugged Franny. "We should be happy for our children and what they achieved. I hoped this day would come Franny. It's perfect." The two of them started crying.

The next morning, everyone was excitedly getting ready. Trevor looked handsome in a black tux and Gina wore a shantung silk sage-green dress. Roxy looked cute in a white dress and a halo of flowers in her hair.

Rio greeted them nervously at the door. Trevor calmed him down by reminding him he and Jae had been together a long time.

Rio suggested, "Let's go smoke a joint. It will help me."

"Just like the old days," they said at the same time. They wandered outside and noticed a few helicopters flying over the house, trying to get pictures of the event. The wedding planner spotted Rio and walked swiftly over to tell him it was time to take his place at the head of the aisle. The ceremony was about to begin.

Rio's eyes welled as he watched Jae walk down the aisle on her father's arm. *That's what weddings do—make you think about love and that special person,* Gina reflected to herself. The ceremony was over in a matter of minutes and the partying started.

Gina walked across the lawn, picking up a glass of champagne from a tray being carried around by one of the tuxedo-shirted waitstaff. As she turned to find Trevor, she saw Brian Mayfield walking out of the house. *How the hell did he get an invite?* Rio wouldn't do that, or did

Brian assume that since everyone in Perfection was invited, that meant him too?

Gina made a beeline for Rio and grabbed his elbow. "Rio, what is Mayfield doing here? Did you invite him?"

Rio was taken aback by her brusqueness. "Hey man, I don't know, but please don't make it a thing on my wedding day."

Gina took a breath and promised to let it go. Well at least in front of Rio. He was right. She shouldn't ride him about this on his wedding day. But she would figure it out somehow.

Trevor came up behind her. "G baby, you good? You look flustered."

"Did you know that Mayfield was coming?"

Trevor wrapped his arms around her and spoke in her ear. "No. Why would I even know that? It's fine. We'll ignore him."

"I won't say anything, but you can be sure I'll be keeping an eye on him. We need to get him away from Perfection. You know that."

As the evening progressed, Rio brought out his guitar and Trevor grabbed one too. Rio played a love song he had written for Jae and Trevor sang the lyrics. That song would be on a future album. Next, the DJ played, "You Are the Sunshine of My Life." Mario and Franny, Uncle Tony and Aunt Deidre, Guy and Nari, Rio and Jae all stepped onto the dance floor. Gina remembered the last time she heard that song at her own wedding and cried. Gina noticed that Frankie and MaryAnn look uncomfortable, this wasn't Long Island where they knew how to navigate a social event. It looked like maybe even a disagreement had happened. Poor Ant appeared very distant, aloof. Gina felt that something was going on with her brother. Gina knew she should be better in connecting with him, they had been close when younger. She felt that Ant was distancing himself from the family, but why? Did it have to do with him becoming a lawyer. A profession their father had no respect for, she was in murky waters. It seemed dark, but what?

Gina turned to find Trevor surprising her by leading her to the dance floor. She looked at him, tears in her eyes. "Babe, you're my everything."

They danced for only the second time in their lives. Uncle Tony and Aunt Deidre couldn't be happier to watch their only son marry a truly genuine lady. Good vibes all around and the band got to hang out with each other and enjoy a normal event. No playlists, sound checks, or interviews. Just being a group of friends.

In the morning Rio and Jae flew to Cabo, the same private secluded resort where Gina and Trevor had stayed. They would be gone for a week, and when the honeymoon was over, it would be back to the studio to work out some new songs.

Gina's brothers went home. Franny and Mario stayed a few days to spend time with their granddaughter who enjoyed the visit as much as they did.

LIFE GOES ON,
SOMETHING BREWING?

RIO RETURNED READY TO GET BACK TO WORK. The band was always developing songs, although the label was not pushing for album five. Something they did not expect to prepare for. Having material ready was a benefit.

Jae had a look of contentment but asked Gina if she had heard the rumors about Trevor and Rio going to Brian Mayfield's wild parties. Gina admitted that she'd heard the rumors and added she couldn't imagine when their husbands could have been at any of them since they both were pretty much homebodies. However, this was the second instance of this particular rumor. The seed of doubt had been planted. If the rumors were true, Trevor had a major problem. Gina contemplated hiring a private detective, recalling there were a couple of nights before the wedding when Trevor claimed he was going to see Rio. But did he? Brian Mayfield may need another Gina McNaughton warning. This time she would hurt him.

Roxanne, now six and half entered first grade at Montecito Union School on August twenty-fourth. Like every other parent, Trevor and Gina had to take first-day-of-school pictures. She was happy to start a true full day of school, unlike some children who clung to their parents. "She's growing up too fast," Trevor lamented to Gina. After they dropped off Roxy each day, Trevor and Gina took every opportunity to spend the mornings in bed. Gina believed their lovemaking had gotten better, not stale, like so many women complained. She and Trevor had something deep, despite living in the world of rock and roll. They avoided the pitfalls of success. What could come between them?

Gina and Jae tried to push the rumors out of their minds. Gina spent her mornings in the office working with Skip on the new direction Perfection would take once they produced the fifth album and created their own label.

Gina took a close look at the payroll. She skimmed through and saw Brian Mayfield's name. She walked casually into Skip's office. "Skip, I am wondering why we are paying Brian Mayfield a ridiculous salary. He doesn't do anything for us except create problems. Can you explain it to me? My inference to you was very clear, I wanted him gone."

Skip hung his head. "Gina, you know he's under contract, we would have to pay him out. He does do some things for me—usually grunt work that I don't have the time to take care of."

Gina's anger was written clearly on her face. "Not good enough. Let's pay that motherfucker off. Pay off his contract. I don't want him associated with us. He is evil. Have you heard the rumors he is taking my husband and cousin to drug-fueled, sex parties? If I've heard them, I know you have and yet you are mute on the subject. What's the truth, Skip? I need to protect this band and protect my marriage. I would think you would like to protect your job. Let's get rid of him and stop this rumor mill from getting worse."

Skip knew Gina was serious about Perfection's business and that she hated Brian Mayfield. He needed to a put plan in place before Gina took care of it.

GINA PLAYING MOMMY

IN THE DOWNTIME FROM THE BAND, Gina became involved with Roxanne's school. She wanted her daughter to have some normalcy. As she got older it became more apparent her friends knew her parents were rock stars. Some of the kids at school made fun of her. Some of her friends were fame fanatics. And there were the friends who didn't care who her parents were.

Gina volunteered for bake sales, class projects, and sometimes she was a chaperone on field trips. Gina noticed Roxanne was going to Trevor when she had a problem. She loved that her daughter was close to her father, but she was beginning to feel like an outsider. A few of her mom friends told her, "It's the age young girls gravitate to their dads." It wasn't like Trevor didn't share what Roxanne told him, but Gina felt hurt. She had invested love and time into her relationship with Roxanne. Her relationship with her own mother was different. Maybe life was playing a mean trick on her. She was a rock star, but she was Roxanne's mom.

Over the years Gina met a friendly bunch of ladies, all of whom had husbands who were state senators, lawyers, doctors, or professors. These ladies didn't have a rock star husband, but they were very fortunate ladies. They would go to lunches, spa outings—get-togethers where they talked about their lives and marriages. They treated her as just Gina. She called them the Montecito Mom's Mob—the MMM—and she loved them: Bekki, Christine, Casey, Karen, and Jessica. They were there for each other in any emergency. Their children had sleepovers. It was the first time Gina had that kind of female friendship. Yes, she had Jae and Lisa who had the band in common but found it refreshing to seem normal in a non-normal world. She got to be known in the community as someone who enjoyed the Montecito lifestyle. Gina felt she was fortunate that she and Trevor never lost their connection. Some of the ladies wished their husbands would pay more attention to them and not their professional lives. Gina knew this group would be a lifeline not involved in the music world.

The summer before Roxanne entered third grade, they took her to Disney World and stayed in a suite at the beautiful Grand Floridian Hotel. Roxy loved seeing all the characters in the lobby and at breakfast. To her it was magical. The McNaughtons enjoyed the special treatment. They were able to jump the lines so they weren't recognized. They also employed a bodyguard to keep away admirers. When they were on a family trip, they had hoped fans would respect the fact that this was their daughter's time. Even with the bodyguard, people would snap photos of them. Gina always had to remind herself this was a life she and Trevor chose.

Perfection was asked to play at certain events, mostly smaller venues, which kept them ready for live performances. It had been a few years since they had released an album, but they knew that album five was looming and would be ready when Brown Fence demanded the fifth and final.

They were asked to perform at one of the dreaded New Year's Eve live shows. Just as Gina promised, Perfection performed live with no lip syncing in spite of the freezing cold weather. They also noticed that some of their older videos were getting airtime. They were still on the top of the rock scene.

TURKS AND CAICOS

TREVOR SURPRISED GINA with a trip to Turks and Caicos, a delayed anniversary trip. He wanted alone time with his wife. They rented a private villa that included the services of a chef and domestic staff. Trevor wanted to have sun, sex, and more sex. He sometimes felt that the band and Gina being a mother took away "his" time. Gina thought he was crazy; she always made time for him.

Hopefully there would be no paparazzi with long lenses. Trevor looked around. "This is exactly what I wanted—total privacy. The staff have their own quarters on the edge of the property. The chef comes in the morning and again at dinner. Otherwise, we have the place all to ourselves. We can walk around naked and make love wherever we want and go skinny dipping. I want to do it all, I want you all to myself. I love you. Happy Anniversary." He gave Gina a big hungry kiss.

Gina broke away for a second. "Trev, baby, I love the idea of all this, but do you feel I haven't been present in our marriage? I have always been there for you, wanting you. You feel neglected somehow?"

Trevor pulled her close. "It's not that I feel neglected, but you have been spending a lot of time with the business, Roxy, and all your friends. I just want you to myself, no sharing." Gina contemplated the sentiment it was sweet, but she also felt Trevor was being a bit territorial. She wouldn't say anything, just go along with his plan.

"Well, then come here. You want us to walk around naked? Take my clothes off, nice and slow, and I'll do the same to you. Let's see where that gets us." Gina played the seductress role he wanted. Trevor slid off her dress, leaving her standing in a pair of pink lace panties. He pulled them down slowly and buried his face between her legs. He couldn't resist. He had to have her. He started slowly, using his tongue. Her body caved with him between her legs. She leaned back on a chair and let him have every bit of her, moaning with pleasure. He knew where he was going to take her. She wanted him bad and started taking off his clothes, stopped suddenly and cried out in pleasure. Her sounds aroused him even further. He took her outside to a huge lounge chair, excited by the thought of making love out in the open air, free, under the sun. Gina was willing to do whatever he wanted. He had her legs up in the air and went hard and fast. In just a few moments, they both cried out in delight.

Trevor kept telling her how much he loved her. She smiled and stroked his face gently. He always surprised her, and she loved it. After they caught their breath, they stepped into the pool. Gina felt free, walking around naked. "I want you again, now," Trevor groaned.

Gina couldn't believe how much sexual energy he had. He pushed her against the side of the pool, kissing her all over, returning again and again to her neck. She wrapped her legs around him, but this time she would control him. He was overloaded with pleasure.

When they were done, Gina got out of the pool, found a towel, wrapped it around herself, and handed one to Trevor. He dried himself off and decided he was fine being naked. He walked back into the room and returned a moment later with his guitar. Gina sat next to him, wiping the water from his hair. "Baby, you really turned me on. I wanted everything you gave me. But you were on another sexual level. Have I been that neglectful, or did you take something that made you super sexual? It's okay if you did. I've just never seen you so stimulated."

Trevor reached for her face and kissed her. "Yeah, I heard that Ecstasy is supposed to extend a couple's sexual pleasure, so I scored a few for this trip. I want us to explore everything together. You okay with that?"

Gina was concerned but tried not to show it. "Trev, this is your trip. I'll do everything you want. Just don't ask me to share. I don't want a third party in our bed."

"We don't share with anyone—just me and you."

"So, no surprises, good. Did you notice the time? The chef will be coming soon. Do you feel free enough for him to see you naked? I'm throwing something over me."

Trevor threw on a pair of shorts and a beat-up T-shirt. The chef came, set the outside table, whipped up a magnificent lobster and crab salad, eand topped it off with a lemon soufflé. The meal was light yet filling. He cleaned up and told them he would return at nine-thirty the next morning to prepare breakfast.

Trevor closed the door, locked it, and began to strip off his clothes. "I love watching the sun set. Come on baby, come here with me."

Gina felt whatever he was taking was fairly powerful. "Give me a minute? I want to brush my teeth." She came out and Trevor was lying on the grass, naked, looking up at the sky.

"Aren't the stars beautiful? We don't get to see the stars like this at home. Get naked and lay down with me."

Gina had some concern with Trevor taking any pill, his demons. However, she was very interested in her husband's sexual appetite. Maybe, it couldn't hurt for him to be over stimulated, she tried to look at it as an experience they both would take together. Then after this trip, Gina would tell him no more. She cuddled up next to him. She wondered if she should take whatever Trevor was taking so they could be on the same level.

"Doesn't the sky look beautiful against the water? You know I feel like we did back in the carriage house days. We couldn't get enough of each other. I needed this time with you alone. Our life is beautiful. I love our daughter. Sometimes I just need you. You protect me. I want you, bad."

"I want you too. Just promise me you'll slow down on whatever you're taking. You have never needed that type of help. Maybe I should take what you are taking so we can be on the same level." She rolled over on top of him, bent down and covered him in little kisses. She straddled him and moved slowly giving him every moment of pleasure that he craved.

After they were done, she begged him to get into bed, and he obliged. The next day before breakfast Trevor came out with two pills, one for him and one for Gina. "Baby, I want you to get on the same level as me. If we both take this, God Gina, we will be making love all day and night. It does something extra to you. Are you sure you want this?"

Gina debated about it for a second. "Yes, I want to experience beyond whatever this does sexually. I want to be on your level." Trevor handed her a pill and they took them together.

The chef came for breakfast and cooked a table's worth of food. He said he would be back for dinner, but Trevor told him to take the night off since there was plenty of food. The real issue was both Gina and Trevor were on Ecstasy and he knew they would not want to be disturbed.

As they ate breakfast, Gina suddenly stripped off her clothes, proceeded to pull Trevor's shorts off, and sat in his lap straddling him. "My God, I want to fuck your brains out and I'm going to do it all day long."

A grin formed on Trevor's face. His wife was now insatiably sexual—just as he wanted it. Gina whipped herself in a frenzy sitting on top of him. They continued like this for an hour. Gina was amazed that they could climax and still continue for that long. Trevor then led her to the pool. They touched and kissed and let the water guide them into another sexual game. Gina understood now how Trevor was unstoppable. She became so stimulated that it was never enough.

In the evening after they stopped to eat, Trevor brought her into the bedroom and left the sliding doors open to hear the waves slam against the shore. Trevor took out an old friend of Gina's, her vibrator.

"Trev, where did you find that? I haven't used that in decades, no need for it."

He grinned devilishly. "We're using it now." He turned on the vibrator and he was in control of using it on her. He knew exactly what spots to hit on her. He stimulated her, let her go, then went back three more times. Trevor watched his wife scream with pleasure like he never heard before.

Gina then returned the favor several times, using every way possible to make her husband go wild. They went late into the night until they were exhausted and fell asleep on each other. Gina woke up the next morning a bit out of sorts, but never had she felt the kind of sexual pleasure that both of them achieved the day before. Gina reflected to herself, their sex life was always wonderful, but this took it stratospheric. She smiled at her husband as he started to wake. "Good morning baby, I love you. Everything yesterday was unbelievable. I wanted it all Trevor. But can we both take a break today? I promise I'll play with you tomorrow."

"I brought this for me, but it's so much hotter when we take it together. Yes, I can take a break. Promise me we'll play tomorrow.

Trevor had six pills; he took one on the first night by himself. Then he and Gina each took Ecstasy two different days. They decided to stagger their highly sexual games every other day giving them a rest in between their Ecstasy-driven lovemaking. The McNaughtons returned home on a different level sexually. Trevor got what he wanted—sun, sex, and more sex. Gina wrote a song about their experience. It was filthy but that was now acceptable. She had a working title, "You, Me and Mr. E." Gina felt it was a great working title after their little foray into private hedonism. She wondered what the band would think but didn't care too much. Everyone knew the McNaughtons needed their alone time. Let them guess what transpired in Turks and Caicos. A smile came to her face, reliving their encounters.

MOVING FORWARD
WITH PERFECTION

ON THE FLIGHT HOME, Gina mentioned they needed to have a band meeting to go over some requests for special shows and to put together some type of recording sessions. They also wanted to get on Tommy's schedule. Trevor agreed there was work to do but he felt so invigorated that he wanted to write some music. Gina felt he was back to normal, otherwise she would have happily joined the Mile High Club.

After a few days back from vacation, Rio and Trevor started working out some music and Ian and Jeff joined soon after. Jae was happy to have Gina back. She stopped over and brought a book that Roxanne wanted. Roxanne had good manners. "Thank you, Aunt Jae. I've been wanting this."

"You enjoy it." Jae couldn't wait to hear about Gina's trip. Gina made lattes and put out homemade lemon poppyseed bread.

"So, did you have a relaxing time?"

Gina looked around. "Honestly Jae, all Trevor wanted to do was have sex. He took some Ecstasy and that heightened his performance, which meant it was never enough. At first, I wasn't complaining, but I think somehow, he feels neglected, or feels at times he needs me for himself. I don't know where he got those pills or why he needed them. We don't have issues in that area. However, seeing him so sexually charged, I decided to try it myself and see where it would take me. Knowing Trevor would buy into the whole idea, which he did. Jae, it was the most stimulating thing I could imagine. It took us places I thought we always got to, but this was a whole new level, even dropping acid didn't compare to the heights of pleasure I felt. I did it two nights with him, with the promise we take a day off in between. I'm getting goosebumps just thinking about it. It was heaven."

Jae looked stunned. "Wait. You are telling me that he took the Ecstasy one night, then you joined him for two nights? That's all you did while you were away?"

"Yes, I love him, so I would do whatever he wanted. I wanted to be where he was, it was so powerful I had to experience it myself."

"Well, I had an experience similar to that, but it was only one night. Rio started to be extremely sexy. Of course I went with it, but it didn't stop all night. I wondered how he was managing to do that. He wanted me more and more; I was just trying to keep up with him. So, you are telling me it made your lovemaking even better? Now I'm curious, but I wonder, where did they get these pills. Any ideas?"

"Wait a fucking minute. I bet that fucking Brian Mayfield gave them those pills. I guarantee you he didn't mean for them to be used with us. It's typically used as a sex party drug. I'm sure if Mayfield knew that if they used them with us he would be pissed. It makes me feel those whispers couldn't be true. But Mayfield is capable of spreading them. I need to get rid of him. I hate him so much, now he's trying to interfere in your marriage. We get the last laugh because it just made things better for us both. Screw you Mayfield, our husband's chose us not a sex party." Gina wrote two songs about their experience on Turks and Caicos.

"You, Me, and Mr. E"

You told me you needed me; you wanted me for yourself. I didn't understand, I am yours for always. Convinced me about sun and fun, I was with you to enjoy the fun. Everything was perfect, you know me so well. The ocean smell and sound relaxed me, I didn't care when you said I want you now. We had hardly arrived but I caved into your desires. You wanting me now, all the day and well into the night. I wondered how long you could last, it just never stopped. I told you I loved you that just made you hotter. Again and again, you took me every way hour after hour. I told you I loved you and you kept coming for more. I asked you how you could keep it going.

You then told me you had a friend, you pulled out your hand, your friend Mr. E. It kept you hard, it kept you coming. I thought it was sexy, loved your love all over my body. Your face hidden way between my legs made me melt. Then I knew you wanted me to go down on you, I did it over and over. I wanted you more. The euphoric high, joy, intoxication. I wanted that exhilaration. Then I got you, loving all of what you have it's my special piece of you. That all belongs to me.

Chorus: You, Me and your friend Mr. E I tried it, I want it, I have to have you. Again, again bring me to that place. Where we find the heights of our pleasure and just simply the desire. You make me wet; I want you hard. You want me and I want our friend Mr. E. He'll take us to places that give us more than just thrills. A place of ecstasy and beyond. You, Me and Mr. E. We are more than fine.

I first was afraid of your friend Mr. E but now I can't wait until we take our next ride. Love is sometimes a game but not with you and me. You wanted me all and I gave much more. You are master of all that is mine, take it all, I want you so much more. I love your body the way you fit into mine. There's nothing more gratifying for me than to take you all in, after all, your body belongs to me. Thank you for introducing me to your Mr. E.

Chorus again: I love you more words don't describe. Our love is majestic, powerful, I have you and you have all of me.

"That Place"

We speak loudly, we love emphatically, our lives are legendary with no boundaries. Look around the crowds are aroused. Strutting across the stage like the cat who's on the prowl. Desire on the faces that watch us perform, who gives a shit it's just a show. But when the audience has long since gone. We will have our own show, only for us. Years may have gone by, we still look the same and our devotion, lust, passion remains the same. That place that is yours is totally mine. Attraction, passion, yearning to get to that place. Love may be something that eludes most but do they love with such a powerful force. We love, but we go to that place.

MUSIC DECISIONS AND FAMILY DECISIONS

PERFECTION SORTED THROUGH THEIR MUSIC to see what they were willing to put on an album and what they wanted to keep. To have that many songs ready was a coup for the band.

Tommy Whelan had a busy schedule, but he tried to come up to Montecito twice a week to record. As usual he wanted Gina and Trevor to come in and do vocals toward the end of a song. There was always the chance the vocals and music would need to change. Skip scheduled live performances once a month including an award show and some football pregame shows. Perfection was still on the radar without releasing any new music.

Tommy let one of the songs out as a tease. The management of the music was very calculated in how it was being brought out to the public. Gina, being part of the business end of things, dealt with other band managers—talking about their music drops and other changes in the music industry. She and Trevor began a nice friendship with Brent Nolan from Orange Wave. They had forgotten about him trying to come on to Gina and telling Trevor to marry her. It had been so many years ago. Everyone knew Trevor and Gina had a great marriage, so there was no reason why they couldn't be friends. They would have lunch occasionally or meet at an awards show. Trevor long since forgot all those earlier missteps.

Lisa and Jae came over more frequently as the band started to rehearse, record, and write. Gina needed to make time for writing also. She had the two songs she wrote after their vacation. The Perfection ladies all enjoyed their time together, shopping, visiting each other's houses, just trying to be normal in the crazy world of the rock and roll music scene. Lisa had two boys who were a bit older than Roxanne. Both boys were into sports. Lisa was constantly driving them to practices. Gina also enjoyed spending time with her other ladies, real friends, Karen, Casey, Bekki, Christine, and Jessica. Their daughters were all friends.

The families decided to go Vail, Colorado, for skiing over winter break from school. Gina was comfortable with her friends. Trevor was different from their husbands because of his profession, but he tried hard to fit in. Everyone but Gina and Trevor were skilled skiers. Even Roxy had become a good skier because she had been invited on past trips to Vail with her friends. Each family rented a house next to each other and took all the girls for one night so each couple could have a "free night."

Trevor and Gina tried skiing. It was hilarious seeing the two of them trying to get down the slopes. Because their livelihood counted on their hands and legs, they decided they would go tubing instead. Lower risk of injury. Roxanne was slightly embarrassed that her parents couldn't ski.

At the lodge one evening they were recognized, and the crowd asked for a song. They were caught off guard and even their friends led in the chants for a song. Trevor said he didn't have a guitar and one appeared. He and Gina wondered what they could sing. It had to be an acoustic version. They chose "Found You," the love song Trevor wrote about meeting Gina for the first time.

The entire lodge gave them a standing ovation. They appreciated the response but wanted to go back to being Roxanne's parents on a group ski trip. When they got back to their villa, Roxanne petulantly asked her parents, "Why do you have to be rock stars all the time? Can't you be normal?"

Trevor never gave Roxanne a cross word, but he was firm when he replied, "Roxanne, your mother and I were minding our business when people recognized us and asked us to sing. That's what we do. We will never be sorry or apologize for what we do for a living, and you shouldn't be either. It makes me sad that you're embarrassed by us. You can go to your room. Good night."

Gina was shocked. "I don't think you were wrong in what you said, but I don't think Roxanne has ever heard you talk to her like that. It's fine baby. She'll apologize in the morning. Let's go to bed, you rock star of mine."

The next morning, Roxanne came down for breakfast and said to her father, "Dad, I am still embarrassed, but I have always understood what you and Mom do for a living is different from my friends' parents. My friends think everyone connected with the band is so cool. I get to do things my other friends don't, like seeing other bands my friends would die to see."

Gina interjected, "You are a very fortunate young lady, Roxanne. The people you get to meet and be around."

Roxanne shot her mother darts. "Geez, Mom you never listen. I said that." This conversation marked the beginning of Roxanne thinking of Gina as the "mean parent."

It was 1993, and the internet was entering nearly every home around the world. Gina hired an agency to create a website and fan pages for Perfection. The site listed future tours with links to buy CDs. Perfection's business was booming, Skip and Gina had to manage that. The rest were still writing music and enjoyed becoming golfers. They had their foursome any day of the week they wanted. That weasel Brian started showing up. Gina started thinking that "golfing" might be a term they used for other activities, but she was reassured knowing that Ian would never participate.

Gina was starting to let her jealousy creep back. She remembered the pills she and Trevor took on their trip. She was sure Lucky Charms had supplied them, intending for Trevor and Rio to use them at one of his sex parties. Next time she saw him she would give Brian a beatdown.

She tried not to think the worst about Trevor's golf games and involved herself in Roxanne's school activities. The MMM ladies were so real and gave her real people advice, not like in the entertainment business. It wasn't like the McNaughtons were the only celebrities who lived in the slower city of Montecito. There were others. Why fixate on them?

Gina was in the office when Skip came bounding through the door. "Gina, I got an awesome offer for Perfection." It had been a good five years since they actively toured. They had made six videos that still aired regularly.

Gina sat back in her chair. "Okay, Skip what is this great offer?"

Skip tried to get it out quickly. "You know how they induct people into the Hall of Fame? Well, you have been asked to sing three songs that will be simulcast for a show for the inductees. They want you to do it at the LA Forum. I think it's great to get your faces out there some more. We have been dripping out Perfection appearances, but this is just three songs and televised. They do want one thing. They want you and Trevor to do a love song together onstage."

Gina laughed. "Of course they do. Do they want to see us do anything more? I'm laughing because it's always something they want to see us do. Skip, gather up the troops and let's discuss. Can we pick the songs, or do we have to sing something from the artist? That's big. We would have to learn their music."

Skip shook his head. "Gina, you're always one step ahead of me."

Gina got up. "No Skip. You're great. I'm just thinking of my own workload. By the way, where is the band? I haven't seen anyone here in a couple of days. Trevor gets home around six. He says he's golfing. I'm not believing it anymore!"

Skip was blindsided by her abrupt subject change.

"Rumors are Brian Mayfield has my husband, my cousin, and my friend Jeff, who is a public relations nightmare, doing unsavory things. Mayfield supposedly has them going to parties with starlets and strippers, and I have no idea what else. I'm sick of the rumors. Get ready. If that asshole shows up here, I am literally kicking his ass. I went through hell years ago getting Trevor clean. I won't have him destroy my husband again. Do you hear what I'm saying?"

Without giving him a chance to reply, she continued. "If you know something, you better get the word out that Gina McNaughton is in combat mode, I'm taking down anyone who gets into my personal life. Find those morons and get them in here."

Skip knew Gina meant every word she said. He would have to find everybody and was hoping like hell they really were on a golf course somewhere. Skip wasn't sure what the truth was and wasn't. He also didn't even want to know.

Within an hour, cars started pulling up to the house. Trevor got out of his car first.

He looked concerned as he walked up the steps. "What is so important that you pulled me off the golf course? I had a great game going." He leaned over and pulled her in for a kiss.

Gina voice was singsongy with sarcasm. "I'm so sorry honey. I hate to ruin your fun, but we have business to discuss." She whispered in his ear, "I'm hearing rumors that you haven't been golfing, maybe playing some other sport. I hope for your sake it isn't true."

He whispered back, "I only fucking love *you*. Stop this, Gina."

Everyone trailed into the house and Skip gave them the details about the LA Forum gig.

Rio was excited. "This is fantastic. We always get gold dropped in our lap. We can sing a cover. It's okay, fantastic. Can we pick what we want, or do we have marching orders?"

Skip stepped in. "There is one caveat. They want Trevor and Gina to sing a love song to each other. People want to see them together. Anyone have an issue with that?"

Rio took control. "No, we get the whole McNaughton thing. We will think of two songs. It's up to you two to figure out what you're singing."

Trevor looked very cocky. "Gina and I got this, no worries."

Skip closed the meeting, "Okay, you got two weeks."

Gina got up and walked into the studio and there he was. She was true to her word. She walked up to Brian Mayfield, standing up against a wall in the studio. "Brian, what are you doing here? I thought I was very clear that you weren't invited into the studio." Before he could answer Gina cocked her arm and punched him right in the face, knocking him to the ground. She landed another punch in his solar plexus while he was down. "You asshole. I warned you so many times to stay out of my marriage. You got my husband addicted. You are trying to destroy his life, sobriety, and marriage. Now you're going after Rio. It's like you want to live in their shadow. I won't let you get away with it."

Brian looked up at her, speechless, wiping the blood from his lip.

Gina landed a high-heeled boot in his ribs as she walked out the door. "Get the fuck out of my house."

Rio and Jeff heard Gina yelling from the other room and got to the door as she was storming out. She heard Rio yell to the other band members, "Gina just decked Brian. Holy shit. She's on the warpath. Run."

Brian was still on the floor, milking his minor injuries and enjoying the chance to be dramatic when Trevor walked in. "You need to stay away, Brian. Gina could actually kill you the next time. You should go."

Trevor walked up to the house and found Gina calmly preparing a bowl of ice cream for Roxy and listening to their daughter talk about her day. No way he would bring the incident up with Roxanne home.

It was obvious Roxanne loved her father, but Gina felt that Roxanne didn't like her as much. Gina, her mother, who did everything for her, but Trevor was her world. "Dad, have some ice cream with me. I was telling Mom what I learned in school today. They started giving us sex education, it's very interesting."

Trevor and Gina exchanged a look with each other. Trevor sat down and asked playfully, "Mom, can you give me some ice cream too?"

Gina knew he was aware of what transpired with Brian in the studio. And Trevor knew that getting her mad was not an option.

Roxanne went on about school, her friends, and her soccer games. Trevor was intoxicated by his daughter's stories. Gina asked, "Roxanne, do you have homework?"

Roxanne lowered her head, "I have to study for a science test and read some history."

"Okay Roxy, why don't you go in your room or Mom's office and do your work. If you need help let me know."

As soon as Roxy was out of hearing distance, Trevor looked directly into his wife's eyes. "Gina, did you punch out Brian? Don't answer. I know you did. You fucked him up bad. I told him to leave, or you could kill him."

"Trevor, you actually backed me up. I'm shocked. I won't have that snake slithering back into your sobriety or turning you into some adulterous piece of scum. I also know that those wonderful sex enhancement pills we took on our vacation were probably from him. But they weren't meant for me, but some party you were supposed to attend with him. He's a piece of shit and wants to see us fall down. That's what he wants. I know it and somewhere you know it too."

Trevor sighed. "Gina, I love you. I told you a million times. You are the only woman I want. Now, what love song are we singing? Or can I pick, and we practice? I thought we would do an acoustic version to make it more intimate."

"Babe, I love that idea. Can we practice tonight?"

Trevor looked interested. "Yes, are we talking about practice, or do you have something else in that mind of yours?"

"I'm saying yes to both. Let me help Roxy with her homework and heat up dinner. Marisol leaves early."

The three McNaughtons ate dinner and Roxy dominated the meal with her chatter. "I love you, Dad. You're the best dad in the world,"

Trevor leaned over to kiss her. "What about your mom?"

"Dad that's silly. Mom knows I love her."

Trevor added, "I love her too."

Roxy laughed, "I know that too, Dad. Everyone in the world knows that. You guys are always kissing and stuff."

"Roxanne, time for you to take a shower. Your father and I have some work tonight."

Trevor and Gina sat downstairs at the piano. Trevor picked up the acoustic guitar Gina had given him years ago and started playing a love song they both knew. It was pretty and soft, and it took a bit of work to get the harmonizing down. But that was it. That was the song. Rio had the other songs ready, he always made sure that he and Trevor were on the same path.

The night at the Forum came fast and Perfection rocked out the two songs. They kicked ass—hard core rock and roll. The lights dimmed and two stools were brought to the center of the stage. Trevor perched on one of the stools and started to pluck his six string. Gina slowly strode toward him. Instead of sitting, she leaned into his shoulder. The two looked so much in love singing to each other. As they began the last verse, Roxanne walked onto the stage and said "hi" to the audience and waved. Trevor helped her onto the stool and he and Gina sang the verse to their daughter. They had been just as surprised as the audience when Roxy walked onto the stage. They finished and the crowd exploded. Roxanne made the love song better, more powerful. She was the proof of their love.

Trevor and Gina looked down at Roxanne when she fell into bed later that night. She stole the show.

Trevor was riding high from the performance as the two of them made their way to their own bedroom. Trevor looked admiringly at his wife, still dressed in her off-the-shoulder, nearly transparent gown. He wound one arm around her waist and grabbed her face, kissing her hard and long. "You have saved me three times in my life. I would never love anybody but you. Now let me show you how much I love you."

"Trevor, did you take one of those pills? Or are you just excited by what happened tonight?"

"The whole evening was a turn on. You looked beautiful. I'm a lucky man."

"You can just talk me right out of my clothes, can't you?"

The next morning the media was buzzing about how Roxanne McNaughton walked onstage and how Trevor and Gina sang to her. Amazingly, none of the tabloids had learned about Gina decking Brian. That would certainly take the shine off the happy family scene onstage that night.

YEARS
FLY BY

TIME SEEMED TO FLY BY, and Roxanne entered high school.
Tommy wanted to record most of the written work. He would determine
what would go to Brown Fence Records and what the band should keep
for themselves. Perfection still appeared at small venues, awards shows,
and clubs in New York, Nashville, and Chicago to keep their heads in
performance mode.

Seattle was becoming known for its distinctive sound—grunge.
Although Perfection was a hard rock band they still sold out in Seattle and
Austin clubs. They did a televised concert at the Red Rocks Amphitheatre
in Colorado. Fans were finding more of their music online.

They liked trickling out performances to build anticipation for their
last tour for Brown Fence. The band members had settled lives. Ian and
Lisa had boys in high school and attended every soccer game and baseball
game, their pride on display. Gina and Trevor cheered them on too.

Rio and Jae were content strolling hand in hand to gallery openings and
visiting her parents. They spent a lot of time at the McNaughtons. Jae and
Gina drank wine and chatted in the kitchen or by the pool, while Trevor
and Rio were trying to come up with another building block of the new

label. Gina wanted to know more about that, however they insisted there was "nothing to talk about yet."

Roxanne excelled in school and was on the cheerleading squad. With all of this came boys. Every couple of months Roxy was "in love" with a new boy. Her friends were a tight group and Gina could overhear them during sleepovers, having deep conversations about which boys they liked. Hearts were broken and mended in a matter of weeks.

Trevor did not like Roxy's obsession with boys. He was convinced every boy was having sex with his daughter. Gina tried to ease his concern. "She's fifteen. They just want to be able to say they have a boyfriend. Doesn't mean they're having sex."

But for good measure, Gina felt she needed to have that conversation with Roxanne and didn't look forward to it. Roxanne was a Daddy's girl, but this subject was not for Trevor to venture into.

Gina and Roxanne were planning her sweet sixteen party when Gina started the conversation.

"Roxy sweetheart, you are getting to an age when boys, or young men, start having ideas about girlfriends. Some might try to get you to have sex, maybe before you're ready. All young men think about it. Have any of these boys tried to get you in that type of situation?"

"I can't believe you are asking me this Mom! Why would you ask me that? It's private."

"Your reaction tells me that you may have already had sex. Am I wrong?"

Roxanne was furious. "No! Just so you know, I haven't. God Mom just because you and Dad are so sexual you assume everybody thinks like you two. It's disgusting knowing that your parents are like that, and all my friends see it."

Gina was pissed off. "Roxanne, your father and I love each other. I'm sorry it offends you, but tough shit kiddo. We make a living off of being that couple. You have a great life based off the fact that your father and I are, oh, how do I say this without offending you more? We are rock stars who use our sexuality onstage. It's what made Perfection stand out from other bands. Get a grip sweetheart. If you are having sex, I will take you to a doctor and put you on birth control. Figure out which side you're on Roxanne. You should be happy it's me you're talking to and not your father."

Roxanne blasted back, "Dad would never ask these types of questions. He wouldn't."

"Because he would probably find the guy and beat the crap out of him. Don't think for a minute your father would be okay with whatever you are doing. He has a watchful eye out. He knows what young men want. Go ahead and have a conversation with him. See how that works out for you. I'm trying to help you. It's your choice."

Gina's last statement was hard for Roxanne to hear. She always saw Trevor as the good guy.

Gina needed a cigarette. A little break would give Roxanne time to cool down. With the whispers of Trevor and Rio partying, the band business, and an increasingly rebellious teenage daughter, Gina found smoking was a stress reliever.

Jae found her there, gazing at the ocean. "How is the sweet sixteen party coming along?"

"She hates me. I tried to have a real discussion about sex with her and she blew up at me. Let her try and talk to Trevor. It's funny when we were first together, he had no issues with living with me and being my lover while we lived on my parents' estate. He was all good with having sex with my father's daughter. Now that he has his own daughter, he thinks so differently. I find it interesting. What's up with you?"

Jae sounded a bit stressed. "Do you have any idea what Trevor and Rio are trying to do with this new label? I'm getting pieces of conversation about checking out new talent. What does that mean?"

"Get ready Jae. I think we are heading for a bumpy road, and I expect Brian Mayfield may be involved."

SWEET SIXTEEN AND COLLEGE MOVES

ROXANNE'S SWEET SIXTEEN was an extravagant affair held at a nearby country club. Over 200 people were in attendance. Everybody in the band, Gina's Montecito Mom's Mob and half of the sophomore class were there. Roxanne was co-captain of the cheerleading squad, which meant football and basketball players were also invited. Trevor was eyeing every boy who even glanced at Roxanne.

He found Gina near the bar. "I can't figure out which of these guys I should shake down first. They all seem interested in Roxy."

Gina looked at him. "Your daughter thinks you are so cool about these boys. I'm laughing that you're worried about her having sex. It didn't bother you when we stayed in the carriage house. I was someone's daughter."

"That was different! You were older. You were what nineteen or twenty, we both knew we had past relationships. Anyway, she's, my daughter. I don't like it."

Gina reached for a pack of cigarettes on the bar. "Well babe, you tell her. I'm the wicked witch. She won't listen to me."

The party was the talk of Montecito the next week among the people who attended and those who wish they had been invited. Everyone was impressed with the elegant styling and delicious catering.

Trevor had that conversation with his daughter, and she listened without any argument. She even told her father about a boy she liked but promised Trevor it wasn't serious.

Gina felt like an outsider, hurt because Trevor was Roxy's confidant. Trevor told Gina, "Just don't bring up boys with her. She doesn't want to share that with you."

Gina felt a stab in her heart. What did she do to make her daughter feel that way? It was almost time to start touring colleges and Gina looked forward to those road trips with Roxy. She wanted them both to enjoy the time together without the awkwardness that marred their current relationship.

Roxanne applied to University of Texas, Colorado State University, University of Alabama, and Stanford. Gina hoped she would choose Stanford, it would keep her only child close by, in California. Roxanne's focus was getting on the cheer squad and chose all big-time football schools. Gina told her she could decide for herself without any interference from her and her father. Roxanne was accepted to all of them. It was her choice.

In 1999, Roxanne would be graduating from high school and going away to college. Gina couldn't believe that life went by so fast. Life was about to change; would Roxanne feel the same way about her father in the coming year?

TROUBLED
MOVES

TREVOR AND RIO STARTED PRODUCING some up-and-coming bands, which resulted in Trevor going out a few nights a week. Gina was dubious, especially when rumors started circulating back to her through her music connections and even some tabloids. She heard again about her husband and Rio getting blackout drunk. Could he remember what he did? Gina was terrified by the thoughts running through her head. She was older now, still very attractive but not in her twenties. Maybe it was time for the private detective she thought about years ago. She wanted to speak to Jae first, since both Trevor and Rio were doing this together.

Jeff had resolved his paternity issues. In one case, he was found to be the father, and he was ordered to pay $10,000 a month in child support. He didn't even remember the woman. Even though the other paternity test turned out negative, both cases left a PR stain on the band.

Ian and Lisa were very happy in their life. Once in a while Ian would pick up some studio work with other musicians, while Perfection waited to do their last album under contract for Brown Fence Records.

Jae too had a gnawing feeling that something wasn't right and called Gina. Jae wanted to stop by to see Gina and talk about what was going on, or what she felt was happening.

Gina said of course, but her radar was up since it was ten o'clock at night.

Jae came in through the kitchen door and Gina poured them both a white wine. "Gina, I think Brian Mayfield is starting trouble. I know you have said it for years, but I see him manipulating them. Rio has come home stinking drunk. I wondered how he got home. What about Trevor?"

Gina put her hands on her face. "Oh no. I knew something was surfacing. Trevor and I have always had a loving marriage, our sex life has always been good and regular, except when he drank, did cocaine and whatever Mayfield was feeding him. Remember when Trevor had Ecstasy and it made us so sexually overcharged? What if they're taking those pills and going to parties? Are our husbands having meaningless sex with strange women and not remembering a thing? Most nights I'm sleeping when Trevor comes in. He gives me a kiss, says 'love you' and passes out. I sometimes smell him to see if I smell liquor or perfume. I look at his clothes for traces of makeup. I have even tried to see if I smelled sex on him. My gut is telling me something bad is happening. Brian Mayfield is involved for sure Jae."

Gina started weeping. "I'm going to lose my daughter to college and my husband to those fucking demons again. This time I'm not sure if I can save him or want to save him. Why? Why would he do this now?"

Jae was more than sympathetic and got weepy too. "Gina, I'm scared. I gave up on my master's to be at Rio's side because he wanted that. Why would he hurt me this way?"

"Because he's drunk, stoned, and anything else that will stroke his ego." Gina felt broken. Maybe it wasn't true, but her gut told her otherwise.

Jae's cell phone rang from inside her spacious purse. She fished it out, looked at the screen and her eyebrows went up.

"Yes?" she answered.

Gina didn't make any attempt to ignore the one-sided conversation. There was no doubt what had happened.

"Are you fucking kidding me Rio? No, that's not the point. Explain to me why you would go to a party like that. Are you high now? What else have you done? I'm furious, you playing the typical fucked up rocker dude. Yes, I'll come bail you out. What? Have bail money for Trevor? You two are together? You were drunk *and* high while you were driving? Well, I'm at Gina's now, so yeah that's a problem for both of you. What station are you at? Are you fucking kidding me, that is over two hours away. Maybe we'll come and bail you out. Maybe we won't. Why don't you think about that Rio?" Jae missed regular telephones that could be slammed down.

Gina looked up at the ceiling to keep the tears from coming down her cheeks. It was at that moment Roxy returned home. "Mom what's wrong?"

Gina couldn't answer right away.

But Roxanne could see the look on Jae's face and the tears in her mother's eyes. "Mom, I know when you're upset. What did Daddy do? I know he has been coming home late. I also heard some older girls talking about parties in BH and that Dad and Uncle Rio went to some. That's it?"

Gina unleashed on her. "You really want to know? Your father and Uncle Rio have been arrested for DUI. They're both off the charts drunk and high on something, so we need to go and bail them out. You wanted the truth, you got it. Your father's making some really bad mistakes. I've got to go. Aunt Jae and I are driving to Beverly Hills. You're okay if I leave?"

"Yes, go! Don't let Daddy stay in jail."

While Gina was bringing Roxy up to speed, Jae had been on the phone with their business attorney. He assured her he would put them in touch with a good criminal defense attorney and not to worry. Not to worry? Yeah, right.

Gina grabbed her keys and followed Jae out the door. Trevor was slipping. Could she bring him back this time before he made an even worse mistake? She wasn't sure. Jae drove Gina to the police station, parked, jumped out, headed for the front door. Gina sat in the passenger seat and cried painfully for the next five minutes. Once she got that out of her system, she straightened herself up and walked in.

Jae had already talked to the desk sergeant who told her bail had been arranged by an attorney whose name she didn't recognize. Why should she? Who would have ever thought she'd need a criminal attorney? Gina joined Jae on a wooden bench and looked around at the gray walls and filthy floor.

They waited for two hours before they heard a shuffling coming down the hall toward them. Trevor and Rio looked like shit and smelled even worse—alcohol, weed, sweat, and shame. Rio kept apologizing to Jae, but she wouldn't hear it. Trevor didn't even look at Gina. He knew it was not going to be a pleasant drive home. Despite the late hour, photographers were already assembled on the steps out front. Tomorrow morning the world would know.

Gina sat in front with Jae. The two newly arrested rockers were in the back seat while both women navigated through tears as they drove.

Trevor, daring to speak quietly said, "Look I'm sorry, it just overcame me ... and—"

Gina stared at him, her eyes dripping with tears. "Fuck off Trevor. You're not sorry. You're not. You keep doing this and you want me to pull you out every time. Do you ever think of how much you hurt me? No, you don't. What about the promises you made? Those don't count. I don't know what's in that goddamned head of yours, but it's not me and it's not your daughter. Did you think of her? The embarrassment she will feel tomorrow when she goes to school. She's a senior in high school. She's not a kid."

Gina was screaming now, "I honestly think you don't care what we think, or you just don't love us enough to stay clean. What whore has you thinking you are so hot that you do no wrong? That's it."

Jae looked in her rearview mirror at Rio. "Gina's right, what young thing has you believing you are a fucking Rock God Rio?" Jae also found it hard to hold back her emotions.

Rio simply said, "Jae, Babe. I fucked up and I'm sorry—"

Jae stopped him. "Save it I don't want to hear your lame ass excuses tonight."

Trevor knew he was in deep. "It's not that way. Can you please stop saying I'm cheating on you? I haven't. I mean, I could have, but never thought of ever doing that to you."

Jae jammed on the brakes, adding more fear to both her and Gina's frazzled nerves. Gina yelled, "Oh, you could have, but you haven't? That makes me feel so much better. And I could have fucked Brent Nolan years ago, and I didn't. How does that feel? Remember the one that said he could take me away from you? Then *YOU DECIDED TO MARRY ME*. Go, fuck off Trevor. How dare you say that shit to me. Your asshole friend Brian Mayfield is destroying your life and that dumbass cousin of mine and you both allow it. Well, I devised a way to get rid of him. I'll have him deported. I'll have my Uncle Tony and Skip rescind his papers. I don't know why I haven't realized it before. You can count on that happening."

The rest of the drive back to the McNaughton house was silent. Trevor and Gina climbed out of the car. Gina slammed the door and Jae drove away.

Trevor slinked behind Gina and grabbed her shoulder. "Can we not yell in front of Roxanne when we get in the house?"

Gina wasn't having it, "Will that make you feel better? Once she smells you, I don't think your daughter will be too happy with you. She should be in bed, but I know she'll be waiting up for you. She knows what happened."

Gina walked into the house, marched straight to the bedroom, slammed the door behind her, and locked it.

An anxious Roxanne was waiting on the living room sofa and got up when she heard her parents come in. She looked at her father, "Why Dad? You know you can't drink, and you probably did some drugs. I know what goes on at those parties. I know who goes to them. Sometimes I think Mom is way too jealous, but she's not wrong this time. I'm going to bed; I hope you have some answers in the morning."

Trevor couldn't bear his own stink and desperately wanted a shower. He got a knife and jimmied the lock on the bedroom door.

Gina sat up. "What are you doing in here?"

"It's my bedroom too. I'm your fucking husband."

"And what? You want to make mad passionate love so it's all okay? You can't even get hard anymore. You're not sleeping in this bed until you get that filth off you. Try boiling water, that should work." Gina pulled the blanket around her and sobbed.

Trevor came out of the shower, a little more sober but still high, and sat down on the side of the bed. "Gina. G. Please don't cry. I know what I did. Rio and I have gone to a few parties scouting out bands. They are crazy. I know I've been wrong in not telling you, but I knew what you would think and what Jae probably thinks. I never should have gone to this band party. We went to talk to them, not realizing what we were walking into."

Gina remained silent and Trevor kept hoping to talk his way out of this disaster. "Rio and I knew we were in trouble. Yes, there were women who came up to us, but we weren't interested. We did drink, and they had some kind of drug that wasn't cocaine, but it was extremely powerful. Someone called it Oxy, I'm sure it was OxyContin. We snorted it. It was potent. We got out knowing we were too drunk and high and thought we could make it home. But the police were waiting outside the party for anyone to leave so they could bust them, that was Rio and me. Now it's going to be a story. If I could take it back I would, but I can't and I don't know how to make you feel better."

Gina shot him daggers. "Trevor, please don't. Talking only digs you into a deeper hole. It's going to take me a while before I get through this. You will have to live with that."

Trevor tried to put his arms around her, but she wasn't having it. She was furious, hurt, and exhausted. As she turned her back to him, for the first time since the birth of Roxanne and the loss of their babies, she heard Trevor cry. She didn't feel bad. Now he knows how it feels.

The next morning, the television in the kitchen was turned on to the morning news like always as Marisol made breakfast. "Rio Poole and Trevor

McNaughton arrested for DUI." Marisol looked at the screen out of the corner of her eye without turning her head or saying a word.

Roxanne, who was standing at the counter eating a bowl of cereal, turned off the TV before her mother walked in. "Mom, it's all over the news. I want to drive to school before I see too many people."

Gina felt like she was bulldozed. "Roxanne, I don't know what to say. I don't have the answers."

Trevor stayed in bed and slept it off.

Gina's cell phone rang. She snatched it up. "Yeah?" It was Skip.

"Skip, I don't have answers."

"Gina this looks really bad. Brown Fence may want their album sooner than later. Especially if they think Trevor and Rio have issues."

Gina bluntly said, "Then you should talk to him. I'm too angry to talk. I have some soul-searching to do. This is my marriage, my husband. I love him, but I won't put up with this."

Skip was cautious. "This is the band, you, Trevor and Rio. Are you thinking of something drastic like breaking up the band?"

Gina scoffed. "No, it's not the end of Perfection. I've worked way too hard for the last twenty years to make this a brand. But I want you to rescind Brian Mayfield's work visa. I'll talk to my Uncle Tony. He won't have an issue doing it, but I also need you to do the same. This is not open for discussion."

Skip added, "With this incident plus Jeff's paternity suits, and let me add that Mayfield has let out you punched him, we need to hire a public relations firm to stop the bleeding."

"You want to bring a PR person in? No, not now. I'll deal with my personal issues."

Skip tried to be forceful, but it was difficult to be firm with Gina McNaughton, "Gina, we have one more album and potential live dates coming up. We need to answer all these questions. Before they come knocking at our door. You need to think about it, okay?"

All Gina could muster up was, "We'll talk later."

Marisol meekly asked if there was trouble. Gina told her yes, but not to worry. After she cleaned up the kitchen, Marisol left to run errands and go grocery shopping.

Trevor waited until he heard Marisol leaving the house before he came out of the bedroom in the bathrobe he hated. He went down to the kitchen, leaned over and kissed Gina on the head. "Baby, baby, can we talk or are you going to give me the silent treatment?"

TROUBLE RISES

THE SILENT TREATMENT. Every woman uses it to get her point across without having a useless discussion.

Trevor looked around. "Did Marisol make breakfast? I'm starving."

Gina placed a platter of scrambled eggs, pancakes, and bacon that Marisol had left on the back of the stove in front of him. Trevor looked up at her. "Thank you."

Gina's cell phone rang. She just knew it was Franny. "Hello Mom." She answered wearily. "Yes, it's true. What? Yes, he's okay, he's just stupid. Mom don't ask me those questions now, please. No, he is not in jail, he's eating breakfast. No, I don't think you should talk to him. You want to pray for him? You better do a lot of praying; he's going to need it." Gina hung up the phone.

Gina sat across from Trevor looking directly into his eyes, trying to read him. "Well, the way I see things Trevor is that you have three options. We can get a divorce, and you can do whatever you want. You would be out of Perfection. The second option is that you and Rio stop all of your producing bullshit. Most important, you and Brian cut ties immediately You don't need to be taking that on, we have our own band. We're a business. The third is you spend more time at home. I will not have my husband in the middle of a rumor mill that has you cozying up to twenty-year-olds who find you so attractive. At least I know where you are and if there is a function that needs to be attended, we do it together. And if that sounds like I don't trust you, you're right. I don't, not now. I also want to know what you are snorting or taking. It's not cocaine. It must be the new thing out there. Is it OxyContin? Are you taking those pills that make you want to have sex at every opportunity also? I'm not there, so who is it? Oxy is extremely addictive. You need to stop now. What is it going to be Trevor? This is the last time I save you."

Trevor was wounded. "Why would you ever consider divorce as an option? And me out of the band? Why is that even on the table, Gina? Is that what you really want? You answer me that."

Gina laughed. "You really have a set on you. Why is that an option? It's what they call the nuclear option. Are you ready to blow up everything we worked for? I don't want that. I have no idea where your head is. Make me believe you want your family, that you want to see your daughter graduate high school, that you want to take her to college. Those are family events. Do you want to be part of that?"

Trevor hung his head. "You know I want my family."

"Do I Trevor? If you want it, then act like it, and don't fuck me over again. I promise you, there will be no more chances. I can't do it." Gina started weeping.

"Gina, come here, please … that Oxy shit is like heroin. I might go through withdrawals again. Please don't be mean to me. I love you. I swear I do. No one could ever replace you."

"Then prove it, and you will have my love and support. Don't screw this up."

"Can I kiss you?" he implored.

Gina was a sucker for his need for her. She walked over and let him hug her and give her a long kiss.

Gina's cell phone rang again and continued to do so for the rest of the day. The Montecito Moms were calling to make sure Gina was okay. That's what real friends do, check on you when you're down.

It took about two weeks after the DUI before Trevor felt somehow normal. He knew he still had the urges and Gina was nursing him through his rough patches. Trevor sat both his girls down. "I'm working on getting the Oxy out of my system. I promise you both I'm not going to hurt you again. Please forgive me Gina, my beautiful wife, and Roxanne, the daughter I cherish. I love you both."

Roxanne ran up to her father and forgave him instantly. Gina was hopeful, but unsure of how strong he really was. Gina walked toward him and told him flatly, "You are the only man I will ever love, ever."

Roxanne wanted to go out to dinner to tell her parents which college she chose.

"It's a celebration! I want to share my decision with you."

Trevor jumped at the chance for a normal family outing. "We're excited to hear your choice. Yes, let's go out, celebrate."

Roxanne was firm. "Dad, you can't drink."

Trevor assured her. "I got it Roxanne. It's not an issue."

The three of them called ahead for a table at Roxanne's favorite restaurant, an old-fashioned steakhouse that was a mainstay in the neighborhood. After they ordered, Roxanne announced, "I really wanted to go to Texas, but after a lot of thought, I think it's wiser for me to stay in state. I'm going to Stanford. I'm going to be a psych major."

Gina grinned, "Are you worried about us Roxanne? If you really want to go to Texas, we would be okay with that."

"No Mom, I want to be here in California, and it's a good program."

Trevor beamed. "We are thrilled with your choice."

All three of them enjoyed a lighthearted dinner. As soon as they pulled into the driveway, Roxanne announced she was going out with her friends and walked over to her own car.

Gina and Trevor walked into the living room. Gina took out one of her pastel cigarettes. "You want one?" she offered Trevor. They sat on the sofa, smoking and enjoying the expansive view of the Pacific Ocean.

Trevor spoke first. "She is going to Stanford to keep an eye on us, you realize that?"

Gina let out a huge exhale. "Of course she is. She wants to keep her eye on you."

Trevor shook his head, "No, she wants us to be okay, normal. We haven't returned to normal."

Gina laughed "What does normal look like to you? Is it that you want us to be intimate again?"

Trevor took the cigarette out of her mouth. "That's one thing. I also want you to share things with me. Band business, but mostly us."

Gina shook her head. "I want that too. I'm just a little fragile. Can you understand why?"

Trevor knelt on the floor in front of her. "G, my love. I feel you next to me every night, and I don't know how to do that without touching you, being with you, wanting you. I'm still your husband."

Gina knew she would cave, but she wanted to least pretend that he had to work for it. "Why do you think I'm still with you? To be hurt? No. Is it because I have loved you since I first laid eyes on you? Have I ever looked at another man? Not ever. We've been through some really sad events together, but we endured, we made it through. Tell me that we will make it through this too."

"I always need all of you, Gina. Would you give me that chance?" Trevor took her by the hand and led her up to their bedroom. He kissed her like he missed her for months. Gina wasn't sure how she felt making love to him. She was still wounded by the events that had transpired. Gina loved him desperately, but also was overcome with emotion of some sort of betrayal. Trevor held her after the kiss, he whispered how much he loved her and needed her. Gina knew how he wanted her and mostly needed her. After all, she was the love of his life but more importantly, she was his protector. He pulled the zipper down the back of her dress, knowing he would find the lace lingerie she always wore.

Gina still felt all torn up. She wanted him, but her mind raced with awful thoughts of him being with someone else. Jealousy was still front and center for Gina McNaughton. She pulled away. "I need to know Trevor, before I let you continue. Did you do anything that you can't take back? Please, I'm begging you for the truth."

Trevor stopped kissing her neck. "G, what? Where are you going with this? How many times have I declared my love for only you? The only woman I have wanted and still want. Baby, we always go through this. Why do you think I want something else? Please, I miss you. I want to feel you. I want you to touch me, love me. You can tell I want you I'm so hard right now just the idea of you loving me."

Gina had tears in her eyes. "Answer the question. Did you make a mistake because you were very high and drunk? I need the answer."

Trevor picked her up and put her on the bed. He wasn't aggressive but pulled off her lingerie, then planted his face between her legs, "I'm going to give you the answer by just going down on you and eating every piece of you up. That's my answer. No, it's always been you. Now I'll show you."

For Gina, it was over. She was his. Trevor took his time savoring every bit of her. Gina felt the pure rapture of his love. Gina started ripping off his shirt, kissing his chest, feeling his arms. She reached down, unzipped his jeans and pulled them off. She turned to him and stroked his penis. "This belongs to me, and I will take it and have every bit of you. I love you Trevor. Don't ever make me feel bruised again." He devoured her once again and made her feel that blissful euphoric feeling. Gina sat on top of him, leaned down and gave him little kisses around his face. Gina became her bewitching self; she kissed him long and hard. His mouth landed on her breasts which put her in a frenzy. "Baby, get ready because I'm going to give you everything you asked for and more." They both knew how much they needed each other. "Oh, Trevor did you lock the bedroom door?"

ROXANNE ALL GROWN UP

ROXANNE'S PROM WAS A WEEK AWAY and she still hadn't bought a dress. Gina called to Roxanne, "Let's go, if we are driving into Beverly Hills, we need to leave now."

Trevor came out from their home office. Gina had involved him more in Perfection's business.

"You're still here? Where is she?"

"She's still upstairs. I wanted to get in and out of BH. It's bad enough that there will be all the paparazzi trolling Rodeo, looking for a shot of anyone. Now I guess we might be one of their targets."

Trevor yelled up the steps. "Roxanne, come on it's a long drive. Don't keep you mother waiting."

She glided down. "I'm here, let's go."

Trevor stopped her. "Hold up Roxy. Who is taking you to prom? Do I know him?"

Roxanne was testy. "No, you don't, but he knows who you two are, so we're good."

Gina was anxious to leave. "Babe don't argue with her. I want to go."

It took two hours and twenty minutes to get to Rodeo Drive and took Roxanne forty-five minutes to find a dress. Gina told Roxy she could have had her stylist drive up and pick out a dress. What a waste of time. Gina asked, "Who is this young man? He's not a boy. Who is taking you? I'm your mother. Tell me."

Roxanne hated this banter. "You know, just because you and Dad are together, like I know you two are, you know, TOGETHER. Doesn't mean I have to—"

"Yes, Roxanne it does. What's his name?"

"Fine. Daniel Rivers. He's cute, but he's not my boyfriend. He's just a friend."

"Well, friends still want to have sex on prom night. Remember that."

Roxanne was done. "You and Dad suck. Just because everyone knows how sexual you are, you think everyone is."

"Okay, enough."

Roxanne turned on the radio and of course it was her parents' music. Gina laughed.

Prom night came, and Trevor scared poor Daniel Rivers. Roxanne looked beautiful. As she had gotten older, she looked more like her mother, but had her father's blue eyes. She had Gina's full head of hair and was tall like Trevor. Gina always saw that in Roxanne. There she stood looking amazing in a white sparkling dress that fit her curves perfectly. She had grown into a woman.

Gina and Trevor offered to host the after-prom breakfast at their house. They didn't want Marisol to cook for all those kids, so Gina hired a caterer. It would be easier for everyone. They didn't realize Roxy had so many friends. Or was it because of who her parents were—but a lot of kids showed up. There were all types of breakfast foods and desserts, but definitely no alcohol. The breakfast was a success, and Gina got to share it with her good friends, the Montecito Moms Mob.

Gina had hoped her parents could come out, but they had business they couldn't reschedule and were sad not to be able to see their granddaughter graduate. The McNaughtons were like any parents, proud of their daughter.

They took lots of pictures of Roxy in her cap and gown. Roxanne graduated with honors. When her name was called, Gina broke down and cried. She no longer had her one and only baby. She would be leaving home soon, going to college. A major life event. Gina was sad when she thought of not seeing her every day. But life moves so fast, especially when you live a high-paced lifestyle.

August came, and it was time to drive Roxanne to college. How did it happen so fast, that little baby into this woman? They arrived at Stanford early to move Roxanne into her apartment and get her everything she needed. She also needed to be there for freshman orientation. They insisted she have a roommate. They didn't like the idea of her alone in an apartment. They found a nice girl looking to rent a room. When it was time to say goodbye, Gina broke down. Her only child was growing up. It made her sad, but happy.

Trevor was a bit teary, "Okay Roxy, we have a five-hour drive ahead of us. We love you and will call when we get home."

The drive was pleasant, but Gina didn't recognize the same landmarks she saw on the way to Stanford. "Trevor why does this look different?"

"We are going to stay in Carmel for two days, a mini vacay. We can take walks on the beach and forget about the world. Sound good?"

"I hope I have clothes."

"Just like Vegas, baby. You won't be needing much."

Trevor and Gina truly reconnected with each other. They found a place in Carmel that had little cottages where they chose to reflect on where their life was now. They were now empty nesters. Gina lay her head on Trevor's lap and asked, "Have we spent too much time on our careers to notice our daughter growing up so fast? I thought I was consistently there for Roxanne. I feel she resents me somehow; I tried to be everything for everyone. Was I deceiving myself? I know she loves you entirely, it doesn't make me jealous. I guess I wanted a relationship different than my mother and me. It's karma."

Trevor lifted her head and looked into her eyes. "Gina you are a good mother, she just knows you are sensitive. She uses that against you. I see it. I'm flawed so she feels I am fragile; she handles me differently. You have me. I'm not going anywhere. Does that count?"

Gina touched his unshaved face. "Trevor, you count for everything in my life. Without you there would be no Perfection, no Roxanne, no love of my life. I never want to lose you,"

Trevor smiled. "Can I show you how incredible I think you are?"

"You haven't trimmed your face. You have those sexy whiskers. I want to feel those whiskers on my thighs. Can we do that?"

"I'm happy to help you with that."

They made love sweetly.

The next morning, they found a breakfast café and walked the breezy beach. When they returned to their room, Trevor lit a fire in the fireplace, they wrapped the comforter around them and just looked into the fire and held each other. Gina started to get ideas for a song and together they wrote the beginnings of a new song. It was personal but they could add their hard rock spin.

Life Flies By ...

One day you wake up and your life is perfect
Your days are filled with dreams and love
The world creeps in, and takes your time away, away
From the happiest of memories, will you still be there
For me, I'll be there for you, even through life's terrible
Moments we have been warriors fighting for our world.
Our life doesn't need to fly along like paper in the wind.
This love is a lifetime when a lifetime seems fleeting.
I would live a thousand years along your side, if I could wish
For that I would. Making love to you sends me to the most
Divine of places, erotic, playful and sweet. All you have is
Mine and all I have is yours. That part of life hasn't flown by
We will be together for a lifetime even when life around us is
toxic, and people try to divide us. I will hold you closer, and
Then let time fly by. You can try to catch it as it goes by, but still
life is meant to fly by like angels rising to heaven, time flies by.

Chorus
I will love you even when life flies by, I will always
Love the way your face looks every morning, no matter
How much life flies by, you're my everything, every day
No matter, how long it will take, will we let life fly as long
As we are together, and when we leave this
world, we must remain together.

They planned to record it when they got home.

PERFECTION BUSINESS AND PUBLIC RELATIONS

ONCE THEY RETURNED, it was time for Perfection business. After the last album was recorded they would do a tour, then it would finally be time to start their own label and produce their own music. It was an exciting time but their last commitment to Brown Fence was looming.

Gina was alone in the office when Skip came in. She asked, "Did we get Mayfield deported?"

Skip was afraid of Gina's reaction. "He was one step ahead of you. After you punched him, he angled himself for a job with another band, so he's still around, just not with us. They picked up his work visa."

Gina was dumbfounded. "Are you shitting me right now? He's still in LA and we can't do anything?"

Skip looked downward. "No. We have nothing. He's around." Gina grew terrified. "He's going to take my marriage down."

Trevor was walking down the hallway and overheard. "Who is taking our marriage down?"

"Mayfield got a job with a band in LA. Did you know that?"

Trevor seemed resigned to the information. "No, I didn't. But he always tends to land on his feet."

"Snakes usually do. Enough of him." She turned to Skip. "What business do we have pending?"

Skip winced as he said, "Well, I have to tell you. Rio got another DUI last night."

Gina banged her head on the desk. "No, no. I wonder why Jae didn't call?" Then Gina remembered she and Trevor were in Carmel, with her phone turned off.

Skip addressed the situation. "Look, this is his second DUI. Jeff lost a paternity issue. The story is out about you punching Mayfield. He let it out to embarrass you. We are starting to have some real PR issues. I think it may be time to start looking at agencies. With all this, Brown Fence might really want to squeeze the last set of recordings out of you. That might happen sooner than later. I think we need to call a band meeting."

Trevor agreed. "This is too much. I know I contributed to this, but we need to stop the bleeding PR wise."

Gina wanted to know. "Babe, we have enough songs to satisfy Brown Fence, right?"

Trevor was confident. "We do. I want to keep songs for us. Do we have PR agencies to look at?"

Skip had a list ready. "These are the top agencies. One comes highly recommended in the music business—Paul Ryan and Associates."

Trevor nodded and Skip left to make the phone calls.

Gina didn't like it. "Do we really want a PR firm? They get into your private business."

Trevor grabbed her hand. "They also clean up your business, and we definitely have some dirty laundry."

Gina rolled her eyes. "What do you think about the Mayfield thing? He will try to get to you. You know it. I know it. I'll have security at every one of our remaining shows to keep him out."

Trevor looked at her. "He can't hurt us. At this point we are hurting ourselves."

When Rio showed up for practice, Gina stopped him. "What the hell are you thinking? Another DUI. Why didn't you call Jae before you got into the car? She would have picked you up if you were that wasted. You have created a PR shitstorm. What happened?"

Rio dropped his head. "I know. I didn't want to call my wife, knowing she would be really pissed off. Now I have a suspended license . Jae has to drive me everywhere and she isn't happy. I messed up and my beautiful wife has to suffer. Gina, I don't want her to leave me."

Gina hugged her cousin. "She loves you, but you need to stop drinking, dude. If you love her that much, then do it. I love you, please be careful and stop before something worse happens." Gina would stand by him. Rio had to get his act together. Gina really hated the public relations firm idea. She and Rio grew up keeping personal business personal—no outsiders.

Gina needed to call Jae. She was sure that this would impact their marriage somehow. "Jae, it's Gina. I heard what happened. Where the hell! What was Rio doing that he got that drunk?"

Jae's voice cracked. "John Conklin from Striped Snake called him. John told him about this vintage guitar he wanted to buy and wanted Rio's help. After John bought the guitar, they wound up at party in a Summerland bar. I knew when he didn't come home by midnight it was bad." Jae was now crying.

Gina asked, "Why not call you? He has that one DUI with Trevor which is still being handled by the attorney. I can't believe this. You know Skip wants us to get a PR firm. That's not how the Riccis conduct business. I feel this is an intrusion into our private lives. I think my hands may be tied on this one."

Jae then got angry. "I now have to drive him everywhere. I don't know Gina. I feel this is a point that I have some hard choices to make."

Gina pleaded, "Jae, no. You love him. He loves you. He fucked up that's true. Don't make a decision that you can't take back. Please. We will fix this."

Jae's response simply was, "Gina I'll try. Let me go."

Trevor came to see Gina. "Rio is too emotional for us to get work done. I'm not a saint but this sucks. We have to have a band meeting—Skip, Tommy, all the guys. We would be negligent if we didn't look into those PR firms. I'll have Skip arrange the meeting as soon as possible. Probably tomorrow, everyone will be here anyway." Trevor leaned in and kissed Gina on the forehead. "I got you baby, no worries."

However, Gina did worry. All this shit was piling up. She felt for the first time, Perfection business was getting away from her. Gina held onto Trevor just a little bit tighter.

PAUL RYAN AND ASSOCIATES

TWO DAYS AFTER RIO'S SECOND DUI everyone met at the studio. The discussion was about the music that was already written. Not including the songs Gina and Trevor wrote, Perfection had twenty-five songs ready. Rio was aggravated, "Let's finish the Brown Fence crap. That fucked up clause that they put in doesn't sit well with me. Let's finish with them. Then we don't owe them anything. We're out and we create our own label."

The band had to pick the songs they were willing to put on their last album with Brown Fence. After a few hours, they narrowed it down to seven songs they were willing to put on the album. Practice went on for a couple of days, with some minor changes to the material as per Tommy's rearranging. They wanted a kick ass album, especially if Brown Fence Records wanted them to tour.

Skip and Tommy came in. Skip started, "Look Tommy and I agree. Perfection needs a solid public relations overhaul. It's not going to be intrusive. We need to show you as good role models, not what's out there now. Each one of you are guilty of some negative publicity. Lucky for you Ian, you're exempt. I called Paul Ryan and Associates. Paul Ryan himself will be overseeing our account. Gina, don't even say anything, it's done."

Gina was resigned. "When is he coming to meet us? I'll put my good girl hat on."

Skip had already arranged a meeting with Paul Ryan for the next day. After everyone left the studio the McNaughtons walked up to the house.

"G we all understand you have an intense dislike for this PR idea. We will be united together. We can't keep going on with our shit all over the tabloids, on MTV, everywhere. You never wanted Perfection to be the band who has crap out there. We will do what we need and let them ride off into the sunset."

Gina teared up, "I have a feeling, this is not going to end in a satisfactory conclusion for us. Don't ask why I feel this way. It's the Brian Mayfield feeling all over again. Speaking of that piece of shit, he is lurking. He wants to get to you."

Trevor had a great idea. "Let's eat dinner in bed, watch television, and cuddle up. You like that?"

Gina half smiled. "Sure, I would love it. Just promise me you will protect us."

Trevor kissed her. "I will always protect us." Until Trevor was unable to keep his word.

MEETING
PAUL RYAN

THE NEXT DAY EVERYONE ASSEMBLED at the studio waiting to meet with Paul Ryan. They all knew this would be unpleasant, because all of them had added to the PR debacle. Skip walked in with Paul Ryan and made introductions. Gina was surprised to see he was a very handsome man. He made a point to introduce himself personally to everyone and stopped at Gina. He took her hand in both of his and looked directly into her eyes. In a near whisper he said, "I've been waiting to meet you in person. I couldn't wait to see the sexy siren herself. You have a very alluring, bewitching, captivating, seductive presence onstage. I have closely followed your career. I cannot wait to sit down with you and find out all the ins and outs of Gina McNaughton. Any man would be envious of having this opportunity to find out all about you."

He was flirting with her in front of her husband, and it made her feel uncomfortable.

Trevor reached across Gina and shook his hand. "I'm glad you follow my wife's career. We are a team. So, if you follow her, then you follow me. Thank you."

Paul met one-on-one with each of the band members who had issues, to figure out how he could redeem them from the bad press. Gina and Trevor made it clear that he would talk to the two of them together.

Paul instructed Jeff to spend time with his son. That would show he wasn't shirking his responsibility. Child support wasn't enough. Be a good father. Jeff was pissed off at this suggestion, having only seen the child once. Ryan's strategy was to reinforce that the other paternity suit was thrown out of court and that the woman was a gold digger who wanted to get a quick cash payout. Gina thought the whole thing made Jeff look sleazy.

Paul arranged for Rio to record public service announcements on the dangers of drinking and driving to show he took responsibility and was remorseful.

As for slugging Brian Mayfield, they would spin the story saying Gina felt threatened.

A press release was written for Trevor, claiming he was a passenger and unaware of how inebriated Rio was.

Ryan was less concerned than Gina about the rumors surrounding Trevor and Rio with the sex parties. None of them had ever been substantiated. Trevor and Gina McNaughton were happily married with a beautiful daughter attending Stanford University. Nothing to see here.

Paul warned the band to avoid any distractions while recording album five. Everyone played like good soldiers.

Gina was working in her office, looking at the paperwork for the last album due to Brown Fence when Paul Ryan rapped on the doorframe. Gina looked up. "Can I help you with something?" She continued before he had a chance to reply. "You know, I'm glad you stopped by. I want to get something straight. When I first met you, I felt like you were flirting with me in front of my husband. It made me feel uncomfortable. It isn't what we hired you for is it, to flirt with the wife of another man? Who I happen to love entirely. So, what was it?"

Paul Ryan pulled a chair up to Gina's desk and admitted. "I *was* flirting. A bit. You are a very provocative, attractive woman. Men desire you. Do you know that? You constantly tell the world how much you love your husband.

I wonder if the McNaughtons are real or a front. Sometimes people who are unhappy flaunt a united front of the perfect marriage."

Gina was furious. "Are you fucking serious right now? You admit you were flirting? I'm uncomfortable with that. You did that in front of Trevor. I have loved my husband for over twenty years. No smoke and mirrors here Paul. It's genuine. Does that surprise you?"

Gina noticed Paul had beautiful blue eyes, like Trevor. She felt like he was staring through her, which made her very self-conscious.

Paul dropped this nugget. "I'm just concerned for you. Maybe those rumors have a hint of truth behind them. You are way too beautiful for a man to take you for granted, possibly cheat on you. Plus, I know about his substance abuse. You hear things in this line of work."

Gina stared at him. "If you know something, you should tell me. But don't make accusations unless you have proof. I trust my husband, and as far as any substance abuse, we have dealt with that privately and I appreciate you respecting that privacy. Okay? We straight?"

Paul was cocky. "Gina, I'm going to look out for you. Don't worry."

Gina wasn't entirely sure what he meant by that. She didn't dislike Paul, but she felt he paid way too much attention to her. He also showed no respect for her marriage. A marriage that had lasted decades. She felt he obviously had some type of hidden agenda. Was she the object of that agenda?

After a long day, Trevor and Gina walked up to the house for dinner. As they entered the kitchen, Trevor unloaded. "I don't like that guy Paul. He was blatantly flirting with you, with me standing there. Did you catch that? What is he doing? Is he a fan boy, or some slimy guy who's after my wife?"

Gina put her arm around Trevor. "Baby, you know I only love you. There is nothing he could do to change that. I agree. He has a flirty nature and said some very inappropriate things. I don't take it seriously, and you shouldn't either. Let's eat and go play, Okay? Feel better?"

Trevor smiled. "Anytime you want a playdate, I'm excited."

The next day, Tommy Whelan dropped into the studio with news from the label. "Listen, Brown Fence wants you to deliver the fifth album you are committed to in six months. We need to have it wrapped up by March. April and May we iron out logistics for a tour, then you tour for the last time June, July, and part of August."

Gina stopped him. "Tommy, it can only be into early August. Trevor and I have to take

Roxy back to college. Sorry, but our daughter takes priority."

Skip chimed in. "No worries, Gina. We'll factor that in. Sounds like Tommy has a plan. We're good to go."

Rio was ambivalent about the proposed recording schedule. "I really can't wait until we do our own thing. This is such a grind and it's for someone else who sneaked in an aggravating clause. It makes them more money off our backs. I hate it. I want Perfection to be a leader in music and recording."

Ian piped up. "Look, I can do without the touring, but this commitment has got us. I would rather be with my family."

Trevor said, "Well we have a good week before we start this nonsense. We should have a party—band and crew only—to celebrate the last and final album with Brown Fence. Everyone in?"

Gina looked nervous. "It's not turning into a frat party. At least two of you need to stay away from alcohol. Having a family party would be great, lots of food and music that's not ours."

The ladies of Perfection managed all the food. Jae cooked Korean dishes. Lisa baked pies and mac and cheese. Gina brought lobsters, clams, and oysters and made some of her Italian dishes. Marisol's Mexican food was on point. Band, road crew, Skip and his wife, and Tommy and his family were going to be there. But should they invite Paul Ryan? He seemed to be part of the band now. Gina decided yes, to prove to him that she and Trevor were a happy couple.

The whole Perfection family was there and told a lot of fun stories, recalling the early days. They served alcohol, margaritas, wine, and beer.

But Trevor and Rio did not touch anything. Trevor was aware of being watched by Paul Ryan. He knew he was looking for a slip up. It's not that there wasn't a joint or two lit up. There was. That never seemed to be an issue for anyone, not even Gina who smoked occasionally to relax.

Paul Ryan still made Gina a bit nervous. He sat with the ladies through-out the evening, telling them PR nightmare stories—no names, just events. It ended up being a good time for everyone. Jae, Lisa, and Gina sat back and enjoyed the ambiance of the day.

October 1999 would be the final recording session for Brown Fence and the band practiced for hours on end. Trevor and Gina were trying to get the vocals and the lyrics to fit the songs. Sometimes rewrites were required. The band practiced tirelessly as they were heading into November but took a break for Thanksgiving. Roxanne came home to enjoy the holiday with her parents and brought her roommate, Sophie.

Sophie was a bit overwhelmed to be in the McNaughtons' home—after all, they were rock stars. They kept it family. Rio played the piano, and they all sang songs, covering other artists, not just their own stuff. Roxy returned to school and Gina was glad Sophie kept her company on the five-hour drive.

Perfection was still working on arrangements and reworking lyrics. The songwriting seemed easier because they knew after this the entire band would own everything. The holidays had the band in high spir-its. Roxanne would return home for a three week break at Christmas. Christmas in California was different than New York. Gina decorated the house by herself. She felt it got her more in the spirit of Christmas. This year would be low-key. Christmas Eve at Rio and Jae's and Christmas dinner at the McNaughtons. Franny and Mario wanted to come out, but they just couldn't make it work.

Aunt Deidre and Uncle Tony arrived at Rio and Jae's house in high spirits and with lots of gifts. Aunt Deidre could see that marriage had settled Rio. Roxanne had fun seeing all her friends from high school and spending time with her father. She loved him and enjoyed listening to him play his guitar. She kept a watchful eye over him also. Roxy's parents were proud she maintained a 3.97 grade point average in her freshman year. Roxanne headed to a friend's New Year's party, giving her parents a night alone.

Trevor and Gina were so spent from writing and recording they felt they needed quality time together. They dressed in sweats, ate fast food in their bedroom, and enjoyed having the house to themselves. They lit a fire, brought in a bunch of comforters, and looked at the Pacific Ocean from their living room. It was a romantic evening, one they needed. They enjoyed kissing and holding each other and talked about their past. Gina loved telling Trevor how she fell in love with him the first minute she saw him, and when he touched her back that night, when she ran into him, she knew right then no other man could ever match the love she had for him.

They made slow, joyful love by the fire. The next day Gina remembered what she loved about New Year's Day—college football games. She had all the TVs in the house tuned to the games. Maybe one year Stanford would play, and they would go watch Roxanne cheer.

Roxanne asked her parents if they would come to Stanford for her birthday in March. Trevor and Gina were thrilled she wanted to spend her day with them. They should be almost done with recording the album by then.

They had four of the seven songs recorded. Two of the songs featured Gina's lead vocals. It took several weeks of practice, recording, and rerecording to get them to Gina's satisfaction. She wanted Trevor to harmonize with her. By the end of February, the album was a wrap. The label would have to sign off on the album and choose which songs to release first. The band had one more video that had to be rushed to production before the release party. Perfection didn't care. They wanted to be done with Brown Fence.

The label gave Perfection a bonus for finishing the album a month ahead of schedule. The release party was scheduled for March 1, 2000 at a new hot club, Black Book on Sunset. The band was relieved this would be the final album release party where someone else pulled the strings. Fans and press gathered outside the venue and the band graciously waved to the cameras and signed autographs. When Gina and Trevor walked in and saw Skip and Tommy with their wives, they started to relax. Gina surveyed the room and saw Paul Ryan at the bar. She would avoid him as much as possible. After spending quiet holidays with her husband and daughter, she felt her life was back on track, wasn't it? Trevor never left Gina's side. He had also spotted Paul Ryan, watching them, waiting for some kind of big faux paus on the McNaughtons' part. Even if they had an issue, they were seasoned performers, and would never bring it to the public eye. After all, that's what Gina did every time Trevor would fall back into substance abuse. She learned to hide it.

Rio and Jae walked in and came over to Trevor and Gina. Rio whispered, "I see our friend Paul Ryan is at the bar. I don't trust him. I also don't like the attention he pays to Gina. It's creepy. I want very little to do with him, other than what I promised to do. After this tour, we should get rid of him."

Trevor looked over. "No complaints from me. I think he wants my wife."

Gina chirped up. "That won't happen."

Ian and Lisa came in very happy that this was the last album release party they would need to attend. Jeff arrived with the same girl he had been seen with for a year or so. They all stood around waiting for presentations. Their video played on a loop, their hardest rock song yet. Gina went to the bar to get herself a martini. As she turned to leave, she bumped into Paul Ryan.

"I guess it makes sense our PR guy is here. So, are you working, or are you just having a good time?" Gina was a bit sarcastic.

"A little of both. You look amazing tonight, as always. Where's your husband?" Paul questioned.

"Paul, please don't. Your comments always make me feel there is something behind them. You're a very handsome man. I'm sure you have many opportunities. There are ladies here who would love your attention. I am a happily married woman. Direct your comments to someone who may find it complimentary."

Paul Ryan did not back off easily. "But none of them are Gina McNaughton, are they? There's only one."

Trevor had been watching the exchange from across the room and made his way through the crowd to Gina's side. He knew Paul was playing some kind of game. "Thank you for watching over my wife, but I can take over. Looks like a lotta females roaming around. I'm sure you could find someone who would like your attention."

Trevor led Gina away by the arm. "That guy is really trying to insert himself into your life and our marriage. Just like you said Brian was. Just so you know, Brian is here. I didn't invite him. I don't know how he got in."

Gina became terrified. "Trevor, I want to leave now. I don't want to see him. Please babe, for me, can we go?"

Trevor lifted her face to his. "Of course, if that makes you feel better, let's go."

Paul Ryan was watching. As they were almost to the door, Rio came running up to Gina. "Guess who's here. Lucky Charms. You going to give him the business, Gina?"

Gina felt sick. "Rio, I need to go. I don't want to see that weasel."

Lurking at the bar, Brian Mayfield saw his old friend and that wife of his. He had a plan, and he was going to put it in motion.

SURPRISES AT STANFORD

THE NEXT DAY, Gina and Trevor made the five-hour drive to Stanford to celebrate Roxy's birthday and stayed at a hotel close to the school. Roxanne looked older somehow, more mature. She asked her parents if she could bring a date to her birthday dinner. Who is this person their daughter was interested in? Roxy walked into the restaurant with Zach Allen, a handsome football player, muscular and blond like her dad. Trevor sat back and observed Roxy and Zach. Conversation flowed easily. They talked about the classes the kids were taking and Gina asked which position Zach played. Small talk. When dinner was over, Gina got teary. They were heading back home in the morning and wouldn't see Roxy again until the next semester break. During the ride back to the hotel, Trevor suddenly said, "That dude is having sex with our daughter."

Gina was shocked. "Babe? Are we those parents? We knew this would happen one day. I choose not to think about it. She has to make those adult decisions now."

Trevor sighed. "You're correct, but this is my daughter."

"Okay, Trev. Wow, let's not think of it, okay?" Gina was in disbelief of Trevor's reaction.

TOURING AND ITS ISSUES

ONCE BACK IN MONTECITO, Skip, Tommy, and Paul Ryan called a meeting with Gina to discuss the logistics of the tour. Perfection was the headliner for a three-band ticket.

When Gina walked in and saw the looks on their faces, she felt like she was being set up. "How bad is this tour schedule? The way you all look makes me think something's up. What is it?"

Paul Ryan started, "Brian Mayfield is saying things about you two." He looked right at Gina and continued. "Especially your husband. Are you sure you can trust him?"

That angered Gina. "What the fuck are you all talking about? Trevor and I have not been apart. This is bullshit that Mayfield is starting. I'm not listening to this. I know he's gunning for me. He will try to get to Trevor, but no, no it's not going to happen. I have security to keep him from going backstage. He will be removed."

Skip looked distressed. "Gina, he works for one of the bands you're touring with. We have no control. You will need to be diligent in making sure Trevor doesn't have the same issues he had before."

Gina was upset. "You mean the substances, the whiskey, cocaine, and Oxy? That's what you're worried about, right?"

Paul had to step in. "Gina, we don't want you to be upset. Trevor could fall off the cliff. Touring is his weak point."

"No Paul, you don't know my relationship or my husband. I have saved him four times. He promised me he would never do it again. He knows that he's out of chances. He wouldn't do it. The hell with all of you! You figure out the logistics. I'm out of this. Let me know when you have it done."

The three looked at each other. There was going to be a blow up. Just how was it going to go down?

By the time Gina got back to the house, she was having a panic attack. She knew there was some truth to what they said. She would protect Trevor. She had to or this would not end well.

Trevor was in the kitchen when she walked in and asked, "Hey babe. How did the meeting go?"

"Trevor, promise me you won't be using on this tour, please, please," she begged him.

Trevor looked confused. "What has you so panicked?"

"Brian. He is going to be on the tour with us. I can't get security to keep him away either."

Trevor tried to reassure her. "Don't think about Brian. It's getting you too worked up. Do you want me to look at their logistics?"

Gina was still in full panic mode. "Baby if you want to deal with them, be my guest. I hate them all right now. They don't trust you, or me in trying to protect you."

It was the beginning of April, and the tour dates were set. Brown Fence Records had secured the venues well in advance. They just didn't tell Perfection until April.

Brown Fence Records Presents

June 1 & 2	Jones Beach, Long Island
June 7	Boston
June 9	Philadelphia
June 15	Jacksonville, FL
June 17	Miami
June 22	Chicago
June 26	Green Bay
July 6	Lincoln, NE
July 13	Denver
July 21	Phoenix, AZ
July 28	Seattle
Aug 3	Los Angeles

Trevor protested that this tour was twelve cities and doing a two-night stint in New York. This was their last tour with Brown Fence and they were riding them. The only plus was the tour was going to be a homecoming in Long Island and end back home in Los Angeles. This would take so much out of Perfection. They wouldn't want to tour again for years.

When Trevor walked into the office, Skip, Tommy, and Paul Ryan were there. Trevor was pissed. "You know you have my wife in a full-blown panic attack right now. You're worried about me and all my substance abuse issues. You told her Brian Mayfield would be working on the show. Why would you do that? This tour is riding us, but it's our last for a while. If you have an issue with me, talk to me, not Gina."

Gina had been worked up and she had good cause to worry. Brian Mayfield and the stress of the tour could push Trevor over the edge. Gina panicked. *What will I do?* Save him again, even though Gina told him she wouldn't? Her heart said she would do whatever Trevor needed.

Gina contacted Mimi, her stylist, she asked her to check out what Claire Shipwell had in her studio. She needed at least twenty or thirty new outfits for touring, plus radio interviews, and the meet and greets before and after the show. She always brought the white crochet dress she was wearing the night she and Trevor met. She had to feel it, to wear it. It was also the one she wore in their iconic picture that people still used. With her wardrobe chosen, the packing had to begin. Even though she could buy whatever she needed on the road, Gina was meticulous about packing. She would also pack for Trevor. He never knew what to wear and through the years his wardrobe had expanded beyond faded jeans and T-shirts.

She called her family and told them she would love for them to be at the June first and second performances at Jones Beach. She had a nagging feeling about this tour and wanted her family around. The fan base in Long Island was loyal. That's where they started. People in New York remember them as their local band, who clawed their way to the top. Gina couldn't shake the feeling that something was coming, and it wasn't good.

Gina had her last luncheon with her Montecito Moms crew before leaving them for the whole summer. Trevor and Gina knew the house would be safe with Marisol there. They locked up the studio, which wasn't going to be used while they were away.

Since they were the headliners, the jet would have limited passengers—no groupies, no drug dealers. Although they occupied the majority of the plane, they couldn't control the other bands. Already seated, Gina saw Brian Mayfield board the plane, and had such a visceral reaction, she almost threw up. Trevor reminded her he couldn't hurt them. Skip and Paul Ryan sat with them, going over radio interviews that were set up in the New York market. Gina had no worries there. Those were her people, after all. Every city had at least two radio interviews and meet and greets. She disliked that part of touring, and this was a long tour, the final one that someone else had their hands in.

They landed at JFK. Gina and Trevor decided to stay at the band hotel, rather than the Ricci estate. Franny was not happy. She wanted to see her daughter for as long as she could. The band went right to their rooms, no partying for Perfection. Gina and Trevor settled into their room and collapsed on the bed.

Gina was exhausted. "You want room service tonight?'

"Just order me whatever, I'll eat it." They were so tired after dinner they fell asleep with their clothes on, a first for the couple.

The band and road crew started walking the outdoor arena. They needed more amps to fill the large area. Gina walked around the venue, knowing this was home. She saw the other two bands playing before them. The band members all expressed their gratitude to be on the same billing as Perfection. Gina said, "You're welcome. Make it great because you will be remembered playing here."

As she turned to leave, Brian Mayfield was standing right in front of her. "Well, it's GMac, Mrs. Trevor McNaughton. How are you? I got five stiches from your punch. You're a lady that shouldn't be fucked with." He walked on by.

Gina knew he was up to something. If only she could remove him from this tour. She thought of talking to the manager of the band he was working for, Night Magic. Give him a little background information on how much of a disruptive influence he could be to the band.

Later that day, the Ricci family met at the hotel. Everyone, including Serena and Frankie's now larger family of four children, Ant was in law school in Villanova, plus Aunt Deidre, and Uncle Tony were there. Mario reserved an entire restaurant so no one would bother them. They all enjoyed French cuisine with a specialty wine. Trevor sipped slowly on one glass to make Mario happy. Rio and Jae were very talkative, which was a blessing. Gina was on edge because of the Mayfield situation. Trevor felt his wife's uneasiness and tried to quelch her fears to no avail. Gina loved her family but didn't feel like small talk.

The night of the concert, Gina couldn't wait to get onstage. She opened with one of her songs, which amped up the crowd. Everyone was on their feet, singing along with the band. The next night was the same reaction.

Franny and Mario had seen their daughter perform early in her career and were mesmerized by what their daughter had become. They were proud she had also fit the role of wife and mother into her career. Their pride was overflowing. Mario told Franny, "I'm glad I gave her those eighteen months to make it."

Boston and Philadelphia were a blur, except the radio interviews. Gina had to make sure she said the right city when she claimed to be "so happy to be here."

Jacksonville and Miami were hot. Gina wore a tight mini dress. She didn't want to be the almost naked lady anymore. Paul Ryan was always right there at the end of the show, telling Gina how her sex appeal really enhances the show. He wanted to exploit that.

Gina nipped that thought in the bud. "I do enough. I don't need to raise my game, but thanks Paul."

OLD HABITS COME TO THE SURFACE

ONCE AT THE HOTEL Gina noticed Trevor was starting to show signs of being somewhat disconnected. He wasn't asking Gina for their regular playdates in the shower or otherwise. Gina asked Trevor if he was hungry.

"What G? I'm sorry I didn't hear you."

Gina sat next to him. "Trevor I asked if you were hungry. Baby you seem really out of it. What are you doing? Tell me now. I can't help you if we don't discuss this. You know Paul Ryan is waiting for you to make the big mistake. Please, be honest with me. Paul Ryan wants me to exploit my sexuality. Trevor, I need you."

He heard the last part of that conversation. "That guy wants my wife. He wants you. I see him. I should punch him out like you did to Brian."

Gina laser-focused on Trevor. "Brian has gotten to you, hasn't he? I should have killed him, Trevor, I think you are on something. Please tell me if I'm wrong or stop now. Baby, I can't help you if you don't tell me."

Trevor looked up. "Yeah, I'm hungry, order me anything. I'm going to tell Ryan to fuck off and leave my wife alone."

Gina teared up. "Trevor, I'm at a loss. Mayfield is fucking you up again. Fine. I'll order you something to eat."

Gina felt him slipping, she had a huge decision, was she or wasn't she going to save him. Again. Would future events dictate that decision?

Chicago and Green Bay were sold out. Meet and greets were with real fans, not chicks wanting to get photo ops with a band member. Gina felt that Paul Ryan was ready to exploit any misstep the band might find themselves in. Especially if it was Trevor McNaughton. Trevor was slipping and Gina knew it. She would try to hide it. Rio would see it, the other members might guess it, Paul Ryan would know it. The band was getting very tired. It was summer and they were in a different city every week. Paul made sure he took advantage of every PR situation, adding more work for the band. Gina was trying to keep Trevor close and not show signs of any addiction issues. Mayfield was hovering. How was he getting to Trevor?

Lincoln, Nebraska, was more reserved with smaller crowds, probably because they had been booked at the same time as the Nebraska Goldenrod Fair. Paul arranged for the band to do an unannounced promotional show, and there was a surprisingly large turnout with lots of requests for autographs. Gina's perception of his role was that he was supposed to clean up things, not give the band more work. But maybe that was his game. He wanted to see the McNaughtons' flaws start to appear. How was he assisting the band? It felt like he was working against them. Paul Ryan was working against the McNaughtons to separate them, maybe. Why hadn't Skip said anything? Didn't he see this? It was his idea to have Paul, but he was more of disruptive force. That went against his job description. Why would he? Poor Skip had no idea that Ryan set his sights for a big catch, Gina McNaughton. He wasn't really interested in doing their public relations.

By the time they finished the Denver and Phoenix shows, everyone in the band was showing signs of fatigue. People think touring is one big party. Sometimes it is when you just start out. Everything is out there for the taking—drugs, women, parties all night long. Perfection was dragging to the finish line. Gina kept seeing Brian Mayfield, backstage, around the venue, at the hotel, he seemed to be everywhere Perfection would be. She told security he was not allowed in the dressing rooms or anywhere near the stage. If there was a situation, Gina was to be told immediately.

Trevor once again seemed out of it. Was it touring fatigue, or had he started back on all his favorite substances? He would fall asleep backstage, in the dressing room, and in the car on the way back to the hotel. He was dropping weight. Happy one minute and pissed off the next. Gina knew at this point he was using and Brian Mayfield was his dealer. Even with Gina's persistence of having him away from the band, he slithered in. The only worse thing that Trevor could do was to cheat or be in a comprising situation with a woman. Gina's jealousy along with Trevor's substance abuse would send her over the edge.

One night backstage, Gina found some groupie trying to force herself on him. He was oblivious. Gina pulled the skanky girl off her husband. "Get your disease-ridden hands off my husband. Security!!! Get this skank out of here. Trevor, what the fuck is going on? You didn't stop that girl from touching you. What the fuck Trev, I can't do this. You promised." Gina started to cry. Trevor was unsure what had actually happened. Gina was still in protection mode, she had to be, to save her marriage.

After the concert, Gina gripped Trevor as they were getting ready to go back to the hotel, they had to wait for a car to pick them up. Gina had Trevor and were getting ready to step outside the venue when she saw Paul Ryan. The last person she wanted to see already had some idea of what was going on with Trevor. Everyone did. Seeing Paul was like a nightmare she wanted to avoid. It was too late, he saw her.

Paul confronted Gina immediately. "I think Trevor is using again. Isn't this it? You told me you were done if he started again."

Gina looked at Paul in wonderment. "Why do I get the feeling you would love it if my marriage broke up? Why? You have been flirting with me from day one. If my husband is using, I'll deal with it ... I would appreciate it if you were more concerned with band issues than my marriage. Step back Paul."

They were booked at the hotel for two nights in Seattle. While Trevor was in the shower, Gina went through the pockets of every piece of clothing he had. She found a prescription bottle with the label torn off. Inside were about a dozen small white pills with OC printed on one side. There were also five small brown pills with smiley faces on them. In his wallet she found the corner of a clear plastic bag, tied around white powder—cocaine. How was he getting all this stuff?

Gina needed to address this with Trevor. He was expecting her to join him in the shower for playtime, but the shower was too small. Gina sat on the bed waiting.

Trevor was toweling off his hair. "I missed playtime. Do I need to schedule that through Paul Ryan?" He noticed the look on Gina's face was far from playful.

"What's this? It's Oxy, isn't it? How long have you been doing this? You're completely out of it half the time. You didn't even realize you had some slutty chick all over you the other night, did you? Well, I noticed. You made me cry. Your guitar playing is sloppy. It's this shit, Trevor. I told you I wouldn't pull you out again. Did Brian give it to you?"

Trevor was blindsided. "Since when do you go through my stuff? Gina, I can't take all the bullshit on this tour. I needed something that made me not give a shit. I promise, once we get to LA, I'll be fine."

Gina started crying. "You broke your promise to me. You don't need this. It's like heroin, you know that. Don't you love me enough to stop? I genuinely feel you love the drugs more than me."

Trevor sat next to her. "I know you're angry with me, but don't leave me Gina. Please I need you."

"Do you need me or the drugs? You're blacking out. Do you remember what you did? How do I know you're not cozying up to more groupies? I can't trust you right now. Paul Ryan knows you're using, so everyone knows. I should walk out now, but I love you too much. You're *my* drug that I can't quit, no matter what you do. We can't keep doing this."

"Gina, I want you so badly, come on."

"You can't use sex as the answer when things go bad. Get your shit together. We have tonight to finish, then get back home to LA, where you and I are going to have a big discussion about where our marriage goes from here."

Trevor looked scared. "Gina you're not going to leave me," he pleaded.

"Just get dressed, Trevor. We need to leave in twenty minutes to get to the arena. Then we go on stage in about ninety minutes. Get your shit together."

The concert that night went well but Rio had to pick up some of Trevor's leads. Rio knew something was going on, and he could tell how Gina was behaving it had to do with Trevor's sobriety.

After their encore, Paul pulled Gina to the side. "Why do you let him treat you like that? He's a mess and you clean it up. Why? You don't need a man who's needy, you need an equal."

Gina was not in the mood. "You've never been married, have you Paul? In marriage you make a commitment to that person with all their faults. Trevor has always been my equal, until he uses. I get the feeling that you would love me to just throw him away so you can step right in. Tell me I'm wrong."

"You're not wrong," he admitted.

"Paul don't do this. It's not fair and not very appropriate for our PR person to want to see our lead singer and guitarist fall on his face. Trevor is my life; don't you dare minimize our relationship or take advantage of my husband's faults. It's for me to determine how this shakes out. You actually disgust me Paul, waiting on the side for a tragedy to happen."

BEGGING
AND PLEADING

GINA WENT LOOKING FOR TREVOR. He wasn't backstage and he wasn't in their dressing room. She walked down by the other bands' dressing rooms and saw Brian Mayfield. Next to him was Trevor with three girls hanging on him who couldn't have been more than eighteen, dressed like two-dollar hookers.

She pushed through the people, grabbed Trevor by the hand, and spat over her shoulder, "If I ever see one of you whores touching my husband again, I'll make sure you never follow another band. Remember who I am. Gina McNaughton. And I swear anything I say can happen in an instant."

Trevor put up no resistance as she dragged him away. "I'm the most jealous person in the world. Why would you do something you know I abhor? You're so high, you don't recognize what you're doing. This is the second time I have found you around these backstage whores. How do I know if you did anything with them? You can't be so high you can't recognize what you're doing. Let me put you to bed. Please Trevor I'm begging you to stop."

Paul Ryan had found them in the hallway. He looked at her and mouthed, "Why do you put up with this?"

Trevor woke the next morning with no memory of anything that happened the night before.

Gina was at a breaking point. "We're going home. I can't have you blacking out. I am so close to not caring. I'm pissed as shit with you. What were you going to do with those backstage whores? Would you even remember? Cross the line Trevor and I don't know if I can forgive this time. Don't put me in that situation. I love you, stop please."

On the plane ride to Los Angeles, Trevor slept across Gina's lap. Paul sat next to her. "So, this is what you're married to. He looks like a junkie off the street, draped across the lap of a phenomenal woman. How much are you willing to take? I'll be waiting when it explodes."

"Shut the fuck up Paul. Please find somewhere else to park your ass. Make sure it is out of my sight."

Gina and Trevor took a limo to the Hollywood Hills house because it was close to the venue. She didn't want to take a two-hour drive with a half-conscious Trevor. He crashed on the bed immediately without even showering or eating. Gina went through his luggage. Two empty whiskey bottles. Drinking, cocaine, Oxy and whatever those smiley face pills were. This had made her husband a shell of who she had known for all those years. They had just celebrated twenty-one years together. Was that the expiration date of their marriage?

When Trevor woke up and wandered through the house, Gina was sitting on the couch with the bottles in front of her.

"So Oxy and coke aren't enough. You're drinking too. Are you fucking kidding me?" Gina started crying. "Are you *trying* to end our marriage? Is that what you're doing? Just tell me you want a divorce, for Christ's sake. Don't make me look like an ass. You owe me so much more."

Trevor looked at Gina through bloodshot eyes. "G, please don't cry. I don't want a divorce. I'll get help. I'm just trying to get through tonight, baby. I promise. I want to get help, I want to be the husband you deserve. I'm sorry. I'm really going to get help with you beside me helping me."

Gina was half crying, half yelling. "I've heard this all before, not too long ago. Your promises are stale. Show me something, anything to make me believe that you want help."

They were scheduled for interviews with three radio stations. Paul had set them up at the last minute. Gina believed he did it purposely, knowing how fragile Trevor was. Gina forced him into the shower. Alone. She had clean clothes laid out on the bed for him when he got out. She made him drink two cups of coffee before they left the house. He was somewhat sober.

Gina knew something was going to go wrong. She just didn't know how badly. Trevor seemed more like himself. "After this I'm going to get help, I swear."

"You need to do something. You are sabotaging our marriage and the band." They walked to the dressing room, dropped off their stage clothes, then returned to the stage to do a sound check. Rio pulled Gina over. "Listen, I'm ready to fill in on solos, but is Trevor that bad right now? I didn't realize we were watching him slide."

Gina let out all the emotion that had been building up and sobbed into Rio's chest. "I'm losing him. He can't make himself right. I warned him I couldn't take any more. I'm so torn. I don't know what's going to happen. Now I have to go out and make these people happy when I'm a miserable wreck. He's my everything, Rio."

Rio held her. "I know Gina. He needs help. I don't think you can hide this anymore. I love you; I'll be here for you and for whatever Trevor needs. Perfection needs him."

THE BIG MISTAKE
AND AFTERMATH

IN THE FEW MINUTES they had been talking, Trevor had already wandered off. Gina, still crying, went in search of her husband. She wandered down the hall and opened the door of each dressing room she passed. When she got to the last room on the right, the door was stuck. She shouldered it open and fell into the room. She gasped. Trevor was seated in an old recliner, head rolled back, eyes closed, with his pants around his ankles. There was a girl on her knees in front of him, her head bobbing up and down. Gina grabbed the girl's long hair and yanked her off Trevor. She held onto the fistful of hair and dragged the screaming girl out of the room and yelled for the security team. "*THROW THIS BITCH OUT NOW.*" Gina dropped the stoned girl to the ground and for good measure, aimed a kick at her ribs. "You scum. Just know that Gina McNaughton kicked the shit out of you. Remember that."

She turned and stomped back into the room. Trevor hadn't even bothered to pull up his pants before he passed out. "You piece of shit! Getting yourself a blow job from some half-wit scum. I hate you! I hate you, Trevor! How could you cheat on me like that?" Infuriated that he wasn't even responding, she leaned over him and slapped him across the face.

Gina looked around her for a way to release her wrath. Not stopping to think whose dressing room it may be, she picked up every item within reach and began smashing it on the floor. Bottles, lamps. She grabbed a metal trash can and hurled it at the mirror, causing shattered pieces to fall across the dressing table and onto the floor. Debris from her tirade rained down on Trevor's inert body.

By now a crowd had gathered outside of the dressing room, not knowing if or how they should intervene. Rio, Jae, Skip, and Tommy arrived and surveyed the destruction.

When Gina stopped to catch her breath, she noticed Rio standing in the doorway. "Rio I'm not going onstage. I can't. Do the concert without me. I don't care. I'm not going to perform with him," she cried as she waved her arm in Trevor's direction. "How could he do this to me? How Rio? You know who did this? Brian Mayfield. Let me find that motherfucker so I can kill him now. Destroying my marriage. Show me where he is."

Rio knew at once from Gina's state what had happened. She had caught Trevor cheating. Nothing else could cause this level of hysteria. He made his way into the dressing room, stepping over broken furniture and lifted Trevor up by his shirt. "Dude, what the hell? You don't shit where you eat. This stupid shit could break up the band. What the fuck, man? That's my cousin. All she ever did was love you, and you think a BJ from some stranger is worth everything you will lose?" Rio's anger level was rising to almost match Gina's, but it was also mixed with disappointment. "Do you even understand me? I'm not sure I can protect you now. Gina's gone off; she's not going to be reasonable. Trevor, I'm trying to protect you regarding Perfection. Gina has gone ballistic."

Trevor looked like a ghost, still unable to really understand what just transpired. Jae tried to comfort Gina who sat in the corner, curled up in a ball.

Skip walked over. "Gina. Gina listen. This is a nightmare, but there are tens of thousands of people waiting for you to sing. We can't cancel. Try to pull it in."

Gina, her face red and mascara-stained, answered him. "You don't really expect me to go out there. You should have my back Skip, what the hell, seriously? I won't take the stage with him. I don't want to look at him. Just say somebody got very sick. I can't go on. I won't. *Your* heart isn't shattered, mine is. You want to sing for me? Go ahead. Have you seen Trevor? He can't go onstage; he can't stand up and can't pull up his own fucking pants. Why aren't you dealing with that?"

Jae looked at Skip. "You can't really expect her to go onstage now."

Tommy came over and tried to help soothe Gina. "Gina, of course no one expects you to go onstage. You are very correct in the assumption that Trevor is unable to perform. I saw signs of him slipping but had no idea it got to be this bad. He always bounced back from one of his dives."

Gina begged, "Please get me a car. I want to go home to Montecito. I want to go home. Tommy, he bounced back because I always saved his ass. I probably would have helped him again but not after this."

Tommy looked around. "You guys need to call this now."

Skip was worried. "This will come out in hours."

Paul Ryan walked over and put his arm around her. "I understand you can't do this. We will make up a sickness and reschedule. I warned you, Gina, he doesn't deserve you."

Gina had so much rage. "Hey Paul, can you give me a minute, before you start hitting on me? My husband just cheated on me with some scum. I hate him but I do love him, please just stop, just stop." Then she went into uncontrollable sobs.

Jae turned to both of them. "You're not very compassionate. If you knew how much she loved him, you would just get her a car."

Rio pressed Skip. "I need your help with Trevor. Tommy is right. We need to postpone the concert. She doesn't want to see him. I can't make her go out there and do a show."

Jae looked at Rio. "She wants a car to take her to Montecito."

"Get her a fucking car now, before things get worse. Jae, would you go with her?"

"I was planning to. We need to get her out. I'll get her things." Jae was also upset.

Ian and Jeff were clueless. "What the hell is going on? Jeff and I were out by the soundboard. What happened?"

Rio looked at Paul Ryan. "Isn't your job to fix things? Tell them what happened." Paul Ryan was only too happy to tell Jeff and Ian that Trevor was deep into drugs and was found in a compromising position and Gina walked in on it.

Jeff asked, "Is she bad, Rio?"

"Jeff, you have known her for years. Do you think she's good?" Rio looked at Ian. "We've got to get him out of here. We can take him to the Hollywood Hills house. I guess I'll have to call Roxanne. Hopefully she will be able to get through to her father. She loves him and will want to help him. The faster I can get her help the better chance we have of saving him, for Gina, for Roxanne, and for all of us. I know she will have an idea."

Tommy was concerned for the band he had nurtured from the beginning. It's not like he hadn't seen this before, but he was worried about this particular situation. A husband-and-wife team is a moneymaker, until it isn't. Tommy told Rio to keep him in the loop.

Jae gathered up Gina's things and ushered her into the car. She spent the night, worried about what Gina might do to herself.

RENEGOTIATING LIFE

GINA SLEPT ON THE COUCH. The minute she sat up the next morning, her first words to Jae were, "I need moving boxes. I'm getting his shit out of my house. He can come and get them. Who do we call? I need this to happen now. I don't want to see his shit around this house."

Jae sadly thought *this had become very real and serious.* "Let's wait for Rio, okay?"

"No. I want him out now. That vision is etched into my brain. My beautiful husband, treating me like I'm nothing. With some sleazy whore. I guess I'm not enough. No worries, I'll find the boxes."

Marisol arrived and took her usual spot in the kitchen. She looked at Jae, "This is not good, right?"

Jae answered, "No Marisol, it's not good."

Jae got a call from Rio. "Gina's getting boxes, she wants him gone."

"Tell her to just hang on for a while. I'll get there as soon as I can. I may be here for the night." Rio spent the night waiting for Roxanne and wanted to be there when Trevor woke.

He had to tell him everything and what the next moves would be. He was nervous. It was his cousin who was hurt and his band that could be in danger. Rio took this moment very seriously; he did care immensely for

Trevor, he was family. He slept on the couch waiting for Trevor to wake and for Roxanne to come home. Hopefully, she had some plan.

RIO AND ROXANNE INTERVENE

TREVOR WOKE UP FROM HIS STUPOR, disoriented. He wanted to know where Gina was and why was he still in the Hollywood Hills house. He couldn't remember the events from last night.

"Trevor, man what the hell? What set you off in using Oxy, cocaine and whatever those other pills were? You're also drinking too much—two or three bottles of whiskey or whatever. You committed the worst sin against Gina last night. Some backstage chick gave you a blow job, you cheated dude. Gina found you. She trashed the place. She is furious and inconsolable. That woman of yours is insanely jealous. Trevor, this has to stop. You need help, some serious help. This isn't the dude I know. What happened man?"

Bits and pieces of the night before were starting to pop into his brain. "You mean that wasn't Gina?"

Rio looked at him in disbelief. "You're crazy, man. Your wife doesn't want to see you. She's packing up your stuff as we speak. She wants you out. If we don't fix this, there is no more Perfection. Do you realize that? I can't let you sabotage your marriage or the band. We need to get you help Trevor. Do you understand? I called Roxanne. I'm hoping she has some plan to fix this."

Trevor slumped on the couch and started to cry. He remembered Gina said she wouldn't pull him out again, but then she also said she would help him. Now he knew his wife wouldn't believe anything he said at this point. He was scared of losing her. He knew Paul Ryan was waiting for this exact situation to occur.

Rio called Jae and told her he had a limo going to LAX to pick up Roxanne. Skip showed up at the Hollywood Hills house to find out what was going on. He was nervous about the band, Trevor, and the last thing Gina told him—he didn't have her back. Redemption for Skip was to help get Trevor back from the abyss. Then put his marriage back together.

 Roxanne walked in the door forty-five minutes later. "Dad, what did you do? Uncle Rio, what happened? Is Mom okay?"

Rio told her everything and didn't hold back. "Roxanne, your father has been back on the Oxy, coke, and some weird ass pills, plus he's drinking a lot. He was really fucked up last night, out of it. Your mother walked into a dressing room; this is hard for me to tell you … some girl was giving your father a BJ when she walked in. Your mom trashed the place. She doesn't want to look at him. She wants him out of the house. You know your mom is very jealous. She's a mess; she loves your father, but she has drawn a line."

"Dad, you need help. If you get help, Mom might forgive you. You can't be like this. Don't you want your family? I know how much you love Mom, you need some serious help."

Trevor asked Roxanne, "You think she would take me back?"

Roxanne shook her head. "I know my mother. She loves you more than her own life. But Dad you cross Gina McNaughton, she's stubborn. Dad please you need real help. Like five months of help. I've heard about an alcohol, drug, and sex addiction program in Malibu. You are going to have to be 100 percent invested in getting better. You do realize that there will be a stage of you going through withdrawal, and I'm fairly sure we can't visit you until you pass that step."

Rio told Trevor to lay low in the Hollywood Hills house for a day or two before trying to talk to Gina. Rio held out some hope that Gina was upset and would at least talk to Trevor.

Roxanne shook her head. "She won't do it. She won't want to talk to him, especially if she wants him out. He shouldn't try to talk to her. She won't listen to any promise, apology or how much he loves her. Nothing my father could say would make it defensible. She won't even listen to me or you Uncle Rio. I know her."

Trevor was still a bit high but also weepy. "I need my wife. I want to tell her I love her. I want to see her before I go away. I know I can't see her until I get better. Please don't tell her about the rehab. She won't believe me unless I'm better."

Roxanne didn't know what to say. "You're asking me to lie to Mom? She's most likely a mess. You are her everything and you know how jealous she is. All she sees is you being messed up and with some random chick. Mom is seeing red. Dad you realize she still loves you; she's hurt."

Rio told her. "She's a mess, alright. I told you she wrecked backstage. We all know her jealousy issues."

Skip had been silently listening to the exchange of the family. Now he added, "This is a PR issue. I'll put Paul on it."

Rio looked at Skip. "This is what Paul Ryan was waiting for. He's been hitting on Gina from day one. I don't think that's a great idea. Skip, you should be keeping Ryan away from her. He has no business getting involved in a personal matter."

Skip insisted. "Rio we hired him to fix problems. This is a big one. Where do we say Trevor is for the next few months? Plus, talk of their split will come out. That's why we hired Paul."

Rio looked at Skip in a sideways manner. "I don't think Paul Ryan should be around my cousin. You need to be aware of what he is doing. End of discussion."

Roxanne said she would stay for a couple of days, until they could get Trevor into a program.

ALONE FOR THE FIRST TIME

MEANWHILE, BACK IN MONTECITO, Gina was crying and angry. She was a yo-yo of emotions—hating Trevor and missing the love of her life. Never had she felt these intense feelings toward her husband. Gina packed some of Trevor's clothes and toiletries. But not the two guitars he cherished. She knew he would want them and come to the house. She may be angry, but still loved him. She hid the fact that she was holding out hope that he would eventually come home.

With Roxanne at the house with Trevor, Rio took the two-hour drive home to Montecito. He was actually afraid to be around his cousin. Rio arrived at the house to pick up Jae. "Gina if you need anything, just call."

Gina's anger was palpable. "Tell that prick to come get his stuff. You asked if I needed anything, right? How about getting me that prick Mayfield? Then can you rewind time so none of this happened? No, you can't. There's nothing I need from you."

Rio agreed. "Okay, I will tell Trevor but are you sure you want to go that far? Packing his things is a bold step, Gina."

"What should I do? It's the only way," Gina sobbed. Her phone rang and she saw that it was Lisa. She knew she would have many calls like this. She wouldn't call her parents. She felt ashamed. Her parents truly loved

Trevor. They thought he was the perfect husband for their daughter. Now this. She would deal with them once it became public knowledge.

Jae and Rio left, and Gina walked around the house, still wearing her T-shirt and pajama pants. She listened to every sad song she could think of. The songs were on a reel-to-reel player, and it played in a loop. "Black," "Comfortably Numb," "Yesterday," "Nothing Compares 2 U," "One," "Everyone Hurts," "Alone Tonight," "Wish You Were Here," "Un-Break My Heart," "Call Me,", and along with a few other songs repeated for hours. Each time she thought of another sad song, she would add it. *What more could I have done to prevent this?* She blamed herself for not getting Trevor the proper help. She looked at all the pictures on the baby grand piano, and asked, *Why? How did this happen?* She continued to cry and wonder how her life had gotten so out of hand.

Gina was convinced Trevor was in a drugged state and had taken off with some girl, not understanding the consequences of what he had done. She could hire a private detective to find him, but she was afraid of what she would learn. If he took up with another woman, it would be over for sure. Maybe it was something else that she could hold out hope for them to reconcile. Gina went back and forth loving and hating Trevor.

The phone call Gina was dreading came. It was her parents. Franny shot the questions through the phone before Gina even said hello. "Gina! What's going on? We are hearing you and Trevor are breaking up. How did this happen? Princess, are you okay?"

Gina tried to hold in her sobs to no avail, it was her parents, she was completely honest. "He's addicted to pills and alcohol. I've saved him at least four times before this, but I can't do it this time. He went too far. There was a girl in the dressing room, doing ... something, I can't even tell you. It hurts bad."

Mario spoke from the extension in his office. "Gina, you love this man. One indiscretion isn't a reason to break up your marriage. Men sometimes don't think. If he has an addiction issue, it's worse. Don't throw away years of a happy marriage."

Gina couldn't believe her father. "Dad! He hurt me! Why would you take his side in this? I'm not able to function right now. I don't know life without him, and you think I should just forget about it. I protected him for years."

Franny tried to calm Gina. "I can tell you're a mess. It reminds me of when Trevor had to go back to Canada. Remember how much you loved him and missed him?"

Gina was irritated. "Mom, this is totally different. My daughter hasn't even called. I don't know where Trevor is—probably with some random slut."

Franny may not say the right things, but she knew her daughter was in tremendous pain. "I'm going to fly out. I'll be there tomorrow night."

"Mom, I'll let you know if I need you to come out. Right now, I don't want to see anyone. I'm broken and I don't know what my life looks like alone. Please, let me figure this out," Gina answered firmly.

Mario choked up. "Okay, Princess, but you're our daughter and we don't want to know you're in pain. If we can help—"

Gina was adamant. "Dad. Mom. Please give me space. I know you mean well. I just can't."

Gina spent days barely getting up off the couch. She refused to sleep in their bedroom. She didn't shower, that reminded her of the playdates Trevor and she had. Everywhere in that house marked a spot of their sexual playtimes. Her bedroom was a land mine of memories. Gina was on shaky ground trying to navigate the new normal of her husband gone. Marisol was worried she couldn't get her to eat, despite making her favorite foods. Marisol knew Jae would be making her daily visits, hopefully she could get her to eat something. Gina was feeling more sad than hurt.

Two days later, there was a knock on the door. Gina was so out of it she hadn't heard the gate open. Trevor showed up at the house, calling, "Gina, Gina please! I love you."

Gina stood in the doorway. "Get your shit and go. I can't look at you. All I see is that lowlife with her face in your lap. Get your shit and go."

Roxanne was waiting for Trevor outside the gate. She had begged her father not to go because he was still highly under the influence. Roxanne knew he would have taken something to take the edge off. The drug facility could admit Trevor the day after tomorrow. He insisted to see and talk to his wife. Roxanne didn't want her mother to see her, because she was lying to her, and Gina would know she was lying. Roxy would need to get a moving company to pick up his stuff and bring it to the Hills house and possibly pack some things for the drug facility.

Trevor got back in the car and told Roxanne he was heartbroken that Gina wouldn't see him. Now he knew he had to make his rehab a top priority. He was deathly afraid of Paul Ryan trying to sweep in to take his wife. He told Roxanne he was committed to getting better.

Two more weeks passed. Gina's moods swung from volatile—banging doors and drawers—to weepy, not bothering to wipe the snot off her face. She listened to Fiona Apple, Nina Simone, and Roy Orbison, which made her even sadder. She wrote her own lyrics, pouring pain and heartache onto the page. She wrote a song, "No Moon Tonight."

No Moon Tonight

How could life be so cruel to have me look at an empty sky,
No stars, no moon tonight. There's no shine on the Pacific
Tonight no shine since you went away. You and I would look at the
Moon, when at home or those private beaches we loved. Making love
At a moonlit sky. No there's no Moon tonight

Chorus
How can it be that I miss you beside me, tell me that you miss me. We
made a mistake, can you and I make it right? I thought our love was like
The Moon in the sky never ending always

there, but there's no Moon tonight.
Please tell me you love me and this was a scare.
The nights are lonely and dark
When you are not there. Both making mistakes
we wish we could take back.
The nights are empty, I still stop and stare.
When will the sky once again be bright because
without you, I look at an empty
Sky devoid of light and you are not there for there's no Moon tonight

Chorus
So please think about me, I'm missing you, wait-
ing and wanting to hold you
I'm sorry for all that I did, please forgive me.
No Moon tonight. But if you
Give me a chance I'll light the sky with the sweet-
est love. You know we are
Meant to be, we have always known our love was endless like the
Moon and the stars. I'll wait but still there's no Moon tonight.

Chorus
I love you, remember always how much I love and need you,
please bring the Moon back on one of these nights.

Jae visited Gina every day. Rio was having a hard time lying to Gina and his own wife. He knew where Trevor was, and Gina could read him like she did Roxanne. On one visit Gina was sitting on the couch with a pile of Valium and bottles of wine. She finished two bottles that Jae noticed and started the third. She was listening to "Comfortably Numb." Numbing herself is how she dealt with her pain. Jae asked, "How many of those pills did you take? Plus, with the wine, you are going to make yourself sick. I need you to stop." Jae started to put the pills back in the vile.

Gina stopped her. "You want me to feel this pain? A pain that doesn't stop. Look around. All I see is him. Together, happy. What should I do? This pain is excruciating. I hate what he did. I always knew of his demons. I can't. It's too much. Tell me how I go on when he has been my entire adult life." Gina started to break down, Jae was her consoler along with Marisol. Jae urged her to take a shower, she smelled badly. Gina went upstairs to Roxanne's room to shower. Marisol made her some soup, hoping they could get her to eat something. She tried to eat a bit to make them happy. Gina was prepared for her lonesome evenings; Jae went home to Rio and Marisol went back to her apartment. Gina was left to feel the pain. She wondered where her daughter was. Skip also made himself scarce. Lisa would check in and always tell her, "Trevor is trying to get himself together. He will be back." Gina knew she would never be anything but positive.

AN UNWANTED INTRUSION

GINA HAD BEEN LIVING WITH THE PAIN for a month. She felt she showered off some of the deep pain she was feeling, but not really. Early the next morning, she finally gathered enough energy to take a walk on the beach. She made her way slowly along the edge of the surf. Still thinking of Trevor and their walks on all the beaches they had visited. Sweet walks, loving walks that ended in marvelous lovemaking. The tears welled up in her eyes thinking about her husband. Today she felt both hurt and anger. How could Trevor do what he did? Gina continued on her walk until she realized someone had stopped in front of her. Paul Ryan. Was he the catalyst that pushed Trevor over the edge, along with Brian Mayfield the supplier?

Gina was startled. "This is a private beach; how did you get here?"

Paul proudly told her, "I'm renting a house, three doors down. We're neighbors."

Gina didn't care. "Paul, you need to stop. I'm not in any mood for your advances. So you rented a house close to me. It makes me think you may have some ideas that might not benefit you. It's actually weird that you have done that knowing the situation. Why Paul? Why?"

Gina continued walking. Paul followed her and asked, "How are you doing? Really. Have you kicked him out? It's been over a month Gina."

BETH PELLINO-DUDZIC

Gina stopped. She couldn't believe the gall. "Paul, you are our PR adviser. Stick to your job and stay out of my private business. It's starting to leak out to the press. What are you doing to clean that up? I'm shattered, Paul. I need to have space. Please respect that."

Gina turned around and headed back to her house. She walked in the kitchen door and sat down at the counter with Marisol. Gina grabbed a cup of coffee. "Marisol do you mind making me a piece of toast?"

"Mrs. Gina I'm glad you want something to eat. I thought your walk on the beach would make you feel better. The salt air, the calmness of the waves."

Gina was aggravated. "I started my walk and who do I see? Paul Ryan. He rented a house three doors away. He is up to something and I don't like it. I think he believes that he has an opportunity to get to me. I am beginning to hate men."

She wondered why Roxanne didn't reach out to her. She deduced that Trevor got to her. Maybe she had met his new girlfriend. Gina's head started to spin with wild ideas. All she knew was that her daughter was MIA. Gina knew she was always close to him, so the hurt doubled by not hearing from her. She wanted to call but she was afraid. What would she tell her? Gina didn't want the truth right now.

Marisol had the kitchen television turned on as always and the morning news hosts were droning on. News of the split was starting to slowly make its way into the media. Stories started to circulate about Gina's backstage destruction. She didn't care.

Her friends in Montecito showed her love by checking on her. They came as a group with tea sandwiches and scones and listened to Gina recall that night's events. She tried not to cry as she did. Karen told her to let her emotions out. All the ladies gave her hugs and told her she would be in a better place soon. The Montecito Moms left the house worried about their famous friend. They could tell Gina was not in a satisfactory condition. Everyone decided that they would take turns calling Gina and stopping by. A check in, the MMM knew that their friend was in pain. Every lady wished they could pull her out of it, but nobody could make her feel better. She was alone for the first time in decades. The only time Gina had lived alone was for those few months she lived in the carriage house before she met Trevor. Her parents thought she was disruptive when she and Rio started their first band, Vision Skye. Coming in at all hours of the morning prompted her parents to let her live in the carriage house. That was it, a few months. Then one Trevor McNaughton entered her life

Everywhere she looked she saw *him*. Every family picture. Every award. Roxanne's graduation pictures on their piano showed their love for each other. Her friend Karen and her husband, Charles, were both painters. Charles (everyone called him Chip) and Karen had presented Gina and Trevor with an oil painting of their iconic photo. The four feet wide painting hung in a prominent place in their living room. It seemed like it followed her. She had to look at it every day. She thought about taking it down but wasn't ready.

Gina wondered if she should see a lawyer. *No, not ready.*

GINA'S UNWANTED VISITOR

ABOUT A WEEK AFTER HER ENCOUNTER with Paul, he showed up at the back door with a bottle of wine.

Gina was annoyed he had the nerve to show up at her house. What was this guy pulling? "Paul, I asked you to give me space. A week isn't exactly the kind of space I need. You don't give up do you? What's that, a bottle of wine? Really. If you had a joint, I might like that better." Gina leaned on the doorframe.

Paul was a bit cocky. "Who says I don't? Come on Gina I come with no expectations. Just a bit of company. I'm sure you are lonely in the evenings. Doesn't Jae go home at night to be with Rio?"

Gina sighed, "Wow, okay Paul, don't know how you would know that. Are you spying on me somehow? It's creepy. Fine Paul, come in, but I'm not good company. I don't know where Trevor is. It's like he vanished. That scares me."

Paul started searching for glasses. "Have you talked to a lawyer yet? I know a good one." He found two wine glasses and set them on the counter.

"Paul, I just told you, I have no idea where Trevor is. How could I possibly serve him divorce papers? Not to mention, I'm not ready to walk down that road. Can we light up that joint, please?" Gina took the joint from Paul and started smoking it.

Paul asked, "Do you like the wine?"

Gina was exasperated. "Ugh, it's fine, Paul. Why do I feel that you are really working me? I told you I wasn't interested, and I am still in love with Trevor. I'm not interested in what you think about that. But seriously, why don't you stop? You are being more than flirty. Are you trying to come on to me? Did you honestly think that I would be so distraught that I would sleep with you? Yeah, no, not going to happen."

Paul had no shame. "Because I am trying to work you. Why do you think I took Perfection on? To get closer to you. Okay I said it. I didn't think you and your husband would have a falling out."

"So why take on Perfection to get close to me? If my marriage was all good and healthy, what would be the point to getting close to me? Paul that makes no sense. Did you have anything to do with getting my husband addicted again? Please tell me now before I find out some other way." Gina was amazed by his bravado.

Paul didn't respond so Gina continued. "It's not a falling out. It's more like a total shattering of my heart. I feel like part of me died and I'm mourning my marriage. You can't possibly understand that, can you?"

They finished the bottle and Paul left, telling Gina on his way out the door, "I'll give you some space now." Paul Ryan was playing the long game.

TURQUOISE SKYE REHAB, VISITING TREVOR

TREVOR WENT THROUGH SEVEN DAYS of heavy withdrawal at the Turquoise Skye Malibu Rehabilitation Clinic. He was not allowed visitors until he went through the horrors of the first two weeks, possibly three of withdrawals. Roxanne called the psychiatrist every day to check on her father's progress. She was told he had a difficult time kicking the alcohol and drugs, but it looked like he was past the worst.

Roxanne asked when she could come see her father and was told—at this point anytime, it might help him to have visitors. The doctor told her Trevor was constantly asking for his wife. They also told her they thought he hallucinated her during withdrawals. He was constantly telling the doctors she was there and asked why she did not come every day. They suggested it would be a good idea if she came to visit him.

Roxanne was adamant. "No, that can't happen yet. I want to see how strong he is first. If his withdrawal was so bad he hallucinated my mother, he is not ready for her."

Roxanne called her Uncle Rio. "Dad is allowed visitors now. Can you come with me, please? They said his withdrawals were bad and he even hallucinated Mom was there. I have no idea what condition I am going to see him in."

Rio wanted to check his progress. "Of course, Roxy. What day? Make sure your mother has no idea."

Roxanne winced. "He's been asking for her, but I know she won't go. I don't think it's a good idea at this point until he is stronger. Remember he wanted to be clean before he saw her."

Two days later, Rio picked Roxy up from LAX and drove her to the clinic.

Rio's guilt kicked in. "Roxy, I'm really uncomfortable keeping all this from your mother. She's in a lot of pain. She also asked why you haven't reached out to her. You should call her."

Roxanne shook her head. "No, Uncle Rio. I can't. I can't lie to her face or even on the phone. She would know. I'd rather she be mad at me. She will understand when Dad is better."

Rio started to get pissed. "Your mother is a mess. And that guy, that opportunist Paul Ryan, is trying to cozy up to her. I don't think Gina is playing his game. But let's see how your dad is first."

The facility looked like a spa, relaxing and sedate. It resembled a first-class hotel or an island resort more than a health facility. The entry featured a waterfall installation and marble floors. The subtle logo on the facing wall looked like a soft blue wave. Lights sparkled from the chandelier. The nurses' station looked more like a hotel concierge desk. Melodic wind chimes tinkled softly.

Roxanne and Rio didn't know where they should go to ask for Trevor. A nurse walked by in tropical print scrubs. "You look lost. Can I help you?"

Rio spoke up. "We're looking for Trevor McNaughton's room."

The nurse walked them to the nurses' station. After checking the approved visitors list and their ID, the receptionist directed them, "Down the hall. Make a right. He's in Room 148."

Rio turned around, "I have to tell you this gives the appearance of a first-class hotel not a rehab facility."

The nurse smiled. "Many of our patients find it more helpful if they feel they are on vacation and not in a facility. It helps with morale, plus a quicker recovery. We have been very successful."

The hallway led past a reflection pond. Trevor was on Harbor Blue wing, Room 148.

Rio and Roxanne were nervous, not knowing what they would be walking into. Trevor was sitting on the bed in old jeans and a T-shirt, playing the acoustic guitar that Gina bought him so many years ago.

Roxanne spoke first, from the doorway. "Hi, Dad. Are you doing okay?"

She walked in and gave her father a huge hug and kiss. She had missed him and their conversations.

He looked sad and withdrawn. "Roxanne, I love you for coming. Oh, Rio, you came too. I'm glad I can have visitors now. But I know Gina was here."

Roxanne looked concerned. "Dad, Mom wasn't here. I think you hallucinated her during your detox. You said you didn't want her to know until you were clean. Don't you remember?"

Trevor looked confused. "She was wearing a white satin nightgown. She told me she loved me and to get better. She misses me and forgives me."

Roxanne started to tear up. "Dad, Mom wasn't here, but I think she feels all those things. Remember you still have some really important work ahead of you." Roxanne was feeling the weight of her parents' situation.

Rio had seen Trevor when he was using but this was something different. "Hey, Trev I hear you're over the worst. But seriously, where's your head at bro? You can do this correct? We all want you ready to be that superstar guitarist and singer."

"I know I have to be here, but I want to go home and be with my wife. I know she misses me and wants me home; she told me."

Rio leveled with him. "Trev, do you know what you did? Roxanne is once again correct, you dreamt this or something. Gina wouldn't come here. She's still mad, but she's also extremely sad, and I'm sure she misses you. But she won't admit it. Your wife is stubborn."

Trevor started choking up. "I was really fucked up. I was really high, and some girl came in. I don't remember what happened. I know it had to be something really wrong if Gina is that mad at me."

Roxanne started to cry. "Dad, you committed the most horrible transgression against Mom. Some girl … I can't even say it."

Rio flatly said, "Trev man, some girl came in and gave you a BJ and Gina caught you. She went fucking nuts. She destroyed the entire dressing room. She won't go onstage with you. We have to fix this, or we won't have a band and you won't have a wife. So, I need you to work real hard at getting well. I believe Gina may need that time to figure out her feelings and I know from Jae she feels her life has stopped. You have been together most of your adult life. Give it time Trevor. I have Jae watching over her."

Trevor became very quiet. "I know I have a lot of work to do. The doctors said it's a process. Before I see her, I want to be me, not this half person I feel I am now. I still want to be her husband. I love her. Does she still love me? She has kept me from those demons for years, but I messed up bad this time. She knew I was falling and told me to stop. I couldn't. I failed my family."

Roxanne started to cry. "Dad, I haven't seen her. I can't. At some point she will know I'm lying to her about knowing where you are. She thinks you are with some girl. Uncle Rio is right. She's mad. I know that somewhere underneath all that anger she still loves you. You need to be rid of all these addictions. Let's get you there and we will fix it with Mom. It's a deal, right?"

Rio sat down next to Trevor. "Hey man, I don't know if this helps, but Jae goes over every day, and Gina cries and plays sad music. She's mourning your marriage. Jae said she listens to the music and strokes your pictures. Your life is all over the house. She hasn't taken them down, so that's hopeful. She loves you, however, your wife makes it so difficult to be compassionate when she's angry. I'm like Roxanne. I can't be around her for a long time. She can read me. It's some weird talent she has reading people. She would know I'm lying to her about something. She would connect it with you since everything in her world is you."

Roxanne had gathered some strength from her crying. "I need you to be strong. You have four months to go. Can you do this? Please say yes. I want our family back together. It's been interesting spending my whole life with two people who really love each other. A lot of people don't have that."

Trevor was shaken. "Will she wait for me? Did she get divorce papers? I need to have some type of hope. Do we know what Paul Ryan is doing? She cries listening to music? She misses me?"

Rio assured him. "She hasn't had papers drawn up. But she might. She doesn't know where you are. I'm not sure a lawyer could actually help her, since you both own everything jointly. She would need to negotiate a settlement. I'll try to keep her from making any moves with a lawyer. We are lying to her. I'm doing it for you Trevor. I believe you can get better, and then we can get the band working again and most importantly put your marriage back together. This is the hardest thing you will probably do in your life, but you need to do this for your entire future. And, hey remember I'm lying to my wife also. She is too close to Gina."

A nurse knocked on the door. "It's time for group therapy, Mr. McNaughton."

Roxanne hugged her dad. "Daddy, I'll be back in a week. You know you can call me anytime if you need me. Here's my number in case you forgot it."

Rio hugged Trevor too. "Bro, I'm counting on you. We need you. You can call me on this number. Jae doesn't know that I have this other phone. It's for Perfection business but mostly for you to call me on."

Rio and Roxanne left. Trevor followed them out the door, turned right, and slowly walked down the hall to group, his eyes welled with tears.

Rio told Roxanne, "That was hard as fuck." It was about to get harder for Rio.

His phone rang. It was Aunt Franny. "Rio, I need to know what's really going on. Where is Trevor? Roxanne and you must know where he is. You're keeping a secret. How bad is he? I'm going to fly out and see him, so just tell me. You know I can find out other ways. This would be so much easier."

Rio was shocked by the call. "Aunt Franny, he's very fragile. I am not sure you want to see him like this. Gina hates him right now."

"I spoke with Princess. I can't get through to her. She's a total disaster. I want to see Trevor. Just tell me where he is. I have seen him broken when they lost their babies. I can handle it."

"Aunt Franny, we are all lying to Gina about Trevor. Do you want to be part of that? Gina won't forgive any of us."

"I can handle Princess. She can be mad at me for a while."

Rio gave her the details and told her she needed to clear it with the head of the facility before visiting.

Trevor walked into the group therapy room where everyone discussed how they got addicted and what life would look like after their treatment. Trevor hadn't shared the origins of addiction yet. He knew this time he would have to open up. He looked around the room and noticed some A-list celebrities. Others were CEOs and high-level attorneys. He wasn't the only known person in the room. They started the session with the Serenity Prayer, nothing religious, just a statement for going through recovery.

The therapist started by asking Trevor to share. He explained that his mother died when he was thirteen and he started drinking and doing drugs shortly after. He told the group that both he and his father tried grief counseling, but his father was unable to continue. He had never shared that with Gina. He started stealing alcohol, drinking a bottle or two a day for four or five years, then started doing drugs. He stopped going to school and was in and out of juvenile detention. Sometimes his father saved him, other times he left him there. He said music was his saving grace. At that point he wanted to explore the music world, which helped him get straight. Knowing he was one drink away from his demons. He quickly shifted to Gina—how he fell in love with her immediately and they truly had a beautiful love story in spite of his demons. He also told the group that she pulled him out of his addictions many times and this time she refused. He understood why and was going to get clean because he loved her that much. After he shared, he broke down. The therapist in charge told him it was appropriate for him to go back to his room.

LIFE IN MONTECITO
ALONE

IN MONTECITO, five weeks after the blowup, Gina was still extremely depressed. She hated Trevor, but still loved him. Where was her daughter? Jae came over every day and would ask. Marisol, "Did Gina eat? Did she shower? Most importantly, did she listen?"

Marisol shook her head, "I am so sad for her. I don't know what to do."

Everyone was bombarding her with advice. Her friends, Jessica and Bekki from the MMM, were married to lawyers. Their advice offered a glimpse into what she could expect. She realized that a divorce would be extremely complicated because of all the band business, their finances, the houses. It wasn't going to be as simple as everyone thought. She couldn't have paperwork drawn up, that was clear. Her head filled with all the torrid thoughts that came across her brain about what Trevor could be doing.

Skip and Tommy stopped by and said there was some band business they needed to discuss with her. Skip was nervous broaching the subject with her, because she was still hostile. She had commented to Skip that he didn't have her back. He wasn't sure of the reception he would receive. Tommy was there for Gina after her meltdown. She felt safe with him.

Gina opened the door and invited them in. She was sarcastic, "What Skip, this is Perfection business. Are we sure we still have a band? Because

I have no idea where Trevor is, and I don't plan on recording with him or ever going onstage with him."

Skip treaded lightly. "Gina, we can work around this if necessary. The band has over twenty songs in the vault. Let's not put an end to things quite yet. You're hurt. We all understand. Just take time. You know there are bands that hate each other, and they record separately, that could be a possibility."

Tommy tried to be less impersonal. "Gina, I know you feel lost right now. We don't need to think about recording right now or how we manage it. I am more concerned with you, Gina McNaughton, and how your life is at this moment. To be honest, Gina, I don't believe Trevor is doing anything harmful to your marriage. I believe he feels ashamed and is hiding until things aren't so public. He loves you. When he is ready, he will come to you. I sincerely believe that."

Gina gave Skip one of her narrow stares as a warning. "Yeah, okay. If my life falls apart so do all of yours. How's that Skip? I can't think about it now. Thank you, Tommy, for your inspirational words. I only wished I believe like you."

Skip backed off totally. "Okay, Gina. I'll check in with you in a bit. Hey, has Paul Ryan talked to you about PR issues?"

Gina laughed. "No, not about PR but how he would like to be in my life, in my pants, in my bed. You realize he has been actively pursuing me, even before Trevor, well, Trevor did what he did. It's not in his job purview is it, to try and get in my pants?"

"Gina, no one is stronger than you. I know you don't believe it right now. If his advances are bothering you, tell him. Look, I have to go. I'll check in with you in a week or so." Even Skip did not feel comfortable lying to Gina McNaughton. She could sniff you out when something didn't seem right.

Tommy lingered for a moment. "Gina, take this time and reflect on all the beautiful memories you have with Trevor. I can't fathom you throwing them away. Take your time Gina, and if you need to talk, I'm happy to drive up. Maybe I'll bring Anne with me. You let me know. I should go now so Skip doesn't get too out of sorts. He's afraid of you." Gina did have some thinking to do. What Tommy said was hopeful she wished it was true. She clung to the negative thoughts. Gina closed the door behind them.

Paul frequently found an excuse to show up with takeout. He knocked on the back door and Gina held the door to block his entry, "Hey Gina, I thought you might like to share some dinner with me. I brought food, the wine and even have a joint."

Gina was too tired, "You just keep coming, don't you? I'm a little hungry so come in. I want that joint first."

Paul looked at her from head to toe. "You look like a wreck. You haven't been taking care of yourself. You're a beautiful woman. You're allowed to continue your life. Don't you think it's time to pick up the pieces and launch something new in your career?"

Gina was taken aback by that comment. "Paul I have no career without Perfection. I created that. It's just like my marriage. Where do I pick it up from? You don't understand. You came in when we had a small blip. You don't know how we clawed our way to get to the top. You may do PR for bands, but you have no idea what it takes to get here. The dirty clubs, never thinking you're good enough. Suddenly making it and wondering if the fans really like your music or like what they see onstage. And as far as the way I look, I prefer you not comment. We good? Because I'm hungry. No more talk about anything that might piss me off."

Paul knew not to push. "You're right Gina, I don't, and I don't pretend to know what you're thinking now."

Gina couldn't help her self-deprecation. "I'm in a big pile of shit and I don't know how to get out. Can you please just try to be a friend and not someone who wants to jump in my bed?"

FRANNY
MAKES A VISIT

RIO TRIED NOT TO TALK to Jae about Trevor and Gina. It was hard holding back on her. Jae curled up next to Rio. "Babe, I can't stand watching Gina torture herself. She still loves Trevor but can't get past what he did. Do you think she should see a therapist? She might listen to you."

Rio was holding a secret. "Gina does what she wants. She always has. She needs to think of it herself. I know you want to help. Just let her process her feelings."

Jae was shocked. "Rio, she's like your sister. I'm not feeling compassion from you."

Rio tried to bullshit it off. "I just know her. She has to work through this." Rio knew Jae was right. He hadn't visited Gina in over a week.

Franny Ricci flew into LAX and had a car take her to Turquoise Skye Malibu Rehab Clinic. She didn't want to upset Trevor but felt that maybe she could help him. She asked to see the facility director.

She was immediately taken to the head of the facility, Dr. Jorge Hernandez. Franny spoke first. "Doctor, I need to know how bad his addictions are. Has he gone through withdrawal?"

Dr. Hernandez explained to Franny it was rough, but after three weeks,

Trevor had come through. "He's been asking for his wife. That is your daughter, correct?"

"Well, that's why I'm here. I'm not sure if you know that my granddaughter, nephew, and now myself are lying to my daughter as to where Trevor is. Trevor wants to walk out of this facility 100 percent clean. At that point he and Gina can start to put their life back together. My daughter is exceedingly stubborn. She won't believe him until he is clean. Please let me see him. I'm sure he is very fragile. I can handle it. Please take me to him."

Franny walked purposefully to Trevor's room and paused at the door. She knew by looking at him it was rough. Franny knocked, "Trevor, it's me Franny."

Trevor looked surprised but happy to see her. "Franny …"

"What can I do to help you? I have to say it to you Trevor, you look ill and despondent. Are they truly helping you get better? We can go to another facility if necessary. My goal is to get you back home to my daughter. Trevor, always know, that no matter how Gina may say otherwise, she will only be in love with you. I saw that in her eyes when she first brought you to the house. Her love is still there. It's the hurt she needs to get over."

Trevor couldn't believe she came and started crying. "Franny, Gina hates me. She doesn't want me. Rio told me what I did but I don't remember. She made me promise to stop and I failed her. She warned me. I didn't stop. I messed up bad. I need her. She's my wife, my one and only. She's the only family I have ever really had."

Franny sat next to him. "Gina has a tough shell when she's hurt. I know what happened. She loves you. I want you to get well. Remember when we prayed after Gina's miscarriages? Let's pray now that God will intervene and make her see the truth, that her love for you is stronger than any addiction you might have had."

Trevor looked at her through the tears. "Can we pray she takes me back?"

Franny hugged him. "Yes, that's what we will pray for. Talk to me about this facility. Is the food good? Do you just sit in your room?" Franny left an hour later and flew back to New York.

VISITATIONS

THE NEXT DAY RIO AND SKIP went to visit Trevor, who had been in rehab for two months. On the drive, Skip admitted, "I have to tell you Rio, I hate keeping this from Gina. She is not someone you want to piss off. Remember Brian Mayfield?"

Rio agreed. "Gina is not someone you want to get mad. What the fuck happened to Mayfield anyway? What is he doing?"

"He is doing grunt work for some band. I heard he was backstage during the whole incident. I think he may have been getting back at Gina by getting Trevor fucked up."

Rio pulled in a parking space by the front door. "I haven't seen Trevor in over two weeks. I hope all this therapy is making him stronger. If my calculations are correct, he has another three months give or take. Depending on his progress, they said they could let him out a touch earlier. We'll see."

They checked in and walked down to Trevor's room. He was dressed better; not the baggy sweatpants, torn-up jeans and raggy T-shirts he had been wearing since admission. Roxanne most likely had dropped off nicer clothing. Roxanne would want him to look like Trevor McNaughton the Rock Star, not the addict. Even though he had put on some weight, he still looked sad and lost. Rio wasn't sure any therapy could take that look away. Only being back home in Montecito with Gina would change that.

He looked up as the two men came through the door. "Hey, thanks for coming to see me. Roxanne and her boyfriend Zach are coming this weekend. You know who came to see me? Franny. She flew all the way out here just to pray with me. I always knew she cared about me, and she really went out of her way to spend time with me. How are things with the band? How's my wife? Is Gina still sad?"

Skip spoke first. "Trev, she is still hurt and angry. She believes you ran off. I'm trying to calm the waters. Gina has and will always be territorial with you. She is not easy to deal with, especially with that question as to where you are out there."

Rio jumped in. "Trev man, I know you don't want her to know. We promised to keep your secret and we will. Skip is spot on. It's hard when she thinks you're out whoring around and still using. Like you, she feels helpless. She thinks she will never have the love of her life back. It's painful to watch her according to Jae. We are keeping a major secret as to where you are."

Skip added, "I don't want to bring this up, but Paul Ryan is making moves on her. She hasn't been interested. She's actually fairly pissed off. Gina reminds me I hired him, and that I need to remind him that he works for Perfection. She claims I don't have her back."

Trevor shut his eyes. "He wants to sleep with my wife. I knew it. She's not interested?"

Rio said, "No she's not, but hopefully we can get you out of here before that happens. I don't think Gina would let that happen Trevor, seriously."

Dr. Hernandez stopped by Trevor's room. "Hi Trevor. I'm happy you have visitors. When do you think we can get your wife here?"

Trevor said. "No. I want to walk out of here cured. I don't want her here. I'm more sure of that fact now. If she came it would remind her of my weakness."

Dr. Hernandez did not look like he agreed. "Trevor, you don't think she would be proud of your accomplishment and that you did this out of the love you have for her?" Trevor shook his head. Dr. Hernandez added, "If you think that's best. I think differently, that's okay."

GINA
STRUGGLES

OTHER THAN HAVING LUNCH with her friends in Montecito, Gina didn't leave the house. All the Montecito ladies were supportive. Bekki and Jessica's husbands helped by laying out legal information. Casey's husband was the contractor to the stars and helped with some work around the studio, while Christine advised her on her financials. Karen tried to take her mind off things by painting flowers together. Gina appreciated the help, but it became a blur.

What was going on with Roxanne? She was hoping the reason Roxanne hadn't reached out was that school was very hectic or even Zach kept her busy. That would be an acceptable answer. She believed that Roxanne might know where Trevor was, and that was why she didn't reach out. Roxanne loved Trevor and would protect his secrets.

Paul Ryan thought that after two plus months of no pressure that he could get Gina to go on a vacation to Hawaii, so he went ahead and bought the tickets. He dropped off food at her place a few days later and set them on the kitchen counter along with the take-out food bags. This way she would see them after he left. The next time he showed up at her house he would see what her answer would be.

When Gina found them, she was furious. Poor Jae had to listen to Gina's wrath, "What the fuck kind of shit is this guy pulling? Why, why would I go anywhere with him? Can you imagine what those rag magazines would make of that? If anyone saw pictures like that, I would look like a villain. Absolutely not, I don't even know what to say to him without wanting to punch him out."

Jae thought for a moment, wanting to word her response correctly. "Gina, you have barely left this house for over two, almost three months. It might be okay for you to get some sun, get away, different scenery. I'm not saying sleep with the guy but getting away might not be a bad idea—just for a few days. I'm not in your head but it's not the worst idea either."

Gina couldn't figure this out. "If I go it's to get away from myself and this house. I don't want that man thinking he has a chance with me. He doesn't. You think I should get a break from myself. Why not come with me, this way he definitely knows there isn't any romantic intent from my perspective. If I had you there, I would feel much better. As you said getting away from everything that is Trevor in this house. Please Jae, come with me."

Jae smiled at her. "Wish I could, but something is going on with Rio. He seems extremely worried about Perfection. Trevor's disappearance has affected him. I think he is lost but not the same as you are. Perfection is his baby also. I can see something in his eyes. He's not himself. He doesn't want to talk about it either. I can't leave him right now. You should go Gina, just for a few days. Maybe when you get home you can think of things with Trevor differently. Go. Just don't give him any chances for anything. It's just a friendly trip. Although I don't trust him, I trust you. You love Trevor and you are having a hard time reconciling those thoughts of what he is doing. You're mad but I know you still love him. A rest away from all this might allow you to see things clearer."

Gina was still defiant. "Jae, I'll listen to your advice, but I am thinking it will be an issue. I will make ground rules with Paul. He annoys me; however, he is our public relations person. I can play this as he is helping me, nothing else."

Paul Ryan was smart and waited two days before going back to see Gina, hoping for a positive answer. "So, you want to go? I got us adjoining rooms. No pressure. You should get away. I promise I'll behave no worries."

Gina sighed. "Paul, I don't feel like leaving. Separate rooms are fine. But attached? I'm not sure I trust you, and I'm sure my daughter would not be happy. Roxanne loves her father. Any man she might see me with would not make her happy. Although, I haven't heard from her. She's protecting her father somehow; I don't want to know what that is. It scares me that she knows where he is. I need you to understand that."

Paul countered. "We are just going to have a relaxing time nothing more. You need to get away and get some sun."

Gina admitted, "I could use some Vitamin D and sunshine and to get away from all these memories I'm living with. Paul, you need to promise—please no pressure. I just can't deal with it. We are not having any type of tryst. For all I care you can find someone who interests you while we are there."

Paul Ryan promised. He wasn't interested in the idea of anyone else. But even so he was handsome and mostly honest. He would try to make some moves, mostly into Gina's bed. A week later, they left for Oahu, on the North Shore.

HAWAII ISN'T PARADISE

THE RESORT HAD BEEN THERE FOR YEARS and had been redone. The open-air lobby was grand. When you walked in you could see straight to the ocean. Gina and Paul were greeted with purple vanda orchid leis. There were several little shops, mostly Hawaiian touristy stores, and a couple of women's and men's resort wear stores. Maybe Gina would buy some Aloha Wear. Adjacent to the lobby were two restaurants that Gina noticed—one run of the mill type food and one fancy.

After checking in, Paul and Gina wandered down to the hotel tiki bar on the beach. They grabbed a table in the sun and enjoyed the trade winds. Paul was wearing a loud tropical shirt, but they were in Hawaii. Gina put on a good game face and was pretending to enjoy herself. They ordered dinner at the bar, and waited for the Hawaiian sunset, hoping to see the elusive green flash as the sun hit the water. Most people would kill for this atmosphere—a Hawaiian sunset, fresh seafood, beautiful table by the beach, tiki torches lit, and the sounds of a ukulele.

She had always noticed how attractive Paul was, but it was merely an observation, nothing that meant anything to her. She was still in love with her husband. Nothing would change that. Would the eleven weeks of being separated from Trevor change her mind? Gina's mind was doing cartwheels, but always ended with loving her husband.

Paul was a gentleman; he knew not to overplay his hand with Gina. He did have a game plan. He was cleaver.

The next afternoon, Gina was relaxing in one of the king-size hammocks that dotted the beach. Gina hated the idea of sand in her bathing suit. Occasionally a waitress would stop by and ask if she wanted a drink. Of course, yes. Gina finally decided since she was in Hawaii she would try to relax. She was half sleeping, relaxing when Paul climbed into the hammock with her, leaned over, and gave her a kiss.

It startled Gina. "Paul, you promised not to try anything. You may be very persuasive with other ladies, but I just can't. I'm not interested. You promised. Please, I'm trying to relax and do some soul searching. Why can't you understand?"

"What type of soul-searching Gina? Your husband is an addict and cheated on you. I'm trying to understand."

Gina retorted, "Paul, you have never been married, nor have you been with someone for over twenty years. I have spent a lifetime with Trevor. Sorry, I'm not going to justify anything with you."

After her little speech with Paul, Gina took in the sun, walked on the beach, and waded in the waves. Paul never seemed to leave her side, which Gina found annoying. They weren't a couple.

Gina wondered, "Paul, have you seen any paparazzi around? This would be very disruptive if this got into the public. I already feel that people have noticed us here. You're not Trevor. That would be a story. You're the PR guy. The optics look really bad. Never mind what my entire family would think. They would hate it."

Paul countered, "Gina, technically you're a free woman. Your husband disappeared. You're free to pursue what you want."

"I'm not free. I'm still married. I may be very angry, but Paul, you don't understand. Trevor has been my life. I just don't want to declare I'm a free woman. I don't feel that way. If he saw pictures of us … I might never know where he is. I can't, I just can't."

"I understand Gina. I'm here waiting for when you rid yourself of these feelings. I told you, I'm a patient man when it's something I want." Paul was more than confident. However he never would best Gina McNaughton.

Gina walked out of the surf. "I can't continue this conversation. I am going to shower and get ready for dinner."

Paul was eager. "Yes, let's have a lovely dinner. Maybe you can forget what's happening for a few hours."

Gina dressed in a flowing tropical print jumpsuit she had picked up when she went to Turks and Caicos with Trevor. She thought to herself, *Even my clothes remind me of him.* She teared up remembering that vacation. They were so much in love and their sexual appetites were off the charts.

Paul knocked on the door and Gina let him in. "You look beautiful and very tropical."

Gina smiled. "Thank you. Let's ask to be seated at a private table. I get a feeling that there are eyes on everything we do."

Gina was correct. Reporters from weekly entertainment magazines were there and Paul was the one who tipped them off. He wanted to create the public perception of a romance between the two of them.

Gina didn't know that the people closest to her were keeping a huge secret. If the lies were exposed, Gina would be filled with bitterness and anger.

Gina and Paul were given a table in the back of one of Hale'iwa's highly rated restaurants. Gina ordered a Mai Tai. Before long she had three more. Even the three-course meal didn't sober her up. Paul didn't stop her either.

They taxied back to the hotel and went to Paul's suite. He turned on Al Green's "Let's Stay Together" and pulled Gina into a close dance.

Gina was very nervous and very drunk. Paul smelled so good. She wanted to stop him before things progressed. She never adhered to the obvious adage that she was too drunk to realize when someone was putting on the moves. Big Time! Gina started to feel uncomfortable in Paul's embrace. She had a feeling he wasn't going to respect the fact she was still mourning her marriage. She pulled away, "Paul, you promised not to do this. Can't you respect that?"

"You had many mai tais, let's see where that gets us."

Before she knew it, they had danced right into his bedroom. The one thing Gina didn't want to happen, she succumbed to. She was horrified that she actually allowed it to happen. He wasn't Trevor, the man who captivated her heart. She couldn't shake her feelings. In the middle of the night, she got up, returned to her own room, and cried. She knew she had made a terrible mistake.

Gina couldn't believe how she had allowed Paul to think he had a chance to be the man in her life. *Now he'll think this is going to happen every night we're here.* She knew it would only be this one time. She had done exactly what Trevor had—cheated on their marriage.

No, she couldn't continue this. Paul gave her a hard press; he was obviously in love with her. She never gave him any reason to believe she returned that love.

The next morning Paul noticed that Gina had gone. He got dressed and knocked on her door. "Gina, you left in the middle of the night. Why?"

She refused to answer his question as to why. Gina was ready to go have breakfast in the restaurant in the lobby. Since it was open air to the beach the birds flew in. Paul of course went with her. Gina could see the disappointment on his face and she didn't care. They asked for a table for two, preferably by the beach. Gina of course was noticed, no denying who she was. They sat at the table and the first words out of Gina's mouth were, "What happened last night was a mistake. I'm not ready for that type of relationship with anyone, except my husband."

Paul might have women looking him over, but he was not her guy. The two left the next day. They both felt it was for the better that they leave.

PERFECTION, NEXT MOVES?

IT WAS HARD FOR THE OTHER BAND MEMBERS to rectify what happened. How did things spiral out of control? Gina and Trevor were the main problem of the next moves for Perfection. However, Rio seemed preoccupied with something. No one could figure it out. The rest of the band knew Rio's preoccupation had to do with the band. He wasn't sharing with anyone either. Everyone knew Jae would be watching over Gina. She was floundering, not sure of her next moves.

Ian, Kevin, and Jeff felt like they were left out of everything that was Perfection. They went to visit Gina. Gina half smiled at them, but she was happy to see them. "I missed you guys. Ian, how's Lisa and the boys? Well, they are men now. I miss Lisa. I know I'm not great company. Jeff, what the hell is going on with you pal? Remember we started Perfection ..." she rattled away.

Gina put on coffee, and they sat at the kitchen counter. Gina was hoping Trevor would not come up in conversation. She was afraid of what her reaction would be. Crying or anger.

Jeff knew Gina well. "Gina, we are worried about you, and we don't know what's going on with the band. We're in limbo and that's frustrating. We all know what happened and why you destroyed a dressing room and part of backstage. I also know you are wondering where Trevor is, we all are. It's an uncomfortable feeling."

"Well, if anyone knows where Trevor McNaughton is," she snipped, "maybe we can have some clarity. I'm in touch with Skip and Tommy. We still have a band, but going forward I'm not sure what that looks like. We have over twenty songs that we haven't given to Brown Fence and won't. I don't know what recording will look like, with or without Trevor." Gina started to choke up. Jeff consoled her. He knew as everyone did, she was still in love with Trevor.

Ian spoke softly. "I know Trevor well. I think he's somewhere trying to get better. I need to say that to you before you do something you can't take back. I know Trevor has those demons; they escape. With that said, I know him, he still loves you. Please don't forget that."

Kevin agreed with Ian. "Us Canadians love passionately. Gina, he is fixing himself. I have seen it before with him. Trevor will always find his way."

Jeff reached for her hand. "Gina, I'm here for you. Call me. Keep us in the loop. This is our band too. He's not easy to nail down, you know. I know Jae comes here every day. Is *their* marriage okay?"

Gina smirked. "Don't feel bad. Rio hasn't come to see me either. Something is going on with him and it's not Jae. Skip and Tommy stopped by. Skip was an asshole, but Tommy is giving me space, which gives us some time to figure things out. I love you guys and I'm sorry this is happening. It affects us all. I do apologize."

Gina gave them all a loving hug, they were family. Gina's expression was one of feeling lost. The guys saw that in her face. There was nothing they could do, maybe try to find Trevor? Or would they be opening up a hornet's nest finding him? As they left, Ian promised he would let Lisa know to come and visit.

TREVOR'S TREATMENT

TREVOR'S TREATMENT WAS MOVING forward—sixteen weeks into the program with three weeks to go and he was making good progress. He seemed more together and could only think about going home to Gina. He also knew he would have to explain being away so long. The prospect of Gina turning him away crept in.

Skip, Rio, and Roxanne visited him every week. The doctors told them he was making incredible progress, but still felt that his wife should be there before he leaves. Roxanne was adamant. "Absolutely not. If she came, he might regress."

Rio told Trevor, "Dude, it's going to be tough. Gina is still angry and sad. I know she loves you, but she is stubborn. We have to tell her what's going on if you are leaving in three weeks. One of us has to tell her. She is going to be outraged. Just so you know, Paul Ryan has been around. We all know he wants Gina. Jae told me he was trying to push her to start working on divorce papers."

Roxanne knew she had to tell her father about Hawaii and was petrified by what his reaction would be. She handed him a copy of *People Magazine*. "She went to Hawaii with him, unfortunately there are these pictures. It doesn't look romantic."

Trevor started to cry. "She's still my wife. She hasn't filed divorce papers? Why did we hire Paul Ryan to clean up things? He's having his own PR nightmare by falling in love with my wife. I need to get home."

Rio was encouraging. "We want to talk to your doctor and let's see where you are at in your treatment. We don't want to rush this, but if they think you're doing well it would be great to get you out sooner. It will mean that one of us will have to tell Gina the secret we have been keeping for over four months."

The trio went to see Dr. Hernandez. He asked them to sit down. Roxanne started, "We were wondering how my dad's treatment is going? I know he wants to go home, but is he ready?" Rio seconded the sentiment.

Dr. Hernandez leaned forward in his chair. "I honestly feel he can leave in a week to ten days. Where is he going?"

Rio said, "We will probably take him to their Hollywood Hills house. Roxanne and I have to have a very difficult conversation with Gina. She will be livid that we have known where Trevor has been."

Dr. Hernandez frowned. "That's why I thought she should come. If she observed the progress he has made, this would not have been an issue. Trevor and I discussed this during a session. I'm not breaking any ethical codes here by telling you this. Have any of you thought what would happen if his wife doesn't take him back?"

Roxanne spoke up. "I know my parents. My mother will cave the minute she sees him. She loves him. She's stubborn, yes, but the two of them have this incredible need for each other. I never understood it, but I know the both of them. My uncle is correct that the conversation with my mother will be difficult. But I think I should be the one to tell her."

Everyone started shaking their heads in agreement. Dr. Hernandez had one last bit of news to tell them. "I just want you to know that we received a call from a gentleman who tracked down Mr. McNaughton. He wanted to know when he would be released. I told him I wasn't allowed to give out that information. He said he worked with the band."

Rio looked confused. "Was it the press looking for a story? Did he give his name?"

Dr. Hernandez was quick to tell them, "Yes, I was surprised he did. He said his name was Paul Ryan and he handled PR for the band. He called about a month ago, I'm sorry I forgot to tell you."

Rio took that in. "Thank you for that information. It's important, appreciate it."

All three were in disbelief. Rio was aggravated. "That asshole. He has known where your father is and tried to get Gina to file divorce papers. That dude is trying to separate them. Gina would never go through with it. Skip this is your guy. I don't trust him. We need to find a way to break that contract. What a fucking jerk-off, wait till Gina finds out." Paul Ryan was playing a serious game and had to be stopped.

GINA'S REGRETS

IN MONTECITO, GINA WENT TO THE OFFICE for the first time since she and Trevor split up. She looked at all of Perfection's press materials and found the picture from so many years ago—Trevor with those long blond curls. She had wild hair and was wearing her beautiful white dress. She started to cry. She touched his face in the picture. "How did we get to this place Trevor? How?"

She spent a few days alone in the office—no Skip, no band members. Even Paul Ryan couldn't pull her out of her depression. Ryan was playing a game for Gina's affection. A game he would never win. He would arrive with a bottle of wine in the evenings. He was smart, he timed it when he knew Marisol would be home. He placed it on the counter and lit a joint for Gina. She was getting tired of whatever game Paul was playing, she knew it would have to stop. Allowing him to come over with food and a joint wasn't a good enough reason to allow him to show up. She needed to stop it. While over the house one night he gave Gina a bag that looked like ice cream from her favorite place in Montecito. In the bag was an engagement ring—a beautiful round diamond measuring ten carats. Paul was confident or rather hopeful that he had swayed things his way. Apparently, he forgot who he was dealing with, Gina McNaughton, *the bad ass bitch*.

Gina was stunned. "I can't accept this. I'm still married. Paul, seriously I have never given you the impression that this was serious or that I was even interested. Why would you do this?" Paul's answer surprised her. "What about your divorce? You haven't filed yet? I'm basing our relationship on your divorce. You need to file right away."

Gina was uncomfortable. "Why in the hell would you think that would be easy. Trevor and I have so much of our life intertwined with each other. Stop asking me to file. I feel pressured by you and you don't have the right. I haven't promised you any type of relationship. Please don't. I think you need to leave. Please take that ring with you."

Paul took the ring out of the box and placed it on the counter, "Gina, I love you. I never wavered on that. I'll give you some time. Try to file some type of papers. If Trevor can't be found you could be free. Then we can be together." He turned to leave and tried to give Gina a kiss. She turned her face, so his kiss landed on her cheek. Gina knew most definitely she needed to stop Paul Ryan's intrusion into her life.

Gina reluctantly picked up a ringing phone later that evening.

"Hey, how are you? What do I owe this phone call to?"

Brent Nolan laughed at the other end of the line. "First, I'm checking on you. I know you have been through fucking hell. You okay? I mean everyone knows Trevor isn't with you. You were a great team. I would be blown away if this breaks up the band."

"Brent, I am more concerned about my marriage. If I have a marriage we have a band. If something were to happen to Trevor and me, I don't know if I could continue. It would be too hard to pretend."

Brent continued. "The reason I'm calling is that we are playing an anniversary gig at one of the clubs on the strip in two weeks. I would love it if you joined me and sang a couple of songs. Don't know if you're up to it."

Gina considered it for a minute. "You know what? I haven't sung anything in over four months. Yes, I'll do it. I may be rusty ... but if you're willing to take that chance."

"I will always take a chance on GMac. I'm sorry. You still using that?"

Gina sighed. "It's fine, everyone knows GMac. Give me the songs you want me to sing. Thanks for thinking of me. You're a good friend, appreciate it."

GOING
HOME?

DR. HERNANDEZ CALLED ROXANNE and Rio and requested a meeting to discuss Trevor's next steps to move out of rehab and ease into living outside. He would be required to attend weekly therapy sessions. Where would they be?

Rio picked up Roxanne at the airport. "They are talking about your father leaving in five days. We have to have that talk with your mother. You know he wants to go home. We can probably have him stay at the Hills house for a few days, but he wants to be back home in Montecito. One of us has to have that awful conversation with her. She is going to go off the rails. Do you still want to be the first?"

"Yes it should be me, Uncle Rio. I haven't spoken to her in months. Now I can tell her why. She will not take this well. We know that. I'm prepared to do it. Especially if that brings them back together, they love each other. I can't wait to get Paul Ryan away from my mother."

Rio looked at Roxanne. "Trust me, I'll get the second wave of your mother's wrath."

Dr. Hernandez was waiting for them when they arrived. He ushered them into his office, "As you know, Trevor had a rough go detoxing. It took three weeks and he asked for your mother constantly. As he went through the program, we noticed he was determined to return home and resume working with the band, which helped him focus on his rehabilitation. We are ready to let him go home in two days. Where will he be going? I advised you to have Gina here, but that's not an issue at this point."

Roxanne spoke up. "Well, I am going have that uncomfortable conversation with my mother. We have all lied to her about my father's treatment, you knew that. She will not handle this well. I think I will have my father stay at our Hollywood Hills house for a week and soon after I will bring him back home to Montecito. I would appreciate it if we could wait that week or until he gets established in his living situation before we get him outside therapy."

Dr. Hernandez said, "You're his family, you know what's best. Let me emphasize this, he has made phenomenal progress."

With that Roxanne and Rio walked to Trevor's room. He looked healthy and was playing his guitar. He looked up. "Hey, I can go home in two days! How's Gina? Is Paul Ryan still hanging around? I'll take care of that."

Rio told Trevor, "Roxanne has to tell Gina the truth that we all knew where you were. You know your wife; she's not going to take it well. Honestly, we are both fucked with Gina, and Skip too. You may have to go to the Hills house until Gina takes in this information. We will do everything to get you back home to her. She still loves you. She's just being Gina the bitch. You know better than anyone. Are you good with our plan?"

Trevor was determined. "If it gets me home to Gina, I'll do whatever. I love her and I need her. I always needed her. She makes me a better human."

Roxanne hugged her father. "Dad, I love you and we'll take you home. You and Mom will be fine." Roxanne was hoping. She now had to tell her mother that Trevor had been in rehab all this time to show her he was clean. Gina thought he had taken up with some young thing, which was the reason she didn't want to go looking for him. That pain would have shattered her heart further.

THE TRUTH
REVEALED

ROXANNE DROVE TO MONTECITO to see her mother. This would not be pleasant. Gina wouldn't understand. She would discover that Rio, Skip, and her daughter had lied to her. Roxanne knew she would be met with tremendous anger from Gina. Roxanne punched the code into the fence on the driveway, alerting Gina someone was at the house.

As Roxanne came through the door, Gina said, "Well what the hell, my long-lost daughter. What has it been? Four months? Five months? Too busy to see your mother? Hmmph, okay Roxanne. What's going on? Busy with school? Zach? Did you get married? You're not pregnant so where have you been? Visiting your father and his new girlfriend?" Gina felt wounded by that last comment, what if that was true? Still, Gina was happy to see her only child. She walked up to her daughter and gave her a kiss and huge hug and saw her daughter's discomfort. "Roxanne, what is it? You are actually scaring me."

Roxanne took a deep breath. "Mom, we need to talk. But before you interrupt me, please let me finish what I have to say."

Gina looked worried. "What is it, Roxanne? You in trouble somehow? I can call Poppi."

Roxanne was both scared and knew she had to get this out. "No Mom! Let me just say what I have to say. I know where Dad has been, so do Uncle Rio and Skip. We put him in a rehab facility. He has worked really hard to get healthy and he's finished. He's at the Hills house now and wants to come home to you."

Gina was stunned. She fell backward, tears streaming from her eyes. She felt betrayed by her daughter, cousin, and manager. She screamed, "Roxanne, your assumption, to keep something of this magnitude from me? This is a fucking joke, right? Why would you do that to me? Why? Who the hell do you think you all are? Your father is all better, huh? I've been mourning my marriage, and you all have let me go down a black hole of pain. I was thinking he went off with some young slut. How could you do that? My own child. You lied to me."

Roxanne got snarky. "Well, it's not like you have been mourning that badly. You went to Hawaii with that opportunist Paul Ryan, and I'm sure he's spent a night or two here."

Gina was hurt and astounded by her daughters claim. "How *dare* you. That's not your business. You know what your father did. He humiliated us."

Roxanne shot back. "No Mom, he humiliated you, not me. He's my father. I wasn't happy with him, but I never threw him out of the house like you did. You haven't filed divorce papers yet. I wonder why? It's because you still love Dad, but you have too much fucking pride. All you see in your brain is his indiscretion. What about all the years you have been madly in love with each other? You have no answer because you still love him. Forget your fucking pride, Mom."

Gina looked at her, tears running down her face. "You hurt me Roxanne—my own child that I tried so hard to have, my everything. Wasn't I a good mother? You didn't come and see me because you're a liar." Gina was sobbing uncontrollably. "Rio, Skip—they lied to me also. Why did I deserve this? I've been a mess, depressed, walking in a nightmare, and you led me down this path. How could you all interfere in my marriage? Since you have protected your father all this time maybe you should go, be with your father."

Gina was floored, she never suspected this. She sat back and took all the information in. Trevor was getting help all this time. She knew why. He wanted her back, he loved her.

Roxanne was crying now too. "Dad made all the progress because he never stopped loving you. He said you made him a better human. Do you really want to give up on the one person beside myself that loves you unconditionally? I am so angry that you are choosing to lose Dad and Perfection. You don't think that you and Dad *are* Perfection? You're so selfish. I hate that you can't even consider this. You need to rethink what's in your soul, Mom. You're not that person. Have you turned into that ugly person? That's not the mother I grew up with."

Gina was livid and hurt but knew her daughter was right. It was her pride. "Roxanne, please leave. I can't look at you right now, you liar. Just go."

Roxanne warned her, "Dad will come here, so you better prepare yourself for that."

Gina fell into a panic attack and took four Valium. She had to confront Rio. How could he have kept this secret? She was getting ready to head to his house, still crying hysterically. As she opened the door, Paul was standing there. Gina closed the door behind her. "Sorry Paul, I have to go see Rio."

Paul noticed she was crying. "Is everything okay with Rio and Jae?" He had spent five months maneuvering this relationship and wanted to take it further and really didn't care if Rio and Jae were okay. Gina still blocked the door. He tried to read her face, "Gina I was just checking. You have my ring. You know I'm serious about us."

"Paul, I have no time for games. I just had a huge fight with my daughter. I need to go see Rio."

Paul noticed the ring on the dining room table and pushed past Gina. She was in awe that he took that bold move. The ring was exactly where he had left it. "Gina, that ring is my commitment to you after your divorce." He stopped and looked at the dining room table in disbelief. "Are those legal papers you had drawn up? You haven't filed?"

Gina was pissed at all the bullshit she just ingested. "No, Paul. I haven't done anything, okay. I don't think you and I need to discuss my divorce or non-divorce. I need to go. Paul, please, I asked you not to give me this."

Paul stunned her. "I think you're wrong. I'm basing our relationship on the fact you are going to divorce the man who cheated on you. I'm here waiting for you. Gina, please consider this. I'm going to go. I'm going to leave the ring, so you remember there is someone who *does* love you. I know Roxanne upset you. I'm sorry she doesn't want another man in your life. I get it."

Gina couldn't get him out the door fast enough. "Well it seems I have some thinking to do. I need to leave, so I would appreciate if you go now."

Gina got in her car, crying and furious. Did Jae know all this time? Did she lie too? Gina drove the ten minutes to their house. She entered the gated community that Rio and Jae lived in. She knew the guard at the gate and waved at him as he let her in. Gina pulled up to the house and stopped the car suddenly. She walked into the house without knocking. Jae looked up from her book. "Gina, oh my God, you look terrible. What happened?"

Gina was still in tears. "You mean you don't have any idea why I'm here?"

Rio was there. "No Gina, she has no idea. Let's get this over with. Yes, I lied to you. That's why I couldn't be there the way you needed me. You had Jae. I was concerned with getting Trevor well, and for us all to continue with our lives, and for Perfection to start to work again. We have a label to start."

Gina went up to his face. "You're fucking kidding me right now. It wasn't about me, your cousin. It was about the band! You cocksucker! How dare you! You saw me broken and you figured that shit was okay to have me fall to pieces. Rio, I hate you. How dare you treat me that way." Gina pushed him and he fell hard.

Jae was in disbelief. "What the fuck is going on right now?"

Gina was breathing hard, upset, "Your husband lied to me about where Trevor was all this time. Him, Roxanne, and Skip put him in rehab so he could get clean. They lied Jae, they lied. You know I sank to the bottom, and they allowed me to be in pain, rather than tell me the truth. All those nasty horrible ideas and fears I had about where Trevor was and who he was with—they allowed me to sink so deep."

Jae looked at Rio. "Babe, tell me this isn't true. None of you had any compassion for all she went through. You lied. Why? Why not tell her Trevor was trying to get help? Rio please don't tell me this is all about the band. I can't believe you would hurt Gina this way."

Jae pulled Gina next to her. "Gina, if I knew anything I would have told you."

Rio stood up. "That's why babe. I knew you would tell her." He looked at Gina. "You hate me now. I bet you want to kick my ass. Go ahead, do it. Trevor didn't want you to know until he was totally clean. He didn't think you would believe he could do it. But he did it, for you. He never stopped thinking about you. When he was at his worst detoxing, the doctor said he kept calling for you, he was in the midst of horrible withdrawals. He hallucinated you being there in his room. He doesn't remember anything from the backstage debacle. He was out of it. He actually thought it was you. Just so you know, I pushed him around when I got to him. I defended you. You're a real fucking bitch. You can't see that we all just wanted to save your marriage. You can tell me a million ways that you don't love him, but you're the liar. Get the fuck over yourself Gina. Get your life back on track. You're just lost. Oh, and here is the best part. Your friend Paul Ryan found out where Trevor was and was asking about his release. So, he's known for over month where Trevor was. I bet he has been pressing you to get some sort of divorce papers signed. Don't answer. I know how this guy operates. I can't believe you care about him. So, go ahead and give it to me."

Gina crumbled into Jae. "Rio where do you come off, saying that I care about Paul in that way? I can't believe this; Trevor thinks he can just come home? Am I supposed to forget that he, too, kept his rehab a secret?"

Rio was disgusted at this point. "You know what Gina? Figure it out. No matter what, Trevor is part of Perfection and you two together make it better. There are at least ten people who are part of the band. You want them to lose their jobs? Are you that selfish? You're just a fucking bitch. Do some soul-searching."

SOUL SEARCHING

GINA STORMED OUT THE DOOR and took two more Valium when she got home. She sat in the living room like she had just been hit several times in the gut. Even looking at the beautiful Pacific Ocean view didn't make her feel Zen. She did have some soul-searching to do, now knowing that her husband never stopped loving her. She put on the sad songs and looked at her life in all the pictures with Trevor and Roxanne, all the awards. She started chain-smoking knowing what her heart was saying, *Was Rio right?* Trevor did this all for her. That was obvious. Paul Ryan was lying to her, pressuring her to file divorce papers. He had a diamond ring ready to go, waiting for her to leave Trevor. There was no way she could trust him, ever again.

The doorbell rang. *Is it Trevor already?* She opened the door to find Paul standing there.

Gina was disgusted by seeing him, now knowing his plan, "What are you doing here? I told you it's been a miserable day."

Paul played a great game of really caring. "I wanted to check on you. I know you had a bad day. I have to go out of town, I'll be home in a few days. Remember Gina, I'm the man who cares deeply for you. Get those papers started, for both of us."

Gina smirked. "I know you want me to get those papers started. I told you. Trevor and I have too many financial issues, which complicates a just sign and go. What is really interesting to me is that you knew where Trevor was for over a month. That's a tidbit of information I found out, so you are also a liar."

Paul asked to come in and explain but Gina remained blocking the doorway. "Gina, I overstepped obviously. I thought we had some kind of connection. We did spend a wonderful evening together. Everything I did for us, to be together and not with that loser you are married to. Let me come in and try to explain."

Gina had pure contempt in her eyes. "Paul you are a liar. It seems like lying is the theme for today. Please go away. I don't want you in my house. I want to be alone. By the way Paul, if you ever mention anything of that night, I will bury you. I will deny it. I will never acknowledge something that never happened."

The next morning, Marisol found Gina on the couch and shook her shoulder. "Mrs. Gina you, okay?"

Gina still felt blindsided. She also started thinking of her part in her separation from Trevor. "I'm not sure. Marisol. Do you think of Mr. Trevor?"

Marisol looked concerned. "Mrs. Gina, I do miss him. The question is do you miss him? I can tell he loves you much. I know you're mad at him. But it would be nice to see his face. Can I get you some breakfast?"

"Just coffee, thanks." Gina dragged herself into the bedroom and sat on her bed, her mind racing, recalling all those nights she and Trevor made love in that room, in that bed. She thought of the nights they had hot sex, sweet lovemaking, all of it. On her dressing table was one of her favorite pictures. It was taken the night Roxanne came onstage while they sang their love song. Digging into the dresser drawer, she found Roxanne's baby footprints, a lock of her hair, and a picture of Trevor holding a newborn Roxanne. Tears running down her face, this was indeed her life. Her anger melted and made her feel like she could leave it behind, but she knew her heart needed to regroup after being shattered.

She found her two wedding pictures—the one taken in Vegas when they were so happy, and the one from the wedding her mother made her have. She was happy then too. She shed more tears thinking about the two babies they lost before Roxanne.

Together they withstood many adversities. Was this just one more? She heard the doorbell ring. *Is it Trevor?*

It was Jae. Gina opened the door and motioned her on in. She wondered how this conversation would go. She asked Jae if she wanted some coffee. Gina grabbed her a cup and they sat in the living room.

"Hi Gina. How are you today? I was very mad at Rio yesterday, but I did listen to him. He did everything out of love for you. He remembered the night you and Trevor met. It was electric. That's how he described it. You two were always meant to be with each other. Can you search your heart?"

Gina looked up at the ceiling, trying to stop the tears from rolling down her face. "I can forgive him. He always told me he had demons and flaws. I loved him totally in spite of the times he fell down. I would just pick him up. He wanted to prove to me he could do this on his own this time. I'm sad he didn't think I believed in him enough. Honestly, I wasn't sure he could do it. I feel like I let him down. I was a fool. I should have trusted him. I should have helped him. I let him down. He loves me."

Jae put the coffee mug down and grabbed Gina's hand. "Gina, if he came here tomorrow, you would take him back. I see it in your eyes."

Gina was shaken by all the information she'd had to digest over the last twenty-four hours. "I don't know if I'm ready. But whenever I see his beautiful face, I want to kiss him. I want him to know that I'm sorry. I always trusted him, until he started drinking or using whatever. I failed him. I want to love him again. I want him to follow me into the shower. I want all those things back. We look good together, right Jae? We match, like we fit together, right?"

Jae teared up too. "Yes. Let yourself think of all those things. Your heart will fix itself. I'm going to go. But if you need me, just call."

All Gina could do was shake her head. All that love rolled over her like a wave. She wondered when Trevor would show up but wanted it on his time. She wondered if he would be mad at her for not believing in him. Would he forgive her and pick up the life that they lived so beautifully?

WAITING GAME

GINA WONDERED CONSTANTLY over the next few days when Trevor would show up. Would she be ready to admit she, too, was wrong? It seemed overwhelming, but Roxanne told her he would show up. It was the not knowing that made her feel uneasy. She made sure she showered and got dressed every morning, never knowing when he would come home. She waited.

Several days went by, but she wasn't going to call Roxanne, Rio, or Skip. If Trevor wanted to come home, he needed to be ready. She was ready to see him. What would she say first? "I love you" or "I'm sorry." She was actually nervous at the idea of her husband coming home. As she walked into the kitchen to get a cup of tea, the doorbell rang. It had to be someone who had the code. She was hoping it wasn't Roxy, Paul, Rio, or anyone she couldn't deal with at the moment.

She opened the door. There stood Trevor, beautiful as ever, but thinner. He was still her husband. She still wore her wedding ring and when she looked down at his hand, so did he. She stood still, not knowing what to do.

Gina pushed her open palm into his chest. "Roxanne was here, then I blasted Rio. I know everything but what I don't know is why. Why would nobody tell me? I thought you went with some young girl. I have been living in my own hell missing you, needing you, wanting you. God Trevor, I hate where we landed with all of this."

Trevor's words were clear. "I needed to prove to you that I could do it this time without you. I needed you to know I was strong enough for both of us to do it alone. You protected me all those years when I fell. I know you thought I deserted you, but I could never do that to you. Gina, can I come in now please?"

She stepped aside, allowing him through the door. Trevor looked around. Nothing had changed. She hadn't taken pictures down. Trevor returned his gaze to Gina. "Can I have a hug from my wife? We are still married. I have missed you and thought of a million ways to tell you I'm sorry. But I know nothing I say can tell you how lonely I am without you. I called for you when I went through withdrawal. I thought you were there, but I know I dreamt you, hallucinated you. It was an awful few weeks. You were always there for me when I needed you. It seemed normal to see you at my bed, or when I was crawling on the floor, you telling me to get up. You told me you forgave me for my drug-fueled fuck up. You told me you would always love me. I couldn't tell what was real in those moments."

Gina's voice quivered and tears streamed down her face. "Baby, I'm so sorry you went through that. Maybe you were hearing what I would have told you if I saw you. You don't know how lonely I was. I went into a deep hole and never expected to ever climb out of. Every day seeing your pictures here, every bit of this house has been our life. Our life together. It became too much, too much without you. We need to talk."

Marisol walked into the living room and saw Trevor. "Mr. Trevor, you look too skinny. We need to get you some food."

Trevor stood up and gave Marisol a hug, "I need to do a lot of things Marisol."

Gina was holding back so much emotion. "Marisol, I need to talk to Trevor, do you mind?"

After Marisol left, Gina looked at Trevor. "I know Mayfield was giving you those drugs. Even when I warned you, you didn't listen. That hurt me Trevor because you know it was true. He set me up. He knew if he provided you with enough substances, you would make some mistake. I knew you were sliding, and I was wrong. I told you I wouldn't save you. I should have done something the minute I saw you passing out and those girls flocking to you. I knew you were in a spiral. I blame myself for how bad things got even though I recognized all the signs. I didn't intervene. I could have stopped so many things. But my pride, my pride got in the way. I believed you didn't care enough to stay clean for me, Roxanne, and Perfection. You told me one night during the tour you would get help. You did. I didn't listen. I was tired of protecting you. That was a terrible decision. I see it now. I understand why you didn't want me to know. You wanted me to see that you did love us, and you had to prove it on your own terms. I spent five months in hell. I'm still not okay with everyone lying to me. That hurts. They all saw what I couldn't—that what we have, always had, is the truest love two people could have. I should be asking you to forgive me for being such … I don't know what word I should use." Gina exploded with tears.

Trevor drew her close. "Gina, we both made mistakes. I think we can recover from all this, right? We have a love most people never have; we will always overcome the fuck ups that we create. Look at me. I missed your face."

Gina was still sobbing. "Hold me closer. I missed your arms around me. I missed everything about you. Did you think I could ever stop loving you? But I hate you at the same time. I just can't not love you. Maybe it's not healthy. Maybe you're *my* addiction but it's the truth. I missed everything so much, I slept in Roxanne's room. Sleeping in our bed brought back too many memories."

Trevor held her tighter, smelled her hair, and looked into her eyes. He brushed her hair back and cupped her face in his hands.

She looked into his blue eyes and ran her fingers through his hair. She touched his face softly. He was really in front of her. She hadn't imagined that the next time she saw him it would be loving. She went limp, like the first time they kissed. Yes, she remembered everything about that night. Now he was here. She hated how much she loved him. She whispered in his ear, "Can we just hold each other like this?"

"We can do whatever you want. I want to kiss you. I have waited so long to kiss you again. I missed your kisses. The little kisses around my face. I missed it all."

Gina leaned in and gave him little kisses around his face. She waited one quick second and gave him a real kiss, one that they both had wanted and waited for. "I don't want to rush one moment of this …"

"I just want us to be who we always were," he told her.

"Trev, I want to enjoy everything we used to, but right now I want to savor every moment, so I never forget." She took out her pastel cigarettes and looked at him. ". Do you remember those things from that first night? I replay it in my head. Everything perfect."

They were both waiting for that moment. They both wanted it to happen. They missed each other physically. It was very hard to hold back, and Trevor said, "I want you. I waited five months to be able to touch you. I'm used to us being together every day, every night. It drove me crazy."

Gina stared into his eyes. "Yes, I'm burning. I want you. We are fooling ourselves in waiting. But I want to take my time. I want to enjoy every bit of you. I need to just look into your eyes so I can believe this is all real, no dreams."

Trevor picked her up and took her into their bedroom. She kissed him softly and lovingly. He returned her love, kissing her neck, remembering how she melted when he did that. She whispered in his ear, "I want to take your clothes off nice and slow. Will you let me do that?"

Trevor told her, "Do whatever you want. I've waited for months. I can wait a little bit longer." Gina slowly took off his shirt. She kissed his bare chest and ran her hands over his shoulders and arms. She unbuttoned his faded jeans, letting them slide down. She reached underneath his boxers, felt his backside, and gripped it tightly. She pulled his boxers off exposing his naked body. Still staring into his eyes, she grasped his hard penis and stroked him. She was dying, she wanted it so badly. Trevor was hard as rock. She missed that perfect penis of his. Gina told him softly, "I will have this, just not yet. I missed your body. I missed you against me."

He stood there, at this point, naked. Gina couldn't stop running her hands over his body. Not breaking their stare, Trevor kissed her lips and took off her shirt, exposing her breasts. Trevor broke their stare, leaned down and fondled her breasts. His mouth found them, and he kissed them tenderly. He looked up at her and continued rubbing her nipples. He knew what got her excited. He reached down and pulled her sweatpants off. Gina stood looking at him in her while lace panties. Just like that first night. He put his hand down those lace panties and started touching her, that simple motion had Gina crying out. She wanted him inside her, but not yet. She turned around, took his hand and led him to the bed. They lay there, touching each other, they savored every touch. They felt that electricity. Gina slithered down his body, her mouth moving lower and lower until she got to his penis. She kissed it and loved it. She reached down, taking her time to fondle his balls.

He whispered, "If you keep doing this, I might not be able to hold back."

Gina was getting anxious. She wanted to have him inside her. She took off her white lace panties and sat on top of him.

Trevor laughed and rolled her over. "You think I don't want a taste?"

She grinned. "I won't be able to hold back."

He smiled. "I know that, but then I'll take you again. You won't hold back again." His mouth was wild all over her. Gina moaned with pleasure and grabbed his hair, her back arching with every flick of his tongue. It didn't take her long before she reached that moment of pure pleasure.

He looked at her. "What's your next move, baby?"

She sat on top of him and guided him inside of her. She looked at him with so much love. "Trevor, I'm going slow, however if you want me to move faster show me." Gina moved rhythmically like a song. Trevor sat up and grabbed her back and together they couldn't hold in what was building for all those months. Their pleasure satiated for the moment, Gina fell onto his chest. Gina looked up at him with tears in her eyes, "I love you, Trevor. Look, I'm wearing that diamond necklace you bought me all those years ago. Baby, promise we never do anything stupid like this again."

"Gina I'm never leaving your side no worries." He kept telling her how much he loved her.

Gina cried into his chest, "I couldn't sleep in this bed, so many nights. Just thinking of making love to you. It was so hard. Now I have you here." He traced her face with his finger. Their kissing grew passionate once again, like teenagers having their first sexual experience.

Trevor held her close. "G, you know you are my addiction too, one I am happy to have."

They lay on the bed naked, looking at each other, still feeling each other's bodies. Trevor lay his head on her chest while Gina stroked his hair. They knew how to make love to each other. They mixed up their repertoire but always knew what each wanted. It took about thirty minutes and Trevor had to have her again. This time he lay on top of her. She wrapped her legs around him and wanted to take all of him. She kissed his lips every time his face came close. They made love in a playful manner this time. After they finished their second go around, they fell into each other's arms. Later, as they sat in bed, Gina told Trevor she didn't have *The Times* crossword puzzle. They laughed.

Trevor kissed her hand. "Baby, I missed this whole life we built, and I'm blessed that we truly love each other. I need to tell you, while I was in the clinic, your mother flew out to see me. She wanted me to pray for our marriage and told me that God would make it better. She flew back home the same day. I never thought she liked me that much."

"Trevor, how could you say that? Franny liked you from the first time she met you. Remember? It was Thanksgiving. She told me she liked my

Trevor. I was shocked that she took to you so quickly. Plus, my parents bought us two houses and came out to help when we lost our babies. She has always cared about you. She even danced with you at our wedding." Gina thought about what Trevor just told her. That Franny, she was always a surprise. She was the only person she wasn't angry with. Her Mother was trying in her way to fix their marriage by praying.

THE TRUTH ABOUT MAYFIELD

EVEN IN THE AFTERGLOW of their lovemaking, Gina wanted to ask the question Trevor never wanted to answer. "I need to know. What does Brian Mayfield have over you? It's something. Just tell me."

Trevor moved Gina to the crook of his arm. He wanted to look at her when he told her the story. "G I told you, when I was younger I got into trouble. After my mother died, my father couldn't handle … well honestly, anything. That's why I don't feel close to him."

Gina touched his face. "I'm sorry my love. I can't imagine what a loss like that could do to you. But wait, that was the beginning of the demons, correct?"

Trevor stroked her hair. "Yes, however not only did we drink and do a lot of drugs around fifteen, but we would also steal things. Break-ins at some small store for stuff we could sell for drug money."

Gina interrupted him. "That was just small-time stuff."

"Yes, it was, I remember Ian, Brian, and some guy you don't know. We broke into a convenience store. We grabbed cigarettes and beer. Next thing we knew, the police were called. I grabbed what I could and ran out the back door. Brian was caught by the police."

Gina commented, "That explains his shitty attitude. You were all young when that happened."

Trevor's face changed. "Brian had a trial and was sentenced to eighteen months in juvenile detention. He never told the police about the three of us. He could have snitched, and he didn't."

Gina lifted her head. "So is this like some payback because he didn't turn you in?"

Trevor was very clear. "After he got out, Brian reminded me all the time how he saved my ass. Years later when Ian and I started Stanley Park, he would show up, wanted to be part of the scene, hung out with us. Being around the band, he met women, did drugs with us. We couldn't shake him until we went to New York."

Gina grimaced. "He wants to shine off your star. I told you he was a prick."

Trevor continued, "When we were back in Vancouver to fix the visa problem, he found us and wanted to go to New York. Ian and I didn't know what to do. He was still using his threats. I didn't want to risk anything coming back to you. We knew he couldn't do anything to help the band. On the visa papers it says he is a band coordinator. I guess it was overlooked during the process."

Gina sat up and leaned on his chest

"You were kids. Knowing this, I hate him more. But he's out. He's not our problem. He's just a grunt worker in a small band now."

Trevor grabbed her face. "My beautiful wife, you saw through him. He did want me to drink and do cocaine with him, go to parties. He knew I was a married man, but he never respected our marriage. He wanted me to fall as payback. Now all he does with that band is parties."

Gina had pegged that asshole right from the beginning. She didn't want Trevor to go to a bad place by thinking about all the drama. Gina smiled. "He can't do anything to us anymore. If he tries, I'll deal with him. I guess it's the Ricci way. I will make sure he remembers the beat down I gave him. Next time, he might not get up."

Trevor touched her face. "G, I love you. Brian is not worth it."

GETTING BACK TO NORMAL

THE CALIFORNIA SUN WAS SETTING, and they lounged around in bed, being very touchy with each other. Gina sat up, exposing her breasts. "I am ready for round three. Are you in?"

Trevor laughed. "I want you; I can't get enough of you. I missed you horribly, and know you missed me." Trevor reached for her exposed breasts, fondled them, kissed them.

Gina whispered, "Love them, it feels so good having your hands on me."

Trevor rolled her over on her side, taking one leg and placing it on his shoulder. He wanted to get as close as possible to her body. She gently took him inside of her. They fit like a puzzle piece. While making love, they kissed passionately. Gina loved to nip at his lips. He knew she was whipped up in passion. Once again, their eyes locked into one another. They moved together like they were playing a song—their love song. Gina was loud and vocal when they both reached their crescendo.

Gina lay on top of Trevor. "Baby, we are so good together. Damn, I love you." Gina sat up. "I'm so sorry, baby. Are you hungry? I'm a bit starved myself."

They walked into the kitchen naked, freedom knowing no one would bother them. Gina started moving things around the fridge. "I haven't cooked in a long time. I know Marisol has something made. She was worried I wasn't eating and so she left me meals. Let me look." Trevor sat admiring his wife from behind. Gina was singing, "I found some food Marisol made. Chiles rellenos and some cilantro-lime rice. You are hungry, right? Trevor you're home, act like you always did when I found Marisol's food."

Trevor looked at her laughed. "G, I assure you, I realize I'm home. I'm guessing we're eating naked. What would Franny Ricci say?"

Gina giggled, "You're funny. She probably never thought of doing that. I heated everything up in the microwave, so be careful, you have some delicate parts exposed." They sat together at the kitchen island, feeding each other. The love factor was off the charts. They ate, talked about nothing.

Then Trevor said it. "Baby, we need to address Perfection, but let's do that tomorrow. Tonight belongs to us."

Gina put the food away and found Marisol's homemade flan, Trevor's favorite. Gina placed it in front of him, "That flan was meant to be here, waiting for you. Enjoy it."

Although the rehab facility had wonderful food, Trevor was enjoying every bit of being home in Montecito, not Hollywood Hills, here with his wife. Gina cleaned up, grabbed Trevor's hand, and led him back to the bedroom. "I'm ready for round four. Is that something you are interested in?"

They stood there for a moment. Trevor raised her head toward him and kissed her. "Do I get to choose how I want to take you?"

Gina teared up. "Whatever you want, beautiful man. I'm yours."

Trevor placed her face down on the bed. She knew what was coming. He would take her from behind. Gina knew he would go hard and fast, the way she liked it. She clutched the sheets and begged him to go harder and faster. He accommodated her wishes. After their session of lovemaking, the two settled into bed wrapped up in each other's bodies and fell asleep. Both of the McNaughtons slept well for the first time in five months.

APOLOGIES

THE NEXT MORNING, TREVOR SMELLED COFFEE and bacon and leapt out of bed. "Let's go have breakfast."

Gina started laughing. "Trev, I love the look, all naked. Your perfect body, your perfect face, your perfect penis, everything. However, I don't think Marisol would enjoy seeing all that. Then again, maybe she would. Here …" She walked into the bathroom and got those old bathrobes that Trevor hated. They walked together into the kitchen.

"Marisol, I missed your breakfasts. The food where I was—not bad, but not your cooking."

Marisol was happy he was there. "Mr. Trevor, it's so much nicer that you're back. Mrs. Gina was so sad."

"Marisol, I'm sorry were you speaking to me?"

"No, Mrs. Gina, just happy to see everyone together."

Gina hugged Marisol. "Yes, our family is back together, as it should be."

Marisol had made bacon, eggs, and the waffles Gina used to make. Marisol made them better. She also made a homemade berry sauce. Trevor sat down at the dining room table to eat and saw the divorce papers and the ring that Paul Ryan had left.

Trevor waited for Gina to sit with him. "G, did you start divorce papers? And what the hell is this? A ring? Is that from Paul Ryan?"

Gina teared up again. "Listen baby, I could never file any papers. You and I are so tied together, financially and otherwise. I couldn't file. The only way was to have you sitting across from me dividing everything we worked for. I knew I would never go forward. Unless you left me for someone else, then it would have been war. But that's over with. We need to go forward, right? The McNaughtons together. No talk about divorce, it's not going to nor was it ever going to happen."

Trevor was eating and looked at Gina. "Ryan was trying to get you from the beginning. He never respected our marriage. But the fucking nerve to give you a ring. Was he high, or just a plain asshole? I can't imagine you encouraged this. Did you?"

Gina would never tell Trevor the mistake she made. That one night when she had too much to drink and Paul was able to have his way with her. Gina would never admit or acknowledge it happened. "Baby, I did everything to make him go away. I told him I wasn't available. He kept coming at me. You know me. I put someone in their place. I did, and he didn't care. He thought there was an opening, but there never was. I told him to take it back, but he left it here so I would be reminded of his intentions. I also found out that he knew where you were. He was trying to find out when you were leaving. We need to find a new PR firm going forward." Trevor snatched up the ring, "I'll make sure he gets this back. Let me handle this."

After breakfast they sat together and enjoyed the view of the Pacific. Trevor gave that look to Gina. "Baby, it's time for our playdate in the shower."

Gina smiled. "I missed you. Every time I took a shower, it reminded me of you. Yes, let's have a playdate." It was like the time away from each other faded away. They took their shower, washing each other, kissing each other. Gina felt he was hard and ready to take her. She asked, "Baby, how do you want me? Tell me." He positioned her back against the shower wall, water running over their bodies. He pulled one of her legs around his waist and took her, gently and lovingly.

After they dried off, Trevor asked, "Do I still have clothes here? When you packed up my things, I never looked to see what was there. I didn't unpack the boxes."

"Take a look in your closet. I could never get rid of anything important. I packed things in the boxes you never wore. I used to come in and smell your clothes. They smell like you." Most of his clothes were still hung perfectly in his closet.

Trevor grabbed Gina as she was getting dressed. "You are a little bitch, making me think *all* my clothes were packed up. I love you; all my favorite stuff is here."

As they got dressed after their shower, Gina remembered to tell Trevor, "I agreed to sing with Brent Nolan and the Orange Wave. He was worried about me. I told him I would do two songs with him. It's not for a week. It's an anniversary party for one of the clubs on the strip. I need you with me. I haven't sung anything in five months, except some sad songs. But Trev, we will be together. Everyone will know we are back. Perfection will be back. You good with that?"

Gina wanted and needed all of Trevor to be back home. Even though she boxed clothing he almost never wore, she wanted all of him back home. She told him, "We need to get the movers to bring all those boxes back here." She kissed him and came out of the bedroom into the living room where she took out her pastel cigarettes. She knew she had to call Roxanne to apologize and let her know that the McNaughton household was restored. Gina also needed to call Rio. He made her see the truth, so she owed him that. Then she would call Skip. Perfection needed a band meeting. Perfection business was ready to reboot.

"I need to call Roxanne. I was very cruel to her. She needs to know that we are back together. She loves you so much, I want her to know that I love you very much also."

She called Roxanne and it went right to voicemail. She started to leave a message, "Rox, it's Mom. I'm sorry. I was very cruel when I yelled at you. I want you to know your father and I are back together. You made me see what I almost forgot, how much your father and I love each other. I couldn't go on without him."

Roxanne picked up before Gina finished talking. "Mom, you took Dad back? You forgave him? Everything he did, I did, Uncle Rio did, was because we knew you could never love anyone but Dad. He wanted to become a better man because of the love he has for you. You're good right?"

Gina choked out her words. "Everyone made me realize I was to blame for not seeing things clearly. My jealousy and pride always overtake me, then I can't see beyond it. The last five months were hell. You know I could never love anyone but your father."

Roxanne was quiet for a moment before she responded. "Mom, I can forgive you. I have my parents back together. That's all I wanted. But what about Paul Ryan?"

"It looks like I have to find another PR firm. Paul Ryan knew where your dad was and kept that from me hoping I would fall into his lap. But that was never going to happen. I think your father and I need to take a trip to Stanford to visit you, sound good?"

Roxanne started to cry. "Yes, I would love that. I love you both, just know that."

Gina looked at Trevor. "And we love you too. You have always been our everything. Bye for now."

Trevor sat close to her. "Baby you did good. Don't worry she'll be fine. Do you need to call Rio?"

"No, I'm going to have him and Jae come over. I need to do this in person."

"I'll be right here with you. It's all fucking good."

Jae picked up on the first ring. "Hey, could you and Rio come over as soon as possible?"

Jae asked nervously, "Gina, are you okay? I mean I've never heard you and Rio fight. It was unnerving to be honest."

"Just drive over now, okay?"

Jae was concerned. "Sure. I'll get him. He's writing. He never stops. We'll be right over, promise."

Trevor comforted Gina. "I know that was hard. Rio will be cool once he sees that everything is the way it should be. Come here. I want to kiss you, my beautiful wife."

They relaxed looking over to their ocean view, waiting for Rio and Jae. Trevor walked over to the piano and started to play music that Gina knew but couldn't recall.

"When did you started playing the piano? I love it."

"They had a piano at rehab."

"We could use you in the band," she laughed.

When Rio and Jae walked in, Rio looked pissed. "So, Gina why did you have us run over here? Are you going to fucking blast me again?"

Jae stopped him. "I don't think that's why we are here, don't." Jae saw Trevor by the piano.

Gina walked up to Rio and hugged him. "I am terribly sorry for the things I said. I was hurt because everyone knew where Trevor was, but me. I realized what you and Roxanne said was true. I couldn't see beyond my jealousy and pain. I came home and had an epiphany. I saw Trevor spiraling out of control. I should have stopped it, like I always did. I'm to blame, and Trevor wanted to prove to me he could do it by himself. We know that we belong together, and our love will always endure. We're back, stronger than ever. I hope you accept my apology. I love you."

Jae screamed, "I knew it. I'm so happy! We missed you together."

Rio shook his head. "Gina, you're a real fucking piece of work. If it took us having a fight to make things right, I can accept that."

He looked at Trevor. "Welcome home. Now you can deal with this crazy bitch cousin of mine. You are the only one who calms her down. The next question is, what about Perfection?"

Trevor took over. "We need to call Skip and have a band meeting and take the next steps. Yes, it means starting our new label. We will come back as a stronger player, as the best hard rock band today. Plus, our own label. Rio you good?"

Rio put his hands in the air. "Thank fucking God. That's what I'm talking about. Damn, it took you two to go through this shit to get us where we need to be. I'll call Skip now. When do you want to meet, tomorrow?"

Trevor waved him off. "Hey, I just got home. I want some alone time with my wife. Next week won't change anything. Please Rio, let us have time."

Rio shook his head, "Yeah, okay I get it. You two have to fuck your brains out."

Jae scolded, "Rio, oh my God!"

Rio kissed her. "I know these two. I'm not wrong. Well, let's go celebrate. Dinner? Come on, it will be good for people to see you out."

Gina asked, "Do we need to Franny Ricci this? Or can we go now, just like us, rock stars."

They chose a nearby open-air bistro. They ordered food and Rio ordered a bottle of wine. He realized that he may have made a mistake. "Trev man, I forgot I can return the wine." Trevor said in a strong voice, "I'm fine with people drinking in front of me. It's my reality. I don't expect people around me not to drink. Go ahead, G have a glass of wine. I'm good."

Their food came rather quickly. The restaurant recognized the famous rock stars sitting in their restaurant. There was some small talk going around the table. Rio wanted Trevor to know, "Hey, so Tommy really did it. He left Brown Fence Records to work with us exclusively. That's a coup. He is the best and we got him."

Trevor acknowledged Rio with, "We are getting off to a great start then."

Gina mentioned, "I'm going to sing a couple of songs with Brent Nolan and the Orange Wave next week, at some club on the strip. Please come. I haven't sung in months. I'm kind of nervous."

"Of course we'll be there," Jae assured her. As the two couples waited for their cars, Rio was pumped. "Trevor knowing you are home we can start to use the studio again. Gina had locked it. She didn't want anyone there. Hey Gina, no hating just speaking the truth."

Gina pointed. "Look Rio there's your car. I'm sure Skip will call when he schedules the meeting."

PIANO PLAYING

THE MCNAUGHTONS WENT HOME, Trevor played the piano again, and Gina sat next to him on the piano bench. "Trev, you're turning me on. Keep playing." Gina unbuttoned his shirt and slid her hands down his pants to squeeze his behind. She unzipped his pants. Trevor raised his butt slightly off the bench so she could slide them down to his ankles. She bent over to taste him—slow and hungry.

"How can I play with you doing that?"

Gina reached under her gauzy sundress and pulled off her lacy panties, flinging them to the floor. Trevor pushed the bench back from the piano and Gina straddled him. "Play while I'm riding you."

Trevor reached his arms around her and placed his fingers on the keys. "I can't do it. I'm concentrating on what you're doing and it's making me so fucking hot." He stood up abruptly, holding Gina in place and walked over to the buffet, placing her bottom on the cherrywood surface.

Gina gently bit his neck, her moans revealing she was close. From there they moved to the bedroom. At one point Gina asked, "You didn't take one of those pills, like Turks and Caicos, did you?"

"It's all me. I told you I missed you."

Rio was right. They were doing exactly what he said, enjoying each other in every way possible.

They gave Marisol the week off and called the movers to bring all of Trevor's boxes back home.

PERFECTION REBOOT AND GINA SINGS

SKIP CALLED THE BAND and told them to meet at the Montecito studio. No one knew what to expect, except Gina, Trevor, and Rio. Even Skip was nervous. Trevor exchanged hellos and hugs with Ian, Jeff, and Kevin. The roadies were called in to see if they still wanted to work for Perfection. Everyone was thrilled to see Trevor looking well and Gina looking like her glowing self.

Trevor started the meeting. "Well, it's good to see you all. I have handled all my addiction issues and have this beautiful lady by my side. Perfection is back, we have twenty songs in the vault, and we are getting all the business paperwork for our record label. We will need to start practicing and writing. I can't commit yet to the timetable. There are some things Gina and I need to take care of first. By the way, Gina has been invited by our friend Brent Nolan from Orange Wave to sing two songs with him and you're all invited. I'm sure Gina would love the support."

Jeff looked at them together. "Dude, glad to see things are the way they should be. You take your time hanging out."

Ian hugged his Canadian brother. "It's good you're all the way back. I missed you. I always knew you would try to fix yourself. I never believed you would leave Gina. I'm sure Lisa will be thrilled to spend time with you both."

Everyone left the studio excited about starting work again but wondered what the timetable would be. They all knew Trevor and Gina would be making up for lost alone time.

It was three days before Gina was to sing with Brent and his band. She asked Trevor to help her. They practiced on his guitar and piano. Gina felt her voice was a bit off, but Trevor promised her, "No worries I'll get you where you need to be. I got you."

"You always got me. Do you think we should call Roxanne and Zach? She would be happy to see us together."

Trevor put his guitar down. "I thought it was a great idea until you added Zach. He's sleeping with our daughter. I'm not thrilled with that."

Gina wrapped her arms around him and kissed his neck. "Roxanne is a grown woman. She makes those choices. I told her to protect herself, so we have no surprises. Baby, we did the same thing. Don't dislike him, become his friend. Roxanne loves you so much. Be the man and accept him. What they do privately is their business. Just as what we do is ours."

Trevor acknowledged Gina's assessment of their daughter's situation. "Oh, G, it's weird that she grew up so fast."

"She was our baby and now she's spread her wings. It happens. Look at us." Gina kissed his neck again. "Come on, I need to practice some more, then we will call her."

They practiced for two more hours then made the call to their daughter. Roxanne said it might be hard to get there because she had some heavy schoolwork, but yes, she wanted to see her parents together.

The day of the show, Rio went over to the house and wanted to understand the delay in getting back to studio work. "Hey, you two are barely dressed. Jae and I will be there all decked out, rocker style. I want to see you do the same. Trevor, you said something at the band meeting. I'm trying to understand what's in your head. Perfection is back. We are already selling merchandise ahead of putting out new songs. The 'This Is What Perfection

Looks Like' T-shirts that are in stores are selling sold out. We need to get out there. Now is the time."

Trevor heard him. "Agreed, things are getting hot now. I need to readjust. I want to make sure everything that resurfaced from rehab is dealt with. I also want to make sure my sobriety is solid. I have an idea for Gina and me. But everyone can use the studio and work and write. I'll be reachable. That's all I'm going to say for now. Glad you're coming tonight. It will be a Perfection coming out party."

Gina slid into a fierce-looking skintight black, off-the-shoulder dress with a deep V in the back. Trevor was in black pants, a nice black T-shirt, and he found the leather jacket Gina bought him years ago.

She noticed that he was wearing the necklace she had made for him many years ago. It was a replica of his favorite guitar, his Les Paul.

She walked out of their bathroom into the bedroom all made up. "Trev, is this too much?"

"Baby, you're a knockout. I'm the luckiest man to have you. Let's go rock and roll."

They definitely looked like the rock and roll couple that they been for over twenty years.

Gina had a bad feeling that Paul Ryan would show up and wanted to make sure Trevor was warned to avoid any confrontation. It was obvious that Gina and Trevor McNaughton had reconciled. Paul would be upset, maybe even heartbroken. Gina didn't care. He showed who he was by lying and forcing her into decisions she was not willing to make.

She shared her worry with Trevor. "Don't be surprised if Paul shows up."

"Good. I can give him this." Trevor reached into his pocket and pulled out the engagement ring.

They entered through the club's backstage entrance. Everyone was happy to see the McNaughtons back together. Everybody in the band had gotten all decked out. Gina gave kisses and hugs all around, keeping an eye out for Roxanne, but she hadn't arrived.

Brent Nolan came up to Trevor. "Hey man I'm glad you worked everything out. You're back and with that lady over there and I'm guessing Perfection will start getting new music out. You know sometimes we have to hit bottom to get back to the top. I've been there. I'm excited for this tonight."

Waiting backstage, Gina got the adrenaline rush that comes with performing. Half nervousness, half high. She kissed Trevor and whispered, "I love you much."

Brent asked Rio to introduce Gina and the spotlight moved to where she was standing. As she walked out, she was met with cheers. She nodded at the audience and took a mic from her cousin and gave him a kiss. Seamlessly, Gina and Brent started singing and a round of applause nearly drowned them out. From the corner of her eye, she saw Paul.

Trevor had seen him too from his spot backstage. The two men locked eyes for a brief moment before Paul continued making his way through the crowd.

Trevor turned as he heard someone approaching. It was Roxanne and Zach. Roxanne asked, "Did I miss anything?"

Trevor kissed her and told her, "Just the crowd in love with your mom."

Gina and Brent sang two more songs together. Gina came offstage, the look of relief that she pulled it off clearly written on her face.

The band played their set and after their last song, Brent announced, "Tonight, not only do we have the one and only GMac, but her husband is here. Maybe we can get them on the stage to sing one of their songs."

Gina and Trevor were shocked and had no idea what song they would sing. Trevor didn't have his guitar, but the guitarist in Orange Wave handed Trevor his. Trevor whispered to Gina, "The only song that makes sense is 'Found You.' You up to it? Acoustic version?"

Gina agreed. "We got this."

They asked for two stools and sang the love song Trevor had written for Gina so many years ago.

Roxanne teared up and said to Zach, "Those two have so much love for each other, it's epic."

Paul Ryan got a very clear message and was hurt. Gina had never wavered in her feelings for Trevor.

They walked offstage to enthusiastic applause and Trevor made a beeline toward Paul Ryan. "Did you think you could take my wife away from me? If you did, you're a fool. You lied to her about where I was, and you were pushing her for a divorce. You thought from the first day you met her, you could have her. But you were wrong. Then you give her a ring—what balls you have man. Here you go mate, you can have this." Trevor pulled the ring out of his pocket and thrust it at Paul.

Paul glared at Trevor. "So you are all cured now, right Trevor? You really have Gina wrapped around your finger. She would do anything to protect you and it's sick how she puts up with your issues. You will fall again, and if you do, I might just be there again to get in your way."

Trevor laughed. "You will be waiting a lifetime Ryan; it's never going to happen."

Gina, who had been watching from a distance, sighed with relief as Paul walked away. Everyone stayed around for another hour, partying. Trevor was good with ginger ale and both his girls by his side.

GOING ON THE ROAD(TRIP)?

GINA WAS IN THE KITCHEN when she heard a rumble coming up the driveway. She opened the door and saw Trevor climb down from a huge RV.

"G, baby come out here!"

"What did you do Trevor?"

"This is what we are going to do for as long as we want, just drive around the country and not be rock stars, just be us, no pressure, just us enjoying nature and each other. What do you think?"

Gina was amazed at the massive RV. "I'm in, but I'm not a nature girl. I'm an Italian girl from Long Island. Nature for me is a mall with plants, but as long as I have you, anywhere we go I'm fine." She didn't want to quell Trevor's enthusiasm but had major reservations. "We're not camping people. We know nothing about camping and what we need. Let me ask this, is there room for Roxanne?"

Trevor smiled, "Of course, it has two bedrooms, two baths."

That's all Gina needed to hear. "Let's start packing. When do we leave?"

PLAYING HIGH PLAYLIST

Maybe I'm Amazed	Paul McCartney
*Who Knows Life Would be Like This**	Perfection
You Are the Sunshine of My Life	Stevie Wonder
*She Got It**	Perfection
Light My Fire	The Doors
*Time is Now**	Perfection
Brass in Pocket	The Pretenders
*What Do You Want to Know?**	Perfection
Roxanne	The Police
Murder By Numbers	The Police
*Like Marble**	Perfection
*Life Flies By**	Perfection
Plush	Stone Temple Pilots
Rock 'n' Roll Fantasy	Bad Company
Every Breath You Take	Police
The Big Empty	Stone Temple Pilots
Ava Adore	Smashing Pumpkins
In Your Eyes	Peter Gabriel
If I Ever Loose My Faith	Sting

GINA'S SAD SONGS

Alone Tonight	Genesis
A Whiter Shade of Pale	Procol Harum
Nothing Compares 2 U	Chris Cornell
Comfortably Numb	Pink Floyd
Nothing Else Matters	Metallica
Tears in Heaven	Eric Clapton
Black	Pearl Jam
Wish You Were Here	Pink Floyd
If Leaving Me is Easy	Phil Collins
Separate Lives	Phil Collins
Since I Been Loving You	Led Zeppelin
I Want to Know What Love Is	Foreigner
In Too Deep	Genesis
Throwing it All Away	Genesis
Fell On Black Day	Soundgarden
The Long and Winding Road	Beatles
While My Guitar Gently Weeps	Beatles
Loser	3 Doors Down

ACKNOWLEDGMENTS

THE SECOND BOOK OF THE *Perfection Saga* is very personal to me. I put a lot of myself in this book—the way Gina acts, the way New Yorkers have their own way of speaking, the gritty life in the music scene. I wish I could thank all of those friends who I spent time within that moment. Unfortunately, some of them are no longer here. I would have loved them to see this work.

I have gained such incredible knowledge the second time around in the self-publishing arena. I am a very lucky person to have a team who is hands down the best of the best. I would like to thank the hardest working lady I know who helped build the team, Polly Letofsky, of My Word Publishing. She helped me produce and publish my books with clear wisdom.

You can say we kept the "band together" for Book 2 *Playing High*; it has served me well. My editor and another awesome woman, Maggie Mills, has always understood my vision, and she gave me some great ideas for enhancing a powerful second book.

The amazing artist Victoria Wolf created magnificent artwork for my book covers. She also manages my website, which grows in content every week; she never misses a beat. Finally, Victoria is the last resource in laying out my book.

My proofreader Cheryl Isaac did another great job in proofreading my work, offering insightful suggestions without changing my story. We both had fun working in the New York colloquialisms.

The hardest job of writing a book or series is marketing. I found a treasure in Mary Walewski. She produces spot-on trailers and videos for *Playing Hard*. She works hard marketing me as the author, a semi-tough job. Mary is on it handling my social media. She has introduced me to many different avenues for promoting my book(s). The fun part for both of us is finding those resources. This fall, with Mary's guidance, I will be going to book festivals all over the country. An author's dream. The *Perfection Saga* series has a fabulous "A" team. I can't imagine doing this series without any one of them. How lucky can a girl be!

A big shout-out to my friend Keri Berk. She runs the Nickelback True Fans page on Facebook. Through the year she has honored me with as an administrator on the page. I take it very seriously. A truly beautiful and best friend, my rock when I need encouragement. She allows me to keep my rock and roll presence through the fan page. Obviously, I love it.

I would also like to thank my closest friends who stood by me when I first decided to write the *Perfection Saga* and encouraged me to keep writing. Their belief in me was unwavering. My besties Beverly and Lynda, who I have known for decades. Truly a supportive group of ladies, all part of the Boykin Lakes Ladies Book Club—Karen, Bekki, Casey, Christine, Chris, Jessica, Lynn and Rachel—have all kept me going. Especially when I thought I was crazy in taking this all on. I know they were correct.

Last, my family who I love dearly, encouragement and love pours out of them while I continue to navigate the publishing world. My heart and soul, my three daughters and my Miss P., my love for them is deep and enduring. They might think their Mom is crazy for doing this, but somehow, they still cheer me on, understanding my dream. In the end, they believe in me.

Life is groovy. Let the Universe guide you; it will take you to places you never imagined.

ABOUT THE AUTHOR

BETH PELLINO-DUDZIC was born in the Bronx, New York City. Beth grew up in Westchester County for most of her life. She received a BA in Business Administration. She then moved to Honolulu, Hawaii, where her three daughters were born. She came back to Westchester to raise her girls and worked at IBM upon her return.

Although the story is fictional, it was part of the author's early history. The story developed over decades in her head; it was waiting to be written. The *Perfection Saga* series has become Beth's passion. The characters and events in the story are close and personal to her. When not writing, Beth's favorite pastimes are cooking and baking; she claims to make the best New York Cheesecake. She also hosts a monthly book club with her friends. Beth is an avid football fan of both college and the NFL. Beth has another other passion: her miniature dachshund, Truffle.

www.ingramcontent.com/pod-product-compliance
Lightning Source LLC
Chambersburg PA
CBHW051531250626
47156CB00001B/311